# LAURA NAVARRE

# GEMINI WICKED

***They say I'm too wicked to be the next queen.
I'm not the Cinderella story they signed up for.***

When you're the celebrity bad girl and wild future queen of the witching world, you pretty much expect scandal, secrets, paparazzi, and bad press. Like those salacious pics plastered all over *The Witching Inquisitor* of me—Zara Gemini—getting hot and heavy with my whole warlock harem.

Like I care about the gossip? My guys'll burn the world down to rule at my side.

What I don't expect is to be betrayed, humiliated, and dethroned by my backstabbing ex-boyfriend and my lying ex-BFF. Because, you know, I'm so "wicked." And thanks for ruining my birthday bash on live TV.

Now I'll need to use every trick in my dark witch academy spell book to win back my throne, pay back my enemies, and prove I'm worthy to the whole witching world.

Never mind that I'm only a freshman at the Icarus Academy, juggling an ever-expanding curriculum of magical superpowers and unpredictable superheats I can barely control. Or that adding the obsessed, possessive, tortured, and twisted Dark Fae King to my limited list of Academy allies splits my found family of warlocks right down the center.

Suddenly I'm the mad, bad, totally rad rebel Cinderella of the witching world resistance.

But hey, if the glass slipper fits…

*Gemini Wicked* is a spicy, shifty, paranormal adult academy why-choose romance and the scandalous sequel to *Gemini Wild*. Get ready for teacher-student forbidden heat, wolf and dragon shifters, dragon riders, bi awakening, all swords crossed, seven seductive warlocks, and a confident queen who never needs to choose. This series is guaranteed to whisk you away from your unmagical day and set your schoolgirl skirt on fire!

# Chapter One
## Zara

The whole world is watching.

And, no, I'm not exaggerating.

The whole world is specifically watching *me*, the celebrity bad girl—basically the royal wild child of the witching world—celebrate my twenty-first birthday at a star-studded gala on the royal yacht.

In the fiery glow of a Mediterranean sunset, helicopters are already circling the sleek white wedge of the *Aquarius Queen,* where she's anchored in the deepwater harbor off Icarus Island, like great whites circling a shark cage.

As we chug across the harbor toward the yacht in our borrowed boat from Racetrack's dive shop, I can already feel those cameras trained on me from all angles. To me, they're predators closing in for the kill.

The choppers circling and chuttering overhead.

The scrum of speedboats churning up the harbor.

And especially the mob of star-powered glitterati already aboard the *Aquarius* for the party. Betcha that school of piranhas already smells blood in the water.

Mine.

"Hey Zara! Gemini queen!" A pair of paparazzi on a jet ski zip past. *"Show us your tits!"*

Fuck.

In the balmy warmth of the June breeze flowing over my skin, my stomach churns worse than the sea in that jet ski's wake. My pulse hammers harder than the electric beat of the globally famous pop diva on that party boat who's performing exclusively for me tonight.

Scandal or no scandal, we're live in five on WNN.

The Witching News Network.

Racetrack pilots the dive boat through the choppy turquoise surf with her usual take-no-prisoners badassery. She's not any happier than I am about this whole shitshow or the media circus this latest invasion of my privacy's unleashed. So she swears like a pirate whenever the *kamikaze* choppers dive-bomb our deck, or the paparazzi speedboats cut it too close buzzing past. She scowls into the blinding blaze of flashbulbs and ignores the news hounds' vulgar shouts.

Let's just say my housemate at the helm isn't Miss Congeniality.

Me?

Teeth gritted, I smile tightly and wave like they all expect. The wind lifts my heavy mane of teal curls, freshly colored for my big day, and sends it swirling around my bare shoulders.

Or maybe that's my power rising.

I don't trust those cameras.

Especially not now.

Twitchy with nerves, I recross my legs in my sequined skirt, grip my silver clutch, and wish like hell this designer gown I'm wearing offered a concealed carry for my stiletto.

Too bad it doesn't. Which is, like, a design flaw.

This party frock is so skimpy I'm barely wearing a goddamn thong—

"Now stop fidgeting, darling, *do,*" Vasili purrs from the seat beside me, where he's lounging like a pasha in his own designer threads. "You don't want to spoil my masterpiece. Which is *you.* You've already been positively *wicked* for spurning the royal purple."

"Sorry to violate the dress code, Goblin King. Maybe you should throw me in detention, huh?" Despite my steadily worsening jitters, I sneak a peek at my outrageous alpha wearing that flamboyant getup.

This time, my smile's a real one.

Vasili Romanov.

He's more than one of my seven mates. More than the holy terror of the Icarus Academy. He's the Scorpio scion of the whole witching world. Which means he's got connections in the fashion world from New York to Milan. He basically dresses both of us for these fancy-shmancy parties.

"Besides," I murmur, all low and sultry, because just the sight of him makes my tummy flutter, "I'm pretty sure the real center of attention on that yacht tonight's gonna be you, bad boy. Same as always."

My appreciation triggers one of his sexy growls. "Hmmm. Just the way I like it."

No doubt about it. He's rocking that skinny violet tux, flown in and expertly tailored to fit his tall slim frame, like nobody's business. His dangerous eyes hide behind the violet frames of his fashionable rock-star spectacles, his cruel mouth glitters with a slick of pale lip gloss, and the ocean breeze flirts with his gilded mop of punk-rock hair.

Yowsa.

I'm literally shacking up with the warlock equivalent of David Bowie.

Among others.

And, despite those stalkerazzi pics of me and my guys popping up left and right in *The Witching Inquisitor*, this bad boy's never minded being filmed.

Unlike me.

Under my admiring eyes, Vasili gives a sultry smirk for the news cams and preens on the dive boat bench like the sexy-pretty diva he is.

"Hey, you're the birthday girl." On my other side, Neo's big warm hand lands on my naked knee and gives a gentle squeeze. "They're all here for you tonight, babe."

Neo Mercury's my fated mate.

More than any of my warlocks, he always knows what I'm feeling.

Now I meet his earnest green eyes, shining down at me through the stylish frames of his bookworm spectacles, with his soft purple curls all wind-tossed around his cleancut face. His broad shoulders and chest fill his crisp white tux to perfection, and his lavender bow tie complements his hair.

For his sake, to keep him from worrying, I dredge up another smile. I swear, he's too good for me. And not just because he's First Boy on the Dean's List. With him, I'm mated to the Clark Kent of the witching world.

That's how honest and sweet and good he is.

"Sorry, baby." I cover his hand with mine. "That latest batch of *Inquisitor* pics has me all on edge. I'm not used to living my life in the spotlight like you are. You're a senator's son. I'm a fucking cat burglar—"

"A *reformed* cat burglar," Lucius murmurs.

My wolf shifter headmaster's sitting quietly across the way, so close that our knees are brushing. With his vintage tux, imperial purple ascot, and Hungarian accent, Lucius Aries is pure Old World aristocrat. His keen eyes are hidden behind John Lennon sunglasses, Renaissance curls sleeked in a tidy knot away from his wary face.

Did I mention I'm also mated to the young and dapper Gary Oldman version of *Bram Stoker's Dracula*?

Especially when his fangs drop.

Racetrack swerves hard to avoid a daredevil speedboat that roars past out of nowhere. Sweet Jesus. We just barely escaped a head-on collision that makes Neo gasp and Dez yelp.

"I swear to fuck, Z." Racetrack scowls after the speeding moron. "These media sharks are gonna get you killed."

"We'll have to become accustomed to attracting attention. Both with and without our consent." Now Lucius is all growly, thanks to that barely averted threat, but he makes the effort and retracts his fangs. He's an intensely private guy, and I know he's no happier than I am about having his naked ass plastered across that scandal sheet, all wolfed out and madly fucking five of his own students (including me).

Thanks to our poly relationship—now openly exposed to the whole witching world—he's barely hanging onto his job. Which is one he treasures.

He definitely doesn't need *The Inquisitor* rubbing the Dean's nose in it.

"That's bullshit. I'm not gonna have your privacy violated like that." I lean forward to grip his hands, all hard and callused from running wild on all fours when he shifts, and gaze fiercely into his eyes. "Not on my account."

"We accepted that kind of attention, all of us, when we mated you." His fingers tighten around mine with a reassuring squeeze. "The Gemini queen."

"Queen in waiting." I glare as a chopper roars past like a gunship, strafing us with an arsenal of telephoto lenses that bristle through the open doors. "And we're not even officially mated yet. How much worse is this gonna be for you once we are?"

"We've all made our choice, Zara." Lucius gives my hands a firm squeeze to ground me. "My dear, we've chosen you. We've chosen *us*. We've chosen all of us."

The worst of the tension eases its viselike grip between my shoulders. He always knows what to say to make me feel better.

Out of all my mates, Lucius is the one who makes me feel safe.

I release him and settle back in my seat with a sigh. "Anyway, the Aquarius queen who's throwing my birthday coronation bash doesn't seem much like she wants to step down. We gotta share that throne—somehow—till she does. Which is another reason I'm really not looking forward to this shindig. Like, at all."

I don't have to say it.

But there's a whole fucking list of reasons I'm not looking forward to tonight.

Reasons related to my conflicted and begrudging feelings about surrendering the last of my hard-won freedom and permanently taking on this whole ball-and-chain queen gig.

I have mating bonds with all the guys in my harem.

Which means, when I'm dreading something the way I'm dreading tonight, they can smell it.

Me refusing to wear the royal purple to my own coronation?

That's just the tip of the iceberg.

"Zara's just sulking because she hasn't had her birthday spanking. *Yet*." Vasili smirks at me over his rock-star spectacles. "That's a gift from Lucius and me you'll have to wait for, little queen. But not for long."

Well, shit. *That* gets me squirming in my seat. My bare thighs rub together under my slitted skirt in a way I definitely notice. And the way Lucius leans forward and growls, deep in his chest, sets my heart skipping and my pulse skyrocketing for a whole new reason.

A little spanky-panky for me from my warlocks?

Oh, hell to the yeah. Sign me up, baby.

Just what I need to take the edge off. At least we can finish off this whole shitty day on a high note.

Lucius smells my mating scent perfuming the briny ocean air, which makes his nostrils flare. Behind his dark specs, his eyes pulse red.

That's his wolf rising.

Dayum.

Now my thong's getting damp.

"Not every girl gets a bloody crown for her birthday, does she, love?" That's Ronin Pendragon, standing in the prow with one booted foot braced on the gunwale, which means he's not smelling me. (But he's a wicked telepath, so he's definitely feeling me.) His long sleek hair streams behind him in the wind in a black silk banner of hotness. Under his tuxedo jacket and plum silk button-down, his painted-on leather pants cup his traffic-stopping ass in a way we all appreciate.

Despite our collective unease.

Shit. There's just no denying it. This morning's paper threw us all off balance.

Like, we really didn't need the whole witching world knowing my nipples are pierced.

"Yeah, no, not feeling the love." I scowl at a passing speedboat and barely resist the urge to flip those intrusive cameras the bird. "Even if this whole coronation—assuming Messalina does plan to crown me tonight, since we're all kinda guessing—is literally the only reason I'm even here."

"Along with the chance to party with the glitterati, yeah?" Dez pipes up from where she's tucked against Racetrack at the helm. The sparkles from Dez's orchid party dress glimmer against her sorrel skin.

Those two girls—Dez and RT—look comfy and settled together in a way I refuse to let myself envy. I mean, I'm not jealous of them together or anything (even though I'm bi). I'm just acknowledging the simplicity of having one mate who's totally settled in the relationship. Instead of the uneasy seven (half of whom distrust and actively hate each other) that I'm somehow rocking.

Including my other shifter mate who's late to this party—assuming he deigns to show up at all—because glitterati parties really aren't Maxim's scene.

Not to mention my two skittish Fae, who've been totally MIA and incommunicado for weeks.

Fuck.

The dive boat bumps gently against the stern of the yacht. Which gets me out of my head and back in the game.

Even if there's no one down here to greet us except a surly-looking deckhand who isn't much for conversation. Unsmiling, he grabs the rope Ronin tosses him and ties us up alongside.

"Huh. Not much of a welcome party." Racetrack gives the setup a sharp look as she cuts the power and pockets the key. "Not that you mind, I guess, if that bitch Messalina's not waiting right here for you with that crown on a goddamn cushion."

With her short blond hair and Ellen DeGeneres power suit, RT's got her don't-fuck-with-me face on. Suddenly I really appreciate having her with me tonight.

Strength in numbers, you feel me?

"I don't mind at all, believe me," I mutter. "Whatever Messalina's got planned, the sooner we get this shitshow behind us and our asses back to the Academy, the better I'll like it."

Neo helps me to my feet in my stilettos and gives me an anxious look. He's kinda hovering, they all are, because they feel what I'm feeling. "Is that your foresight acting up, babe?"

"It's not witchcraft. It's performance anxiety." Vasili sneers at a passing chopper like he's going to light it on fire (even though that's Ronin's power and not V's). The gust from the thing's noisy passing blows my hair around my head. "For fuck's sake. Better put your game face on, little queen, *do*. Or these Aquarius piranhas will eat you alive."

"Thanks for that, Goblin King." I give his disdainful pout the stink eye, but I do pull my shit together. "And don't be a dick tonight. I mean it."

He hums, but doesn't bother to answer.

Great.

If he's feeling pissy, he's gonna be a problem.

Then we're all scrambling out on the afterdeck, with me cursing these strappy shoes Vasili's talked me into, but grateful as fuck for the front slit I insisted on when he picked out my party frock. Which means my skirt's split all the way up to mid-thigh.

I need to know I can run or fight if I have to.

Even if I'm not armed.

I mean, the conventional way.

Ronin leaps out ahead of me, graceful as a panther on the rocking deck, then gives me a nice firm hand onto that treacherous sleek-ass yacht and slips an arm around my waist in that possessive way that always heats my hoochie. He's the Leo scion—a fire sign—so he literally runs hot anyway.

And it definitely doesn't hurt, having Ronin's unstoppable hotness squiring me up the stairs toward that well-dressed pack of cackling hyenas on the poop deck.

Or having Vasili and Lucius, two of my badass alphas, both looming at my back like sexy bodyguards.

Hopefully Maxim, who's kind of a loner but makes a ferociously intimidating third alpha, will turn up on his own.

"Stay tight and stick close, okay?" I call back to Neo and the girls, pitching my voice to carry over the throbbing bass from the live band and the pop icon's syrupy croon. "Just till we know what's what."

*No worries, babe,* Neo says, sweet and patient, through our mating bond. *I'm not going anywhere. You're permanently stuck with me.*

Which is about the nine hundredth reason why I love that guy.

His loyalty.

Unshakable.

I pull in a steadying breath and try to look relaxed and in control, like the next goddamn queen of the witching world, even if that's not how I feel. Those salacious pics of all six of us, snapped from some stalky angle outside my own bedroom window, have definitely knocked me off my stride.

But fuck if I'm gonna show it.

Any of it.

The party's already in full swing, with the oyster bar and the champagne fountain seeing plenty of action on the poop deck, the dance floor on the main deck rocking under laser lights and a mirrored ball, and the megastar and her band set up on the quarterdeck under a massive LED screen screaming *Happy Birthday, Zara Gemini!!* that lights up the twilight like a second sun.

Every deck on this superyacht is packed with the glitterati of the witching world, famous faces from all twelve clans, from the Senate to the WNN newsroom. All dressed to the nines in Tom Ford tuxes and Vera Wang gowns, mingling over champagne and canapés, sipping poison and swapping secrets, swaying to the tunes under swoopy strings of festive lights that glow against the violet sky.

No one makes any kind of announcement or fuss of any kind over our arrival. Which is kinda weird, but I'm definitely not complaining.

Still, I'm still the guest of honor (I mean, allegedly?) and we're kinda hard to miss.

Heads are already turning all over this deck, hands rising to cover the sibilant hiss of whispers, venomous eyes skittering over all of us like spiders. Over the floral notes of high-end fragrance and the dry fizz of bubbly, the dark spice of Mogadon pheromones—Vasili's, mine, the biochemical hit of sex and aggression from half the crowd on this party boat—is making my head spin.

Cheese on toast.

Why do I feel like this shiver of sharks is closing in for the kill?

These days, I'm a famous face myself. (Thanks for that, WNN). My spangly gown with its icy blue discs catches the sunset and throws flashes of light in all directions, my eyes glow purple with psi fire when I'm nervous (like now), and I'm definitely the only guest on board with a wild mane of teal hair that falls to my ass.

Not to mention Ronin towering at my side, with his powerful frame and leather pants and waist-length black mane, golden eyes flaming in his feral face while all those eyes devour him.

Thanks to those stalker pics, everyone on board knows he's packing a pierced dick behind his zipper.

Hell, right now, his Prince Albert is probably the most famous piercing in the witching world.

"Fuck, it's already famous. Half this lot have already seen it up close, love, believe me," Ronin says easily, because of course he's following my thoughts. Deftly he snares me a glass of bubbly from a passing tray. "I fucked half the bloody aristocracy before you came along, didn't I?"

Of course he has.

Till I came along, Ronin was just living his best bisexual manwhore life. He doesn't seem to miss it, but I love the way he owns that shit.

Vasili snickers as he slithers up alongside us. His cool fingers rescue the silver clutch I'm gripping too tightly (which looks better on him anyway). His free hand laces through mine.

That's my Goblin King staking his own casual claim.

On me.

"Yeah, well Sir One and Done is officially off the market. So they all better get used to that." I glare at a trio of bitches by the oyster bar, who aren't even trying to hide the way they're eye-fucking Ronin.

"Too right, he is. I'm taken." Ronin slips his champagne glass into my free hand. Then he smolders at V and nuzzles my ear with his hot lips in a way that makes me shiver with sudden need.

Vasili watches the two of us connect and hums with appreciation.

*Finally*, those three bitches look away. Good. I'm a goddamn alpha myself and they better show me—and my mates—some fucking respect.

Ronin eases away before we can take our PDA to the next level so he can collect glasses of bubbly for Neo and the girls. Which is fine. I'm definitely not planning another of our infamous public orgies in this joint.

I sip the crisp dry fizz of my Dom Perignon and play it all casual for the news cams.

But still.

It's weird. I wasn't expecting party favors or a table piled with presents. I don't know these people. And what little I do know, I don't like.

But no one comes to greet us. No one even throws me a token *Happy Birthday*.

Yet heads are turning our way all over this goddamn boat.

There's a world-famous rock star performing live to the starboard side. A spectacular Mediterranean sunset blazing away to port. Two good-looking girls with runway-quality bodies in barely-there party frocks making out on the dance floor.

And this whole joint's fixated on *us*?

The snap and pop of a nearby camera makes me flinch.

Which I fucking hate.

"Better get used to it, babe." That's Neo, bringing me a little cocktail plate piled high with fancy nibbles. We cluster around a tall standing table and try to ignore the attention. "Once you ascend, this is gonna be your court."

"Yeah, kinda, I guess." I nibble on a chocolate-covered strawberry, the sweet fruit and milk chocolate melting on my tongue, and study the crowd with a wary eye.

I don't see Messalina, who's supposed to be our hostess with the mostest. And the current queen of the witching world should *not* be hard to spot.

Plus there are other familiar faces I'm looking for and not seeing.

"Where's Daddy Dearest, I wonder?" Vasili, who prefers vodka to champagne, swirls an olive around his otherwise untouched martini glass and looks dangerous. "Mick Gemini is hardly known for being bashful. He should be front and center to see his little darling crowned queen."

"Guess he stood me up." I give an eloquent snort. "Or let me down. Again. Go figure."

Sure, my dad's a piece-of-shit casino czar who spent years after I ran away posting a bounty on my rebel ass. Last intel I heard, he was offering a cool two mill to whoever brought him my head in a bag.

But allegedly we're past all that, with me now tapped to be the next queen.

So, yeah, I figured my asshole dad would be here.

"Back at the Double Gemini in Vegas, counting his millions?" Racetrack's abandoned her bubbly for a longneck, she's not into frou-frou drinks, but none of us are drinking much. "My moms aren't here either, and I figured they would be. The Prynnes are big shots in the witching world."

"Speaking of big shots." Dez scans the scene with her pretty brow puckered. "Where's Neo's old man? Senator Mercury. Figured he'd be front and center for the beanfest, yeah?"

"He was definitely supposed to be." That's Neo, who's been trying to reach his dad on our finicky landline for days. We don't have functioning internet behind the magical wards that conceal the Icarus Academy from the mortal world. This is one of the times that sucks. "For both political and personal reasons, this isn't an event my dad would ever miss."

"For that matter, I was also very much expecting the Dean." Lucius isn't even pretending to drink. My headmaster's prowling around our table like a hunting wolf, his glasses tucked away now that darkness is falling. His sherry-colored eyes pulse with a reddish tinge. "Quite possibly, of course, her failing health has kept her away. But my own grandsire, as head of the Aries clan, should also be in attendance. In fact, he wrote me a letter to expect him."

My nerves tingle and plink with alarm like a plucked harp. Sharply I glance around our table at the circle of worried faces.

"That's, what, six no-shows? And all of them our allies—I mean, except my dad." I watch Lucius' nostrils flare as he paces and scents. Ronin's eyes glow golden with psi fire against his tawny skin. Resting on the table, Vasili's deadly casting hand twitches.

If V closes that telekinetic fist of his and means it, he'll crush half the people on this boat.

"Plus our so-called hostess," I finish. "The queen bee, as in bitch, is totally MIA."

Across the table, RT's flinty gray gaze locks with mine. She sucks in a breath and thunks her longneck down. "Yeah, something's fucked. You think we should motor, Z?"

Fuck. That's exactly what I'm thinking.

Neo, the senator's son, the most political of all my mates, looks downright alarmed. "Wait a minute, we can't just take off. This is Zara's big night. It's her coronation—I mean, maybe. But it's definitely her birthday. She's the guest of honor. There's like a million cameras filming us live right now—"

"Yeah, and they're filming for a reason. But it might not be the reason we think." I abandon my champagne, grab my clutch, and spin toward the stairs. "Come on, guys. We're outtie."

This time, no one argues, not even Neo.

Racetrack's already powering down the stairs for the afterdeck and our ride, towing a worried-looking Dez along with her.

My warlocks close ranks around me, all protective. Ronin on one side, Neo on the other, V and Lucius dropping back to guard my six.

But I haven't taken more than two steps away from the table before someone else slips into my escape path.

Actually, make that two someones.

My eyes are lowered, sweeping the deck for spills or other obstacles that could trip me up in my mile-high stilettos. Now my gaze slides up a pair of long legs sheathed in a sparkly evening gown in a purple so deep it's nearly black, poured over the tall slim lines of a supermodel physique, framed in a sleek curtain of merlot hair.

I know that hair.

And I definitely know that body.

I jerk to a halt like I've just been knifed.

My stunned gaze drills into a pair of wide violet eyes, set in a famously stunning face. Those are eyes I thought I'd never look into again, except from the cover of *Vogue* or *Vanity Fair*, where they're regularly featured.

I wonder if I could possibly be hallucinating. Like maybe those three sips of champagne I've taken have somehow gone straight to my head.

Then those lush lips, slicked with mauve, part around the purring Italian drama diva voice I remember like it was yesterday.

*"Ciao, bella.* Surely you're not leaving us already. Not without saying *arrivederci."*

Sweet.

Fucking.

Jesus.

I'm not hallucinating.

My mouth is open. I close it so I can swallow, because my throat's gone dry as a goddamn ashtray. Then I pull my shit together, plant a hand on my hip, and give her and her partner in crime—the good-looking guy in a spiffy tux who's hovering submissively at her heels—a cool once-over.

Yep. It's official.

My celebrity-studded twenty-first birthday bash is a goddamn fucking ambush.

I'm standing three feet away from my backstabbing bitch of an ex-BFF.

*And* my lying sack of shit ex-boyfriend.

"Well, there goes the fucking neighborhood," I drawl. "Cleo Ferrari. And Xiao Long Zheng. You two come all this way just to finish the job you royally fucked up in Singapore and kill me?"

# Chapter Two
## Vasili

It isn't often yours truly is caught by surprise.

Anyone at this Academy will tell you. I've built my horrible reputation around being hard to startle and easy to enrage.

Yet here I stand, caught flat-footed and slack-jawed, like the village idiot. Reeling as though I've just been sucker-punched.

Is it the sight of my little queen getting ambushed at her own birthday bash? Going toe to toe while the cameras roll with the bitchy bestie who betrayed her *and* the ex-lover who did his damnedest to get her kidnapped or killed?

Well, I'm certainly not amused.

But that isn't the reason I'm reeling.

I'm reeling because I've just made the staggering connection between Zara's ex-BFF (whom she never cares to discuss) and my own family history with the fishy bitch.

All through my cold and loveless childhood, the Ferrari girl now stealing the limelight was the favorite deadly *protégée* of my fucking father.

Nikolai Romanov.

His name alone is enough to trigger the ugly landslide of loneliness and shame I've never really left behind.

And to ignite my rage.

Especially when that arrogant former flame of Zara's—Xiao Long Zheng—prowls in close, all sleek muscles and dangerous attitude, looking like a fuckable feast in an Armani tux that's open to show off the gold chain at his throat.

Dear fuck.

I'm incensed, but I manage to close my mouth, fix my face, and pull myself together. This is simply not the time to deal with my truckload of unresolved  queer-boy-rejected-and-tossed-away-by-Daddy  emotional garbage.

It's time to deal with Xiao.

Surely, he can't be planning to kiss her?

"Looking good tonight, *bambina*. Even if you're out of uni. Didn't you get the memo about the purple?" With a cocky grin, the bastard reaches for her.

I really can't imagine what she'll do.

Zara may be the only guest on this party boat (including the pop diva) who's not wearing the royal purple. But Zara isn't the same girl these two betrayed in Singapore. Since then, she's claimed her power.

She's become the Gemini queen.

In fact, my darling girl is already levitating in her Jimmy Choo shoes, floating a few inches off the deck, teal hair swirling around her shoulders, violet sparks dancing along her fingers. And the fact that Ferrari bitch and her boyfriend—who is clearly no warlock—aren't batting an eye?

Color me suspicious.

"Don't even think about touching me," Zara growls at both her exes. If those two had any sense, hearing the spooky metallic resonance of her lightning voice, they'd be pissing themselves. "What are you even doing on this yacht?"

"Invited." That bastard ex-beau of hers gives a cocky shrug, but he's smart enough (barely) to keep his distance. "Guess the gloves are off now, aren't they? I tried to tell you about Cleo that night in Vegas, but did you listen? Nope, instead you were obsessed with—"

"Enough, *bello*." The Ferrari bitch doesn't even twitch. But her cool voice reels him in like a fish.

Lover Boy falls silent and retreats to Cleo's side, where she clearly prefers him.

Now he's sulking.

Truly, it isn't a good look.

Zara lowers her floating form to alight on the deck. I slink into the shadows near the bar to regain my famously cool composure. There I lurk like the rattlesnake I am, just waiting for some unsuspecting fool to annoy me.

Then I'll strike.

Magically speaking, I'm the biggest threat on this megayacht. I'm the most lethal warlock in our polycule, not to mention the most actively homicidal. Especially now that I've grasped the connection (which can't be a coincidence) between Zara's ex-BFF and my funnel web spider of a father.

Yet, somehow, both members of Zara's former *ménage* seem to have overlooked me. Which isn't easy to do. I'm a gorgeous six feet-plus of celebrity warlock fashionably sporting a violet tux and a gilded mane of rock-star hair.

From this vantage, I can't see my little queen's face. But her voice is positively stony. "She's a grifter. You're a hacker. I was the one who took the risks. I had your backs. *Always.* But you—didn't have mine."

Finally, Zara's brittle voice fractures. "How many more secrets are you hiding?"

My little darling's pain makes me more than annoyed. I'm positively murderous. My eyes narrow to slits and my chest burns with a rising tide of rage.

"*Bene.* The time for secrets is over. Tonight is the night I finally tell you mine." Cleo Ferrari has all the poise of a runway model, including the ability to strike a pose. Every move this girl makes is calculated. Now she shifts a sinuous hip under her sleek designer gown and touches a manicured finger to her pouty lip. "You know. This doesn't have to end unpleasantly for you, *bella.*"

Now my own lip curls in a snarl.

What *I* know is that Ferrari bitch was far more to Zara than her partner-in-crime or even her BFF. What I *don't* know is how much of her former… affection… for this duplicitous and deadly creature Zara might still be harboring.

"I could say the same to you." Zara hums in her special lightning voice and raises a deadly hand. Purple lightning spills from her fingers and crackles down her arm. "You said it yourself. The gloves are off… *bella.*"

Thunder mutters in the twilight sky. The tinny reek of ozone seeps through the air. A few random looky-loos edge away from my electrified darling, which is certainly wise.

They wouldn't like her when she's angry.

"Careful, my dear," Lucius slips up behind to murmur at Zara's ear. Of course, with my shifter senses, I too can hear him. "This is no random encounter. You're the future queen, and this vessel is awash in journalists. Don't give these two the reaction they're clearly seeking."

He's right, of course.

The words have barely left his lips before a chopper buzzes past, cameras protruding from the open door. The breeze from their passing swirls Zara's teal hair around her shoulders and plays with the spangly mirrored discs of the ice-blue gown around her sleek legs. In that moment, she's every inch a lightning witch.

Lucius looms over her, utterly alpha and deliciously lurky, while his wolfish mating scent perfumes the air. Zara leans into his touch by reflex.

But she gives no indication whatsoever that she's listening.

My, my.

Our wolf nuzzles her bare shoulder and smolders at her ex-lovers with his red-tinged eyes. To his beast, those two are sexual rivals for Zara's bed.

I'm not entirely certain he's wrong.

Lucius bristles at the pair, but he's far too mannerly to growl. Instead, he stalks to the rear of our cozy ensemble. He's searching the crowd, scanning the clump of dancers wiggling under the main deck stage where that perky diva's still belting out tunes despite the sudden threat of rain.

"Messalina Aquarius," Lucius snarls at me through his fangs as he prowls past. "Where is she?"

"No idea," I say briefly.

Wherever the Aquarius queen is lurking, it's more than obvious that wicked witch is responsible for this entire welcome party. Clearly she's invited these two troublemakers to spoil Zara's special night.

And whatever web his black widow *protégée* is spinning, Nikolai Romanov must somehow be involved.

I grit my teeth and fight viciously through the ugly emotional snarl of my daddy issues.

Meanwhile, Cleo Ferrari tilts her head and looks thoughtful. The rising wind flirts with her burgundy mane.

Ronin and Neo have closed ranks around Zara. No one's getting past

Ronin, of course, but I'm not certain how Neo plans to defend her. Perhaps by hurling a textbook at someone's head? Or challenging our enemies to a spelling bee?

Instead, our bookworm quietly takes Zara's clutch.

In case she needs to fight.

For that small gesture alone, for the absolute belief in her it signifies… well, that's why we all adore him.

"Aw, *bambina*, don't be like that." Zara's ex-boy toy pipes up again, trying everyone's patience by speaking. "We weren't the only ones keeping secrets, were we. You didn't exactly sashay up to Cleo and me the night we met in Bangkok and say 'Hey, before I fuck the two of you six ways to Sunday, just wanted to let you know I'm the Gemini queen.'"

"Because I *wasn't*," Zara fires back. "Messalina's daughter—Cybelle—she was supposed to rule. She was supposed to be the Aquarius queen. I only got shackled with this whole queen gig after Cybelle got killed. That's what made Messalina the last Aquarius. And me the first Gemini."

For a heartbeat, Cleo's brow puckers. Her bony supermodel shoulders tighten with a subtle tension.

Hmmm.

That's the first flicker of genuine emotion I've seen from that walking mannequin all night.

Zara plants a hand on her hip. "Besides, hello? I thought you two were fucking *mortal*. Which I guess you're not. Since you're here."

"You thought what everyone thought. Ensuring the entire mortal world believes the same… well, this has been my role." The Ferrari girl sighs. "*Bene*. I never meant to find myself in this position. In this, you are not alone."

Lover Boy gives a cocky shrug that makes me want to slap him. "Well, we're here now. No reason the three of us can't pick up where we left off, right, *bambina*?"

My breath hisses and my eyes narrow.

Never mind that the thought of another woman—*any* woman—joining Zara and the rest of us in our bed is revolting. For fuck's sake, I identified as gay until Zara came along.

But these two, in particular, are joining our polycule over my dead and decomposing body.

Fortunately, my girl shuts him right down. "Yeah, no, not happening. There's not, like, a vacancy in my bed. And even if there was? My guys and me, we vote on that shit. You two wouldn't even be on the ballot."

Neo hasn't said a word, because he knows this is Zara's show. But at this, he gives an earnest nod.

Of course, that sweet boy fondly imagined he was straight until Ronin deflowered him.

But it's clear the Ferrari bitch isn't getting his vote either.

"You sure we can't change your mind?" That pure idiot of a Xiao simply won't take no for an answer. In fact, he's fool enough to slink toward Zara.

Ronin's warning growl puts a stop to that. My boyfriend's taller and broader through the chest than Xiao, and Ronin's eyes burn gold when his power rises.

He's fucking deadly. And he's on a hairpin trigger.

*Careful, darling,* I purr at him through our bond. *Bloodshed makes such a mess. And that Dolce & Gabbana tuxedo jacket you're wearing requires dry cleaning.*

My boyfriend's the strongest telepath in our polycule. But our bond is weirdly silent. It's atypical, but I suppose he's distracted by this unexpected encounter.

Still, I don't like it.

The last thing I need to feel tonight is more alone.

Lover Boy shoots Ronin a cautious look, then retrains his broody gaze on Zara. "Guess not then, huh. You, me, her? Too bad."

"Not really," Zara shoots back.

"Too bloody right," Ronin mutters in disgust.

Now Lover Boy's eyes turn shifty. "You know this isn't personal, right? Like we were ever gonna say no when a sweet deal like this falls right in our lap?"

My skin prickles in a cold trickle of warning.

"What deal?" my girl snarls.

"It's not personal, *bambina.*" Xiao's handsome face hardens. "But it's not an offer we could refuse."

That's when that arrogant ass whips a fucking *pistol* from his tux.

And points it straight at Zara.

Somehow no one ever expects anyone to bring an old-fashioned handgun to a witching party.

He's fast. I'll give him that. He's trained and he's lethal and he's fast. Plus that slippery bastard chose his moment with exquisite care. The moment when he's too close to Zara to miss.

I hiss with alarm. My casting hand sweeps up.

The whiplash snap of my witchcraft coils and crackles through every synapse.

Ronin's already firing into motion with his own killer instincts, snarling and shoving Zara into Neo's startled arms, then diving in front of them. All too clearly, he intends to take the hit himself.

No.

*Not* Ronin.

That's simply not happening.

Lover Boy flips the safety off and gives my boyfriend a nasty grin. In a sort of hideous slow motion, his trigger finger tightens—

With a sweep of my ringed hand, I let my bad side out to play.

The telekinetic wallop of my witchcraft sends that bastard hurling backward through the air, gun flying from his hand, before he can tighten his grip. I launch Xiao airborne across the deck before he can lay a single fucking finger on Zara or Ronin, who are both fucking *mine*.

Lover Boy's flying form crashes into an unsuspecting waiter, toiling along under a tray of empty glasses, and knocks both of them sprawling into a bulkhead with a cry.

The pair crash to the deck in a tangle of startled limbs and a shower of broken glass.

Oh, dear. Collateral damage.

Despicable me.

A heartbeat later, the handgun hits the deck and goes off with a deafening bang that sets my ears ringing and leaves a bullet hole in Messalina's starboard bulkhead. Across the deck, scattered screams ring out. The nearby looky-loos scatter for cover.

Through a tide of fleeing bodies, I stalk from the shadows with a vicious grin. Apparently, when it comes to protecting my mates, I have a violent streak.

Who knew?

If Lover Boy had any sense, he'd stay down, right where I put him, and beg for mercy. Instead, he scrambles to his feet with an offensively catlike grace and shrugs out of his ruined tuxedo jacket.

Does he really imagine he's going to challenge… *moi*?

"Well, well, Lover Boy," I purr like the villain I am. "Look who has a death wish. Bring it on, *do*."

I'd love nothing better than a little homicide.

Looming between Zara and the threat, Ronin growls at him, "Haven't met Vasili yet, have you, mate? I'd bloody well stay down if I were you."

"Well, he isn't wrong," I murmur. "But don't let that discourage you."

Typically, I hide my horrible fangs. They're repulsive, and they don't retract like Lucius'. This once, I bare those horrid incisors I'm cursed with. I bare them in a bloodthirsty grin.

That's shifter instinct. An intimidation display.

Sadly, my victim doesn't appear intimidated. An ugly look lurks in Xiao's face. He rolls his shoulders with fluid grace and pads toward me with a panther's deadly intent.

With an idle flick of my casting hand, I send the fallen handgun flying over the rail to splash into the night-dark sea.

Truly, there's no point taking chances. Mere seconds ago, that thing was pointed at Ronin.

"Know all about you." Xiao's menacing glare flickers between Ronin and me—the primary threats he imagines he's facing. "I know about *all* of you. I know how you fight. I know how you fuck. I know who you bend for, Pendragon. I even know Romanov snores in his sleep."

As if!

"Well, I never." I expel a huff of outrage. "I've never snored in my life."

Lover Boy gives me a sly smirk.

Of course, everyone knows more about us than I'd like since *The Inquisitor*'s gotten so… inquisitive. But that scandal rag certainly doesn't come with a soundtrack. Obviously. What this one's just said proves it.

Still, there's something happening here that's very much amiss. Something off with this entire setup. The Ferrari girl and I rarely interacted growing up, and she doesn't betray the merest flicker of recognition now.

But my identity is no secret, so she's surely well aware.

With or without my father's lethal star pupil in his corner, Lover Boy can't imagine we're going to let him anywhere near Zara. He's deliberately provoking all of us, especially our little queen—and not in a good way.

He's not even a warlock, for fuck's sake. Trust me to know. So what's his game?

More to the point, what's hers?

Cleo Ferrari arrests her sidekick in his tracks with an impatient look and a fusillade of Italian I can't follow.

Xiao's fists clench and his jaw knots. But her curt command stops him.

For now.

I saunter over to lurk at Ronin's side. My boyfriend's teeth are bared in a savage scowl. Flames flicker and burn in his topaz eyes.

His own gift is rising.

A stern-faced Lucius pads into our path and inserts himself between the warring parties. "Ronin, Vasili, all of you—stand down. Kindly allow me to handle this situation."

"Oh, very well, pet. If you must." I pout.

Truly, he can be a terrible spoilsport.

Sparing me a narrow look of warning, Lucius frowns at our enemies. "I'm Lucius Aries, headmaster of Villa Augustus at the Icarus Academy. In the Dean's absence, I speak on her behalf. In the event you're unaware, I must advise you that violence within the island wards is strictly forbidden by the Academy Codex. Those wards were lowered to allow this vessel into the harbor. As guests, you're bound by those obligations."

For Lucius' sake, I manage not to roll my eyes. Of course he intends to de-escalate the crisis, like the responsible headmaster he is.

But this entire dynamic is far too volatile for even his cool head to manage.

Too bad, of course.

"Hey Teach, sorry to rain on your parade, but these two don't give a single shit about the Academy Codex." Zara slips out of Neo's protective arms, strides over to Cleo, and gets right in the Ferrari bitch's face.

"That stunt Xiao just pulled. Is that what you came here for?" she demands of this girl whose smoldering face I'll never see gracing the cover of my *Cosmo* in quite the same light again. "To finish the fucking Singapore job and kill me?"

Now that the handgun is out of play, this reunion is drawing an audience to rival the pop diva's synchronized gyrations on stage. In fact, we're attracting an actual crowd, and the cameras are definitely rolling. As for that witchy bitch Messalina Aquarius, our hostess is still nowhere to be found.

But Cleo Ferrari only has eyes for Zara.

"You never understood what the job even was," the supermodel says tightly. "For you, it was always a sort of game. To protect your precious freedom. To thumb your nose at your horrible father. Someone must take the broader view, *bella.*"

Zara clenches her fists and pushes in closer. I don't think the dear girl even realizes she's floating. Levitation is one of the newer manifestations of her ever-expanding repertoire of witchy powers.

"Is that what this is, Cleo?" she grits, low and ugly. "You taking the broader view? Or is my asshole dad still bankrolling your fashion fix?"

Cleo Ferrari's runway pout curls in a scowl of contempt. "Mick Gemini was never the one calling the shots. *Cavolo.* Why won't you listen? I tell you, I didn't come here to kill you."

"Oh? Your sidekick certainly could have fooled us," I murmur.

Ronin snarls in agreement. He's still tracking Xiao and shifting to keep his own beefcake build between Lover Boy and Zara.

As for Zara and Cleo, their gazes are locked together. Neither one spares anyone else on the scene a particle of attention.

"Well, that's a relief," Zara drawls. "That you're not actually trying to kill me. You know, what with the cameras rolling and all the little kiddies watching at home."

I hum with admiration for my girl's general badassery. She's fearless. She's a goddess. Only we—her warlocks—sense that she's hurting.

She doesn't trust easily, she's tender-hearted, and her former *ménage* knifed her in the back.

Normally I'd be sensing all this firsthand through our mating bond. But the psychic bond that connects me with all the mates I've bitten— plus Ronin, spared my horrible bite but bonded to me all the same—those psychic bonds are silent.

Which can only mean someone in this crowd is carrying a nullifying object.

Something else about this entire setup that sets my nerves on edge.

Cleo is saying, oh, something or other to Zara about her tedious wish to talk. She even lapses into earnest Italian (which Zara speaks) in an apparent attempt to demonstrate her sincerity. But that Ferrari bitch has lost her audience.

At least, she's lost *me*.

I, Vasili Romanov, am no longer entertained.

That little fuck toy Xiao is eyeing Ronin, trying to sidle closer to Zara, and generally looking shifty. His hand hovers near his trouser pocket in a way that makes me suspect he's carrying another lethal weapon.

He can't imagine he'll succeed in getting anywhere near her. Still, all too clearly, he's up to no good.

I summon my power with a slash of my casting hand that shoves that wretch backward, snarling, through a sea of broken glass until his back hits the bulkhead. There I pin him to the surface like a bug.

I'm seriously tempted to crush him.

While the cameras roll, Lover Boy bears his teeth and hisses at me like a rabid cat.

"By all means, *do* keep struggling." I fish out my compact to check my lip gloss. "I can easily keep this going all night."

"Vasili, my dear," Lucius murmurs. "I beg that we not make this unfortunate encounter any more of a public scene. Especially since we're being televised."

"Oh, so we're being discreet, are we." I snap my compact closed and give the entire mess a vicious look.

Cleo sighs something in Italian that sounds exasperated, the poor dear. Then she snaps, *"Xiao."* Without even looking at her poor minion.

Abruptly, Lover Boy stills in my telekinetic grip and gives her a narrow look.

"Mr. Romanov," my headmaster says quietly, which is oh so civil of him. But I know a command from Lucius Aries when I hear one. "I won't ask again."

When all's said and done, he's still my headmaster. (Except when he bends for me.)

"Oh, very well. *Fine*." Pouting, I splay my manicured fingers to release my hostage.

Sneering, Xiao scrambles free of the bulkhead, tugs his clothing into order, and touches the gold chain at his throat.

"Zara. *Per favore.*" That's the Ferrari bitch again, never looking away from my girl (who used to be *her* girl), and quite possibly wanting her back. Cleo's picture-perfect supermodel face goes soft. "Xiao plays his own game, as always. A game I've told him he will not win. Me, I only wish to talk."

Slowly my girl stops levitating and lets her stilettos graze the floor. But her hair keeps swirling around her shoulders in the psychic wind.

Another chopper roars past. Ronin glares at the thing like he's seriously tempted to set it on fire. But Lucius' demand for restraint holds him too in check.

"Then talk," Zara clips out, glaring at Cleo. "Make it snappy."

Cleo tries to touch her arm, but Zara knocks her hand roughly aside.

The other girl covers the awkward moment with a smooth shrug. "It is true, yes? I'm not what I claim to be. But I was given no choice."

Zara shifts her weight impatiently. "What, did my dad hold a gun to your head and order you to take his money? Besides, Lucius told me how the Academy got you on board when he nabbed me in Singapore. Didn't sound to me like you needed much convincing."

"You do not wish to be queen, no?" Cleo's perfect teeth sink into the violet matte of her lower lip. "And I—don't you see—I have no choice to be anything else."

I'm really not following all the swirly undercurrents of this overdue *tête-à-tête*, certainly not with our mating bond all muddy. But Lucius sucks in a sharp breath.

He's putting all the jagged little pieces of this puzzle together in a way I'm suddenly quite keen to follow.

Zara folds her arms across her chest and scowls at her ex-BFF. "Yeah, sure, I'm not all yippy-skippy about the whole queen gig. But I'm dealing with it. What are you trying to say?"

The Ferrari girl's mile-long lashes sweep down.

Perhaps she's genuinely pensive about whatever scandalous secret she's about to impart. But, more likely, the bitch is deploying the finely honed weapons of deception and misdirection she learned from my fucking father.

Because why waste all that drama?

"For me, this was never about the money. Or the title. None of it." Cleo shakes back her merlot hair. "*Merda!* I have a… responsibility… I was never allowed to ignore—"

"What the fuck, Z? We going or staying?" That's our Racetrack, appearing abruptly at the head of the stairs to the afterdeck where our getaway vehicle awaits.

She and Dez, lucky girls, made it down before the shitshow started. Clearly, they've both been biding their time.

RT's sudden appearance interrupts Cleo's confession and seems to shatter some sort of spell for Zara too. I know the Ferrari girl meant more to her than a partner in crime, more even than a trusted ally. What I don't know is how Zara still feels, in her heart of hearts, about the backstabbing bitch.

Or what that backstabbing bitch has planned for Zara.

My little queen glances around at all of us. The pop diva's fallen silent and is being hurriedly ushered offstage. The choppers circle at a watchful distance.

Now the entire ship's watching us. Watching in an eerie silence that confirms every one of my horrid suspicions.

Something about this entire scenario is about to explode in our faces.

The pregnant silence is broken by the low growl of the dive boat motor.

Clearly, that's Dez at the throttle.

"Whatever this is, I don't want any part of it," Zara says curtly. Her turquoise gaze veers to find me. "We're going."

"An excellent notion." Lucius dips his chin in a nod of relief. "I'll just remain behind to make our excuses to the queen—"

"Actually," Lover Boy says from his safe spot at Cleo's side, "you're staying. You all are. For the ceremony."

Zara barks out a laugh and gives her vivid head a violent shake. "Yeah, no, I don't think so. For some reason, you know, I'm just not feeling it?" She shifts into motion and strides toward Racetrack, with Ronin and Neo falling right in behind her. "Not gonna be any effing coronation tonight—"

"There will be a coronation tonight, Zara Gemini, I assure you." A familiar female voice, ringing with authority and projected to carry, jerks my startled gaze toward a sudden blaze of electric light from the stage that nearly blinds me. "A coronation to crown the next queen. The queen with whom I willingly share my throne and my power. But that queen won't be some trashy casino slut of a Gemini who gets photographed carousing in a naked orgy."

Scattered murmurs sweep the ship. The assembled crowd of looky-loos is nodding like bobble heads.

Morons.

Messalina lowers her voice for effect. "Or a reckless, willful, wicked girl who kills her own mother and wipes out half of downtown Vegas in a temper tantrum. That wicked girl is unworthy to be anyone's queen."

Zara stumbles in her stilettos and sucks in a ragged gasp.

In the twisty maze of my brain, a fiendish recognition of this entire diabolical setup finally snaps into place. I tingle with an electric flood of rage.

"That manipulative Aquarius *cunt*," I hiss.

"What the fuck?" Ronin spins around looking murderous, black hair flying around his powerful frame, psi fire burning in his eyes.

My stare sweeps over Zara's whitening face—it's truly a low blow, attacking my girl over that ancient history, due to her mother's piss-poor judgment, when Zara was just a child—then swerves back to Messalina.

Our hostess with the mostest is standing at center stage, looking regal and unstoppable in her glittering purple gown, and using the diva's own mic to make her public service announcement.

"I'm crowning the next *Aquarius* queen," Messalina announces to the world at large. A murmur of interest ripples through the idiotic crowd. "I'm crowning my daughter with my late husband Oberon, the last Dark Fae King."

"Oh, crap," Neo breathes beside me.

Still patiently holding Zara's clutch, he's pale under his magenta curls. His free hand shoots out to grip Zara's, anchoring her against what he clearly sees coming.

Zara stands perfectly still, eyes wide with shock. Against her bubblegum lipstick and cobalt eyeliner, her gorgeous Hollywood face is etched with an emotion that, on her, is unfamiliar.

A soul-wrenching emotion that looks hideously like… shame.

Then that Grade A Ferrari bitch glides forward, cool and composed like she's walking a Paris runway, and poses for the crowd.

Messalina sweeps a royal arm in the bitch's direction and announces, in a ringing voice that resonates with pride and triumph, "All hail! Tonight I crown *her*. My long-lost, half-Fae, twice-royal daughter. Cleopatra Regina Aquarius."

Now Messalina swings to pinpoint Zara with a commanding finger. "I call upon *you*, Zarina Selene Gemini, to be the first of my subjects to bow down to her in homage. To renounce your claim and worship this worthy Aquarius scion, who was always destined to be the witching world's next queen."

# Chapter Three
## Zara

Oh, hell to the no.

That's all I can think.

Because I'm not gonna dwell on the way my whole body just shriveled up with guilt and shame. I'm not gonna spiral like a goddamn pinwheel over the shit that went down with my mom.

I fucked that up. I did. I couldn't control my own lightning. I took the roof off the Double Gem. I was a kid, I was just coming into my power, I was hurt, attacked, terrified, trying to help, blah blah blah.

Here's the bottom line. Eighty-seven innocents ended up dead. Including my mom (who wasn't exactly innocent). I can never atone for that.

Never.

Yeah. Maybe that means I don't deserve to be queen.

But that doesn't mean Cleo does.

I mean, where was she when Avalon was dying, due to the late king Oberon not having an heir? If she's who she says, that was *her fucking mess* I just cleaned up over there. Not that I'm complaining about hooking up with Ash and Zephyr. But the Dark Fae King's definitely making life for me and my guys even more complicated and contentious.

Long story short? I'm sure as shit not about to *bow down to her in homage.*

I lick my upper lip, sticky with glitter gloss yet somehow dry as fuck, and search the sea of accusatory faces turned toward me all over this party boat. I don't know these people from Adam, they're all witching world aristocracy, sleek and well-bred, the way a runaway wild child casino rat like me could never aspire to be.

They're pedigreed greyhounds.

I'm a junkyard dog.

But, fuck, the look on all those faces is identical. Unfriendly. Judgy. Condemning me for more than what I did.

They're condemning me for *who I am.*

These people don't know me. They only know what the media—and that bitch in heels on stage who calls the shots—wants them to know.

Still, that look of collective condemnation, like I'm something they just scraped off their shoe, makes me want to shrink in my stilettos.

"Take a breath, babe." Neo's gripping my icy hand firmly in his warm grip, which is part of what's keeping me anchored. "No one's making you do anything. It's all some kind of mixed-up misunderstanding. We're gonna sort this out. Together."

"It's a blooming lie, that's what it is." Ronin's looming protectively at my other side, still scowling and planted like a tank between me and my exes. "That Oberon kid fucking *died* due to Messalina's shit. That's the whole bloody reason Zeph kidnapped you, Zara. Either Messalina was fibbing to him about her kid being dead all those years, or she's fibbing to the whole witching world now. Either way, she's a liar."

Lucius is standing guard on his own, crouched like a hunting wolf, staring intently at the stage. He's all sober and respectable in his vintage tux and tied-back hair, brow furrowed and eyes fierce.

But he's not as civilized as he looks.

A continuous growl rumbles from his powerful chest.

Shit, I really hope he's not gonna shift. The last thing we need right now is him wolfing out.

Plus I can't tell what anyone's thinking, because someone in this mob's apparently packing a nullifying object.

Yay.

That's when my snake slithers into the spotlight and saunters straight into the sea of news cams.

"Talk about a fairytale," Vasili sneers in a cool voice that carries from stem to stern. "A lost Aquarius queen. A dead Fae princess miraculously risen from the dead. *That's* certainly an imaginative story. Manufactured in the nick of time by a failed queen who'll obviously say *anything* to cling to her pathetic crown. Truly, darlings, are we buying it?"

He jabs that pointed question right at our viewing audience, then deploys the lifted Romanov eyebrow for effect. He's really talking to the witches and warlocks at home. Like, the commoners who are my real subjects, the ones who can't have kids and are scared and helpless and losing their witchcraft due to this endless succession of weak and unmagical Aquarius queens.

The ones who need me.

The ones going extinct.

A few of the looky-loos on board shift and mutter. These aristocrats might be like the spoiled citizens of the Capital in *The Hunger Games*. But they're not all Team Messalina.

Yet.

A tiny trickle of hope seeps through the burning weight of my shame. I lift my head, straighten my shoulders, and stare straight into the cameras I've been avoiding my whole life.

*Gimme a chance here, people,* I'm trying to say. *Gimme a chance to save us.*

Hips swaying, lips smirking, the focus of every eye in his violet tux, Vasili catwalks to the rail that looms over the main deck. Then he sneers down his perfect nose at the queen bee on stage.

"It's really too bad for you," he purrs, "that it's the witching world Senate, not the lame-duck queen, who holds the constitutional power to elect our next sovereign. You'll just have to get with the program, Lina. They've chosen *her*. Zara. The Gemini queen."

Messalina strides to the platform's edge to meet his challenge. She's elegant as fuck in her glittery purple gown and heels, electric light sparkling in the tiara that crowns her twist of fiery hair. All spiffed up in a way that looks effortless.

And just totally at ease in the spotlight. In a way I'll never be.

In that one way, she suddenly reminds me of Cleo.

"After tonight, Vasili Romanov," Messalina breathes into the mic like she's Marilyn Monroe, "knowing there's another claimant—a *worthy* claimant, one whose discretion is flawless, one whose commitment to duty is unimpeachable, one whose reputation is beyond reproach—I assure you, the Senate *will* reconsider. I've already petitioned, as is my right under witching world law, to bring a vote to the floor."

My blood congeals to a slurry of ice.

My gut clenches in a fist of dread.

Wow. That's, like, a blow. She's obviously been planning to shake up the succession for a while. Probably since those first scattered rumors about a rival claimant popped up in *The Inquisitor* last winter.

Neo tightens his grip on my hand and whispers, "Oh, sugar."

Which is his way of swearing.

"You 'lead' the Senate. In. Name. Only." Vasili cracks each word like a whip. He's standing on familiar terrain and crackling with confidence, because he teaches our Foundations of Witching World law class as part of his adjunct professor gig, and he's a holy terror behind the lectern. (I'm not kidding. He literally makes his students cry.)

So he has no problem contradicting the queen, natch, with total Vasili snark. "Your role in the Senate is purely a ceremonial function. And it's *barely* even that."

That's my Goblin King. Sticking up for me.

"So, um, he's actually right, Your Majesty." Much more respectfully, Neo trots up to stand right next to him. Of course, since we're linked, my bookworm draws me forward with him. Even when more hostile scrutiny from this unfriendly crowd of bluebloods is literally the last thing I need. "My dad's president pro tem of the Senate. Bringing a vote to the floor, well, that's his responsibility. And he supports Zara."

He sounds all polite and apologetic for contradicting her, but totally determined in a way that warms my cold and shellshocked body.

My guys are with me. They're solid.

Even the three who are missing.

Right?

Besides, I'm common-law mated to half the scions of the twelve major clans in the witching world. For fuck's sake, I'm the Gemini scion myself. By mating Zephyr, I'm actually legally married to a political ally, if you buy into that whole Dark Fae custom. (Which is, like, a major bone of contention in my harem. And wouldn't it be great if Zephyr were actually here tonight, instead of being MIA?)

Anyway, my point is, she can't get rid of *all* of us.

Can she?

Obviously, Neo's argument would hold more weight if Senator Mercury was standing here next to us. The way he's supposed to be.

Across the crowded deck, Messalina looks right into my eyes and smiles in a way that makes my skin crawl.

"I'm afraid Senator Mercury has… reconsidered," she whispers into the mic. "Now that the whole witching world has seen… *this*."

Right on cue, the huge LED screen behind her lights up in a blaze of color. The familiar contours of my bedroom flash into view. It's a video feed, my room at night, lit by the warm golden glow of my study desk lamp. Judging by the angle, this view was shot from inside the vacant *domus* across the street.

My stomach sinks to my stilettos.

"Oh, fuck," I whisper.

The stalkerazzi strike again.

There's my sweet Neo, all buff and nakey, kneeling on hands and knees in my big medieval bed. With Max's dick stuffed in his mouth and Vasili's cock buried in his ass, at the perfect pornographic angle for all three of my guys to be fully visible. Max is gripping a fistful of Neo's curls for control, his lithe body pumping strongly into our bookworm's sweet mouth, with Max's buttery blond hair slithering loose around his suntanned shoulders and his shifter eyes flaming with purpose.

Sleek and supple, Vasili's undulating into our bookworm from behind like the snake he is, his pretty face ruthless, his icy gaze burning into Max's over Neo's back the whole time.

Framed in the next window over, there's me. Standing mother-naked, with my wild mane of teal hair floating everywhere, my hands gripping the frame for balance, and my tan lines and pierced nipples on full fucking display.

Again.

Goddamn it.

Behind me looms a half-shifted Lucius—bestial and snarling, fangs distended and eyes burning red—gripping my hips in his taloned claws and pounding into me with savage intent. My mouth is open, my eyes are closed, my face is ecstatic, and my tits bounce with every one of Lucius' pistoning thrusts.

The only one of us whose modesty is quasi-preserved is Ronin, who's sitting between my legs and lurking mostly out of sight, except for his muscled arms wrapped around my hips and his sleek black head buried between my thighs.

Cheese on toast.

Whoever filmed our magic moment literally couldn't have chosen a more pornographic visual. You could charge money for that shit back in Vegas.

Not exactly my most regal look.

We all look fucking debauched.

And this X-rated peep show's streaming live on WNN for the whole witching world to see.

I actually recognize that scene from a few nights back. That was our scorching hot reunion, right after Max got back from wherever he's been vanishing for days on end. Still shots from that same scene are splashed across the last *Inquisitor*. Now, clearly, someone was also recording us.

Like, with sound.

We don't have neighbors, the cobblestone streets are so narrow the houses practically lean into each other, plus our *domus* is the only one on our street that's occupied.

So our windows were wide open to the balmy spring night.

Which means the speakers are projecting Neo's throaty moans as he gets reamed and teamed by our two alphas. Along with Lucius' rhythmic, guttural, half-human snarls as he hammers into me.

"Want you to spill inside me, Teach," my magnified voice breathes into the titillated night. "Want you and your wolf to rail me with that thick dick. Want your cum dripping down my thighs. All over Ronin's face."

Standing stock-still at the rail, the real-time Lucius swallows an audible groan. He's always been the most discreet of my guys, super mindful of the need for propriety to protect that teaching gig he lives for.

God, the poor guy is mortified.

I never realized the way his face shifts when he fucks me from behind, eyes glowing like embers, fangs enormous and dripping, scholarly features distorted, wolf ears poking through his Renaissance curls. Like monster porn. It's hot as fuck.

But even I gotta admit that look's not so good for his academic reputation.

Me, I'm way past mortified.

At this point, I'm enraged.

"Blooming hell, we get the picture," Ronin mutters. "Turn that shit off."

As the scene plays out larger than life, massive and glowing on the screen, Max pulls out of Neo's breathless mouth to fist his barbed dick, which is complicated and shifty and shaped like a devil's forked tail.

I know what comes next. Pumping hard and fast, Max is revving up to spurt all over Neo's face.

Because we recently discovered (kinda by accident) that our innocent bookworm really likes when we make him all filthy.

I don't have to look at the actual Neo next to me to know he's appalled, beet-red with humiliation, waiting in agonized dread for the entire witching world (including his famous Ted Kennedy dad) to see *that*.

The cum shot.

Hell to the no.

That's not happening.

In my desperate grip, Neo's hand feels like lead. I hum low in my throat, release my guy, and thrust my arms overhead. An electric current of power and rage crackles through me and erupts from my lungs in a vengeful scream.

A bolt of ultraviolet lightning forks from the sky. I hurl all that amperage like Thor son of Odin, straight at the offending image.

The LED screen explodes with a deafening *crack!* A blinding shower of sparks and shrapnel sends people screaming and diving for cover all over the deck.

Ronin wraps himself around me, protecting me with his own powerful build, which I have all kinds of issues with. That's twice tonight he's thrown himself between me and physical damage.

When it should be me protecting him.

That's what it means to be queen.

I protect *them*.

Before we can be shredded by that sea of flying glass, Vasili sweeps an arm sideways and hurls the blast wave away from all of us. His witchcraft flings that airborne debris harmlessly out to sea.

Messalina was thrown hard to her hands and knees, so the shrapnel passed harmlessly over her head. She's clutching her tiara to keep the thing on. Still, she lifts her face to find me across the sea of screaming chaos I just created all over her yacht—and nails me with a look of blazing triumph.

What the actual fuck?

Once the blast wave passes, the shipboard racket goes out like a snuffed candle.

*"Cavolo, bella,"* Cleo says softly into the ringing silence. Gracefully my ex-BFF straightens from where she's crouched at the bulkhead and slips free from Xiao, who's flung himself over her to protect her. "Always so predictable. You've given her exactly what she hoped for, Zara."

"She's lucky I didn't flambé *her*," I say, wrathful, in a voice that carries. "How's that for predictable?"

"Who says we still won't?" Ronin growls for emphasis like the bully he is and tightens his grip, pulling me hard into the muscled heat of his chest.

"Do you see?" With a degree of poise I gotta respect, Messalina climbs to her feet, settles her tiara more securely on her head, and speaks into the mic.

But she's not speaking to me.

She's speaking to the scattered sea of news cams that survived my pyrotechnics. To the witches and warlocks watching this debacle from their living rooms all over the planet.

Addressing all her subjects, she demands, "Does the witching world need this wild, willful, wicked Gemini? Is *this* what we deserve for a queen? Zara Gemini is paranoid. Psychotic. Psychologically damaged and congenitally dangerous. She slaughtered her own insane mother in a fit of rage. The next time she snaps, it could be *your* loved ones she slaughters."

Well, fuck.

*Fuck.*

She's not wrong. Is she?

"What the *hell*," Ronin snarls. He doesn't need telepathy to feel me clenching up in his arms. "That's bonkers."

Vasili hisses in vicious protest and rivets me with a sharp look (even though he can't hear what I'm thinking). Grimly I evade his searching gaze.

"Don't you believe her, babe," Neo whispers earnestly, reaching for my hand. "Don't. You're not like that. You're *good*."

I shake my head and pull my deadly hand away. When I'm this worked up, I'm dangerous to touch. She's right about that.

"Let me go, Adam." With deliberate care, I wiggle out from the shelter of Ronin's protective arms. Ronin (who's a dead ringer for Adam Driver, hence the nickname) is super reluctant and grumbles in protest. But he knows I mean it, so he gives me my space.

I give all my guys some distance, for their own good.

Now I stand alone.

All around me, stunned spectators are struggling to their feet. I've overturned the champagne fountain, destroyed the stage, skinned elbows, bloodied knees. Sure, these people might be mostly assholes, but they're also my subjects.

I didn't mean to hurt them.

Yeah, I've killed the feed and protected what little is left of poor Neo's privacy. I've done what little I can to protect all my guys.

But at what fucking price?

"As for the Senator." Messalina extends a queenly arm to point at Neo, who's looking confused and hurt as he tries to process why I pushed him away. Damn it. "Theo Mercury is understandably concerned for the moral welfare of his only son, who has fallen under the influence of this wicked creature. The Senator understands the importance of placing duty before sentiment. So, yes, I fully expect that he *will* call the vote."

Poor Neo looks totally crestfallen.

When Ronin prowls over to take Neo's hand and tug him gently into the strength of his body, I'm silently so grateful it makes my chest ache.

God, I love these guys. They're a huge part of the reason I'm even trying to do this whole queen thing.

I square my shoulders and make myself step forward to grip the rail. I want to whisper, but I pitch my voice to carry.

"I never wanted to be queen. That's no secret. It's why the guys had to kidnap my ass in the first place and drag me off to Icarus." I clench the rail and lean forward. "But the witching world needs a queen. A real one, with actual power and shit. We're dying here. We're an endangered species. Some of the old bloodlines, like the were shifters, they're already extinct. That's the whole reason I took the gig."

Now those cameras are pointed at me, and I can see at least some of the looky-loos are listening. Messalina lifts the mic to her mouth, but I rush ahead before she can get a word in edgewise.

Because that bitch has already said plenty.

"I'm talking here. You can go when I'm done. And, hey, newsflash." I scowl down at her. "It happens to be *good* and *healthy* for the four witching world races when the queen fucks. When she takes lots of mates and she fucks and she likes it. That's why we're poly, all of us royals. The queen has, like, magical and symbolic value for the whole witching world. Like we all saw in Avalon when I mated the Dark Fae King, the way your actual daughter was supposed to. When I cleaned up your mess."

I don't really wanna say the rest. But I gotta.

This is part of the issue, because her legit heir Cybelle got killed, and this queen's too long in the tooth to make another one. Besides, Messalina has to be making this shit up about Cleo, who doesn't exactly have pointy Fae ears and a dragon she rides, like the Unseelie royals in Avalon.

So I brace myself and say the F word. "I'm still figuring out this whole business. But that's how the next queen's gonna save the witching world. That's how you queen it. It's a power thing. And, uh, a fertility thing."

"Fertility?" Messalina pounces on that word I had such a hard time saying like a cat on a ball of string. "How can you possibly claim to embody *fertility* when you're deliberately preventing your own conception?"

I suck in a startled breath. My mouth pops open before I can hide it.

Yeah, sure, I'm taking BC shots right now, for reasons. For one thing, I'd prefer to avoid getting knocked up while I finish my stressful and eventful and kinda overwhelming freshman year at the witch academy, so excuse the fuck outta me for that.

Even though my aversion to getting preggo is causing real strain with my shifter guys, who have this really powerful genetic need to breed.

But that shit's private.

It's fucking *private*.

"There you have it!" Seeing me knocked off balance, the queen rushes ahead. The cameras swing toward her like spectator heads at a tennis match. "Even believing what she claims to believe, this so-called *Gemini queen* is under medical care to prevent conception! Fortunately, a loyal subject leaked her medical records to the *Witching Inquisitor*. This shameless slut's infamous exploits with her so-called *mates* are far from noble. It's debauchery and whoredom. Plain and simple. It's shocking. And sinful!"

In this dump truck of fuckery that's backing into me and upending this load of garbage on my head, one stinking gobbet hits me square between the eyes.

Somehow my medical records from the Academy clinic are getting pubbed in the *Witching Inquisitor*.

Great.

Man, whoever's acting as Messalina's inside man in the Academy? That POS has wicked access.

I bite my lip and scan my surroundings. With the sun sunk below the horizon and a breeze kicking up, it's getting chilly out here on the ocean. Beyond the dark tower of the abandoned lighthouse in the harbor, the jagged bulk of Icarus Island looms against the starlit sky, with only a few scattered lights twinkling in the Roman ruins of the village and the Gothic church where we hold our classes.

I grimly resist the urge to hug myself and shiver in my skimpy dress. With Messalina throwing around ten-cent words like *debauchery* and *whoredom*, I kinda wish I had a wrap to cover my cleavage.

But fuck that shit. I'm decent. Me and my guys, we're in love with each other. (I mean, leaving Zephyr and Ash outta the full poly love equation, just for now.)

Anyway. We literally did nothing wrong.

While the breeze raises goosebumps down my bare arms, I try to think warming thoughts and glare down at this royal witch who's turned into such a pain in my ass.

"Look, sure, I've got personal shit I'm working through, okay? I never said I was perfect. That doesn't mean Cleo would be an improvement." I twist around to glare at my ex-BFF. "I mean, where the hell were you when Avalon was dying? Where were you when I laid my ass on the line and almost got killed by Mad Queen Maeve breaking that fucking Unseelie curse? You do realize what happens over there affects what happens over here, right? That these two separate planes are, like, linked?"

Cleo's supermodel lashes fall over her gaze.

Figures that when I actually need her to talk, she's totally silent. She's a goddamn sphinx.

I huff out a breath of frustration and spin back to the cameras. "Sweet Jesus. Do any of you even *know* this woman?"

"That isn't your call to make," Messalina says sternly from the stage. "Renounce your claim. Acknowledge Cleopatra Aquarius as your rightful queen. Then you can return to your schoolbooks and your homework—or abandon the classroom and return to your budding career as a cat burglar, for all I care. That's all you have to do. Renounce your claim and bow to her. Then Theo Mercury will convene the Senate to ratify the vote."

Neo rushes over and wraps a protective arm around my chilly shoulders. "Don't you agree to that, babe. I'm gonna call my dad as soon as we're off this boat."

I don't know anything about Theo Mercury. I don't even know if I deserve to be queen. I really don't.

But what I do know is this.

I don't like the way I'm being manipulated. There are way too many unanswered questions still lurking. At the very minimum, we all need time to talk this through, like Lucius keeps saying. I mean, what's the hurry?

And I'm definitely not gonna tolerate my guys getting spied on and violated.

Just the thought has my power rising.

"Zara," Lucius growls through his fangs, so guttural I can barely follow him. He's literally struggling with human speech, because his wolf perceives a threat to me, and he's clawing at Lucius to let him rise.

Still, Lucius drags a taloned hand (practically a paw at this point) through the falling-down knot of his chestnut hair and manages to say, "Let me handle this from here. I beg you. There's—a time and a place— for this discussion. It belongs with—the scions and—the Senate."

Yeah, he wants me to stay calm and show restraint. But he's barely staying bipedal himself.

Bottom line up front? I feel like the time for restraint has passed.

That's why I glare across the deck into Messalina's gloating face and announce where I stand, loud enough for the whole witching world to hear. "Keep dreaming, dancing queen. I'm not renouncing *shit*."

"That's truly unfortunate, Zara." The queen's voice hardens. "Because I'm not asking."

She snaps her fingers like some kinda cartoon character of a witch. Then it's mayhem.

Doors fly open to port and starboard from the living quarters on my level. A double row of purposeful guys in police uniforms, with broad shoulders and stern faces, tromp out on deck, clutching literal electric shock sticks like you read about. Only these guys are wearing indigo instead of blue.

In a flash, I recognize those unis. They're enforcers from the AIB.

The Arcane Investigative Bureau.

Those boys are like Imperial stormtroopers from *Star Wars*. They're bad news. They're muscle for the queen. And their reputation is, like, unsavory.

Electricity crackles through me, my hair swirls around my shoulders, and my feet rise from the deck.

But I don't dare summon lightning.

Not with my guys and a bunch of civvies standing right here. Not with the memory of what happened with my mom at the Double Gem front and center in everyone's mind.

Especially mine.

Fuck. For all I know, this entire shitshow was designed to make me lose it on live TV.

While I hesitate, my guys spring into action.

Hair swirling around him in a cloud of ink, Ronin flings Neo behind him, spins clear of all of us, and cocks an arm like a pitcher winding up at Yankee Stadium. A flaming ball of golden psi fire erupts from his palm. His fireball sears across the deck like a comet and barrels into the nearest heavies.

Those guys go sprawling in all directions, electric batons abandoned in favor of yelling and beating out the flames engulfing their imperial unis.

Ronin grins fiercely, eyes flaming gold and teeth gleaming white in the billowing smoke, and winds up to pitch another fireball at the second wave of stormtroopers—who are now uber-focused on *him*.

While Ronin deals with the incoming, Vasili streaks airborne across the poop deck (levitation is one of his gifts, he can fly like fucking Tinkerbell). With a sweep of his casting hand, he hurls a wall of telekinetic whoop-ass that slams both doors shut on the heavies still trying to push through.

Cue the muffled shouts and pounding while the backups try to shoulder through the barrier.

The living quarters of this megayacht are not exactly Fort Knox. Those doors won't hold long, and there have to be other exits.

Still, I call out, with lightning lurking in my voice, "Way to go, Goblin King!"

Since our psychic channel's still blocked.

Meanwhile, Lucius gives up a losing battle and let his wolf out in a blinding flash of light. He's a timber wolf, all gray and chestnut, shaggy and slavering and freaking massive. His wolf gallops across the deck and launches himself into the back of some guy who's climbing on a table to get behind Vasili's hovering frame with his shock stick.

Those two crash to the ground, leaving V untouched, with the stormtrooper screaming. The wolf's fanged jaws lock into the back of the guy's neck and shake him like a rat.

"You tell him, Lucius," I mutter. Because his wolf doesn't follow human speech.

I drop to the deck and spin to check on Neo. He's the only one of my guys who isn't trained to handle himself in a fistfight.

That's when some asshole from the crowd—a heavyset guy in a tux who isn't even one of the troopers—makes the mistake of grabbing my arm in his big sweaty paw. His ruddy face scowls down at me.

"That's enough, you Gemini bitch. Call off your fuck buddies or I'll—"

I'm torqued pretty tight, and this rough handling I didn't ask for and wasn't expecting really sets me off. With a flash of lavender light and a staticky crackle, the electric shock I call the little lightning rips his grip off my arm and hurls that asshole halfway across the deck.

He slams into the bar and slumps to the deck. Where he lies pretty much unmoving. While the cameras roll, a fussy-looking older woman in a purple feather boa shrieks and rushes to his side.

Her shrill scream splits the night. "He's not breathing. *He's not breathing!*"

"Oh, fuck me." I look around wildly, spot the defibrillator unit mounted on the wall, and rush toward it.

I'm in the middle of ripping off the plexiglass cover that protects the gizmo when another scream—a heart-stoppingly familiar one—drags my attention to the stern.

Dez is standing at the head of the gangway, with the biggest brute on the whole damn boat twisting her arms viciously behind her back to cuff her. She's really struggling, and the heavy—who's snarling and blistered red and still smoking from a hit of Ronin's psi fire—is handling her so roughly he's about to rip her arms off.

Dez's pretty face twists tight in fear and pain.

"Hey!" I shout. "You leave her the fuck alone, you big bully! Pick on someone your own size."

Dez is, like, the real innocent in this whole shitshow. She's my housemate. She's my friend. She's literally only here to support me. She's not athletic, she's delicate, she doesn't even know how to fight. Her gifts are telepathy and precognition.

She's defenseless.

She's scared.

And she's hurting.

The poop deck is a mess, civvies running and screaming, troopers bellowing commands and trying to impose order and then arrest us I guess, the doors splintering despite V's solid efforts to let more of the brute squad barrel through.

I can't find Racetrack in the fray. And all my guys have their hands full.

My flying skills are still a work in progress. But I snatch the defibrillator, shoot erratically above the scrum, zip over to the bar to shove the thing at the freaked-out chick with the boa (who just about rips the unit from my arms), then hurl myself airborne to help my friend.

Before I can ride to Dez's rescue like the Lone Ranger, Neo (another innocent) rushes across the deck and tackles her attacker.

What my fated mate lacks in skill, he definitely makes up for in brawn and bravery. Through sheer body mass and determination, Neo does manage to knock the jerk into a wall.

Dez stumbles clear of the scuffle, wrists shackled behind her. Face frantic, dress torn, hair falling down in spirals from her sleek ponytail, she scrambles out of the way through the chaos the best she can—

Then her head jerks up and her eyes widen with alarm. Her mouth opens in a horrified O.

That's when she winks out of sight.

Gone in a blink.

My friend. The gentle one. The only one of us who's totally, truly innocent.

She's… just… fucking… *gone*.

Now I'm the one screaming.

*"Dezzz!"*

# Chapter Four
## Ronin

Bloody fuck.

Sure, the rough surface of psychic friction from this whole shitshow's been chafing me since I set foot on this blooming boat. The atmosphere on board's been bristly enough to give any Valyrian telepath the hives. Even after that nullifying object some bloke's carrying numbs me out like Novocaine.

But Zara's scream rips through my deadened senses like a Sawsall.

Snarling with fury, I lob a flaming fireball at the wall of assholes powering toward me and take those bastards out like ninepins. All screaming like blazes, some doing the drop-and-roll to extinguish their smoldering shirts. Others run to hurl their flaming bodies over the rail into the sea.

With any luck, they'll drown.

I've got kilojoules of blistering rage crackling through every synapse.

No one—and I mean *no one*—fucking touches my girl.

I pivot to find Zara losing her shit, eyes glowing ultraviolet, lightning crackling round her hands. She's staring at Dez's glittery purse, lying on the empty deck where our housemate was literally just standing.

But I've also got eyes on Racetrack, crouched on the bar behind Zara in a sea of shattered glass, with one arm outflung, eyes burning silver, and her hard face all wicked with witchcraft.

"Oh, bloody hell," I mutter.

RT's witchcraft is teleportation. No shocker then. She's teleported her girlfriend out of danger, probably straight back to the *domus*. Even though teleporting a whole girl that kind of distance, kilometers back to shore, would drain anyone's psychic battery.

In this case, my housemate's judgment sucks.

"Fuck me, RT!" I bellow. Her freaky gaze snaps toward me. "You got anything left in the tank?"

Racetrack hesitates, then jerks her chin in a nod.

Not exactly the ringing endorsement I'm hoping for. But a bloke takes what he can get.

"Then get Zara the hell out of here!" I snap.

Zara swings round and scopes out the sitch. Her panicky worry for Dez vanishes in an eyeblink as she grasps what's gone down. Her face fires with awareness. "Oh, hell to the no. No way. Not me!"

Of course, my girl's not down with getting whisked out of play herself.

For shit's sake. I'm already pissed. Now my aggravation ratchets way up. That's bad news for the big trooper who barrels into me from the side. His body mass sends me flying. I tuck and roll into the impact, then come up from the deck snarling. He's right on top of me, but my booted foot snaps out sideways to hammer that asshole into next week. Bone cracks under the force of my side kick. The guy flies back and drops like an anvil.

I let out a satisfied growl and spin back toward the fray—

That's when the shock stick slams into my chest.

From that other bloke I never saw coming.

The hit delivers an electric jolt that fries every cell of my body. That jolt of juice rattles my wits like peanuts rattling in a jar.

My pores crawl. A sensation like stinging bees swarms through my skin. Pretty sure smoke's rising from my ears.

When my brain stops sizzling, I'm sprawled flat, face down on deck, limbs limp and heavy as a load of wet laundry. Basically, I'm in no state to avoid the steel-toed boot that slams into my ribs like a baseball bat.

I absorb the sickening impact with a groan.

Through blurred vision, I can just make out Xiao's sneering face looming over me. With the fucking shock stick that hit me still swinging from his fist.

"Not such a badass now, are you, Pendragon?" he gloats down at me. "His Royal Hotness doesn't look so hot when he's drooling."

Fuck, am I? My face is way too numb and tingly to tell. I'd like to sweep that asshole's legs out from under him. But my body's not responding.

My circuits are fried.

My bleary gaze drifts through a sea of running legs to catch a fractured glimpse of Zara kicking some royal ass. I know she's afraid to hurl lightning in this crowd, but she's a spinning fury of fists and knees and elbows—even in her stilettos. She's single-handedly fending off three AIB assholes.

She trained for this shit, but she can't hold them off forever.

Especially with those shock sticks in play.

*"Racetrack,"* I groan.

My housemate's the only ally in sight. She's got to get Zara the fuck out. Now.

I can just make out RT, still standing on the bar, scowling and kicking some fool in the face with her shitkicker boot.

Xiao's foot slams into my diaphragm. My sternum ignites in a red blaze of pain.

I curl into the blow with an *oof!* Try to clear my head. Order my limbs to function.

No joy. I'm limp as a clubbed fish.

"You'd better… fucking… run," I grind out, with my chest on fire, "before I… fucking… kill you."

"Wow, *Adam.* I'm really scared." Xiao sneers at my rubber-lipped threat.

"Not me, RT!" Zara's gritty yell spirals through the buzz in my brain. "You got anything left, you help Neo! Then Ronin!"

*That* gets my heavy head off the deck in a hurry.

Blast.

There's my sweet Red, handcuffed and struggling, getting perp-walked (more like dragged) between two grim-faced coppers toward the cabin. His white tuxedo jacket's all sooty, his glasses are knocked askew, and his horrified gaze is locked on me.

Hearing Zara's yell, Neo's desperate face swings from me to Racetrack. "No way! Not me. I'm not leaving Zara. You help Ronin!"

"Bollocks," I groan.

I know what my girl's doing. Neo's a civvy, a noncom, he's helpless in a fistfight. Zara feels like it's her responsibility to protect him first, then the rest of us.

Never mind that it's our job to protect her. Pulling that sweet lad of ours away from Zara while she's this deep in the shit will kill him.

Xiao's foot swings toward me like a wrecking ball. I flop away from the kick and manage to avoid the worst. Still heavy and tingling with shock, I swing my leg round, clumsy and uncoordinated as fuck. Through sheer brute force, without any of my usual panache, I knock Xiao's feet from under him.

He crashes to the deck with a yell. The shock stick he's gripping clatters out of reach.

Over his sprawled body, I catch a glimpse of RT charging up the old battery to do her thing, with eyes like molten lead and the ends of her short hair floating.

Poor Red's fiercely protesting the whole plan as he's muscled toward the cabin. "No no no, not me! Ronin—"

*"Abigail Prudence Bulworthy Prynne."* Zara roars in the lightning voice, edged and humming with the voltage of a good strong Compulsion spell. Because that mouthful's RT's proper name, and names have power in the witching world. *"HELP. NEO."*

RT's face hardens with resolve. I bark out my own protest—it's Zara who's the target, Zara we've got to save—but I'm too bloody late. Racetrack's Compelled, and her arm sweeps wide.

Neo's desperate protest ends in mid-syllable. Our bookworm's solid body vanishes in a blink.

His two bullies bellow in surprise and outrage.

"Hell." I flop onto my gut, get a knee under me, use my wobbly arms to muscle my aching chest off the deck. "Red."

He'll never bloody get over this.

Gods willing, Neo's already materialized back at the *domus*. With any luck, he'll find Dez on the landline ringing up the Dean.

My head's still muddy, so I barely register the flash of steel. That fucker Xiao's back on his feet.

Coming at me from my blind spot.

With a blooming knife.

*"Shit."* I push up to stand, but my clumsy palms skid in a puddle of spilled booze. I crash back to the deck, hard enough to bite my tongue. The metallic tang of blood fills my mouth.

The blade slices past with a thin seam of fire that licks my shoulder blade.

Now I've really gone round the bend. That prick just ripped my D&G jacket that Vasili picked out for me. I'm probably bleeding all over the thing. When Vasili sees the damage, I'll never hear the end of it.

Growling with fury, I roll hard into Xiao—hard enough to bruise—and knock that six feet of trouble right to his knees.

"What's your bloody problem anyway, mate?" Forcing my heavy arms into action, I pin his knife hand above me, holding the blade at bay, even though I'm still wobbly and shocky as fuck. "You jealous of me or what?"

His lip curls in contempt.

"It's not about you, hot stuff. It's about *her*. About what it'll take to make her lose her Gemini shit on live TV." He's got leverage in this position and he uses it, pitting his full weight against my numb and tingling arms, glaring into my eyes the whole time, teeth bared in a grimace of effort. "I figure—this'll do it."

Hell, he isn't wrong.

Despite all I can do, that shining blade's inching, inexorable as fuck, toward my neck. If he buries that blade in my throat, he'll make Zara mental. Not to mention what it'll do to Vasili and Lucius, who'll both blame themselves.

Plus he'd put a serious damper on my whole day.

I haven't got shit for leverage. But I manage to twist my hips and knee him a decent knock in the junk.

He yelps and collapses on top of me, nearly skewering me like a damn kebob. I barely catch his wrist, a breath before he'd give me that involuntary tracheotomy he's jonesing for.

He hisses out a curse in his native tongue.

"That's got to smart a bit, yeah?" I grin into his agonized face.

But he's still in the game.

Fucker literally hurls himself at me.

We're scuffling and swearing and scrabbling for the knife when a snarling blur of chestnut fur streaks over me and drives Xiao's weight right off my body.

I push up to sit with a gasp of relief, then scramble to my feet, weak and knock-kneed as a fawn. Totally fucking helpless to do anything but watch while Xiao and Lucius' wolf tumble end over end, knife flashing, the prick yelling, the wolf growling and snapping…

…right through a gap in the guardrail…

Over the side of the ship.

Still locked together, the two tumble out of sight with the wolf's surprised yip.

A long second later, the silence splinters in a heavy splash.

"Lucius!" I stagger to the rail, swaying like a drunk, and stare wildly down into the night-black sea. *"Lucius!"*

Where in blazes are they? The inky sea's all choppy, but they're nowhere in sight.

Gripping the rail for balance, I twist for a lookabout to see if, somehow, I've missed them. Most of the action on board seems to have shifted to the lower decks, except for those losers we've left scattered in various piles of moaning incapacitation on the poop deck. There's gallons of spilled blood splashed about. Looks a bit like *The Texas Chainsaw Massacre* up here, because Lucius' wolf tore through anyone who threatened us, and he's savage with those wicked chompers. Plus my psi fire's taken a bunch of blokes off the board.

The remaining action on this deck's centered on Zara.

Her face has gone incandescent like the goddess she is, eyes pulsing platinum, hair writhing round her face like Medusa snakes.

Now my girl clenches her fists and does this foot-stomp trick, with an echoing cry that summons her little lightning. An electric jolt of ultraviolet whoop-ass ripples outward across the deck, with her at the center, and arcs through those three guys troubling her.

Our queen's way more lethal than a shock stick, even when she's pulling her punches (like now). That crackle of electric discharge puts all three of them on the ground.

Knocked out cold, just like that beefy civvy who grabbed her before. That guy's only now coming round near the oyster bar, while the chick with the purple boa sobs and flutters over him.

Racetrack's down, slumped over the bar, though I can't see any blood. Looks like she's maybe spell-stunned, like she burned through too much juice porting Dez and Neo (who's a big boy, a lot of mass for her to move) kilometers out of play.

Or else she's been thunked on the noggin. Which is a bloody good way to take any kind of telekinetic out of the game.

Speaking of telekinetics…

I can't see Vasili any damn place. But the main deck below is bedlam. Place looks and sounds like it's coming apart at the seams. There's screaming. Running. Random police brutality.

At a guess, that's where I'll find my boyfriend. Right in the bloody thick of it.

*"Ronin!"* Zara races toward me, face wild and hair flying. "My God. You're bleeding!"

"Fuck, it's nothing. Flesh wound." Sure, Xiao nicked me with that knife. My shoulder stings a bit. But I've handled lots worse.

I grip my girl's silky bare arms, her skin cold under my hot hands, and give her a quick once-over. She's lost her stilettos and one strap of her party frock has snapped. Otherwise, thank fuck, she looks undamaged.

Shuddering in relief, I drag her into my arms in a quick hard hug. "Fuck, Zara."

"Sweet Jesus. Ronin." She presses into me, arms winding tight round my waist. Guess whoever has that nullifying object's moved along, because the familiar tingling rush of our psychic bond floods through me. She's trembling in my arms, which totally makes me mental.

I pull her head hard into my chest and tighten my grip.

Yeah, she's shaken, who wouldn't be after this circus? But she's also pissed as fuck.

That's my girl.

I mean to wreak *hari-kari* on Messalina, Cleo, Xiao and the whole lot over this load of rubbish.

"Okay, look." I pull in a breath, lock onto my girl's wide eyes, and make my voice firm. "Time to regroup. Retrench. Circle the wagons. Whatever. First thing we've got to do is get our crew together and get off this blasted boat."

Her teal brows draw together in a frown. "Yeah. Working on that. But Cleo's gone… somewhere… and Messalina's vamoosed down below. I think Vasili's gone after her. Maybe he's gone after both of them." Her alarmed gaze veers to the sea. "Is—is Lucius in the water?"

"Think so, yeah. With your ex." We both lean way out over the rail to look, but I still can't see shit.

I can't find Lucius.

What's worse, I can't *feel* him. Which has to mean that nullifying object's still in play.

Somewhere.

"Lucius?" I'm still wobbly from getting juiced, but I've got enough left in the tank to cock an arm and lob a weak fireball over the water for illumination. Not that there's much to illuminate. "Lucius!"

I can't feel him, but I can feel Zara, and she's spiraling.

She's not afraid for herself. She's afraid for him. Afraid for me. Afraid for all our lot.

I barely manage to get hold of her arm before she lifts off the deck to fly down there and investigate for herself.

"Look, Zara. You'd best get Racetrack into the dive boat." Sensing the protest rising to her lips, I rush ahead. "She's hurt. She needs you."

"God. I know." Zara's teeth sink into her lower lip. Her forehead scrunches with conflict, and the look she darts at RT is poignant with guilt it fucks with my heart to see. "But what about Lucius? I won't leave him, Ronin."

"No one's bloody leaving him." Thinking fast, I'm already powering for the gangway, urging a still reluctant Zara along with me. "I'll get Vasili to have a look round. He's a wicked flier. He can telekinetic our wolf out of the drink, just in case… in case Lucius is hurt. Which you can't, love."

Her mouth pops open in instant protest. She's set on getting her two pence in, she doesn't like admitting there's anything she can't do. But, all of a sudden, I can't hear shit.

Just an earth-shattering roar that splits the night like a tyrannosaur's bellow.

That roar sets my ears ringing. It's the roar of an angry dragon. (Because we've got a few of those round again in the witching world.)

This dragon's massive black form blots out the night sky under the span of his outstretched wings. He soars toward us over the waves. Right over the complete fucking pandemonium of the *Aquarius Queen*.

That's the type of pandemonium that ensues when you're overflown by a dragon roughly the size of a flying Godzilla, bellowing with deafening fury.

It's pandemonium even before his fanged jaws open over the deck below.

When the dragon starts flaming, that scene of pandemonium turns to literal Hell.

# Chapter Five
## Zara

As a column of crimson flame engulfs the swimming pool and ignites the empty stage, my mating bond blazes to life.

*Finally*.

And that psychic wallop definitely packs a punch.

After the muddy sense of psychic deprivation I've been slogging through on this boat, the bracing crackle of Ronin's telepath-potent aggression hits me in the face like a dash of cold water. Vasili's down below, wreaking some kinda havoc in the living quarters. Now my bond with him crackles to life too, ebbing and swelling like staticky radio on a mountain road, lurky with malice and homicidal intent.

Lucius? He's a gaping hole in the tapestry of our group bond. The familiar comfort of his steady alpha strength is, like, nowhere to be found.

Which is freaking me the fuck out.

For real.

But all that's nothing compared to the tsunami of murderous rage that's howling through every pore of my body from my third alpha. The one who just got here. The one who's already circling for another lethal pass.

"Maxim!" I scream.

Barefoot, I scramble up on the bar and wave my arms madly for the dragon's attention.

*Who threatens my mate!* His voice roars through our mating bond, echoed by a dragonish bellow that nearly ruptures my eardrums.

Ronin grimaces and claps his hands over his ears. He too is scrambling, mentally, to throw up some psychic armor against the broadside of Max's fury.

"That's a little loud, love," Ronin groans through the bond we all share. "We're literally right here."

*Gladly will I kill for my sovereign and for you!* Maxim roars like blazes and rakes the sleek glassy prow of the megayacht with a curling firehose of flame.

My dragon shifter's lining up so he can strafe the main deck with his flamethrower breath, while traumatized passengers flee screaming in all directions. Honestly, it's like King's Landing in the series finale of *Game of Thrones* down there.

"No killing, big guy!" Shifty senses are super acute. Still, I reinforce the shouted command with all the psychic voltage I've got. "I mean it. We got civvies down here. Ronin's a little bloody, but we're both basically okay. Lucius and V are, uh, MIA."

Hearing my warning, Max swerves and veers away with a deafening roar of concern.

I know he admires Lucius, in this cute hero worship student-teacher kinda way. Those two aren't together in our polycule (yet). But I'm starting to suspect Max is kinda crushing on Lucius, even though it's taking him forever to act on it.

Anyway. Our dragon's extra protective of Vasili these days. Like he's trying to be V's alpha too. Even though that's an instinct that never fails to make my Goblin King vicious. When those two alphas of mine interact—the snake and the dragon—they're like sparks to tinder.

Right now it's an instinct that works for me, because right away, Max stops flaming the civvies on board. Instead, he redirects his torrent of angry fire to warn off a circling news chopper that's ventured too close.

"Cheese on toast," I yell. "I mean it. No sautéeing the civvies. You got that?"

*If they threaten my mates, I will kill them all.* He broods and wings over the spreading flames. But at least he lets the chopper clatter off unmolested.

Well, that's lucky.

Just in case you haven't figured this out by now, Max is kinda, like, a hothead.

Seriously.

He's way worse than Ronin, who used to be the psycho in this harem.

As flames race across the deck, the whoop of the megayacht's fire alarm adds its voice to the fray, followed by the hiss and sputter of the suppression system. Acrid smoke burns my lungs and makes me cough. I twist my blowing hair into a hasty knot on my head, duck to avoid a gust of flaming cinders, and try to strategize about how to get us all out of this shitshow.

Without, like, killing anyone.

Meanwhile, those hovering choppers and WNN speedboats are still recording the whole clusterfuck. Betcha this night's gonna break the witching world ratings record.

*Lucius is in the blooming drink,* Ronin sends through our bond to Max. My Brit's pacing the poop deck, bloody and disheveled, glaring balefully at the singed and savaged AIB guys as they scurry for the stairs and make for the lifeboats.

*Have a lookabout for our wolf, Max,* he urges. *There's a love.*

*I will find him and I will save him!* Max bellows and swoops to circle the boat. He's flying low above the water, all broody and ominous with intent, which wreaks all kinds of havoc with the speedboats that are trying to mount a rescue operation. His low pass overturns a lifeboat some panicky crew from this party boat are trying to winch over the water. That mishap plunges the anxious passengers, all crowding to scramble aboard, into screaming hysterics.

Sweet Jesus, this ambush is turning into an actual emergency.

The *Aquarius Queen* is definitely burning, with fingers of fire racing across the varnished and (apparently) highly flammable deck in multiple places. We might even be looking at a *Titanic*-type situation, like a sinking (minus Leo DiCaprio and the iceberg).

At least we're close to shore, and the water's not freezing. So there's that.

But I'm no Kate Winslet.

I don't need saving.

The person that does the saving around here is me.

I make up my mind and will myself airborne. I'm still new at this flying shit and I don't have Vasili's style and panache in the air (at least in human form). But I've got enough basic levitation to propel myself over the debris-littered scrum of the swimming pool and the smoke-wreathed chaos of the main deck, swoop in to grab the diva's abandoned mic from the fiery stage, and land (coughing) on the raised quarterdeck above the living quarters.

The air's clearer up here. Plus there's a bright red fire alarm console mounted on the wall right there. I swipe a hand across my stinging eyes to dry my smoky tears, then hit the switch to kill the sound.

With a last whoop, the alarm falls silent.

Thank fuck. My poor ears. They might never stop ringing.

"Listen up, people," I announce into the mic, my amplified voice seeping thin and tinny through the shrill buzz of my battered eardrums. "There's more lifeboats port and starboard, and those paparazzi speedboats are starting to queue up at the back. Everyone needs to form lines and start offloading."

Terrified faces divide their attention between me, the steadily advancing flames, and Max's lurky flight.

"That dragon's mine," I say firmly. Because he is. "As long as everyone behaves, he's gonna hold his fire."

That might be, like, aspirational thinking on my part. But I reinforce that shit though our mating bond and instruct my broody, threatening alpha dragon to play nice.

Max grumbles, but he does begrudgingly widen the circumference of his circle. That gives those rescue boats some space.

A few passengers, all sooty and disheveled and definitely the worse for wear, start shuffling into queues near the lifeboats or migrating aft for offloading.

"Good. That's real good," I encourage everyone. "We're like two kilometers max from the island. That's an easy paddle. We'll all regroup there."

You might be wondering who died and made me queen.

But the actual queen—that duplicitous bitch Messalina—is nowhere to be found.

Yeah, she'd better fucking hide if she knows what's good for her. We'll all be lucky if no one winds up dead due to this stunt she pulled tonight. For fuck's sake, the four witching races are already practically extinct. We need every functioning dick and uterus we've got to sustain the population.

Maybe even… mine?

That furtive question sneaks through my brain, buried deep behind my barriers so I don't set off my shifter guys, a couple of whom are rocking this major breeding kink. Suddenly, those BC shots I've been taking with evangelical fervor don't feel as much like a no-brainer as they used to.

I mean, if I'm gonna be queen… maybe I'd better start queening it.

Like I'm trying to do right here.

I cough again to clear my throat and refocus on the crowd. Ronin's directing traffic down there, looking surly and unsafe and therefore not much comfort to the terrorized passengers. But they need the direction. Those flames are spreading fast, the smoke's making it hard to breathe.

Long story short? This whole boat's teetering right on the edge of panic. Wouldn't take much to nudge the whole shebang into hysteria.

A scuffling fistfight erupts in the milling crowd near the lifeboats, punctuated with a flurry of thrown punches and shoving.

"Whoa, easy there. No pushing," I say into the mic. "There's gonna be plenty of room for everyone on those lifeboats. We'll make extra trips if we have to. People who can walk okay, you help the folks who need it."

A tall slim streak of violet swoops up from the main cabin to alight at my side.

With a blend of relief and unease, I give the side-eye to my dominant alpha.

Somehow Vasili still looks like he'd be right at home walking a Fashion Week runway in Paris in that violet tux, even with his gilded shag of rock-star hair all windblown, a streak of soot striping his sharp features, and a dark spatter of blood (hopefully not his) staining his crisp cuffs and his narrow ringed hands.

He looks like an escapee from a Marilyn Manson MTV video. Honestly, he's so flamboyant he steals my thunder without even trying.

But I'm so relieved to see him I totally don't mind.

"Shit, Goblin King, where the hell have you been?" I grumble. "We have a situation here."

"I'll say," he purrs, eyeing the scrum around the lifeboats under his smoky lids. "Who knew that Aquarius bitch has a teleporter at her beck and call? That naughty fellow whisked little Lina off the boat—along with himself—before I could slit her throat in the powder room."

You never know how literally to take him when he says shit like that. But I eye his bloodstained hands and cuffs and feel kinda queasy.

This bad boy always carries a cache of hidden knives. When he uses them, he's fucking lethal.

"Regicide is a felony," I say primly (like he needs reminding). "Uh, not to mention, murder's a violation of the Academy Codex."

"Well, she was whisked off before she could bleed out," he says peevishly. "So no harm done. More's the pity. Fortunately, little queen…" He gives me a sly smirk and slips a hand inside his tuxedo jacket to produce a glittery object. "In her rush to flee the scene, she left a little something behind."

I stare down at the delicate tiara in his hand. Up close, that slender circlet sports actual diamonds, the icy blue-white glitter interspersed with purple amethyst. The thing's real familiar, because Messalina wears it for all her public appearances. It's like a royal heirloom that goes back centuries.

In fact, she was literally just wearing it.

Suddenly I'm feeling kinda dizzy. "Is that…?"

"What it is, little queen, is *yours*." My warlock hums with wicked satisfaction and offers me the ancient artifact with a showy flourish. "You'll want to replace the Aquarius amethysts with Gemini emeralds, of course. Ideally before the formal coronation, whenever that may be. I can assist with that. I have a personal jeweler at Tiffany's."

"Why does that not surprise me." I'm still staring at the thing in this nauseated fascination.

Seriously? This whole moment is pretty otherworldly. My snake's attracting plenty of attention, the way he always does (even in mid-evac), perched elegantly above the fray in his bloodstained violet tux, casually offering me the witching world crown.

The action slows and the seconds stretch.

I feel the weight of this moment, the pressure of all those watching eyes, like a physical presence pressing down on me. A swarm of choppers circles overhead, bristling with those omnipresent cameras.

Then I suck in a breath and lift my chin. My eyes lock with V's.

"Go ahead and put it on me, bad boy," I tell him softly. "You're the Scorpio scion. Plus you're gonna be one of my kings, aren't you? I intend to crown you and all the guys right along with me at the formal ceremony."

Something fractures in his face.

His icy gaze glitters with suppressed longing.

My heart clenches and aches in my chest. I know shit about him that only the guys in our polycule know. Behind his horrible bully warlock facade, I know my terrible alpha will always be the lonely queer boy his father rejected and shipped off to hide behind magical wards at the Academy, just for the so-called sin of being gay. Though he'll deny it with cutting scorn that's sharp enough to draw blood, Vasili's always secretly been afraid we'll reject him too.

I want him to know that's never gonna happen. Not on my watch.

We're all crazy in love with our snake.

Even if, deep down inside, he's still afraid to believe it.

In an eyeblink, his smoky lashes sweep down and his perfect face shutters. Now he's all sneering arrogance, same as usual, as he saunters up close and places the crown delicately on my head.

That artifact throbs with ancient power.

Yowsa.

The thing's so unexpectedly heavy I can barely hold my head up.

And the whole world is suddenly so still and silent, under the crackle and pop of burning wood and the *chukka-chukka* of the choppers, that I can hear my own heartbeat thudding in my ears. It's like the night is holding its breath.

Every eye in the witching world is watching.

I swallow hard and raise the mic to my lips. Even while my gaze clings to V's for reassurance.

"Okay, listen up," I tell the whole witching world. "The Senate voted on the next queen months ago. We don't need a do-over. I'm the next queen. So I'm keeping this." I stick out my chin and glare straight at the cameras. "Anybody wants to take it from me? I got finals this week. Right here at Icarus. Just so you all know where to find me."

Vasili acknowledges my declaration of intent with the Romanov eyebrow. Then he inclines his chin, just a fraction of an inch, in subtle approval. He pivots to stand with me, shoulder to shoulder. His dangerous stare slices through the spellbound crowd in silent challenge.

A streak of chestnut lopes up the gangway and drops at my feet, shaggy fur dripping with seawater.

A ragged gasp spills from my lungs. My legs almost buckle with relief.

My mating bond with Lucius is different when he's all wolfed out—he's, like, not verbal in that form—but it's definitely him. I can barely restrain the impulse to collapse on the deck beside him and smother my headmaster in a desperate hug.

Instead I just drop a hand to my side, so he can nuzzle my fingers with his cold wet nose.

I'll do a lot more than that once we're private.

Though I do definitely wonder what happened to Xiao.

Ronin stalks up the stairs, plants himself squarely at my side with booted legs spread and belligerent arms folded, and smolders at our viewing audience like he's ready to hurl fire at any provocation.

Still circling overhead, Maxim bellows in triumph.

This moment's pretty fraught. So I'm hyper-alert and tingling with nerves. A subtle flicker of movement from the flybridge across the way snags my immediate attention.

That's the highest part of the boat, higher than where I'm standing with the guys, it's mostly used for navigation. I'm a certified diver and I'm comfy on boats. That's how I know the flybridge is usually secured. There shouldn't be civvies up there.

And, actually, that's no civvie.

It's Cleo.

She's standing alone at the helm, straight and regal as a queen. (If I'm being honest.) With her royal indigo gown sheathing her stately supermodel physique and the wind teasing her silky merlot mane. Somehow, even in the middle of this flaming shitshow, with multiple fires raging, she's managed to stay impeccable.

She definitely looks more like a queen than I do, standing barefoot with my motley crew of disreputables, my teal curls twisted in a hasty knot, stray ringlets spilling down my neck, and one strap of my spangly cocktail gown broken.

God even knows where I've left my purse.

In that tense stretch of silence, Cleo meets my gaze across the width of the boat that divides us. Across the literal gulf of fire that lies between us. I lift my chin and lock onto her level stare.

She even acts more like a queen than I do. She always has. She's literally a famous celebrity in the mortal world. She's a supermodel who's lived her whole life in the spotlight.

But fuck that shit.

I'm not stepping down.

Not for her.

The witching world needs me. Far as I can tell, she's left the arcane races twisting in the wind.

*Is this the one!* Max's psychic bellow just about makes me jump out of my skin.

In fact, his telepathic broadside makes all my mates twitch. Lucius' wolf emits a growl of warning as our massive black dragon swoops toward the boat with golden eyes flaming, taloned legs outstretched, and smoke leaking through his serrated jaws.

"Yeah, that's her." I sigh. "No flaming."

Sure, I hate what she's done. But I used to love her. Like, I really fucking thought I was in love with her. That's the whole reason her betrayal back in Singapore—not to mention this new one tonight—hurt me so bad.

Clearly, she needs to be dealt with. But I don't need to see her flambéed right in front of me.

Max snarls and sails toward her, low and lethal.

Shit. I'm not even sure he's listening.

Calmly Cleo slips the straps of her evening gown from her slim shoulders. The garment slithers down her long pale body to pool at her feet. Underneath she's wearing a wisp of black lace that cups her perfect tits, a tiny triangle of matching lace over her crotch, and a garter that straps a baby handgun to her sleek thigh. She poses on the deck like a lingerie model, just long enough for the paparazzi cameras to flash.

"What the fuck," Ronin grouses.

Thank God he sounds totally unimpressed.

Sure, we all share in this harem, that's how it works when you're poly. But I'm not about to share my warlocks with *her*.

While Max closes in with jaws gaping wide like he's gonna swallow her whole, Cleo toes deftly out of her sparkly stilettos. Her graceful arms sweep over her head like an Olympic diver. Then she executes a perfect swan dive from the flybridge.

A blinding white flash obliterates her falling form.

I suck in my breath on a spurt of shock.

When my vision clears, a sleek coil of garnet scales is pouring through the air. That endless spiral, divided by a spine of razor-sharp spikes glittering merlot and ruby in the firelight, slips into the inky sea with barely a splash. Just before the whole apparition that used to be my supposedly mortal, unshifty girlfriend is engulfed in the depths, her forked tail flicks in a flirty wave.

"Sweet Jesus!" I yelp. "What the hell *was* that?"

But I know.

We all know.

Even though no one's ever seen one in the flesh—I've only seen illustrations in the antique books of witching world lore in Lucius' library—what we've all just seen is literally supposed to have been extinct for centuries.

My backstabbing ex-BFF is… a fucking sea dragon.

Max hammers past in a powerful gust of wind and roars in frustrated rage. Next to me, Ronin's swearing like a sailor. Vasili doesn't even twitch and he doesn't utter a sound (he's actually suspiciously silent). But his eyes are narrowed in snaky calculation and his face is hard and dangerous. Lucius' wolf tilts back his muzzle in a long mournful howl.

Which pretty much voices my own turbulent feelings to a T.

Cleo might've just escaped my dragon's vengeance. But I know she won't be going far. I've got something that belongs to her.

The way she sees it, I'm wearing her crown.

And she's gonna want it back.

# Chapter Six
## Neo

My hands are still shaking.

That makes it hard to pour the slug of peppermint schnapps from the vintage liquor cart in our great room into Dez's cocoa. But she really needs it to steady her nerves, so I just suck it up and get the job done.

Since I'm apparently not a candidate for helping in any of the major ways around this *domus.*

At least in Zara's view.

I hate thinking that way, I really do, like now is obviously not the time for me to throw myself a pity party? No one has time to deal with that.

The thing is, that's obviously what she and the guys are thinking. That's gotta be why, when my fated mate was in danger and needed us most, I got whisked away. I was literally the only one of her guys she wanted sent away. She wanted me gone so badly she even Compelled Racetrack (who definitely looked doubtful, with me yelling *no way* and frantically shaking my head at her the whole time) to do it.

Everyone else in the harem (except Zephyr and Ash, who haven't exactly been around) got to stay at Zara's side and fight.

And the fact that my hands are still shaking, even hours later, well after the rest of them got home?

It's like proof that Zara's right.

When it comes to fighting for her and defending her, I really am useless.

Biting my lip, I breathe in the cool bite of peppermint, cradle the steaming mug carefully between my palms, and trot across the great room to the crackling heat and light of the central hearth. Shadows dance and flicker around the high-backed Renaissance sofa where Dez and Racetrack are cuddled together in their jammies.

RT looks grumpy as heck in her scruffy sweats and athletic socks, with a gauze bandage wrapped around her forehead and her fist wrapped around a bracing cup of black coffee. Nurse Lavinia just left, and my housemate's not supposed to sleep, because she might have a mild concussion.

After RT magicked me off the yacht, one of those big bullies from the AIB apparently sucker-punched her. Knocked her out cold.

Snuggled up next to her, Dez is swimming in her big terrycloth bathrobe, dark ringlets still damp from her shower. When I hand over her cocoa, her olive eyes look big and haunted.

"Thanks, copper. That'll set me to rights." Dez summons up a brave smile, but her voice is raspy from crying, and her skin is tight with strain.

She's got bruises on her delicate wrists from being manhandled by those jerks, but I give her total credit. She's no kind of fighter. But Dez held her shit together like a pro.

When I blinked into the *domus*, still yelling in protest, Dez was already getting the Dean (who's like a million years old and had to be woken up and apparently slept through the actual party?) on the landline.

"How about a nip of the strong stuff for yourself, Red?" Ronin's sprawled across the settee, tummy-down and shirtless, with a white square of adhesive standing out against the tawny ripple of his naked shoulder and his head pillowed in Zara's lap. His black hair spills over the edge of the settee and one hand cradles his glass on the floor. There's an inch of amber scotch melting the ice. That's the only anesthetic he'd let Nurse administer before she stitched him up.

I don't want any cocoa. I don't need to be babied.

But I go and fetch the Macallan to top off his glass.

At least that gives me something to do that's useful. I mean, like, it's an alternative to hurling myself at Zara's feet and howling like a toddler throwing a tantrum because she sent me away.

"You're a good lad," Ronin murmurs.

He's kinda sleepy from the scotch and the heat and Zara stroking his hair. He's so brave. I mean, he's so badass I don't think he was even afraid. When Zara's ex was doing his darnedest to ram his knife through

Ronin's throat, I was more terrified than Ronin, who mostly just looked pissed.

Anyway, I'm *not* a good lad.

I'm about to explode with frustration.

My shoulders are all bunched tight with stress.

Leaving three messages in a row on my dad's mobile, which he still hasn't returned, is definitely not helping.

"How's your shoulder?" I say politely, but also with real concern.

Ronin was the one who needed actual rescue. Seeing him tasered and pinned under that jerk, I was scared to death. By the time Ronin showed up here with the others, grim and bloody but thankfully still ambulatory and breathing, I was practically in tears.

"I'll be right as rain, love. No worries." From the comfy pillow of Zara's lap, he eyes my hovering frame under sleepy lids. "I'm a fast healer, aren't I? All those shifter biochemicals I've got from Lucius, yeah?"

My gaze shoots to the kitchen, where I can still hear the soothing drone of Lucius' murmur on the landline. Our headmaster's speaking Hungarian, so I guess he's finally been able to reach his grandpa.

I don't speak the language, and we don't have a mating bond, because Lucius is afraid to bite me (and please don't get me started on that whole topic). But I like the sound of his rolling R's and buzzing Z's and sibilant S's. He's lurking in the kitchen doorway, stretching the long phone cord to its maximum limit. That way he can keep an eye on Ronin and Zara (both of whom he's bitten and thus goes alpha-to-the-max protective over) while he talks to Laszlo Aries.

"If you will insist upon engaging in mortal combat, Ronin Pendragon, you should have more than one mating bite." That's Maxim, getting in his two cents and speaking his careful English, which he taught himself back home in Russia. "My dragon's bite will speed your healing."

Max has been super vocal lately (when he's around, because he's gone a lot) about wanting to bite Ronin, because Ronin and Zara were the first ones he mated, and he bit Zara right away.

It especially comes up when they're fucking.

Which is, like, insanely sexy.

Right now, my dragon shifter boyfriend looks disreputable but yummy, ripped jeans and faded black tee clinging to his wiry frame, buttery blond hair spilling loose around his shoulders. He's scowling and pacing before the sliding doors that open on the *domus* courtyard and the glowing turquoise rectangle of our swimming pool.

Those glass doors are currently closed and locked because A) we're on an island and the nights still get nippy, and B) no one feels safe having any doors open.

Not after what went down on that yacht tonight.

"And have superheats every blooming month the way Zara does? No thanks, love. My heats from Lucius' bite are plenty." Ronin snorts at Max, but softens the rejection with a wry smile. "You dragons are a potent lot."

Max looks kinda disgruntled—I think he literally wants to bite all of us, except maybe Lucius, whom he defers to.

But Max is too focused on patrol duty over there to double down on coaxing Ronin to take his mating bite.

He's been pacing like that since he shifted back. It's actually making *me* tired just watching him.

Zara stirs on the settee and turns to Max with a sigh. "C'mon over here and warm up by the fire, big guy. We gotta talk this thing through, all of us. Anyway, Lucius has wards on the *domus*. We'll know if anyone comes."

Her wary eyes shift to me and soften. "You too, baby. Come right over here and sit with me. We can all feel you. I'm really sorry you're hurting."

Now it's my turn to sigh. Living in a polycule with telepaths isn't all fun and games.

It's, like, impossible to keep anything secret.

Unless you're Vasili.

Who seems to have no problem, ever, keeping secrets.

I eye the ottoman where Zara's bare feet are resting. Her pretty opal toenail polish glitters in the firelight.

But her little feet look cold.

When she came home, she just threw on her favorite yoga pants and a Villa Augustus tee shirt (that's the name of this *domus*, our residential college at Icarus). She's really not wearing enough for a chilly night.

That decides me. I can't have my precious one cold.

I trot over and plunk myself down on the cushion at Zara's feet to face her. It's hard to meet her eyes when I feel this way, but her love and worry for me radiate through our mating bond. Gently I gather her feet in my lap and cup her cold toes (she's, like, icy) in my warm palms.

"That's so nice, baby," she murmurs with a grateful smile. "My feet are freezing. Too worked up earlier to find my slippers."

I'm a little chilly too, but there isn't time right now to worry about me. Until, to my surprise, Max prowls over and crowds onto the cushion with me and wraps himself around me from behind.

Which is just so comforting and nice.

He's a fire sign, he's the Sagittarius scion (only he calls it a prince), and fire signs always run hot.

While I rub Zara's cold feet and massage her soles, Max's sinewy suntanned arms slide around my waist. He spreads his denim-clad thighs to tuck me between them, then rubs the tawny bristle of his five o'clock stubble against the side of my neck.

Goosebumps break out all over me under my Academy polo shirt. I sigh and melt into him.

I love Max so much.

Literally one of the only good things about Zara getting kidnapped this spring was that Max and I got major together time while we were chasing her and Zephyr through the portal and the standing stones to Avalon.

Max and I hooked up over there (finally!) So now we're together too.

"Perhaps it is you I should be biting, hmmm, *kotyonok*?" our dragon rumbles in my ear. His mating scent of leather and brimstone fills my head. "If you will follow our sovereign and these hellions we are mating into danger, then we must keep you safe."

*Kotyonok* means kitten in Russian. I love the nickname. And I love the thought of him biting me (after waiting so long for him to offer!)

I shiver all over with happiness and delight.

Of course, Vasili's in a mood. He's never totally gotten over finding out about Max and me, and he's really territorial. Because V actually *has* bitten me. That means he really is one of my alphas.

Even if he doesn't act like it.

I mean, he never hovers and fusses over me to make sure I'm warm and fed and happy, you know, like an alpha should. Actually, Max is way more hovery.

So of course V has to totally ruin any kind of nice moment Max and I are having.

"Bite him if you must, darling." Vasili sneers at Max from the far corner of the settee where he's draped like a serpent, looking like Mata Hari in a silk kimono, with his gilded hair still damp from his shower and slicked back from his pretty face. "Since our First Boy is clearly into it. Then you can fuck him into a sex puddle and indulge your ridiculous mpreg obsession about filling his nonexistent uterus with a clutch of your revolting dragonets. The same way you carry on with Ronin."

"Oh, man," Racetrack mumbles from the sofa behind her coffee. "TMI, guys."

Ronin gives a surprised snort of laughter and rolls onto his good side to grin at Vasili. "Easy, love. Don't yuck on his yum. Not Max's fault he's got a breeding kink, is it?"

"Yeah, what he said," Zara murmurs. I feel a warm little spurt of gratitude, because she always defends me. "It's just a fantasy, Goblin King. Since Ronin doesn't mind, it's all good. We gotta let Neo and Max have their own thing too."

Her tone is soft with understanding because she gets Vasili, she really does, even when he's being all vile and snaky.

Still, I'm sensing a somber note of sadness and guilt lurking in my fated mate that I don't like her to feel.

When she fiddles with the glittery tiara she's tossed onto the end table next to her, with her gorgeous Hollywood face all pensive, I figure out what's bothering her.

It's all those awful things Messalina said in front of the whole witching world. You know, about how Zara's all wicked and selfish and slutty.

How she's not worthy to wear the witching world crown.

Hearing Zara put him in his place, V gives an annoyed little huff and sulks behind his martini.

But Ronin's really hard to resist when he's shirtless and grinning like that.

Especially when he throws one yummy leather-clad leg over Vasili's lap and rubs a teasing bare foot against V's thigh.

That makes V unbend enough to give Ronin a sultry smirk.

"Just don't expect me to throw you a baby shower." That snake gives a delicate shudder. "You know I despise infants."

Ronin smolders back at him and slides his sexy toes up V's inner thigh. "Bet you'd like mine though. Wouldn't you, love?"

Wow. Okay.

Clearly, Ronin's all sexed up. Even though the moon's nowhere near full and no one's going into heat.

Maybe it's the adrenaline rush of combat.

Not that I'd know anything about that.

Firing with sudden resolve, I turn my head to peer back at Max.

He too is literally smoldering at V (who hasn't even bothered to answer Ronin's question) with his golden eyes flaming and his oblong dragon pupils narrowed to slits. Suddenly I wonder if Ronin isn't the only guy in our harem Max fantasizes about knocking up.

Anyway.

Max might be looking at Vasili, but he's wrapped around me, slipping his hot fire sign fingers under my polo shirt to tease my bare abs. He's attentive and possessive and broody enough about me these days to finally give me the courage to tell him what *I* want.

Like, for myself.

I clear my throat, give Zara's pretty feet a gentle squeeze for courage, and sit straighter in his arms. "Uh, Max?"

Max rubs his bristly face into my neck to scent me. *"Kotyonok."*

I lick my dry lips. "Will you teach me to fight?"

The whole room falls silent. Like, you can practically hear a mosquito breathe under the crackle and pop of the fire.

"Fight?" Max repeats cautiously, lifting his face from my neck to peer at me. "How do you mean, fight?"

"I mean *fight*." My held breath spills out in a rush. "You know, fight fight? Like, with knives and staffs and weapons, the way you and Ronin train all the time?"

Zara's gaze locks on mine and her plush lips fall open. I read surprise and understanding and concern in her eyes. But there's something else pulsing through our mating bond that's an instinct too strong for her to hide.

It's fear. For me. Because she doesn't think I can fight for myself.

That whole reaction just makes me more determined to learn.

Totally predictable that Vasili recovers first.

"Dear fuck," he says into the startled silence. "This is like that moment when you open your express delivery from Balenciaga and realize they've sent you Miu Miu instead."

Racetrack snickers from the sofa. Dez hushes her with a soft murmur.

"Why would you wish to fight, Neo Mercury?" Max sounds so reasonable. "It is my honor to fight for you. As I fight for our sovereign. As I fight for all of you."

"Yeah, I know." My shoulders lift in a frustrated shrug. "I just… I want to fight *with* you. I want to *help*. I want to defend Zara. Against Messalina and Cleo and whoever else comes after her and tries to steal her crown."

While everyone else absorbs this newsflash, Ronin pushes up to sit and sweeps back his long hair with an impatient hand.

"Love," he says to me gently, "you're already helping. Every day. Just by being you. You've got nothing to prove. You don't need to risk yourself—"

"No. I need to do this." I don't like interrupting, but this is way too important. "I'm not, like, some sheltered omega from one of Zara's books. I don't need to be sheltered. I want to carry my share of the load." My face heats with shame and my volume takes a nosedive.

I finish in an embarrassed mutter. "At least let me learn to protect myself."

Ronin's brow furrows in consternation. "Bloody hell."

Zara's been reading us some of those glossy omegaverse paperbacks I had shipped from her old place. Those are some of my favorite times, curled up in a pile with her and the guys in our big medieval bed on a rainy Sunday morning while she reads to us.

So we all know what an omega is. In her books, they're like this special protected mate that has to be taken care of by all the alphas in their pack.

And most—but not all—of the omegas are girls.

"Neo, baby," Zara breathes, because of course she's in my head, just like I'm in hers. "You're never a burden. I love being with you. And so do they."

"Omega," Max says slowly. His tone deepens to a dragonish rumble in my ear. "In Zara's books, these omegas… they become pregnant, do they not?"

Vasili rolls his eyes and voices an eloquent snort of disgust.

Max isn't a natural telepath and he hasn't bitten me, so we don't have an actual mating bond. That means I can't actually read his mind. But I don't need telepathy to sense the sudden addition of an imaginary omega version of me, capable of getting pregnant, to Max's mpreg sexual fantasies.

Racetrack groans and scrambles up from the couch. "You guys gotta do this mpreg shit when I'm not around, for real. But Neo's got a point. He does need to learn how to handle himself in a fistfight."

"Thank you, Racetrack," I tell her humbly.

"Yeah." She shrugs. "Just makes sense. If they won't teach you, I will."

Max makes a disgruntled sound, but I glow up at her. I'm beyond grateful to have at least one ally.

My housemate's beelining for the kitchen with her empty mug when Dez pipes up. "Maybe we should all learn, cobber."

RT stops in her tracks and pivots to eye her girlfriend. Under her bandage, her hard face scrunches up. Clearly she sees the trap she's just walked into. "Shit. Dez… that's… totally different—"

"Except it's not, though, is it?" Dez sits up straight in her big terrycloth robe and looks determined. "Messalina's minions, the AIB, Cleopatra and her boo—they'll all be gunning for Zara—"

At that exact moment, a furtive knock echoes through our *domus*.

Someone's knocking at our front door.

From the kitchen, the comforting hum of Lucius' voice breaks off. A heartbeat later his wary face appears in the doorway.

Wary, but not totally alarmed.

The defensive wards on our *domus* are linked to him. If someone's lurking out there who wants to hurt us, I have to hope he'd sense that.

But this island's crawling with all those refugees from the yacht. All those Aquarius allies.

So it really could be anyone.

In a single catlike twist, Ronin rolls to his feet. Max snarls and coils up to stand with him, shoulder to shoulder.

Vasili lapses into perfect stillness. You'd need to look close to realize he's levitating, barely an inch above the settee. Without even trying, wearing nothing but a black silk kimono and whatever knives he's got strapped to his sexy body underneath, he's still the biggest badass in this *domus*.

Zara snatches her feet out of my lap, grabs the witching world crown, and rams it on her head. Her eyes light up with periwinkle fire and the ends of her teal pigtails start floating.

Which makes me wonder if that bauble we pinched is more than a royal heirloom.

Maybe it's also, like, a magical artifact?

But I shove that thought in a folder to think about later, because that furtive knock—more insistent this time, almost desperate—sounds again. I leap to my feet, but don't know what else to do. Dez and I are just the civvies, the non-combatants in the room.

Same as always.

Anyway, I'm not leaving Zara. I grab the iron poker from the fire grate and plant myself between her and the door. Racetrack stalks across the room and ranges herself at my side.

Like a comrade-in-arms. I appreciate her for that.

Zara levitates six feet in the air and orders, in the eerie reverberation of the lightning voice, "Open the door."

"I'll handle this. The rest of you, for the love of God, try to stay out of trouble." Lucius gives us all a grim look and crosses the room with his measured tread.

Looking all professorial in his cardigan and houndstooth trousers, with his chestnut hair neatly tied at his nape, he pads down the little staircase to the vestibule.

Ronin and Max are right on his heels.

Zara stares after them with her eyes narrowed. I have the feeling she's reaching out with senses I didn't even know she had, like Ronin's clairsentience.

Vasili takes a delicate sip of his martini and watches the stairs like a cobra eyeing a mongoose.

A rush of hushed and hurried voices flows from the vestibule. But I don't have shifty senses, just plain old Kryll ones like the rest of my race, so I can't make out a word.

"Well, well," Vasili murmurs, sounding thoughtful. His icy eyes narrow, but they don't thaw. He does have shifty senses, but he likes to keep his secrets.

"Fuck this waiting shit. Not cut out for it," Racetrack mutters and starts for the door.

But she doesn't get far before they're back. All three of our guys.

But, like, with company.

The whole kit and kaboodle tromps up the stairs and pours into our great room, with Lucius in the lead.

Behind him, a tall skinny girl pushes back the hood of her Academy sweatshirt to reveal a pale freckled face, wide gray eyes, and a soft mouth that's grim with resolve. Her bright coppery braid, which is super distinctive, spills over one shoulder.

"Oh. hey," I say in happy recognition.

Two guys push in on either side like bookends and loom over her, all protective. These are guys I recognize from Villa Hadrian. (That's one of the other residential colleges.) Draco's in my Witching World Law class and pretty hard to miss. Jae's more of a lurker, but I did a group project with him last year in Witching World History.

"Sweet fuck." Vasili sneers. "It's Mallory McSnicker and her magical *ménage*."

"Hey, Zara." To her credit, Mallory doesn't get distracted by that snake. She's laser-focused on my fated mate, who's still floating six feet above the fray. "I know we're not part of your harem. But we're here to join your court. I mean, if you'll have us."

"God save the queen," Draco growls in his gravelly voice and bares his teeth in a savage grin. "We're here to join the witching world resistance."

# Chapter Seven
## Zara

I'm seriously fascinated by Mallory and her *ménage*.

I mean, I don't know anyone else at Icarus who's poly like me and my guys. But I don't want to make my classmate feel weird. Or, God knows, threatened—like the rebel queen's macking on her guys (or on her). So I work really hard not to stare.

Since that's apparently what I am right now.

The rebel queen.

"WNN just finished filming their whole special broadcast from our villa crypt. I guess because it's, I dunno, all medieval and atmospheric down there?" From her uneasy perch on the Renaissance sofa, Mallory wraps up her story with an apologetic shrug and scoots closer to the fire. "So we heard the whole thing right from the source. Messalina controls the media, and they're spinning this whole thing like we're starring in *The Hunger Games* and this is the revolution."

"Am I supposed to be Katniss?" I stare. "Not totally minding. She's badass."

Mal's throat ripples in a hard swallow. "They're saying you and your kings are trying to overthrow the government."

"Oh, please." Vasili sneers and looks totally unimpressed. "As though there's any sort of actual Aquarius government to overthrow. Everyone knows Messalina's reign has been a nightmare. Truly, she's worse than useless. The witching world is practically extinct. First she ignored it, then she denied it. In the end, she's only made the entire crisis worse."

"That's why we're here, true?" Draco Mars rasps in his sandpaper voice, draping a possessive arm around Mallory's shoulders and tucking her skinny frame against his big body to keep her warm. "A shitload of witches and warlocks gonna feel the same way. The way we see it, you boys and her? If we gonna survive? You're the only play for this shithole throne we got to make."

Sure, that sounds supportive, and they're *here*—which speaks volumes. But those Nordic eyes burning in the square-jawed face of Mallory's hulking Icelandic beau are twin chips of blue ice.

Suffice it to say, this guy's not filling half our sofa with his Hulk-sized body at one a.m. because he likes me.

And Mal's other guy—Jean-Emilien Labête (who goes by Jae)—seems even more on edge as he prowls around our great room, barely visible in the shadows with his black hair and black clothes and silent tread.

Let's just say it's no coincidence that my guys have rearranged themselves around me on the settee with V coiled on one side, Lucius lurking on the other, and Ronin looming on his feet behind me with his hot Leo hands literally resting on my shoulders. Max is pacing around the windows again (and Jae's definitely ceding him that terrain).

My surly dragon looks like he might shift and start flaming at the first sign of danger.

While Neo and Dez bustle around getting everyone refills on their coffee and cocoa, Racetrack pokes at the fire and looks grumpy.

I worry that my housemate's head is hurting from her injury (which she incurred fighting for me). But of course, she's too stubborn to admit it and take a numbing potion. Especially now, with these uninvited guests in the house, especially guests that are so alarming. I figure Dez is gonna have to coax her girlfriend into taking care of herself.

Because, clearly, I did enough ordering everyone around—including RT who isn't even my mate—while we were fighting for our lives on that yacht.

"I'll admit the news you're hearing is consistent with what I've derived from my own sources, Ms. McSnicker," Lucius murmurs around a genteel sip of Hungarian *palinka*. The fruity bite of his brandy stings my nostrils, but that bite is familiar and comforting. Comfort is something we all need right now. "My grandsire missed the yacht's departure from the port in Sorrento to attend this evening's festivities only because he was detained by the AIB when he attempted to board."

"What the hell?" Okay, now I'm indignant. "One, Gramps is head of the Aries clan, so he's influential as fuck. And two, he's like a hundred years old. You can't just go around arresting old people. They get heart attacks and shit."

"Except for being inconvenienced by his detainment, he's fine. Although I don't advise that you address him as Gramps when you meet." My headmaster shoots me a wry look and rests a steadying hand on my knee. "More to the point, I fear the same fate has befallen Racetrack's mothers, as well as Senator Mercury… and even Mick Gemini."

"My dad?" Caught in the middle of serving Mallory's cocoa (minus schnapps, because she's pregnant), Neo's so surprised he almost squeaks. "He's under arrest?"

"Whoa." I sit up straighter and carefully cradle my own boozy cocoa, which is way too yummy to spill. "I mean, don't get me wrong. My asshole dad gets arrested on, like, a regular basis. That's what happens when you're an Irish mob boss *and* a crooked casino czar. But I'm guessing that's maybe not the norm for anyone else's parental unit?"

"Let's just say the arrest was a novel experience for my law-abiding and very traditional Hungarian grandsire," Lucius says dryly. "However, a pureblooded Aries wolf shifter—even one of his years—is difficult to confine, as the AIB learned to their dismay. He is at this moment, as I believe you'd say, on the wind?"

*"Bon bagay!"* Jae, who's a lean and kinda slinky-looking Creole with expensive clothes and amber eyes like a shifter—prowls into the light and bares his teeth in a wolfish grin. "The Aries wolves are badass, *oui?* My *fanmi* back in New Orleans, they tell folk tales about Count Laszlo."

"Count Laszlo, huh?" I murmur to Lucius, shooting him a teasing wink. *You been holding out on me, Teach? Am I gonna be a countess once you and I officially tie the knot?*

*You're already a queen.* The gray silk ribbon of my headmaster's mental murmur unspools through the mating bond we share with our guys. *Although it's true my ancestral home is a rather atmospheric medieval castle in the Carpathians. I'll enjoy taking you—all of you—to visit someday.*

That juicy revelation definitely adds to the whole Old World aristocrat vibe Lucius is rocking.

Too bad I'm so worried about everything else I'm hearing, and so relieved Lucius seems none the worse for wear after his wolfish scuffle with that fucker Xiao—someone else who's still on the wind—that I can barely even get psyched about visiting Dracula's castle.

Still, it means something that Lucius (who's super reserved and private, at least when he's not wolfing out) is extending the invite. It means something that his whiskey eyes linger on all of us—all our mates, even Max who he isn't fucking—with that kinda warmth.

Vasili hums with interest and looks intrigued. Still looming behind me, Ronin shifts one hand from my shoulder to rest on Lucius'.

My headmaster's still talking, his affectionate gaze resting on Neo's worried face as our bookworm trots over and snuggles on the ottoman at my feet. "There's no cause for alarm over anyone's parents. I understand Senator Mercury is very capably negotiating with the AIB authorities, and the Prynnes are among his biggest donors. My grandsire fully expects they'll all be paroled and released by dawn."

"Oh, gosh, poor Dad. *Paroled.*" Neo leans into my knees and sighs. "Wait'll the press get wind of that. It's an election year too. No wonder he isn't returning my calls." His face turns diplomatically toward RT. "And the poor Prynnes too."

"Yeah, sucks, but it's nothing they can't handle." Racetrack scowls into the fire. "One of my moms runs a construction crew. She's tough enough to spit nails, so no one fucks with her. And my other mom has nerves of steel—you know, brain surgeon."

"A construction boss *and* a brain surgeon?" Mallory looks impressed. "Wow. Did they meet cute? Someone should write them into a sapphic romance."

RT looks so appalled at that idea that Ronin snickers. "That could be your side hustle, mate. Romance author."

Predictably, Racetrack flips him the bird. "Anyway, they're both pretty hard to shake up. And they're too loaded to intimidate. Neo's dad'll get 'em sprung."

"Which leaves *my* dad," I mutter. "He's got more legal lives than a cat. He'll lawyer up and wiggle outta whatever they try to charge him with. Same as always."

Lucius says quietly, "I'm afraid the charge is sedition."

Hearing the word, I suck in my breath. My heart gives a hard thump.

That ugly word just lies there, on the colorful Turkish rug before us, like a stinking dead rat no one wants to touch.

"The fuck," Ronin mutters.

Maxim lets out a dragonish snarl and resumes pacing.

"Sedition?" I echo, feeling dizzy. "As in, *treason*? If we're all being charged with treason, why isn't the AIB beating down our door to haul us off right now?"

Lucius places his snifter on the end table, right next to my stolen crown, and raises a scholarly hand for caution. "It appears no one's been formally arraigned. Merely detained. Messalina was clearly hoping you'd recognize her daughter, renounce your claim on the crown, and obviate the need for any more dramatic course of action."

"Yeah, no, not renouncing." I scowl at the crown that's causing all this trouble. "Vasili said it. Draco said it." I give a wary nod at the hulking Norseman sitting across the way who's watching us all so closely. "I said it on live TV. The witching world is dying. We're in free fall. We're not making enough little witches and warlocks to sustain the population. If I can figure out how to reverse that, the way Zephyr and I did for the Dark Fae in Avalon when we broke the curse—then we've got a fighting chance."

My point's one hundred percent valid. Still, it hurts to say Zephyr's name, for real. Hot pain pings in my chest and burns in my throat.

Because neither he nor Ash have been picking up (so to speak) from Avalon when I try to call.

Ronin, my telepath, shifts both hands to my tight shoulders and gives me a hard squeeze.

His fierce voice ricochets through our mating bond. *I'll find that bloody-minded Unseelie bastard. And the other one too, I reckon. Can't hide forever, can they? I've got a scrying glass, haven't I? And I know how to use it.*

I can't hold back a mortified giggle, which makes Mal and her guys eye me like I'm psycho. Here I am, the mad queen, giggling into my cocoa over an extinction event that's dooming all four of the arcane races.

"No wonder they're hiding, Adam, with that kinda attitude," I mutter into my mug.

Now it's Ronin's turn to voice a dark chuckle. Which I'm kinda relieved to hear. My sexy Brit's got his own major baggage with my two missing Fae. Enough baggage to pretty much fill all the available space whenever he scrys for my two missing guys.

But now definitely isn't the time to unpack all that.

"Let's try to stay focused," Lucius says mildly, eyeing the two of us with gentle exasperation as we chortle away. "To Zara's point, no one's come to arrest us—even after she announced to the entire witching world where to find us and practically dared Messalina to try. Cleopatra actually fled the scene rather than fight."

"That's one way to put it," Ronin mutters. "A blooming sea dragon. Thought they were supposed to be extinct."

"Not in Avalon," I murmur. Sure, my ex-BFF turning sea dragon shifter was a shocker, but I've had a few hours now to process that shit. "They've got all kinds of dragons over there. And Cleo's apparently half-Fae, born in Avalon, so do the math."

"Even so." Lucius steeples his thoughtful fingers. "Even the AIB aggression on the yacht appeared to be primarily a delaying tactic. This restraint suggests Messalina Aquarius is… uncertain. Not yet prepared to declare open war against you—her proclaimed successor, the Gemini queen—and your powerful allies. In this situation, we retain a certain amount of freedom to… strategize."

I squirm on the settee and sip at my well-fortified cocoa to steady my jittery nerves. Seems weird to think of me—reformed cat burglar and a casino czar's brat—having powerful allies.

But, clearly, I do. I'm the closest thing to a purebred female witch our depleted races can scare up, with DNA from all four arcane races, which is why the Senate chose me to be the next royal. I've got all kinds of uber-scary witchcraft I'm still discovering and coming to terms with.

Plus I'm common-law mated to half the blooded scions in the witching world.

Not to mention semi-officially mated (kinda by accident) to Zephyr, the Unseelie King. *And* semi-officially shagging Ash, the Seelie Prince.

Assuming those two Fae haven't changed their minds about wanting me… us… I mean, all my warlocks. And all our baggage—

"So what's our play?" Draco growls in his gravelly voice. Under his spiky thatch of ice-white hair, his arctic eyes flick over me and half my mates packed like sardines around the settee. His lips twist in a scowl. "Assuming you got one."

This Viking might be Mallory's guy, but I swear the temp in this *domus* plunges ten degrees every time he opens his mouth. Still, Mal's snuggled right up against that Icelandic version of the Terminator like he's not the most alarming thing that's walked into our *domus* since Bjorn the polar bear shifter last winter.

"Don't you mean, assuming we trust you?" Vasili's mouth curls in a silky smile. "You're not exactly your stodgy and responsible elder brother, are you, Draco? Where does the Mars clan stand in the matter of our so-called rebellion?"

Draco's cold eyes narrow and his big shoulders bunch under his spiked leather jacket. Mallory rests a hand on his knee to hold him.

"Draco stands with me," she says firmly. "And I might not look like much—but appearances can be deceiving."

Before any of us can dig into that, Mallory's freckled face fires with determination and she leans forward. "Besides, there's one other thing we came to tell you."

"Oh, we're listening, McSnicker," Vasili purrs. "With bated breath."

Now it's my turn to slide a hand over his silk kimono-clad knee. "Don't be an asshole with them, okay, Goblin King? They really are here to help."

"Yeah, don't be a brat," Neo chimes in helpfully from his seat at my feet. "Zara needs every ally we can get."

V hums with annoyance, but his cool fingers glide over mine (which is the closest he ever comes to an apology). His snaky humor lurks in our mating bond. I'm guessing he doesn't totally mind when sweet Neo calls him a brat.

Especially when, like, he is one.

His cool touch trails up my wrist, sharp black-painted nails tickling my skin like talons. Which is more than enough to get me all goosebumpy and tingling and totally sidetracked.

Yowsa.

Suddenly all I can think about is how vicious my horrible bully of an alpha's gonna be later.

When he finally gets me cornered.

In our bed.

Mallory's Creole boyfriend Jae slinks onto the sofa beside her and leans in to rub his face into her neck (which is classic shifty stuff. He's scenting her.) The beads and juju woven in his sleek black dreads slither over his shoulder.

And now Mal's blushing, because her redhead complexion's too fair to hide it.

"Me, I walk unseen on this island when I wish," Jae says softly, in the musical singsong of his Creole voice. "There is much I see. Tonight I see lot of traffic coming and going from Villa Tiberius."

"That den of vipers." Still vigilant near the glass doors, Max stalks back and forth. By now, he's so suspicious he practically has smoke leaking from his nostrils. "Those creatures are Zara's enemies. And they are mine."

Villa Tiberius is, like, our rival residential college. They bullied me like they bullied Max when we first turned up at Icarus. If Mallory and the Hadrians are Hufflepuffs, those cliquey witches at Tiberius (who all lean Aquarius) are definitely Slytherin.

And us? Given my creative cat burglary approach to the law, Neo's sky-high I.Q., and V's twisty cunning, we're definitely Ravenclaws. Because sometimes we skirt the rules. And we're smart enough and badass enough to get away with it.

I mean, usually.

"Somebody moving in at the rival *domus*?" I rest my empty mug on the floor and sift my fingers through Neo's soft curls to caress his warm nape. That's both for his comfort and mine. My fated mate's always responsive, but tonight he's a little withdrawn. His hurt still smarts in our mating bond.

I breathe in his clean soapy scent of sage and lavender and hope he won't stay upset for too long.

If our sweet bookworm learning to fight is the price I've gotta pay to earn his forgiveness?

Guess I better get used to that.

"Yeah, a bunch of someones are moving in at Tiberius," Mallory says in response to my question. "With a lot of luggage too. It looks like an actual entourage."

"You mean, like, a *royal* entourage?" I stare into her earnest gray eyes. "I mean, sure, we sank the royal yacht. By accident, of course—"

"That was no accident." Maxim growls. "I meant to burn that vessel to the waterline. So that is what I did."

Ronin laughs, which doesn't help, but we're moving past Max and his bloodthirsty ways. I glance around at all my guys. "I mean, why would Messalina move in at Icarus? This Academy is totally our space. It's our power base."

"She wouldn't," Vasili murmurs. "That bitchy witch has almost certainly retreated to sulk and lick her wounds at the Aquarius palazzo in Venice. That's *her* stronghold, where her actual throne resides. You've stolen her crown, darling. She's going to cling to that throne like a barnacle."

"Crikey! New student." Dez pops up suddenly.

Our resident house elf has finally stopped fussing over everyone's coffee and cocoa. Now Dez is tucked up neatly next to Racetrack on the rug and practically vibrating with excitement. "That's what the Dean said when I finally got her on the landline, yeah? I thought she was barmy. Telling me about a new student at a time like this? But maybe she was actually trying to warn us."

In the sudden silence, Vasili draws in a hiss of alarm. His cold fingers close around my wrist like a manacle.

That's his way of holding me close.

For protection.

Max snarls and stops in his tracks to eye me. In his golden irises, his oblong pupils narrow to slits. He's feeling the sizzle of instinct that crackles through my brain like a lightning bolt.

Since my mates all read me like the goddamn Sunday paper, Ronin's hands tighten on my shoulders. "Oh, bloody hell. Surely not, love."

Clearly smelling the tension in the room, even though they're not in our bond, Jae and Draco loom protectively over Mallory. The Viking's eyes flare and pulse with an eerie blue fire.

Even with my shifty senses, I can't be sure in the flickering light, but Jae's fingers seem to elongate, so they're all extra jointy and sprout cruel-looking talons.

Mallory squeezes Draco's thick thigh and grips Jae's freaky-looking hand. Her cautious gaze shoots straight to Lucius, the face of authority in the room. "I don't get it. Why would the Dean warn you about a new student? It can't be Messalina. She graduated from here thirty years ago."

"No, our new resident wouldn't be Messalina," Lucius murmurs. He sounds totally composed, but I know my unshakable headmaster is troubled (which makes my own misgivings worse). "As Vasili has surmised, our queen regnant has very likely returned to her royal seat in Venice. The refugees from the yacht are likewise being flown home on the Academy supply plane. Queen or no queen, only faculty and students are permitted past the wards to reside on this island."

I don't even wanna say this shit out loud.

But, clearly, someone needs to say it.

And then figure out some plan to deal with it.

"Fuuuuuck." I groan, long and low, from the heart. "Fucking Cleo. She just fucking enrolled here as a student."

# Chapter Eight
## Lucius

"I mean, seriously, why is Cleo even here? It's not enough the backstabbing bitch just schemed to get me dethroned and humiliated at my own birthday bash—on live TV?"

Zara's indignant voice floats through the open door of our shared bedroom as I prowl down the darkened stretch of the upstairs hall.

There's currently no electrified light in the drafty corridor of our ancient *domus*, a habitation whose foundations date to the Roman era. Regrettably, the antiquated wiring is fragile and temperamental across the island grid (all the more so since Zara arrived at Icarus, hurling lightning like a vengeful Zeus).

Thus, I'm carrying a lit candle while I conduct my nightly prowl to confirm that all our doors and windows are locked and warded against the unknown night.

As I test the latch on the tall window that spills a pale wash of moonlight down the hall, Zara's fretful words seep through the bedroom door she's left ajar for me.

"Even, like, academically, what's *up* with the bitch's timing? Cleo already graduated from the Sorbonne in Paris or some shit. She's older than us. Not to mention it's literally finals week."

Despite the seriousness of our current situation, with words like *revolution* and *sedition* still ringing in my ears, the prickly annoyance in my queen's voice makes my wolf bristle and pace.

We've witnessed ample evidence that Zara's superheats, which are supposed to sync with the moon, have become far less predictable since she returned from the hidden Fae realm of Avalon. Still, she's diligently maintained her regimen of prophylactic shots at the Academy clinic. As long as I've known her, she's been fixated on avoiding conception.

In fact, when it comes to those shots, she's fanatical in her zeal.

Now I wonder if perhaps, given these unseasonal heats she's having, she might be due for a booster.

Presented with this discouraging prospect, my wolf whines with disappointment. In the witching world, pureblooded wolf shifters are all but extinct. My beast craves a litter of shifter pups. He craves them desperately.

I too am desperate.

I long to see Zara soft and ripe and swelling with my pups.

But this subject is so incendiary in our *domus* that I remind my wolf, once again, to be patient.

Swiftly I pad past the open door of the darkened bedroom Dez shares with Racetrack. Those two are still downstairs, brewing a fresh pot of coffee and murmuring over Dez's deck of Tarot cards, ever since we bid farewell to our guests.

None of us under this roof have spoken our fears aloud. But since Racetrack isn't allowed to sleep anyway (doctor's orders), the two girls have taken up sentry duty.

Our queen is in danger.

As I home in on Zara's bedroom, my steps quicken.

"I can perhaps explain the academic timing." I slip into the firelit refuge where we all sleep—our queen and her harem—piled together like puppies in Zara's big medieval bed. "As a matter of arcane custom, any witch or warlock is permitted to sit for final examinations to demonstrate their magical aptitude, whether or not they've attended classes at this Academy. Cleopatra Aquarius is likely hoping to demonstrate the potency of her magical *bona fides*, as it were, to rule the witching world."

In the startled silence that ensues, I gently close our bedroom door and shoot the bolt, then murmur an incantation—just a scrap of common magic, but I'm quite apt at this sort of thing—to ward our den while we sleep.

"Oh, wow." Looking rumpled and adorable in his Academy sweats, Neo sits up in bed. Clearly, he's been poring over a textbook and determinedly cramming for finals (even at this hour).

"What's that, then?" Ronin glances toward the bed from the window seat where he's sitting cross-legged, barefoot and shirtless, hunched over the scrying mirror in his lap. "No offense, love, but that Honors Alchemy telephone book you're poring over doesn't look all that riveting."

"Oh, Ronin. You know it's my favorite subject. But that's not what I'm talking about." Our bookworm sighs, nudges his glasses up his studious nose, and looks endearingly earnest. "Cleo's going for First Girl on the Dean's List."

From her antique vanity, Zara twists around and stares. She's perched on her stool before the glittering threat of the witching world crown that rests before her, while Vasili coaxes a brush through the vivid mane of teal curls that tumbles to her waist.

Momentarily, I'm caught by a glimpse of Vasili's reflection in the glass. As our mate hovers over her, his pretty, sharp, so often spiteful features are soft with a brooding tenderness.

That unguarded flash of love, which he typically hides and hoards and broods over like a dragon with his gold, makes my heart skip and my breath hitch.

Ah, these mates of mine.

They wring my heart like a dishcloth.

Then Zara's turquoise eyes, wide and anxious as the American icon Betty Boop's, lock with mine.

"First Girl," she says flatly. "That's Mallory's spot. She's had it since midterms."

I swallow a sigh of my own and pinch out my candle, then pad across the room to join her.

"That place could be yours, my dear," I say gently, "if only you'd apply yourself to your studies. The academic merit system is really quite straightforward. The highest scoring students in end-of-term examinations are awarded the honor of serving as First Boy and Girl— or whatever their gender may be, of course—for the coming term. The other high scorers comprise the Dean's List."

Our mating bond prickles with the spike of her irritable impatience. My suspicions about Zara's erratic hormonal status are deepening.

Surely—most inconveniently—our queen's next superheat is looming.

During the grueling and occasionally lethal ordeal of final examinations at this Academy, a superheat is one distraction Zara and our mates could stand to forego.

Predictably, Maxim springs to his mate's defense.

"It is not Zara's fault she was kidnapped by that Unseelie tyrant Zephyr. Or that she missed many classes while she was breaking the Avalon curse." Maxim scowls. "Saving the witching world is more important to our sovereign than having her name blazoned on the Dean's List."

"Blazoned, hmm?" Vasili murmurs with a wicked smirk. "Someone in this harem's been boning up on his English."

Ronin snickers over his scrying mirror.

We're all well aware that our dragon shifter is an indifferent student at best. And that the most recent obsession Maxim has been boning is Vasili.

Tonight, however, our resident dragon is focused elsewhere. He's restless and prowling near the crackling fire, possessive and broody, never straying far from Zara's side. If Maxim were currently in his shifted form, his tail would be lashing.

Obviously, he too is sensing our queen's looming heat.

Maxim has stripped out of his shirt and shoes, leaving him clad in nothing but the ripped jeans that cling to his wiry hips. I swallow hard at the sight of his lean sinewy torso, his sleek skin golden with Black Sea suntan, the twisting flex of his tight abs. The cruel silver barbells piercing his ruddy nipples gleam in the firelight.

He's sensitive there. Exquisitely sensitive. I know precisely how sensitive he is from watching him with our mates…

But I mustn't ogle my student.

Truly, I mustn't.

If Maxim desired my attention in that way, he would surely have invited my advances months ago. When it comes to his libido, an alpha shifter is rarely shy.

All too clearly, Maxim does not view me—his headmaster, his teacher, his responsible co-alpha, his stodgy elder by more than a decade—in a sexual way.

*He submits to us,* my wolf growls inside my skin. *He could be ours. You are foolish not to claim him.*

"Apparently," I say firmly, banishing my amorous wolf and his libido to my mental pantry and closing the door between us, "Cleopatra Aquarius does not share your priorities, my dear. Being awarded the First

Girl ribbon and having her name, well, blazoned at the head of the Dean's List is a respectable academic credential. If Cleopatra manages to capture it, that win will bolster her claim to your crown."

Zara's eyes narrow and her stubborn chin acquires a mutinous tilt. "I never even finished high school. You know, on account of running away from my shitty dad? Plus I missed a whole semester of my freshman year here. I'm just saying—there's a reason I'm behind."

"My dear, no one is criticizing your choices or your aptitude. Least of all myself." Gently I bend to kiss her, and Vasili gives way. I pause to acknowledge his accommodation with a respectful nod.

This is the careful navigation of multiple alphas who share a polycule.

Ours is an arrangement—three alpha males and an alpha queen in the same harem—that occurs so rarely it's generally considered to be impossible.

Still, somehow, we make it work.

Between Zara's teal brows, a worried pucker lingers. But, to my pleasure, she leans into my kiss. Her hot lush mouth parts under mine. I cup her delicate jaw, skin soft as velvet under my rough palm, and nudge her lips apart to taste her. My mate's naughty tongue flicks out to meet mine in a sweet swirl that tastes like peppermint cocoa.

The heady vanilla rose of her mating scent hits my acute shifter senses like a mallet wrapped in velvet.

My wolf lunges to his feet with a growl.

Our queen is scenting… quite heavily.

Vasili growls and slithers closer. His hand closes behind Zara's head to nudge her deeper into my kiss. He tugs loose the tidy ponytail at my nape. My thick curls—long overdue for a trim, but my mates won't hear of it—tumble down around my face.

My groin floods with a rush of tingling heat.

"I've been thinking," Zara whispers against my lips. "What if I stopped taking the shots?"

The entire *domus* seems to suck in its breath.

My queen's words affect me like a hand closing around my shaft. Behind my houndstooth trousers, my member thickens and swells in a sudden surge of need.

Somehow I've fallen to my knees on the cool mosaic floor. I surface from the seductive suck of her kiss to find my hands clutching the soft swell of her hips, my fangs shooting from my palate to fill my mouth, and the creamy spice of her mating scent filling my head.

Desperate for more, I bury my head in her lap.

Her supple thighs, encased in the synthetic fabric of her yoga pants, soften and part. I pull in a long inhale and nuzzle my fangs into her warm crotch. Her breath hitches in a soft gasp.

God help us. My wolf has seized control.

My sharpened senses pick up the sudden rustle of leather from the window seat where Ronin leans forward to watch.

"Bloody hell, love," he says softly into the spellbound stillness. "Reckon you've got our attention. Especially theirs. Your alphas."

Fighting for control, I push Zara's thighs wider and breathe in her sweet musk. Under the insistent press of my mouth, the crotch of her yoga pants turns hot and damp.

"Lucius," she moans. One hand clutches my tumbled curls. Her other hand finds Vasili's and pulls him closer.

"Zara," Maxim rasps, thick and husky. His dragon lurks in his voice. "Did… did you mean it?"

He's looming over all of us, wound too tight to touch, so tight with need he's vibrating.

Vasili too is looming, trapping Zara's hand to inhale the intoxicating sweetness of her inner wrist, dragging his sharp little fangs over her fragile skin in a way that makes her whole body shiver. Under lowered lids, his icy gaze simmers with sinful heat.

Merciful Christ.

All three of her alphas are riveted.

Vasili's been more than vocal about his utter contempt for Maxim's breeding kink (but not mine, perhaps because I've largely kept mine to myself). Vasili's been more than clear about his complete disinterest in siring offspring of any kind.

Yet, tonight, shifter biology has seized even our snake in its unbreakable grip.

"I'm not saying I've decided," Zara warns all of us, edged in the low resonance of her lightning voice. "I just feel like we can't ignore it anymore. Our orgy last winter left half the girls on this island pregnant. Including Mal. What if we could do that for the whole witching world?"

My wolf snarls and nuzzles hard into her sweet pussy. My God, she smells like sex. I'm ravenous to taste the tang of her dripping against my tongue. I want to tear her pants off with my teeth, bury my face in her luscious quim, tongue her until she screams with pleasure.

Then, by Christ, I want to fuck her.

"Be very careful, darling," Vasili murmurs into her palm, between sharp nips that make her gasp and twitch. "God knows, I'm not craving diaper duty and a playpen full of colicky brats in onesies like these two. But even I can tell you're playing with powerful pheromones."

Zara arches under me, thighs spread open around me, her curvy little body undulating, hips rocking slightly into my mouth.

"I'm not playing," she gasps. "I wouldn't be that cruel. I know how you guys… feel. I'm just saying… the witching world needs that."

My fangs are too distended for speech. I rub my face into her thighs to scent her and drag my claws—which have also sprouted, sharp and curving, from my fingers—down the sides of her flimsy pants to shred them.

*"That?"* Vasili's tone cuts sharper than a surgeon's scalpel. "Be a bit more specific, little queen, *do*. What precisely are you referring to?"

She moans out the word. "Babies."

From the bed, Neo's soft gasp fills the sudden silence.

I freeze, panting with a driving need I can barely suppress. Under my claws, Zara's ruined yoga pants lie in shreds around her succulent thighs. Beneath, she's barely wearing the most provocative scrap of panties in lime-green lace that cling to her hips.

I'm a heartbeat away from shredding those too.

"My sovereign," Maxim grates in a voice like gravel. Clearly he too is clinging to control by a thread. "Are you saying…?"

"I'm not saying anything. I'm just exploring the idea." She sounds breathless, because of course she senses the effect her words are having. "A baby is, like, this whole major thing. We should want one for its own sake. I'm just thinking… it's always been part of the plan, uh, eventually. That's part of what it means to be queen, right?"

My palms clutch her silky thighs. With a guttural growl, I rub my face into her cunt. Her ruined garment still protects her from my depravity.

But not for long.

"Lucius," she gasps. "Oh, God. Here's what I'm thinking. What if we… picked up the pace? Tightened our timeline? What if we just… kinda… let loose? Without the guardrails?"

Max voices a dragonish snarl and pounces.

He swoops to claim her mouth in a kiss that screams dominance. His sinewy arms enclose her torso. The leather-and-brimstone bite of his mating scent floods the air.

She arches into his kiss with a soft cry. Her hand clenches around my head. Her eager quim presses into my desperate face.

The sharp snick of a switchblade and the flash of steel in the firelight are the only flicker of warning I receive before one of Vasili's hidden knives slices through her tee shirt in a single stroke.

The shredded cotton falls away to reveal her tight tummy and tiny waist and another swath of lime-green lace. This is that demure little garment she calls a bralette. The lingerie frames her sweet curves and clings to the lush swell of her breasts. The tight buds of her nipples, so cruelly pierced with her silver rings, jut against the lace.

Vasili hisses like a snake and closes in behind her. His narrow ringed hands wrap around her breasts. He dives to nip her soft shoulder with his wicked fangs.

She presses into Maxim's kiss and winds an arm around Vasili's neck in welcome.

I nuzzle her hot slit through her thin fabric until she moans and bucks under my mouth.

Now we're surrounding her.

Claiming her.

All three of her shifter alphas.

Like the predatory pack of monsters we are.

I break free from tormenting her long enough to flex my claws, tear through the remnants of Zara's pants, then rip the ruined garment aside. Hot and throbbing with need, I bury my face in the drenched gusset of her panties. The plump lips of her pussy press against the lace. Through the flimsy fabric, I tongue the swollen pearl of her clit. She writhes under me with a savage snarl.

She too is shifter.

But my earthbound wolf will never meet her in a mating flight.

My beast claws at my skin—he wants *out*, and now, wants to be inside her while she's still human. When I deny him, he tilts his muzzle to the moon in a hungry howl.

Dear God, I can barely keep him from rising.

"Fuck me," Ronin mutters from the window in a voice that's thick with lust. The heavy heat of his arousal pulses through our mating bond.

"Wow," Neo whispers, reverent with awe. "Babe, that's incredibly hot."

I slice that sweet boy a heated glance and find him kneeling on the bed to watch. His wide eyes are riveted on Zara—his fated mate. Textbook abandoned, soft lips parted, spectacles sliding down his nose.

Ronin tosses his mirror aside and prowls across the floor with menacing purpose. He grips Neo's square jaw in a hard hand and claims him with a ravenous kiss.

My wolf growls and lunges against my skin.

My bestial mating scent floods from every pore. This olfactory hit intensifies the head-spinning cocktail of potent pheromones the others are pumping out.

In this polycule, they both bend for me. Ronin and Neo. Neo is shy and Ronin is savage, but they both bend so beautifully—for me and all our alphas. My beast is wild to claim them.

But only after we've claimed Zara.

Shot or no shot.

Tonight I intend to pump my queen so full of my potent shifter seed she'll be dripping with my spend for days.

If not weeks.

"Better hold tight for a wild night, love," Ronin mutters against our bookworm's breathless mouth. "Zara's just pitched the whole bloody lot of them into a mating rut."

# Chapter Nine
## Zara

Sweet fuck. A mating rut?

While Lucius drinks in the scent of my ripening cunt through my panties… while Vasili torments my nipples through my bralette and his fangs menace my neck… while Max's demanding tongue fucks my mouth the exact way I'm pretty sure his cock will shortly be riding my cunt… Ronin's words sear and pulse behind my closed lids.

For a shifter queen, I gotta admit, I'm in an embarrassing state of almost total ignorance about mating ruts. Apparently I threw Max into one when I had my first superheat. And that possessive alpha dragon of mine in rut?

He was… intense.

I mean, even more than usual.

But V's still kinda new to the shifty stuff. He's vicious and unpredictable and I honestly have no idea how he'll be affected. And Lucius is always so restrained. I legit can't imagine my responsible headmaster abandoning all that ironclad control and losing himself in a mating frenzy.

Just the thought of Lucius losing it makes my pussy tingle and burn.

If all three of my shifter guys go into rut, you know, in unison?

Sure, I have an industrial-strength pussy. Like, we need that kinda resilience down there at ground zero with seven horny guys in this harem. But I'm not sure even my royal titanium pussy's cut out to handle three alpha shifters in a mating rut.

Under my drenched panties, my slick cunt throbs and clenches with need.

Clearly, she's ready to give this whole supercharged sex situation the old college try.

I'm still all shivery from the dangerous snick of Vasili's switchblade (which is, very possibly, the exact one he used earlier to slit the Aquarius queen's throat). Now his knife slices through the straps of my bralette, one after the other, with such wicked precision the blade doesn't even graze my skin.

"Hey," I mumble through Max's claiming kiss. "That bra came from my lingerie box from Paris, you asshole."

"I'll buy you another." Vasili's heated whisper spills in my ear. My snake's voice is a sandpaper growl, much harsher than his usual silky menace. "I'll buy you the entire inventory, little queen. Just for the pleasure of seeing your delectable body showcase every scrap while I slice your lingerie to ribbons."

"Whoa." That's Neo on the bed, sounding all sexed up and breathless from whatever Ronin's doing to him. "Dude, you can't just ruin all Zara's underwear."

"That does seem excessive, Goblin King. Even for you." I gasp out a laugh and surface from the hot suck of Max's kiss, just so I can catch my breath.

"Darling, I assure you. You haven't even begun to see me excessive." Vasili's hard hands drag my ruined lace below my tits in a makeshift bustier that offers my girls up like canapés. *"Yet."*

Before I can answer, my snake's cool palms cradle my full tits.

Which pretty much hijacks my brain.

My boobs feel way fuller and heavier than usual. My nipples are swollen and uber-sensitive (all signs of a looming heat for yours truly, which is *so* not the major distraction we all need during finals. Plus, you know, the revolution.)

"Pay attention, little queen." His vicious fingers twist my nipple rings—hard enough to wring out of me a strangled yelp.

That does it. I'm in charge here. He's a bully, but he's not gonna bully *me*.

Still, he *is* definitely gonna fuck me.

"Why don't you make me, bad boy," I breathe. "All of you."

God, I really should know by now when *not* to yank his chain. The Goblin King's practically a sociopath and it doesn't take much to push him over the edge.

But he's *so* good at this kinda foreplay. So good, so good. When he pinches my tingling nipples between his wicked digits, pleasure streaks through the pinch to pool between my thighs.

My breath breaks on a ragged gasp. My thighs twitch and quiver. My knees clamp around Lucius, still kneeling before my cunt like a priest at the altar.

My wolf growls and shoves my thighs wide with his taloned hands, then dives in to nuzzle my starving pussy through the lace. My drenched panties chafe the engorged bud of my clit. Under the ravenous press of his mouth and the scrape of his fangs, my folds get even slicker.

My head falls back and my mouth falls open.

"Oh, fuuuuck," I groan through my teeth. *"Lucius."*

He snarls and laps down my slit in long hungry licks that make me keen with need.

My alpha dragon looms over me, and my own inner beast coils and purrs. Max's eyes lock with mine, all burning with heat and narrowed to slits. Then his smoldering gaze drops to my exposed tits. His nostrils flare to pull in a hit of my mating scent.

Actually, we're all scenting heavier than a fragrance factory.

All these pheromones flooding the air. Including mine. They're making my head spin and my hips writhe under Lucius' hungry mouth.

"Tonight you belong to the snake," Max growls. "And the wolf. Yet you are also mine. If you will breed, my sovereign, it is my seed that will fill you. My dragonets you will carry. I hunger to see you ripen with my clutch."

That dark promise make my pussy ache. Especially when Lucius growls, low and savage, against my cunt and worries at the soaked lace like he's gonna tear it off me with his fangs.

I'm still boning up on shifter biology. I need, like, the 101 section of that class. Because Max seems to think I could maybe lay eggs with him like a goddamn hen. (Even though I'm not pure shifter. Genetically speaking, I'm a mutt.) But that's how dragon shifters do their thing.

Honestly speaking, I'm just not ready for that.

Besides, I *am* still on the shot.

In science we trust.

I'm trying to wrap my head around how to address all this when Max's hand drops to the fly of his distressed denim and pops the button.

Behind his zipper, the thick bulge of his complicated dick shoves against the faded fabric.

Every flicker of coherent thought in my brain turns to smoke and drifts away. I swallow hard at the sight.

Sweet Jesus. I've missed that.

I literally can't wait to wrap my mouth around his potent dragon cock.

Totally unselfconscious, he rubs his dick for me though his jeans. Under his purposeful touch, all those inches swell and thicken.

That's when something new snares my gaze. A prickly circlet of gray ink twining around Max's sinewy wrist.

Huh. At some point while he was MIA, my dragon musta picked up… a tattoo.

That tattoo's like a barbed-wire manacle looped around his wrist.

And I like it. I like it a lot.

"Mmmm." I sigh with appreciation and skim my fingers over his ink. "That's new. I didn't even know shifters could hold a tattoo. I mean, once you shift."

He stills and shivers under my touch. His gruff dragon voice drops two octaves. "We can hold one when there is ground silver in the ink. In Warsaw, there is a place that specializes in shifters."

"Warsaw, huh?" When a sudden plink of caution quivers through our bond, my curious gaze darts to his wary face. "Is that where you were all this time?"

Max never lies. That's, like, a point of honor for him as a dragon. But there's definitely shit he doesn't mention.

Now, he hesitates. He fucking *hesitates.* "There… and other places."

"Hmmmm." Vasili licks and nibbles my mating bite—the one Lucius gave me where my neck meets my shoulder, a spot that's extra-vulnerable and extra-sensitive—with his razor-sharp fangs. Just the threat of that snake's teeth on my neck makes shivers spill over my skin and skitter down my spine.

Even before his wicked fingers tweak my nipples in a way that demands my attention *and* Max's.

Which is a fucking deliberate attempt to distract me. Damn it.

I love my snake, but I never make the mistake of trusting him.

"Barbed wire, hmmm?" the Goblin King purrs, all velvety with menace. "Do you feel like you're in prison, dragon?"

Max's smoking stare lifts from my tits and blazes at Vasili. "Mine is a prison of passion. I remain of my own accord."

Well, dayum.

Something's up with these two. Something's been up with them since Avalon, when Vasili finally stopped making Max's life a living hell and now (*very* occasionally) lets Max have his wicked way with Vasili's sneaky, snaky, sexy body.

And yeah, sure, my snake might bend for my dragon a little these days. But Vasili's definitely topping from below in that relationship. Max doesn't have a subtle bone in his body.

But V? He's a goddamn pit viper.

Vasili knows where Max is sneaking off to. In fact, I'd pay real money Vasili's *telling* Max where to go. Which definitely can't be anywhere good.

Now, eyeing that whole *prison of passion* tattoo our dragon's rocking, I can't escape the feeling Max is in over his head.

At least, I can't escape it until Max eases his zipper down and lets that thick dick of his out to play.

Underneath, that dragon's wearing the world's tiniest pair of cheetah-print briefs stretched over his tumescent bulge. When it comes to his style in undies, Max is a Eurotrash kinda guy.

But I definitely don't mind.

Now he shoves his jeans carelessly down his hips and steps out of them, rakes back his buttery hair with a ruthless hand, and smolders at V and me like he's ready to set us both on fire.

Lucius is still crouched between my thighs and nuzzling at my cunt. He's actually guarding my pussy. That's something he does a lot lately, especially when I'm going into heat and he's wolfing out. Now his chestnut head lifts alertly, nostrils flaring in his broody face. His eyes are crimson and his fangs are out. But he's still Lucius.

Still, he sneaks a furtive peek at Max's junk.

That sneaky peeky gets me mighty intrigued.

They're the only two of my guys who aren't fucking yet. (I mean, when you leave out the two Fae, which definitely seems to be what everyone wants right now.) Ruthlessly I crush another twinge of heartache. I just crush that shit out like a cigarette. That's my standard *modus operandi* whenever I think about Ash and Zephyr these days.

Tonight I'm gonna focus on the one issue in my harem I can actually do something about.

An electric charge races over my skin. Tiny purple sparks crackle and pop at my fingertips.

"Hey Lucius," I say softly, all echoey with the lightning voice. "Kiss Max for me."

Max snarls in surprise. His slitted pupils telescope wide. But his big saber-toothed fangs (which never come out except when he means to use them) punch down from his palate.

That definitely means he's… not opposed.

Lucius lurks around my pussy and looks furtive. But there's no mistaking the sudden spike of wolfish hunger that rips through our mating bond.

With a growl, my headmaster surges to his feet—and drags me up with him. One hard arm locks around my waist and traps me up on tiptoe against his rangy frame. His mouth claims mine in a savage kiss that's tangy with my own taste.

I fist his scholarly cardigan sweater and arch into him. My throaty moan mingles with his satisfied grunt.

"My queen," he says gruffly against my breathless mouth, his Hungarian accent all thickening. "Your wish. My command."

With a ravenous hunger that leaves me reeling, he surfaces from our kiss, grips Max's surprised chin in a taloned hand, and lunges into a hard claiming kiss that makes even Vasili exclaim.

Max stumbles into us, one hot arm sliding around my hips, one hand gripping Lucius' shoulder for balance. I tumble against Max's sleek golden frame with my knees all wobbly. Our headmaster steadies us both, the contact sears through me, and my whole body ignites with heat.

Because I'm already nakey—except for a pair of panties that probably aren't gonna be on me much longer. And Max is nakey except for those tiny jungle-print briefs.

I graze Max's soft hair and stroke back the golden tendrils to keep them out of the way while those two guys of mine are kissing. At the same time, I tug on Lucius' sweater to nudge them closer.

God knows, I'd never push them into anything. But we've all been waiting for this.

We've all been waiting so long.

Plus the thrumming purpose in our mating bond, the desperate way they're both clutching each other and groaning and dragging me up against them, tells me how much they're both into this.

Oh, yeah. They want each other.

I actually think they need each other.

"Nicely done, darling." Vasili's voice, cool with amusement, slithers through the simmering silence.

The whisper of silk is the only warning I get before he rears up behind me like a cobra. "They've certainly kept us waiting long enough."

I nod in agreement. But I can't look away from the savage clash of Max and Lucius, mouth on mouth.

The wolf and the dragon.

I can practically see Max's dragon bating his wings and Lucius' wolf locking his jaws around Max's windpipe. The two of them are fighting to crawl down each other's throats. That's my alphas fighting for dominance in the only way I'll allow.

Before the night gets much older, one of them's gonna yield.

Probably the same one who's gonna bend.

If they regret it in the morning?

That'll be the fault of me and my fucking heat.

"Oh, pretty sure they'll not regret it, love." Ronin's husky voice draws my gaze to the bed. "They're been wanting this like blazes. Both of them. You're just helping them along a bit."

Ronin's a fast mover, so he's wasted zero time getting Neo out of his sweats. Our bookworm's already stripped down to his boxer briefs, his brawny frame pinned under Ronin's prowly length, his soft curls all mussed and his big eyes glowing with happiness at the attention he's getting. Neo's gotten a lot bolder since Ronin and I popped his cherry last winter. Right now he's gripping Ronin's tight ass in his big hands and moaning as he grinds up against our Brit.

Not that all his recent experience stops our bookworm from blushing.

When Ronin dives in to start sucking on his neck, Neo whimpers with excitement and blushes tomato-red.

But he's happy. And he's distracting Ronin, who hasn't been himself since Zephyr popped up—

But I'm not thinking about Zephyr. Remember?

I'm really not.

"Mind your manners, little queen. I'm right here," Vasili hisses against the super-sensitive scars from my mating bite. Because of course he senses when he's lost my attention, and he's not a Zephyr fan (to put it *really* mildly).

I sigh and sneak a hand back to stroke his thigh, long and sinewy under his kimono. "It's okay, Goblin King. You've got me. Don't go crazy."

"You've driven us all wild tonight." Completely unplaced, the snick of V's switchblade prickles my skin. The cruel point traces up my outer thigh. "Wild to fuck you raw. Wild to fill that greedy little cunt of yours until you're dripping with our cum. I trust it goes without saying— I'm not waiting in line."

With a single sharp twist, his blade slices through the narrow band of my panties.

And there's one more piece of lingerie ruined.

The soaked scrap of lace falls to the floor.

His cool hands bracket my hips—under Max's arm and Lucius', because those two are both still claiming me—and pin me tight against his tall body.

Now I'm trapped between all three of my alphas.

It's still hard to look away from Max and Lucius. My wolf's hand has gentled. Now he's cradling Max's face in those savage talons. And Max, who's always so skittish and distrustful, is clinging to Lucius' sweater and breathing so hard he's almost sobbing.

Max has daddy issues (as in, he's never had one—a daddy, I mean) on top of everything else. Right now, Lucius is triggering a kink we never even knew Max had.

*Be careful with him, Teach*, I breathe through our bond, just for Lucius. *He's not as tough as he looks.*

Lucius sighs, and his touch turns even gentler. Even half-shifted, he's so tender and careful he breaks my heart. Max melts into that careful kiss and clutches Lucius' sweater like he's drowning.

Vasili hisses in my ear like an adder. His hand snakes down my tummy to cup my slick and dripping snatch.

Clearly, he's done sharing his toys.

My hips punch into the Goblin King's touch. His palm rubs my clit and one cool finger slides into my heated hole. Around that delicious intrusion—both hot as fuck and yet not enough—my pussy ripples and clenches.

Vasili's ragged moan fills my ear. His hot breath spills down my neck.

I shoot a heated glance over my shoulder to claim a goblin kiss. His silky mouth still carries a tart hint of cherry from his pre-shower lip gloss. His shaggy rock-star mop of gilded hair slithers around his shoulders. It looks like it's literally growing as I watch—all those shifter pheromones at work—and his long-lidded eyes pulse with heat.

Guess that's what a mating rut looks like on him.

I arch my back like a cat and rub into his satiny PJs. "Lose the kimono, Goblin King."

He takes his time about that, slowly unwinding his kimono with one hand and pumping into me with the other. Setting the pace with long slow strokes, skillfully working my clit with the heel of his palm, letting us all hear the rhythmic wet suck of my cunt gripping his finger. The leisurely lick of his tongue against mine carries the dry juniper bite of his recent martini.

When he finally lets me surface from that head-spinning kiss, it's only so he can slide his hand out of my dripping slit and trace my breathless mouth with his soaked finger. The scent of musk and roses fills my head. My eyes lock on his and my tongue flickers out to taste my own slick.

When I encase his finger with my mouth and suck like it's his dick, stroking and kneading the underside with my tongue, his pupils dilate and his eyes narrow.

"Someone's asking for trouble tonight," he gasps on an indrawn breath. "Someone's asking to choke on my cock until I unload down her throat."

The warning rumble of Lucius' wolf fills the night.

"You can have her naughty mouth, Mr. Romanov," my headmaster grates, his beast lurking in his voice. "Mr. Rasputin can have her saucy and spankable derrière. But her delectably fertile quim is *mine*."

Shit.

That wolf of his is definitely guarding my pussy. Clearly, this is one of those rutting alpha shifter traits.

My mouth falls open and Vasili pulls back, but not before V tweaks my nose with a playful wink. "Looks like someone's getting stuffed with dick in every orifice, darling."

Well, he isn't wrong.

With all this shifter rut in play, it's gonna be up to me to make sure my guys get what they need tonight.

All of them.

I slide a hand between Lucius and Max and unbuckle my wolf's belt. But my gaze never wavers from Vasili.

"I told you to lose that kimono," I say in my queen voice. "So do it."

Vasili's cruel mouth curls in a sexy smirk.

Never breaking my challenging stare, he unwinds his black kimono with serpentine grace and lets the garment slip down his long pale body. He's a lingerie boy himself, with a penchant for black lace.

But tonight, he's wearing something else stretched over the supple length of his hard goblin cock. A queer fashion staple.

A jockstrap.

In turquoise.

That's my color. In his own unique Goblin King way, visible to the only ones he cares about, he's wearing it as a declaration of solidarity.

With me.

My chest swells, my throat thickens, and my face heats with a rush of pleasure.

But I can still multitask. I can tease the edge of Vasili's jockstrap and unbutton Lucius' trousers at the same time. I can graze the long swell of Vasili's shaft through the fabric, while he hums and undulates into my touch, and ease down Lucius' zipper around the cola-can thickness of my wolf's fat cock.

Lucius would never be caught dead in a jockstrap. He's definitely a silk boxers kinda guy. And that rich silk fabric's already soaked with wolf jizz precum.

Now this, I can't resist.

I finally break my staring contest with Vasili to sneak Lucius a mischievous look. Max's face is hidden in our headmaster's neck, and Lucius has one clawed hand wrapped tenderly around our dragon's golden head.

Those two are so sweet together the sight of them makes my throat thicken.

I suck in my breath in wonder. I always knew Max never had a dad growing up. Yet, somehow, I've only just realized there's a big old daddy-sized hole in Maxim Rasputin's love-starved heart.

A hole my solid, firm, kind, responsible headmaster Lucius Aries is exactly the right size and shape to fill.

Now, meeting my upturned gaze, my wolf's eyes pulse crimson with need. His lip curls back to bare his savage fangs. That's a mating display, to show me how fierce he is. How fiercely he'll defend our little pack. My own inner beast bates and hisses with approval.

My teeth sink into my lower lip around a grin. Then my fingers slip through the slit in Lucius' boxers to curl around the delicious thick girth of his dick.

The growl that rips from his chest is all animal.

His shaft, hot and veiny, throbs in my grip.

With a sudden spurt of violence, his free hand clamps over mine and shoves his full length into my fist. That's when my hand bumps up against—whoa—an unfamiliar intruder.

Hello.

There's, like, a hard swell of flesh at the base of his cock that's totally new.

What the actual fuck?

That new addition he's packing under his boxers is the size of a freaking *apple*.

"Cheese on toast, Lucius!" I yelp, all squeaky with surprise. "What the fuck is *this*?"

His red eyes blink down at me.

"I fear it's the inevitable consequence of a purebred wolf shifter in full mating rut," Lucius says, managing to sound simultaneously apologetic and primal, while also very much like a lecturing prof. "In a word, well, that's my knot."

# Chapter Ten
## Maxim

The sudden appearance of my headmaster's knot creates a startled silence.

Ronin's soft curse mingles with Neo's gentle gasp of wonder from the place where those two of my mates—both so beloved and so missed—lie entwined and writhing on our bed.

After the ordeal of my recent travels, roaming the backstreet bookshops and antiquities black markets in Rome and Athens and Istanbul—all the ancient cities—in fruitless hunt for secret Unseelie lore at Vasili's command, my dragon is wild for both my mates.

Wild to reclaim them.

Wild to scent them and fuck them and fill them with our seed.

But if our sovereign meant those inflammatory words she spoke, in her colloquial English, about *cutting loose* and *without guardrails* and *needing babies…?*

Then my dragon and I are going nowhere.

We will not budge from our queen's side until her heat is broken.

Until she is bedded and bred.

Until she is so sated and so filled with our potent dragon seed that she wishes to do nothing for days on end except sleep and dream and incubate our young.

During the breeding time—this short precious interlude, so sheltered and so special, when Zara is fertile and conceiving our young—we will guard our lair and keep her safe.

Whenever she wakes, we will fuck.

When you are a dragon shifter, when it is time to breed, that is how it is done.

Already my queen sways in my arms, flushed and breathless from the engine of her looming heat, her lush curves naked and burning like a fiery coal. I wrap one arm around her tiny waist and one arm around Lucius' rangy frame and breathe… breathe deeply… while I wage a desperate inner war.

I pray I will not abandon all restraint and run mad under the blind mindless need of this mating rut.

Predictably, this pregnant silence (an apt phrase, no?) is broken by Vasili. My first love. My first rival. My desperate conundrum and my lethal obsession.

Vasili, who is finally mine.

My sweetheart.

*Mine.*

Of all my mates, Vasili Romanov is the most deceptive. And the most deadly.

"Well, darlings, it's about time," he purrs, rearing behind Zara like a rattlesnake and smirking at Lucius. "I wondered when that knot of yours would make an appearance, pet. In fact, I've rather wondered why he's never made an appearance for *me*."

With fangs fully extended and eyes red as embers in his feral face, Lucius Aries is a breath away from shifting. Seeing my headmaster so close to lost in his own rut makes my bones hum and my groin heat with a low throb of need.

Still, despite the pheromones flooding the air and his wolf growling under his skin and fighting to rise, Lucius manages to level Vasili an apologetic look.

"A wolf's knot is a breeding trait," our headmaster explains patiently, in his rough wolfish timber. "It's an anatomical feature that typically only manifests during a mating rut, when a wolf shifter's mate is fertile. I've, er, never before experienced one. This is my first rut. And, thus, my first knot."

A knot? I ponder.

A dragon shifter does not grow a knot. My dragon cock has other unique anatomical features, which are always present but will be more so now (when we are breeding), to maximize our prospects for conception.

Still, Lucius could sprout tentacles like a sea kraken, and I would not be repelled.

He is Lucius. And I... I am his.

I am his in ways that my dragon and I are only beginning to comprehend.

"Blooming hell, love. A knot, is it?" Ronin rolls lithely out of bed, lean and luscious in those unbuttoned leather pants that barely cling to his hips, with his silky hair tumbled from Neo's eager hands. He gives our bookworm a smoking look, then prowls across the room to join us near the fire. "That's hot as fuck. Any chance after you knot our girl, you'll have a bit of that knot left over for me?"

Lucius' jaw elongates and his nostrils flare. Slowly, but very surely, his gentle scholarly demeanor is losing the battle to his beast. "I'll knot you if you can take it."

"Fuck." Ronin's voice goes husky and his tawny eyes smolder with rising heat. "Only one way to go on then, isn't there?"

The wolf's pupils dilate with hunger. His chest swells in a gravelly rumble of need.

The whisper of bare feet drags my stare away from this riveting exchange. Neo's curly head pokes over Ronin's shoulder, green eyes round behind his spectacles. "A knot? Really? Can I see?"

Neo's wide-eyed interest finally curls Zara's lush mouth, still parted with surprise, into a slow grin. "Hmm, yeah, I think we'd all like a closer look. C'mon over here where you can see better, baby."

Ronin slings an affectionate arm around Neo's brawny shoulders and draws him fully into our circle.

Wearing nothing but a pair of navy cotton boxers stretched tight over his ass, with a damp patch of precum blooming over his bulge, our Neo is a sight to behold.

But Ronin's smoldering gaze never veers from Lucius.

After a questioning look at our headmaster, who permits this intimacy with a nod, Zara works Lucius' houndstooth trousers down his hips. By now, his wolf wants him naked, so our headmaster's trousers are on the floor, as Neo would say, shifty-swifty. Carefully, as though she is unwrapping a birthday present, Zara eases the wolf's conservative boxers—in burgundy silk from an affluent label—over his magnificent package.

"Whoa," she breathes, pausing in her labors to stare.

"Oh, fuck, sign me up for that," Ronin mutters.

I hear myself grunt in heartfelt sentiment.

Zara's shimmering aqua gaze shifts to me. Her teal eyebrows lift. A hint of a smile ghosts across her sweet lips before she is drawn back to Lucius' anatomy—which does tend to draw the eye.

He is thick and girthy, his veiny cock rigid and jutting with need, springing from the thicket of chestnut curls between his muscled thighs. His heavy sac swings beneath, already flushed and swollen with purpose. As I have observed many times, Lucius is endowed with an abundance of dick that pleases all our mates.

He pleases all our mates very well.

Yet it has always felt disrespectful to watch too closely while he pleases them. He is my teacher, almost my father (the kind that stays), he leads this household. We dragonkind are raised to respect our elders.

Besides… he… has never seemed interested in claiming me, as he does all the others.

Even tonight, I think perhaps he has only kissed me—that searing kiss that ignited my entire body into a raging inferno of need that still blazes in my blood—because Zara has told him he should.

I am not as intimately familiar with his body as I am with all the others. Still, I am deferential and careful not to stare.

Even so, the thick knot of hardened flesh swelling at the base of his dick makes my mouth run dry.

My sovereign drops to her knees for a closer look. This arrangement makes Lucius growl with anticipation.

Her mischievous gaze lifts to his. "Does it hurt?"

"Not in the way you're asking, you minx," he says gruffly. "No. But the… tumescence… won't subside until I've been—"

"Milked?" Our queen's pretty hands slide up his strong thighs.

"Satisfied," he growls through his fangs. "Behave yourself, Ms. Gemini."

"Is that really what you want, Teach? Me behaving myself?" Slow and teasing, her thumbs circle the base of his knot. Lucius' eyes close, his head falls back on a ragged groan, and his hips thrust into her touch.

"Wow," she breathes. "You're really sensitive here, aren't you?"

Her little hands cradle his knot, while Lucius' hips twitch and his talons hover around her lightning-blue head. Clearly, it is all he can manage not to seat himself deep in her saucy mouth.

Her thoughtful face tilts toward me. "You want a closer look, big guy?"

I need a moment to realize she is speaking to me.

Now I am torn between conflicting instincts. I am in rut, and my mate lingers close to a rival alpha who is likewise in rut. In these circumstances, my dragon should be savage. He should bugle and rend and tear.

Already, he is trembling with pent-up yearning. For he is a slave to the ancient genetic imperative of all our kind.

That devastating need to breed.

Yet my dragon is also… strangely… subservient.

I am the Sagittarius prince. I am a fully manifested male dragon shifter. I am the greatest of my kind. And I am also the last.

This sense of subservience is… utterly foreign.

Yet it is too overwhelming to deny.

Heavily I drop to my knees beside Zara, curl my arm around her waist to steady her, and bow my forehead against Lucius' muscled thigh.

I close my eyes and pull in a deep lungful of his familiar wolfish odor, mingled with the creamy rose of Zara's mating scent. Her inner beast croons and bates her wings in welcome.

Saints of the northern steppes. Our queen burns to rise in a mating flight.

If she does, beyond all doubt, Vasili and I will rise to fly her.

But Lucius… Lucius cannot follow.

He is earthbound. But I will not leave him behind. My free arm snakes around his leg like a vine. My dragon exhales a soft keen of yearning.

We are his.

"Well, aren't you full of surprises tonight, dragon?" That is my sweetheart, my Vasili, lurking near, who is sounding so disgruntled and so spiteful. "You won't bend for me. But you'll bend for *Lucius*?"

I press my brow harder into Lucius' thigh and close my eyes.

By Christ, I am trembling.

Lucius' taloned hand curls tenderly around my head, as though he will protect me from these jeering words. Still, I take no offense.

My sweetheart is vicious because he is jealous.

I am trying to think how to answer. I am not like our mates, I do not bend. I am alpha.

But I am lost in a strange confusion. The words will not form.

"Take it easy with him, Goblin King," Zara says softly. "He's trying to figure his shit out."

She nestles into my side—so hot, so ripe, so succulent—then reaches to draw Vasili close.

He is sulking, but he comes.

"If we end up deciding we're doing this, you know, for real?" Snuggled up against all three of us, Zara hesitates and looks up at me. My heart thunders as though it will burst from my chest. By *this*, she means breeding. "Then we're all gonna need to be… careful. With each other."

We all grasp her warning.

Lucius mutters in agreement and strokes my hair. I rub my bristly jaw into him—daring to scent him, just a little, near his groin—then nuzzle the hot hairy stretch of his thigh for reassurance.

In a typical shifter harem, the alphas would fight and kill for the privilege to breed their queen.

In our unconventional cobbled-together polycule, we will defy centuries of shifter instinct if we breed her together.

My dragon should be bathing in our rivals' blood. Yet the thought of harming any of them fills me with a frenzy of distress.

"It's okay," Zara breathes in my ear. "There's enough of me for all of you. That's the only way we're doing this. I mean, *if* we're doing this—"

If?

There will be no *if*.

Brutally I drag her into me and twist to find her mouth with mine. The hot sweet suck of her lips burns through me, as though she has wrapped her mouth around my cock. She moans and winds one silky arm around my neck. Her lush breasts, pierced by her silver rings, press into my chest. Behind my briefs, the sensitive barbs of my dragon dick chafe and jut.

The rumble of my dragon's need is a continuous echo that fills my head and crowds out all reason.

*Breed her breed we must breed…*

I groan and sway and cling to Zara and Lucius as though I am drowning.

I sense Ronin's potent heat pulsing through my blood, because he is so powerful a telepath, and I know sweet Neo too is near. But I cannot abide anyone, not even my mates, too near my horribly scarred and tortured back, my Achilles heel that has always been so vulnerable.

So my mates are giving me this space.

*It's okay, big guy,* Zara whispers through our mating bond. *No one's gonna hurt you. Not ever again. We'll all get through this together. You wanna help me make Lucius feel good?*

Lucius is the pillar we all lean against. Even now, he is the physical scaffold that holds our joined bodies upright. Always, he takes nothing for himself.

"Yes, my sovereign," I growl against Zara's eager mouth. "I want that."

*That's good, Max.* She pulls back enough to give me a sultry grin. *That's real good. Let's you and me give all our guys a night to remember.*

Lucius' thick cock is jutting beside her face and mine. He is mere centimeters away.

She cups his shaft in her little hand and gives him a few hard strokes that make him shudder and me groan. Then she leans in to mouth his bulbous cockhead and slurp at his dripping slit.

A ragged groan rips from his lungs.

His hand fists in her tumbled teal curls and shoves her deep onto his length.

She envelops his impressive girth in her plush lips. Then she wraps her hand around his knot to milk him. He flings back his head—brow furrowed, fangs extended, face contorted with primal pleasure—and pumps into her willing mouth in short demanding snaps. With every thrust, he voices a savage grunt.

Zara moans with approval and matches his pace, her fingers kneading his knot. His impressive length swells, growing slick and flushing violet from her attentions.

I think Lucius does not realize he is still gripping my head.

Or that he is insistently pushing me closer to his pumping dick.

My brain is a jumble of old voices, old hatreds, old prejudices. My orthodox upbringing could never abide the simple intimacy of two men in love. Fucking Ronin for the first time was a revelation. Sucking Vasili's cock for the first time was another.

Lucius is my teacher, he defends me from my enemies, he has

mentored me so patiently since the day I enrolled. Clearly I owe him an elder's respect.

But Zara must breed, and she will only agree if I will share.

Besides, he is Lucius. I am his.

This leap, too, I can take.

I soften my desperate clutch around Lucius' leg. My rough palm strokes up his powerful hamstring to spread over the hard flexing globe of his buttock. His breath hitches, his pace stutters, and Zara's dragon croons in our mating bond.

Vasili is lurking and spying, he is jealous over Zara in a way he does not often permit others to see. I think this may finally be the mating instinct to which even he (who jeers at every mention of babies or fatherhood) must yield.

I even think it is possible he is jealous over me.

I push these distracting thoughts from my mind and lean in to nuzzle Zara's petal-soft cheek, while she sucks the wolf off. She hums and backs off a few inches, until she is suckling just his tip.

She is offering me his cock.

I pull in a shaky breath and will my fangs to retract. Then, with a rush of resolve, I lunge to graze his hot slick girth with my lips.

*"Maxim."* My name explodes from my headmaster's throat on a long groan.

I think perhaps this is the first time he has called me anything except Mr. Rasputin.

Hesitant, still new to these pleasures, but eager to please him, I lick along his length as he rocks into Zara's mouth. My lips graze hers while he fucks into her mouth. Our mouths meet, wet and sticky with his precum, around the engorged head of his cock. I find, in this way, I can kiss her *and* arouse him. She tastes like peppermint cocoa. He tastes dark and musky, he tastes like wolf.

Truly, there is nothing to fear here, except the fear that I will spill my pleasure all over his legs, before I can mount my queen.

But this singular moment is not only for me. It is also for Lucius, who will have his first knotting. Cautiously I wrap a hand over Zara's around the hard swell of his knot.

His breath hisses out in a rush and his hungry thrusts quicken. "Merciful Christ."

*Nicely done, love.* Ronin's smiling murmur ripples through my head. He is wrapped around Neo, but they are both watching. *The two of you keep that up, you'll get him off like a blooming rocket.*

"No," Lucius growls, because he shares the psychic intimacy of a mating bond with Ronin. "Tonight I will spend my wolf's passion knotted deep inside our queen."

The burning embers of his stare drop to Zara, her vivid head bobbing as she kneels before him naked and labors so sweetly over his cock. Then his fierce gaze shifts to me. Now I am feeding her his length and milking his knot.

Gently his hand cradles my jaw, curved talons tickling my cheek, and lifts my gaze to his.

"Precious boy," his wolf grates, thick with gravel. "King of dragons."

Still kneeling at my queen's side, with a possessive arm wrapped tight around her waist, I lick the dark musk of wolf from my lips and gaze up at my teacher with all the loyalty and devotion that fills my dragon's heart.

"Wolf king," I rasp.

I am overcome by this moment. I am overcome by this wolf. I am so overcome by this entire situation that my English fails me and I must lapse into Russian. *"If our sovereign will breed, then it is I who must breed her. But to you—you alone—will I yield the honor—to precede me."*

Still lurking in my periphery like a coiled viper upon which one must be careful not to tread, Vasili (who is Russian) utters a scornful hiss.

Well, that is too bad.

Our queen's witchcraft is so potent that the strength of her desire alone, once she wills it, might be sufficient to overcome the perverse effect of those hateful shots she insists upon.

To render her fertile.

By his own admission, as he reminds us all constantly, our snake does not even want offspring.

In this case, our order of precedence is clear. For once in his self-centered life, my spoiled brat of a sweetheart will have to wait his turn.

Lucius does not share my mother tongue, but he peers deep in my eyes, deep into my very soul. I let him read in my face the silent oath of loyalty I am swearing. His fierce muzzle dips in a grave nod that acknowledges my vow.

Then his fiery gaze veers to Zara.

"Now, on the floor, before the fire." When Lucius speaks, his accent is thick as *borscht.* He is fighting not to shift, so his voice is barely human. "I want you on your hands and knees for me, my queen. I want you kneeling when you take my knot."

# Chapter Eleven
## Zara

I'm so hot for that knot, I feel dipped in fire.

I'm already slick and dripping from sharing Lucius' dick like a popsicle with Max for the first time ever. The two of them finally hooking up is the most fabulous birthday gift I could've gotten after this whole shitty day.

Meanwhile, my greedy cunt is opening wide like a mouth to welcome my wolf king's mating knot.

Our scents mingle with the crisp tang of burning applewood from our friendly fire. Max's rich aroma of leather and brimstone smells like oiled dragonhide, while Lucius' dark musk is all wolf. And Vasili…?

Man.

V's pumping out enough caramel and vetiver, laced with potent feel-good pheromones, to take the top of my head off.

Among the four of us who scent, we're kicking out enough pheromones to make our whole polycule high.

"No more dawdling, little queen. You heard our headmaster. He wants you on the floor. That's the faculty talking." Vasili's usual liquid purr is rough as sandpaper. His raspy voice in my ear spills a shiver down my spine.

I sneak him a peek. An uncharacteristic hint of color rides his high cheekbones. A furrow digs between his perfectly shaped brows like he's pissy as fuck (which often happens) or maybe perplexed (which he hardly ever is).

But it's the icy fire raging in his glacial gaze, rimming his pupils all blown wide, that makes the butterflies in my tummy swoop and dive.

Yowsa.

Of all my guys, I always figured me talking about (maybe) making babies would be a massive turnoff for our snake. Like something I could actually lose him over. He's made it one hundred percent clear he despises kids even more than he despises cats.

Instead, for some reason, he's so lurky and possessive tonight he's making me nervous.

Weird.

"You gonna put me in detention if I disobey, Teach?" I shift my sultry stare to Lucius.

Because, no matter what's going down with V, I legit can't keep my eyes away from that knot Lucius is packing.

"No." Lucius' baritone rumble is so gravelly it's practically a bark. "There will be no mere detention for you tonight, Ms Gemini. If you disobey me now, I'll turn you over my knee and finally administer the bare-bottom spanking that saucy ass of yours is begging for." His growly voice plunges another octave. "But first, I intend to knot you. On your knees."

Well, alrighty then.

Very clearly, Lucius is in a mood. I aim to take full advantage before his Old World gentleman manners resurface.

I give my headmaster a bad girl wink and saunter toward the fire, hips swaying, the ends of my curls teasing the base of my spine, my apparently saucy ass on full display.

In unison, Maxim and Lucius fall in on either side.

Stalking me like the predators they are.

To my surprise, Vasili's right there with them, bringing up the rear. So I can't turn tail and run.

Not that I'd ever run from them.

But this aching clench of need in my uterus, these powerful ripples of craving that are swelling my clit and drenching my pussy? This sweet edge of hunger that has my empty cunt clamoring to be overfilled and overstuffed and overridden?

This whole hormonal experience?

Intense.

My heart is pounding so hard it's practically audible in the expectant silence that hums and arcs among me and my guys like an electric current. All my guys—even Ronin and Neo, who don't shift, aren't alphas, and have never seemed overly compelled by the collective *let's all get Zara pregnant now* obsession—are lurking and eyeing me like they're a pride of African lions, lying in wait in the long grass, and I'm the lost baby giraffe that just wandered past.

In other words, I'm dinner.

By now, we're all either naked or stripped down to our skivvies. Ronin's just wearing his leather pants. And we're all sweating. The fire's warmth licks at my skin and bathes the high ceilings and Roman frescoes that dance across the walls of our ancient villa in a cozy light. Shadows coil under the canopy of our big medieval bed.

I hate that my gaze sneaks to the windows—just to confirm what I already know. Our curtains are drawn tight to protect us against prying eyes and judgy news crews.

This is our family.

Our time.

Our choice.

And for once, it's gonna be private.

The warm spot before the fire sports a colorful Turkish carpet whose thick weave cushions my bare soles from the cool mosaic floor. I like to lie there sometimes when I study. Neo's already scrambling for a fat feather pillow to baby my knees.

When he pops back up, I loop my arms around his neck and rise on tiptoe to claim his warm eager lips. He tastes fresh and bookwormy and minty from his spearmint toothpaste.

Neo might not be an alpha. But I don't want him feeling left out.

"I won't be." Following my thoughts without effort, because of that whole fated mate thing, and also because I'm *his* alpha, he sighs and smiles against my mouth. "I'm right here with you, babe. Same as always."

I breathe in his clean comforting smell of sage and lavender and snuggle into his brawny body. My fingers coast over his boxer briefs to squeeze his luscious glutes.

"Will you mind waiting your turn tonight, baby?" I whisper. "If I promise to take care of you?"

"I don't mind waiting. You making changes with your shots isn't this whole shifty issue for me." He wraps his big hands around my ass and tucks me up against his mouthwatering boner. "I mean, we're just talking about it. But even if you decide something? Like if you're ready to come off the shots?"

His earnest green eyes blink down at me through his glasses like a wise owl. "I'm not gonna lose my shit."

"Yeah, me neither." That's Ronin prowling up behind me—literally the only guy in our harem who'll risk getting between me and Vasili when our snake is on the slither. Ronin wraps his sinewy arms around my waist and tucks *his* leather-clad boner into the crack of my ass.

Oh, yum.

I twine an arm up and back, around his neck, and wiggle my sexed-up body between my two guys. Not gonna lie. I love being the meat in this man sandwich.

But I can't get distracted here. This is important terrain we're all navigating.

"So you're good with all this… baby talk?" Geez, I'm almost whispering the B word. That's how charged the atmosphere's gotten in this bedroom.

Just hearing the word makes Max rumble and Lucius growl. Under the fire's crackle, Vasili pulls in a slow hiss.

Ronin snorts and tucks my back into the sleek plane of his tattooed chest, then nuzzles my neck with his hot lips. "I'm the baby of this lot, aren't I? Won't even turn twenty till August. Figure I've got a bit of time then, haven't I? Before I start queuing up for daddy duty."

My former bully's going straight for the jugular—I mean, for the scars of those double punctures Lucius left in my neck from his wolf's mating bites. They're super sensitive.

With a sigh and a shiver, I tilt my head to give Ronin access to the spot.

I always forget how young Ronin is. He's so fierce and capable and totally lethal. But it's a good reminder of another reason I'm holding off on firing up my ovaries to make little witches.

Nineteen (and a sophomore) is way too young to be a dad.

Lucius' worried face appears at Neo's shoulder, chestnut curls tumbled around his bare shoulders in yummy disarray. "Dear God, you're all so very young. In truth, perhaps we shouldn't—"

"Not making any decisions tonight, Teach." I'm answering him, but

I'm reminding all of them. I lock onto my headmaster's intent stare with a provocative grin. "Unless you changed your mind about knotting me?"

That's me punching his buttons.

When his wolfish eyes glow an evil red and he starts getting fangy, I know it's working.

Neo gives my cheek an affectionate nuzzle, then shuffles aside with a grin to make room. Lucius grips my chin in a clawed hand and looms over me. The prod of his fiercely erect cock juts into my belly in a way that lights me on fire.

"On your knees now, Ms. Gemini," he rumbles, all husky and Hungarian. "I'll tolerate no backtalk. Or I'll make you suffer."

Vasili huffs in surprise, because Lucius has just totally stolen his line.

I barely bite back a giggle.

Geez, my hormones must be going haywire. I'm not normally a giggler.

"That's you all sorted then." Ronin snickers into my neck and nudges me toward the pillow on the floor. His hot hands turn predatory as he shoves me hard to my knees. "Teacher's orders, love."

Ronin might not be jonesing for diaper duty, but clearly I've triggered his own inner bully.

My knees sink into the thick pillow Neo borrowed from our medieval bed. I fall forward on my palms, carpet rough under my fingers (we're gonna need to be careful about rug burn), and spread my knees wide to expose my soaked slit. I deliberately tilt my hips to place my ass at the most provocative possible angle and just work this deliciously exposed and submissive posture to the max.

Queen or no queen, I love it when my guys get a little dommy.

I especially love it in the sack.

I let my hair spill forward over one shoulder and glance coyly back at Lucius. He's looming over me like the monster he is, breathing heavy and grunting like a beast in the forest, with his monster dick jutting before him like a battering ram, knot fully engorged and ruddy with intent. He wraps a fist around his shaft to give himself a few hard strokes, baring his teeth when he squeezes his knot.

Then he drops heavily to his knees behind me with a snarl. His wild chestnut curls spill halfway down his back. A thick pelt of fur sprouts across his powerful chest.

Fuck, he's right on the edge.

I really wonder how he's gonna manage not to shift.

Max is lurking right behind him, with his golden dragon eyes flaming and the bulge of his dick shoving against his tiny jungle-print briefs.

Through our mating bond, the powerful vise of our dragon's rut closes around me and clenches.

Whoa.

That bond is so strong it almost hauls me to my feet and drags me toward him, like a telekinetic fist I can barely resist.

Max is holding back out of deference to Lucius. But he's getting really close to losing it.

"I can take more than one of you at a time," I tell my dragon, low and husky. "Why don't you come over here and choke me with your big cock?"

His slitted pupils blow wide and black with purpose. Moving with a carnivore's prowly grace, he stalks to a halt right in front of me. That placement puts his scarred back to the fire, rather than the door or anyone else in the room, so he can bury his childhood demons for a while and focus on us.

Staring down at me with ruthless intent, he sweeps his golden hair back with both hands and twists it into a swift braid to keep it out of his way. The cold lines of his Slavic face harden with a determination that makes my pulse skyrocket.

From my hands and knees, I give him a sexy stare that says *come and get me*. My inner dragon purrs and bridles for her mate.

Holding my gaze, he shoves his briefs brutally down his legs. His exotic dragon dick thrusts before him in all its glory, thick like a devil's forked tail that flares wide, then tapers at the tip. The twin barbs are the pointy bits where his tail forks widest. They're always uber-sensitive, and they lock us together when he fucks me.

I'm used to his junk, we all are. It's part of him, part of the whole Maxim Rasputin experience.

In our different ways, we all love him.

But I'm not expecting the thin shining river of precum that drizzles from his cock. It's, like, a lot.

I think that's his dick's way of warming up for a mating rut.

"Do I please my sovereign?" he rasps, his Russian accent all thick and broken with need.

"Oh, Max." My chest splits wide open with love for him, for all our guys, even when I'm raw and achy from missing the two that are MIA. "You always please me, big guy. Come here and let me show you how much."

A groan rips from his throat that sounds like he's being tortured. He grips my head in one hand. With the other, he offers me his dripping cock.

His hands are shaking. That's how hard this whole rut is hitting him.

Gently I close my hand over his to steady him, then encase his tapered cockhead with my lips. When my mouth closes around his tip, he barks out a hoarse cry.

My dragon queen croons to comfort him. I hum around his cock, which jerks and twitches with need. Then I swirl my tongue around his complicated dick like a lollipop.

The drizzle of precum smeared over his hot silky skin tastes like burnt cinnamon. The tawny nest of curls between his thighs smells like brimstone and leather. I lick over his slit and coat my lips with his fluids, slick as oil (which is another new thing).

All this moisture he's producing is, like, the perfect lube.

*Well, this is convenient, big guy,* I whisper through our bond. *You gonna save some of this for our other mates later?*

He's in my head and he's hearing my thoughts, so a hard shiver runs through him. And I'm definitely hearing his inner narrative, which is all rutting dragon.

*My mate my queen lock fuck breed you will ripen my Zara mine—*

Fiercely he grips my head in both hands. I know he's fighting like fuck not to shove himself down my throat and thrust into me. He's slowly learning to give everyone in our polycule the space we need to navigate his unique dragon anatomy.

Still, I hollow my cheeks and suck him into my mouth right up to where he flares widest, just before his barbs. Because once we pass the point of no return and he's fully seated in my mouth, those barbs of his will engage and lock.

Then it'll be all over but the moaning.

The puff of hot breath against my exposed ass is all the heads-up I get before Lucius' rough wolfish tongue slicks down my taint and dips into my soaked snatch.

A throaty moan rolls through me. My thighs spread and my hips cant higher, basically offering my wolf full access to my pussy like the shameless hussy I am.

He snarls and fucks me with his tongue like he's about to do with his cock.

Like he means business.

Like he can't get enough of the way I taste and smell and sound.

His fierce pleasure, his sense of possession, all sharp and spiky with alpha aggression, surge through our mating bond. Where my neck meets my shoulder, the twin punctures of his old mating bites tingle like vampire bites.

He grips my hips to hold me still and rides me with his tongue while I clench and pulse around the thrust of that slick organ.

I moan and whimper and back off Max's dick just long enough to gasp out, *"Lucius."*

My wolf growls against my dripping cunt between long hungry licks. "Your sweet quim is… already opening for me… my queen. But you're still… very tight."

Under all my warlocks' heated stares, I clench with a gasp around his probing tongue. His distended fangs tease my tender pussy. His gruff wolfish rumble vibrates against my core. "How your hole will milk my knot."

Sweet Jesus. Sign me up for that shit.

My inner dragon purrs with pleasure. Guess she and I are both on board.

Max grips my head and eases my mouth back down around his dick. This time I pull in a deep breath and take all of him, navigating his pointy bits with some skill (we're all learning!) until his fat cockhead nudges the back of my throat.

His barbs flare wide. Wide enough to claim his terrain and secure his place. Too wide for me to back off his dick until after he cums.

But I'm used to this shit.

Max kneads my head and rocks into me. I wanna help, but he holds me steady so he's fucking my mouth. His first few thrusts are slow and careful, he's being polite to start, but he loses that restraint pretty quick.

Now his pace stutters into short hard snaps that heat me up better than the fire crackling behind him. I love it when my guys lose it, love it when they abandon every scrap of control, love it when they fuck me like they mean it and they can't make themselves stop. Max is grunting with every stroke. The nudge of his dick against my tonsils is triggering my gag reflex (since I can't swallow him).

I fucking love every second.

My dragon's rough thrusts shove me back onto Lucius' ruthless tongue, which my other alpha doesn't seem to mind a bit. Instead, my wolf's strong hands spread me wider. He's got my pussy and my pucker on display back there like they're butterflied.

When Lucius' tongue withdraws from my aching core to swipe over the throbbing heat of my clit, my inner dragon spreads her wings. I jerk and let out a keening cry. Of course, the sound is muffled by Max's cock.

"No more foreplay, darlings." That sinister purr is all Vasili. Suddenly, he's crouched right next to me on the carpet, long and pale and sinuous, peeling out of his teal jockstrap like a snake shedding his skin. "Sweet fuck, our little queen's more than ready. For all of us."

Then my snake slithers under our linked bodies, under the London Bridge of me on my hands and knees, spitroasted between Max's dick in my mouth and Lucius' tongue in my pussy.

My tits are hanging free and unmolested. That changes when Vasili's cool hands cradle my girls and his silky mouth closes around one pierced nipple.

He goes right for the pinprick punctures of his mating bite on my tit, because of course he bit me like Cleopatra's asp the first night we fucked. The slick of his tongue over those tiny scars shoots a zinging jolt of pleasure, like Cupid's arrow, straight to my clit.

Fuck. Me.

Now I'm really losing it.

I whimper and arch into his wicked suck.

Vasili's tall body uncoils beneath me, his legs winding between mine and Lucius', all of us shifting to accommodate him. My Goblin King's laser-focused on licking and sucking and teasing my already overstimulated nipples. Under this assault, my tits feel even more swollen and full, like this devoted attention from one of my alphas is having an actual hormonal effect.

Lucius shoves three fingers (claws retracted) deep in my slick and ravenous cunt. When I clench around him with a moan, he snarls with satisfaction.

He's testing my readiness to take his knot.

*Cheese on toast, Lucius,* I gasp through our bond, while he finger-fucks me slowly, with tortuous restraint. *I'm your queen. I can fucking handle you, okay? I can handle all of you.*

I writhe between them, my mouth full of Max's dick, my cunt full of Lucius' fingers, with Vasili's long sexy body undulating against me and his hot sucking pulls on my nipples making me even wetter. All my shifty senses are super acute and honed to a wicked edge, so the tiny moist sounds of Lucius' fingers riding my cunt sound amplified, along with Max's heavy breathing and Lucius' bestial grunts and the slither of leather somewhere behind me as Neo works Ronin out of his pants.

Because we're all linked, I feel the sizzle of every new contact.

Like this one right here, when Lucius' hand drops between us to find Vasili's hard length and starts stroking.

"Dear pet," my snake gasps, sounding breathless and ragged. "Don't tease. We're all waiting for that knot of yours. Why don't you lube him up, Ronin? That's a lot of cock for our little darling to handle."

Now this I'd love to see.

Ronin murmurs something low and sexy and obliging. Lucius rumbles and eases his soaked fingers out of my eager pussy (which is reluctant to see him go, but thrilled for what's coming). Neo pipes up too, volunteering to help, sounding all curious and excited in a way that makes me smile.

But of course I can't see.

All I can see is the tight flex and ripple of Max's Adonis belt. My nose is currently buried in the tawny nest of Max's pubes while I suck him off like a porn star. His dick is pulsing and his pace is quickening in short urgent stutters and he's clutching my head like he's honestly afraid I'll stop.

If I back off an inch, I'll run into an issue with his fully flared and extended barbs.

So I wrap my arms around his thrusting hips and fill my palms with his tight little ass and let his heavy swaying ball sack hit me in the chin with every thrust.

This maneuver arches my spine and pushes my tits even more in Vasili's face, which he totally does not protest.

In fact, Lucius has barely vacated the premises of my hoochie when my snake's cool arms twine around my derrière to angle my hips the way

Vasili apparently wants. V's quads shove into my inner thighs to splay me even wider.

I barely have a heartbeat to register the supple prod of his shaft against my soaked and primed girly parts. Then Vasili arches into me with a single violent thrust that fills my empty cunt with the smooth wet glide of goblin cock.

*You fucking snake!* I voice an outraged groan around Max's dick. *That's supposed to be for Lucius. Vasili—oh, fuck—*

"Well, I did warn you I wasn't in the mood to wait. What did you imagine I meant?" Vasili breathes out on a gasp. "Besides, it's unfair of you to hog that knot of his. I want some too."

He's laughing, that fucking terror of an alpha is actually laughing like the psycho he is, literally while he fucks me.

He got poor Lucius to back off on a total ruse and now he's fucking me himself.

I'd be pissed as fuck if my eyes weren't already rolling back in my head with pleasure.

Alpha shifter spunk is what I need to break my heats, and I'm getting that hit of biochemicals now from both ends. Max is so turned on by V's show of dominance that it's pushing him right over the cliff. Hoarse cries wrench from Max's chest as he pumps into me, hard and fast, cries edged in his dragon's brassy rumble. I'm drooling spit and precum around his thrusting dick in a way that's messy, yet somehow also deeply satisfying. I savor the feverish flex of his ass under my palms and I'm clutching his butt so hard I'm probably gonna leave nail marks (which he'll love).

Meanwhile, my tits are bouncing in Vasili's face with every stroke (which *he* loves). In fact, I'll be really lucky if that snake doesn't take the bait and bite me again—

The hot hairy press of Lucius' half-shifted body engulfs my ass and the backs of my thighs. My thoughts splinter as my headmaster rubs the engorged head of his cock along my taint and roots between my thighs.

And Vasili, for all his horrible bully tendencies, actually downshifts to a slow, teasing, barely-there rhythm that I know is meant to accommodate our wolf.

My durable pussy can handle two dicks at once, and these two like to share. So the first stretching burn of Lucius' cola-can dick pushing into me just makes all three of us sigh in unison.

But the bulbous press of Lucius' knot against my hole makes my breath hitch and my eyes widen.

Suddenly I'm not at all sure how this whole arrangement is even supposed to work.

*"Lucius,"* Vasili gasps, with none of his usual silky eloquence. "I—she's—well, we're full in here."

"Easy, loves," Ronin murmurs to all of us, in a voice that's thick with arousal. His hot Leo hand strokes along my thigh. Thanks to that wicked telepathy he's rocking, he's linked to all of us. "Give her just a little of that knot, Lucius."

Lucius is clearly past human speech at this point, but he voices a guttural growl and presses into me. The slick press of his lubed knot stretches my cunt wide, *so* wide, wider than it's ever been stretched.

But I'm made for this. For them. For all of them. I'm queen of the witching world.

The witching world needs this.

There's nothing wicked or shameful in me loving them all like this.

And I will *not* be denied.

I release a soft sigh around Max's dick and let my cunt unfold around all this cock like a flower.

Vasili shudders and moans like I'm torturing him. Lucius' wolf whines with need. Neo and Ronin, kneeling on either side, ease my knees gently wider to accommodate all this action.

"Take a deep breath, babe," Neo whispers, his strong hands kneading my quivering quads. "You can do this."

Finally, under our combined efforts, my body yields to this supersized intrusion with a shuddery sigh.

Well lubed by Ronin's efforts and my own copious slick, the hot bulge of Lucius' knot presses against my tender folds till my pussy waves the whole flag and surrenders.

When Lucius' knot seats deep inside me, his wolf gives a short bark of triumph.

Vasili hisses with pleasure and rocks into both of us.

Max's dragon trumpets and mine roars.

Behind me, I sense Ronin and Neo falling into each other's arms in a hug of shared victory that quickly turns heated.

"Wolf king." Max pants in his guttural accent, between thrusts that make all our joined bodies rock and sway. "We are yours. We are all— yours to command."

I have no idea where this submissive streak in my incredibly alpha dragon is even coming from. I mean, literally, who knew?

But I am *here* for it.

Then I'm lost in it, this, them, all of them.

Max loses his mind first in a violent climax that spills spurt after spurt of hot cinnamon jizz down my throat. I gulp and swallow and slurp him down till my eyes water.

Neo falls to his hands and knees on the carpet beside me, face turned toward me and glasses askew, his eyes squeezed shut, flushed and whimpering with pleasure while Ronin fucks him deep and long at last.

The sight of Ronin's tawny tattooed body flexing, inky hair swirling as he pounds into sweet Neo from behind like some kinda sex demon, is so hot it's pornographic.

Vasili's coiling and writhing beneath me like he's out of his Goblin King mind, pistoning viciously into the tight vise of my snatch and fucking Lucius at the same time as their cocks glide together inside me. My snake's hot breath and sharp fangs against my defenseless tits are a constant menace.

But I'm his to ravish. In all the ways. Always.

And Lucius.

Sweet Jesus.

Lucius is a grunting, growling, savage beast, his hot hairy bulk pressed into my back, his thick dick hammering into me with ruthless purpose. That monster knot of his locks all three of us together, probably for a good long while.

I'm teetering right on the brink of a climax that's gonna blow every fuse on the island (again).

Vasili's sharp cry and the hot kick of his alpha shifter cum spurting against my inner walls push me hard over the cliff.

Now I'm in free fall, pinwheeling through the night, my blind scream of rapture mingling with the resonant roar of my dragon. I convulse around Lucius' knot, squeezing that fat bulb of flesh like a washcloth, and he joins me in a bellow that releases a gush of hot shifter spunk that floods my basement and inundates V's cock.

Ronin is swearing like a sailor getting off, Neo's yelling with a very unbookwormlike abandon and clutching my hand, my guys are all with me as we plummet.

The pop of the bulb on the desk lamp blowing just adds an exclamation mark to the sentence.

Let this whole goddamn island know we're fucking. These guys are mine and I'm keeping them and I'm ruling with them—all of them—at my side.

And Cleo Ferrari, my so-called rival for the witching world crown?

My backstabbing bitch of an ex-BFF better stay the fuck outta my way.

# Chapter Twelve

## Ronin

When my eyes pop open with a start, a misty dawn's streaming into our digs, right past those open curtains we definitely left closed last night. A summer breeze, crisp with briny sea, tickles my sleepy face.

The balcony doors that overlook the courtyard—the same doors we always lock for security reasons—are swinging wide open.

What the fuck?

At the sight of those open doors, my Valyrian foresight gives a nasty ping.

My alarmed gaze darts over the canopy of our medieval bed to the naked sleep heap of my mates' bodies, spilling from a twist of blankets.

Zara's snuggled up tight with Neo, both smothered in sleeping alpha, with Max and Vasili flung possessively over the top. Lucius is sprawled face down and snoring with one heavy arm thrown over my hips. Plus he's got a territorial palm planted on Zara's lower tummy, right over her womb, which is sweet as fuck.

Thank gods for my mates. When they're about, all's right as rain.

Still, somehow, my jangled sense of unease is mounting.

My anxious eyes chart a course across our peaceful pad to Zara's desk.

*There.*

Just beside a tidy stack of Neo's spell books and alchemy texts, a glassy pair of dead eyes stares back.

I shoot up to sit with a gasp.

Bloody hell.

That's… a severed head. Propped right there on Zara's desk.

A severed head with feral features, pointy ears, and a spill of lavender hair.

That's a dead fucking Fae.

Whoever he is, he's not been dead for long.

And there's a live one sprawled in Zara's chair. With his booted legs crossed arrogantly on Zara's desk.

Holding Zara's crown in his steepled hands.

My gaze skids over the green leather gauntlets gripping that crown, over the knotted bulge of biceps and delts filling out that Avenger suit of supple dragonscale. I lock onto a face so familiar it'll be blazoned on my noggin till the day I kick the bucket. High cheekbones, narrow nose, ruthless mouth so delicate it's deceiving, all framed in a sleek curtain of forest-green hair, held back from a cruel face by the braid that circles his brow like a coronet.

Only the green eyepatch that slants across that familiar puss and covers one socket is new.

But even that I've glimpsed before. From afar. In the scrying glass.

Thanks to my thunderous gasp, he's spied me, sitting bolt upright and mother-naked, dragging a twist of sheet over my hips to preserve what little's left of my modesty.

His single eye, a perfect orb the color of cloudy jade, holds my riveted stare. One slim green brow lifts in a mocking arch.

"Good morrow, Ronin," he murmurs, in that voice like water trickling over rock. His tone's sharp and brittle as glass. "Have you missed me?"

*"Zephyr?"* I scrape out.

Fuck. I can't breathe.

It's him. The Unseelie King. The fucking Dark Fae who nabbed Zara and fucked her and mated her last term. The same Fae who came for my sister, once upon a time.

*Oh gods, Gwen—*

Grief claws at my chest like an angry cat. I rub a hand over my jackhammering heart and fight like blazes to breathe.

Of course I always fancied he'd pitch up here eventually. Fancied he'd come dragging trouble at his heels like the trailing end of a bullwhip. Fancied when he did, I'd be ready.

Now here's him, cool and composed as the blooming Queen of

England (except, you know, for that severed head he's casually nudging with his boot).

And here's me, gasping for air like a gaffed fish.

Locked onto that sly mocking stare, I swallow hard against the fist of nerves that's throttling my throat.

"Took you long enough to pitch up here, mate." My voice is a shredded rasp, but I'm flat out amazed it's working.

Any rate, I've got to keep the volume down, or I'll startle my mates. They'll be startled enough in a tick when they see that Dark Fae and his severed head, won't they?

Of course our drop-by guest doesn't bother answering. Slowly his gaze wanders over my tattooed chest. Over the inky dragon, spewing flames, that claws across my pecs.

He's not seen it before. But he has to suspect the truth.

I did it for him.

For the pain of losing him.

After I fucking killed him.

Every prick of that needle etched the pain of my guilt and my grief and my doomed love for this fucking Dark Fae permanently into my skin.

Now, while I tingle under his cold stare, his suspicious gaze slides down my naked abs. It narrows on the fistful of sheets I'm clenching over my dick.

This has to be the worst possible time in history for me to pop a boner. With him looking like he'd rather slit my gullet than fuck me.

But of course that's what's happening.

Same as always. Even now, under that inscrutable Unseelie stare, I'm hard for him.

Him? Un-fucking-likely he's having the same reaction. He's impossible to read, always has been, even for a pedigreed telepath like me.

And the fact I can't read him makes me mental.

While the awkward silence stretches between us, I scowl into his broody face. "For fuck's sake, Zeph. Zara's been bonkers with worry over you—and the other one. Supposed to follow her right back from Avalon weeks ago, the both of you, weren't you?"

I pause again, but of course he only sneers.

Figures.

Why do I always have to fall for the most difficult blasted men?

I heave a sigh and beg the gods for patience. "Why didn't you bloody answer the scrying glass when I rang?"

His lip curls in a snarl that reveals a tiny hint of fang.

"A scrying glass is not a telephone, Ronin Kilcannon Pendragon. Nor am I an answering service." His whispery murmur turns dark with malice.

Because when a Dark Fae knows your true name, there's naught that comes from it but evil.

Caught short by the threat, I prickle with nerves. Once upon a time, I trusted this deadly creature. I more than trusted him. I blooming loved him.

But he betrayed my trust.

Now, thanks to him, Gwen's dead.

He's no telepath, but I am, and I must be broadcasting my emotional mess on all channels. Against the honed line of his jaw, a muscle flexes.

He pulls in a slow hiss.

"I was… vexed to learn of your sister's passing. As I was vexed to be parted from Zara." His broody gaze drops to the crown he's gripping. "Unfortunately, I was given no choice in the matter. Nor was Ash. I have been… most occupied… in Avalon."

Without even looking, his booted toe gives a careless nudge to the severed head propped against Neo's stack of textbooks.

I'm a trained fighter and I've seen loads worse, so I take a sec to appreciate with a warrior's eye the clean slice across the cadaver's gullet.

Not to be Captain Obvious, but that was clearly the killing blow.

The strike's clean enough to attribute to those crossed swords jutting over Zephyr's slim shoulders. I know those blades, like I know the supple green dragonscale that encases his lethal frame. I know what he's capable of.

It's just the bitter hatred for me that's lurking in his whisper, poisoning his stare like venom, that's new.

Well, I've bloody well earned that hatred, haven't I?

I'm the sole reason for that eyepatch he's sporting.

I clench my jaw and scoot back till my spine hits the high carved headboard of Zara's bed. At the maneuver, my arse gives a twinge, because Lucius finally gave me that knot of his right before we slept. (Which was epic.) We were still locked when I nodded off.

Even now, hours later, my headmaster's arm is still wrapped round my thighs. But Lucius is twitching, his steady rhythm of snores dissolving in a wolfish grumble.

Bollocks. He'll be up any tick now.

I scrub a hand over my face, bristly with morning stubble, and think about popping out for coffee. Gods know, we'll all need it. But I'm naked under this sheet, and I'm feeling more than a bit self-conscious about flashing my junk—complete with hard-on and a Prince Albert piercing he's never seen—to my pissed-off first love.

I settle for airing my litany of grievances. "Why the everloving fuck did you stay away so long? If Gwen only knew you survived… if she'd not seen you plummet from Pendragon Tower…"

Fuck me. I can't even finish. Not out loud.

If he'd answered me in the glass even once, if he'd eased my guilt over killing him for her sake, if he'd done *anything* but what he did, my twin might still be alive. At least, she would've had more petrol in the tank to fuel her fight against Damien Gemini and those witchy bitches who were hazing her.

She might've not… hanged herself… in the midst of our troubled freshman year.

*Damn it to hell, Gwen.*

"Why did *I* stay away?" Zephyr's cruel voice cracks through the air like a whip. "Why did you throw the knife?"

I shoot him a tortured look. "You know why. Bleeding hell, Zeph. What else could I have done?"

He flourishes a graceful hand before his ruined socket, over the green eyepatch that hides his only flaw. That's his souvenir of the night he fell from the roof of the Pendragon family home with my knife buried in his eye.

"Does the sight of me now please you?" His harsh words flay me and claw at the open wound I carry in my chest instead of a beating heart. "To see firsthand what you've done to me? To witness the nightmare I've become?"

The whiplash snap of his voice shreds the morning hush.

Lucius rolls over to his back with a sluggish grunt. "What…?"

Then a flurry of naked limbs and scrambling bodies erupts from the bedclothes beside us.

"Well, now you've bloody done it," I mutter and wait for the storm to break.

"Oh my God." Zara emerges, stunned and disheveled in a wild tumble of teal curls, from her sea of alphas. Color floods her riveted face. *"Zephyr?"*

She flings back the blankets with a happy cry.

Instantly Max dives to cover her naked curves with his naked torso, his dragon eyes flaming, pinning his mate flat to the mattress and growling at this rival male who's invaded our lair. The pungent scent of leather and brimstone floods the air.

"Jesus, Max, take it easy. It's Zephyr!" Zara's simultaneously trying to soothe our possessive alpha dragon and push him aside.

Needless to say, Max is having none of it.

Still in rut then, obvi. Probably will be for days.

Next to her, Neo's rubbing his sleepy peepers and fumbling for his glasses and generally trying to wake up.

With a ferocious snarl, a naked Lucius—also clearly still in rut— leaps into a protective crouch beside our bed. He plants his bristling body between us and the intruder, guarding the shit out of his mates and fighting not to wolf out and just rip Zephyr's blooming throat out.

That leaves center stage to Vasili, who uncoils from our sea of blankets like a cobra rising from a basket.

"Well, well." My boyfriend's malicious murmur drips into the riveted silence like acid. "Look what the cat dragged in. Posed like an artistic composition from the Surrealist period titled *Missing Fae with Severed Head.*"

# Chapter Thirteen

## Zara

"Easy on the alpha there, big guy." I pull in a lungful of our dragon's mating scent that reeks of leather and brimstone.

Fuck. That shit is potent.

Then I rub a soothing hand along the flex of Max's naked ass (because rubbing his scarred back, which is a total trigger due to his fucked-up family history, would really launch him into orbit).

Without giving me an inch of freedom, Max twists around to eye our new arrival with open suspicion and rips out a vicious snarl.

"Hey, I mean it." Knowing where my alpha's coming from keeps my impatience in check and my voice gentle. "You gotta throttle all that rutting dragon shit back a little, okay?"

"Why should I not act like a rutting dragon when I am one?" Guttural with mating instinct, Max smothers my face protectively in his naked chest. His excited heartbeat thunders in my ear.

I'm pretty excited myself, my pulse is racing and my fingers are sparking and my whole body is tingling, which makes it super hard to stay patient and speak calmly to my overprotective dragon. Needless to say, I could summon various aspects of my witchy superpowers and liberate myself that way. But I've dealt with Max enough when he's like this to know if I try to push him while he's all worked up, I'll trigger him.

Next stop for the Max train after *triggered* is *violent.*

Of course, that homicidal streak he's packing won't be aimed at me.

If I'm being honest, he's never exactly been Team Zephyr. This open animosity he's rocking for the Dark Fae who kidnapped me last spring? That's been looming since Day One.

But I don't wanna make it worse.

I can't even see Zephyr—to my total frustration—with my face crushed into Max's chest. Still, my initial rush of elation and relief at seeing my Fae ambulatory and breathing is eroded by an undertow of resentment.

Now that I know he's not dead and lying in a tomb or wherever the Unseelie bury the bodies, I'm twitchy with a mounting prickle of anger.

That fucking Fae is *weeks* late showing up here. Plus he hasn't said a goddamn word. Even now. He was apparently totally content sneaking past Lucius' extremely strong wards (somehow) and watching us all sleep like a creeper.

Long story short? Mr. Johnny Come Lately's got some explaining to do.

But, fuck, I'm glad to see him.

Or I will be, once I can coax this overprotective dragon of mine to ease up.

I raise my voice a notch to connect with my other alpha, whose baritone growl rumbles steadily from somewhere near my feet.

"Hey, Lucius? Could use a little help with Max here, Teach."

Lucius' rumbly warning rolls on without a hitch.

My inner dragon gives a chirp of annoyance. She, too, is bating her wings and demanding to see our Unseelie mate and *his* dragon (who's way too big to fit in my bedroom, but Xhevith's gotta be looming around here somewhere).

My queen wants to see both of them, like, now.

Of course, I've got a dominant alpha, that's Vasili, who's supposed to help me deal with all kinds of shit in our bed and our polycule and basically rule the witching world at my side.

But right now that snake's not even helping me settle our unsettled mates, and I don't bother asking.

Vasili—also not a card-carrying fan of Team Zephyr—will literally be no help. Sure, he's not out of control losing it like my other alphas, he's way too sly to show his hand like that.

But he's still the most dangerous.

I can't even see V with my face smushed into the hot plane of Max's chest.

But his Goblin King aggression skulks in our mating bond like a serial killer lurking in the basement.

"For shit's sake," Ronin mutters to the room in general. "Bloke's not here to do that Hades-Persephone thing this time, is he? Zara's safe as houses. Just… don't be an arse, okay, Zeph?"

Of course, Zephyr says nothing.

Meanwhile, my Brit's scrunched up against the headboard to my right, scrubbing his face with his hands like he's trying to claw his own skin off.

Underneath all this hostility that's roiling the quiet morning air like a spaghetti pot at a lively boil, Ronin's mental anguish tears at me like claws.

For his sake, too, I gotta regain control of this volatile sitch.

I gotta.

With a sigh, I summon up my queen voice. "Maxim Rasputin—"

"Hey, Max, take it easy, buddy, okay?" Neo's also pinned under the press of protective dragon to my left, but he's managed to park his glasses on his nose. Plus he's got enough wiggle room to loop an arm around Max's neck and nuzzle his cheek. "You're smooshing Zara."

"Truly, darlings, why blame Max?" Of course that's my snake Vasili, all wicked with spite. "He's seen firsthand what the Dark Fae *do*. What they covet, they steal. Max is afraid this Unseelie tyrant will steal our mate. After all, he's done it before."

Max's growl deepens to a brassy rumble. His whole body quivers with intensity. Our mating bond floods with his dragon's need to rend and ravage and burn.

*Mine she is mine we will breed I will kill—*

Cheese on toast. If that flying Godzilla loses his shit and shifts, he'll bring down this whole *domus*.

"Don't be a dick, Goblin King." I huff out a breath. "I mean it. I know what you're doing. Stop setting Max off."

"But he makes it so easy," Vasili murmurs, sharp with spite. I swear, that villain's practically rubbing his hands with glee.

In our mating bond, Lucius' wolf mutters and paces.

Dropping my own exasperated F bomb, I squirm against Max's lean hot body and wiggle through the sheets like an eel till I can peer over Max's protective shoulder at my pacing headmaster.

"Lucius," I say firmly, "don't you dare wolf out. I need you to start adulting and help me defuse this situation."

Lucius shoots me a guarded look over one shoulder. His eyes are blood red and he's sporting fangs like Nosferatu. But his fiery gaze drops to Max's bristling body and softens. He stops pacing and gentles his warning snarl from aggression to a protective rumble.

"Precious boy," my headmaster says through his canines. "Maxim, king of dragons. Do not fear him. I will help you protect our queen."

I don't need protecting, especially from one of my own mates. Still, that gruff wolfish promise turns my heart all melty.

These two—I mean Max and Lucius—are still a really new thing, they haven't even fucked yet. But I can't deny our headmaster gets our fatherless dragon in a really deep way.

Lucius is getting through to him in a way Neo and I haven't.

Maxim stops growling and pulls in a long shuddery breath. Then he rubs his bristly face into my neck to scent me and rolls off.

(Finally!)

"Good dragon." With a sigh of relief, I pop up to sit next to him and sweep my wild mane out of my face.

And, yeah, I sneak a peek at myself in the big vanity mirror.

Which is, like, a massive mistake.

For a sec, I flounder in a surge of self-conscious dismay. After last night's fuckfest, I'm literally a hot mess. Hair everywhere, lower lip swollen and bruised from Vasili's savage nip the last time he fucked me, neck all abraded from Max continual whiskery scenting, and the violet bruise of a hicky Ronin gave me clearly visible on my tit.

Not to mention what the mirror thankfully *isn't* showing.

My hidden girly parts. All tender and stretched and overridden from being stuffed by Lucius' knot.

I mean, dayum.

He and V and Max—all three of them—were sex machines.

For real.

Even my snake, despite his well-known daddy aversion, barely pulled out of me all night. Apparently just the suggestion that I might be willing to move up the timeline—and, you know, hang out the vacancy sign on my uterus—triggered some genetic shifter instinct in those guys that's powerful as fuck.

Good thing I heal up shifty-swifty myself, thanks to those biochemicals in my own witchy DNA.

Still, there's no hiding how much I smell like sex. I'm literally dripping with alpha shifter spunk.

But why should I hide it?

I own that shit.

That's what it means to be queen.

I straighten my shoulders, lift my chin, and look straight into the alien face of the Dark Fae King.

Across the width of the room that yawns like a chasm between us, Zephyr's cold jade gaze burns into me. Framed in a sleek curtain of mossy hair, divided by the green slash of his eyepatch, his cold perfect face is so remote and inscrutable he could be chiseled from alabaster. His lithe frame looks invulnerable in his dragonscale armor and boots and gauntlets.

My sparkly antique crown looks fragile perched in his casual grip.

With his arrogant legs crossed on my desk, he literally hasn't even gotten up. In fact, he's sprawled in *my* chair like it's *his* goddamn throne.

That air of aloof entitlement he's packing pisses me right off.

Same as always.

He's literally ten weeks late showing up at Icarus. *And* he's been ignoring all Ronin's pings through the scrying glass.

I mean, would it kill the guy to say hey, sorry I was held up, you must've been worried?

Would it kill him to say he missed me?

"Busy social schedule at court, Your Radiance?" I work hard to keep it casual, because there's no point hiring a blimp to broadcast for the entire island my hidden uncertainty and achy hurt.

Or my lurking fear of rejection.

Zephyr's no mind-reader, but he's perceptive as fuck. He actually does answer to that la-dee-dah title—Your Radiance—at the Unseelie court.

But he doesn't like the way I'm saying it.

Hearing the anger and heartache that edges my tone, his eye narrows and his brow lifts.

"Busy? You might say so. I've been quashing a rebellion in Avalon." His voice is the same, cool water trickling over river-smooth stone.

Even while his glacial tone gives my heart a painful ping.

"Another rebellion? My, my." Vasili slithers up next to Ronin and drapes a possessive arm around his boyfriend's neck. "Never tell me your enslaved subjects are chafing under your tyrannical rule."

Zephyr's cruel mouth turns down in a frown.

"No one in Avalon is enslaved. My late mother's former faction at the royal court has always been treacherous. Now they've turned outright… treasonous." He's answering Vasili, but his stare stays locked on me. "That faction has declared they will never accept a witching world queen on the Unseelie throne."

Great.

Guess that's another throne I'm not worthy of claiming.

But the blow of that rejection's dwarfed by the one I weathered last night, when my own realm rejected me.

Not to mention the personal pain of *his* rejection.

My Unseelie mate.

I mean, not to sound like a broken record. But it's been. Ten. Weeks.

Goddamn guy couldn't even send the Unseelie equivalent of a Hogwarts owl?

Anger burns in my chest like heartburn. I make my voice hard and callous. "I'm not on the Unseelie throne. I was never crowned, remember? Sure, we did that whole ritual fuck practically in public, specifically to break the infertility curse and rescue your whole race from extinction. How's that working out for you, by the way?"

One corner of Zephyr's feral mouth curls up in satisfaction.

"The magic we wrought through our mating ritual has ripened. The curse is clearly broken. More than half the Unseelie females of breeding age in Avalon are with child."

Hearing that news, my heart gives a good hard kick. I suck in a breath and hug my knees to my chest. No matter what else is going down in our polycule, I'm *so* happy we shattered that curse and saved his dying race.

And if we could do that shit there, why can't we do it here? To save the witching world?

"Just what the world needs." Vasili jeers. "Playpens and pacifiers and pointy-eared Unseelie brats crawling through the wards."

Sweet Jesus, he's horrible.

That comes with the whole Goblin King package.

But I forgive him, because he's managed to coax Ronin to stop clawing at his own face. He's captured Ronin's restless hands and he's stroking Ronin's sleep-tangled black mane in a way that broadcasts a possessive *hands off* message that's aimed straight at Zephyr.

My Unseelie—assuming he's still my Unseelie—drinks us all in with his inscrutable stare.

Lucius has taken his wolf firmly in hand. Now my headmaster's quietly and efficiently tucking himself into his lord of the manor *Downton Abbey* pajamas and smoking jacket.

Maxim is looming over me, no longer audibly snarling, but still bristling suspiciously at Zephyr. He unbends enough to accept the ripped jeans Lucius passes him and, after another suspicious look at Zephyr, shoves his legs into the pants.

Ronin tucks into Vasili's side and stares at Zephyr with his topaz eyes all haunted.

Every time their gazes lock, I swear, the air between those two exes is so superheated the atmosphere practically combusts.

Like someone's turned on the gas in here and left it running.

All we need is a single spark to blow us all to Kingdom Come.

Vasili sits straight in our bed like a queen, with the blankets draped gracefully around his slim hips, an unpleasant smirk lurking around his lips, his sex-smudged mascara and smoky liner adding a disreputable dash of rock-star glam, and his tousled shag of gilded hair skimming his shoulders.

Geez, his hair must've grown like four inches overnight, and probably literally while he was fucking me. (That's a shifter thing, and he'll be annoyed he has to cut it again.)

Me?

I hug my knees to my chest, pull the rumpled sheets over my naked snatch and boobs so I don't feel quite so exposed and therefore vulnerable, and wonder why Zephyr's even here.

He hasn't really talked to me, he hasn't made any move to kiss me, and God knows I'm not initiating that shit.

I'm half pissed, half worried, and increasingly suspicious over everything Mr. Taciturn over there *isn't* saying.

Zephyr's cool gaze drifts over my wary huddle, pauses over my various private parts all covered up thanks to my mounting suspicions, then narrows on my guarded face.

I tilt my head and give him a look. "Okay, Your Radiance. Time to spill."

Nothing.

Nofuckingthing.

Of course.

"Look," I say through gritted teeth. "If you're thinking about pulling that cat-got-your-tongue uncommunicative act again, now is *not* the time. You and Ash were supposed to follow me right back here. Instead you've been MIA for weeks. What aren't you telling us?"

A small sigh whispers past his tight lips.

Then he places my crown delicately on my desk, right over my half-written essay for History of Witchcraft class, and flexes his green-and-gold gauntlets in a way that hints at all that tension he's carrying.

"The curse *is* well and truly broken, Zarina Selene Gemini," he murmurs, so quiet I need my special shifty senses to hear. "Despite the fact you are not crowned queen on the Avalon throne. Still, my late mother's faction is… dangerously discontent. They tried to proclaim this one—my moon-cursed cousin Lothian—to be king in my place."

With his booted toe, he gives Cousin Lothian's severed head on my desk a dismissive nudge. "Well. He'll rule among the rats and the carrion crows."

"Dude." Neo pushes his glasses up his nose, scoots up to sit next to me, and looks scandalized. "Are you telling us you killed your own cousin? That's messed up."

Zephyr knows Neo and likes him, so he spares my bookworm a narrow grin that shows a sliver of sexy fang.

"He's only a second cousin." Zephyr gives a shrug that makes his supple dragonscale glitter. "Regrettably, he has a twin—Mordred—who is by far the more troublesome of the two. That one is still breathing. The rebels' treasonous hopes must now shift to him."

"Ooh, translation: trouble in paradise," Vasili says, so coyly even I wanna slap him. "Truly, darling, what a shame."

My fingers drum an impatient tattoo on my bent knees. "And someone broke your scrying mirror too, I guess, huh?"

Zephyr's gaze shifts to Ronin, who's knotting his fists in the sheets, and turns even more inscrutable. "I'm not a demon to be summoned with a magical word."

(Wait, are there demons? Or was that, like, a figure of speech?)

"That's pretty fucking obvi, isn't it, mate?" Ronin slants him a sullen look.

Abruptly Zephyr lowers his booted legs and flows to his feet, with that eerie grace all Fae possess. He's not tall, he's literally my height and I'm petite. But he manages to command the room without effort like the Dark Fae King he is.

The Fae prowls toward our bed with a deliberate intent that makes Max growl and even Lucius bristle, though my headmaster tamps that shit right down and signals Max with a subtle gesture to hold his peace.

While Lucius lingers anxiously nearby, Zephyr halts beside the bed and levels his broody stare into my cautious gaze.

Now that he's close enough to touch (if I wanted that) his rich perfume of burnt amber and sun-warmed dragonscale makes my inner dragon purr with interest.

I pull in a long breath and let my gaze drift over him. My chest swells with a powerful longing. A longing to bridge the awkward gap these long awful weeks of silence and distance have opened between us.

To make him mine again.

I know exactly how sleek and supple that green dragonscale would feel if I slid a hand down the hard plane of his chest. I know exactly how *he* would feel underneath if I caressed the tight flexing ripple of his abs. I know exactly how his eye would narrow and his breath would hitch if I leaned forward to graze the bulge of his codpiece with my lips—

"I am here now, am I not?" he says softly. My gaze veers from his codpiece to his smoldering face. "Zara the Moon-Blessed, Queen of Dragons, Lady of Lightning. The unrest in Avalon will subside once I have crowned my wild Gemini queen. I brought you my cousin's head as a bridal gift."

My heart jumps so hard it lodges in my throat. Dragonflies cartwheel through my tummy. Heat races into my face and a complex tangle of emotion crowds my chest.

He's still claiming me then.

As his mate. And his queen.

He hasn't changed his mind.

I was supposed to be just his consort, his lover, with no political power to rule in his parallel world (at least in that original *let's kidnap*

*Zara and just take what I want like an asshole* scenario he had going). That was before we got so tangled up in each other.

Before I basically fell in love with him.

Before he started feeling… whatever he feels… for me.

The thing is, I still don't know what he feels for me. Not exactly. Like I said before, he's closemouthed and secretive as fuck. Plus he's no telepath—at least, he's not my kind of telepath, I can't read him—and he's never allowed or offered a mating bite.

So we don't have the same kinda intimate, immersive, no-holds-barred mating bond that connects me with my warlocks.

But clearly, bond or no bond, he intends to park my mortal Gemini ass on the Dark Fae throne right next to his royal Unseelie rump.

I'm just not sure how I feel about that.

You know, given all this unresolved baggage between him and my guys.

"We're not actually married," I point out. I've always denied it, no matter what's written in Unseelie lore, even if that ritual first fuck we shared on the night of the new moon equinox did break the Unseelie curse. "You know I'm true poly, like all the witching world queens. If you and I tie the knot, we're gonna do it together with all these guys—plus Ash I guess, if he still wants to—like I said from Day One."

Ronin makes a strangled sound, like the thought of him and Zephyr getting hitched just hit him in the feels.

And maybe not in a good way.

Ronin's psychic barriers are sky high, but I don't need telepathy to know he's a mess.

I shoot Ronin's stricken expression an apologetic look, then give Zephyr the stink eye. "Besides, even if we were married, Your Radiance, pretty sure a fucking dead Fae head would *not* be on my bridal registry."

For a fleeting moment, Zephyr's smooth brow puckers. He actually looks puzzled by my totally unpuzzling reaction. "It's a trophy. A token of my devotion to my bride."

"Yeah, but I'm *not* your bride—" I figure the point bears repeating.

"For moon's sake," he hisses. His fists clench at his sides. "The moment you set foot in Avalon for your coronation ritual, my cousin Lothian would have killed you. Now it will demand all my wit and all my vigilance to ensure his demonic twin doesn't finish the deed."

Shock reverberates through our mating bond.

Yeah. That's the electric jolt of all my mates reacting to this latest threat against my life.

All on its own, my hand shoots out to clamp around Max's wrist before he can launch for Zephyr's throat.

"Cheese on toast. You telling me someone else wants me dead now?" Bitterness bubbles up and seethes in my chest in a witch's cauldron of anger. "What, like getting dethroned and betrayed by my ex-boyfriend *and* my ex-BFF, plus humiliated on live TV, wasn't good enough?"

The furrow between Zephyr's green brows deepens.

Reminding myself of everything he doesn't know (because they don't have TV or even electricity in Avalon), I pull my shit together and dial down the volume.

"Afraid your cousin's gonna have to stand in line, Your Radiance. I mean, if he wants a piece of me." I share a grim look with Lucius. "We've got our own rebellion going on right here at Icarus."

Zephyr's lips part and his eye widens.

While he's processing this newsflash, Lucius calmly intervenes to pass Neo his neatly folded sweats.

"Neo, sweet boy, would you mind terribly brewing us all a pot of coffee downstairs, and perhaps scrambling a few eggs?" Lucius says. "His, er, Radiance must have been flying half the night and is probably quite hungry. And the rest of you are due in class in an hour. It's final examination week. You all need to prioritize your studies."

He's chosen exactly the right angle and the right man for the mission. Our bookworm readily accepts both the clothes and the chore without complaint.

"Sure, I'll whip up eggs and toast and coffee for everyone before class," Neo says happily. "Including the girls, so Racetrack doesn't have to cook while her head hurts. Plus bacon for you, Lucius. You know your wolf always wants it."

Lucius licks his lips and looks hungry.

My fated mate wrestles his Academy sweatshirt over his curly head, then hesitates. Behind his spectacles, his cautious eyes veer from Lucius to Zephyr to Vasili.

Neo clears his throat. "Just, um, keep these guys from killing each other up here while I'm gone, okay, Lucius?"

"You may rest assured I'll tolerate no homicide beneath this roof. Manslaughter is a violation of the Academy Codex," Lucius says wryly. His whiskey-colored eyes linger on Ronin. "Why don't you help Neo in the kitchen, my dear one?"

Our headmaster's tone is so tender it makes my eyes sting. Lucius is very clearly feeling extra protective over Ronin since he knotted our guy last night, I can feel all that broody tenderness through our bond, so it's actually hard for him to let Ronin out of his sight.

Ronin pushes out a breath and rolls away, scrambling lithely out of bed with an alacrity that gives our collective an electrifying flash of his tight ass, all tawny skin and flexing glutes, before he's dragging his abandoned leather pants over his hips.

Vasili hums with approval.

Even Zephyr's unreadable gaze sneaks over to check out the view.

Ronin flings someone's shirt around his muscled shoulders—looks like one of Lucius' Oxford button-downs, infused with our headmaster's comforting scent—then hightails it after Neo out the door without looking back.

It hurts me that Ronin looks and feels so profoundly relieved to leave.

And even though I don't have a mating bond with Zephyr, I've got a feeling it hurts him too.

With a sigh, I pass Max a tee shirt so he can cover up his back, because he won't want Zephyr staring at his scars. Then I reach for my own bathrobe on its hook beside the bed.

That maneuver flashes my boobs, complete with piercings. And yowsa, the way Zephyr's gaze devours me. Like wildfire ripping through a stand of dry timber, consuming every tree in its path, and leaving a drift of ash.

Speaking of which…

Under the incendiary smolder of his riveted stare, I bundle my warm and tingling body into my Academy bathrobe and clear my throat. "Where's Ash?"

Zephyr blinks and drags his focus from my boobs to my face. "Ash is currently acting as my regent on the Avalon throne. Never fear. You shall soon see him."

Resentment curdles in my tummy and floods my mouth, sharp and astringent as vinegar. "Guess you're taking right off, then? To swap places with him in Avalon? Since you can't leave the throne vacant during a civil war."

His chin dips in a somber nod. "I am indeed returning to Avalon."

Before my heart can totally plummet in free fall, he keeps going. "But I won't be returning alone."

"Oh, yeah?" I level him a suspicious look. "Well, I've got finals this week, we all do. So…?"

"My bride." For the first time since I opened my eyes and found him here, his cold face thaws in a rueful smile that makes my heart skip a beat. "I come to you not empty-handed."

My gaze shoots to the severed head on my desk. "Well, obvi."

He chuffs out a breath. Impatience laced with a subterranean note of humor. "Zarina Gemini, I come bearing more than my cousin's head."

Deftly he plucks an envelope I haven't even noticed from the nightstand and offers it to me with a graceful flourish. Green parchment thick as velvet, embossed with my name in swirly gold letters, rich with the scent of burnt amber and summer roses.

It's dangerous to accept anything from a Fae. That's one of the ways they trap you.

But, you know, either I trust the guy or I don't.

My lips part and I reach—

Quick as a striking rattlesnake, Vasili snatches the envelope from Zephyr's grip. "What's this?"

"Hey." I give Vasili my annoyed queen look. "That's mine."

Zephyr tilts his own chin at a regal angle that's positively glacial. "*That* is an enchanted invitation—for all of you—to attend the social event of the Avalon season. The Faerie Ball."

"The Faerie Ball?" I gape up at him. "Is that an actual thing?" When his lofty head inclines an inch, I keep going. "So I'd be going as, like, your date?"

"As rather more than that." Zephyr's remote face turns toward Vasili, who's already slit open my invite (of course) with one of his hidden stash of knives to skim the slanting lines of handwritten text inside. "I've proclaimed to all my kingdom that your coronation will take place at the gala, before all the assembled Unseelie Realm—both my allies and my enemies."

My skin tingles with interest and my hair swirls around me in a gust of psychic wind.

"Whoa," I breathe. "Not like that plan sounds risky or anything. But it's ballsy. Gotta give you that."

Lucius is hovering close to listen, his scholarly face intent as he ties back his wild hair in a tidy knot at his nape. That adjustment completes my headmaster's downshift from vicious Vlad the Impaler to clerky Jonathan Harker.

Now the wary ping I get from my wolf through our mating bond reminds me of all those other, non-Fae issues we need to deal with at Icarus.

A surge of resolve rolls through me and lifts my hair right off my shoulders.

I swing my legs out of bed and hop down without using the little rolling stair that comes with our tall medieval bed.

Then I plant my hands on my robed hips and square off with my broody Dark Fae while my wild mane floats around me like a teal cloud. "Uh, is that whole coronation gig supposed to go down before or after finals? Because I gotta be here for those. I need to defend my own throne from that fucking Cleo."

Now Zephyr's standing right next to me, and he's only taller because he's wearing boots and I'm barefoot. As our gazes lock, a painful flicker of longing fractures his face before he can hide it.

Me? My whole body aches with that same longing.

I need to full-on concentrate just to hold myself back from touching him.

"The moon in Avalon is dark in two days' time," he whispers. "That is when I'll crown you. At the Faerie Ball. Then shall you begin your reign as my queen."

Finally, he reaches for me.

And, shit, I'm leaning toward him.

Before we can connect, Max leaps out of bed in a vicious scramble and shoves roughly between us. Golden hair swirling around his shoulders, my alpha looms over Zephyr with flaming eyes and a ferocious scowl.

"You will take Zara from this place of safety over my dead body," Max says in a thick voice that's guttural with dragon. "Her alphas are in rut and my mate is ripe for breeding. She will not leave this *domus*—neither for your dangerous crowning nor her war with Cleopatra—until her fertile womb is filled with my dragonets."

# Chapter Fourteen
## Zephyr

I should never have come.

That is, very clearly, what they're all thinking. My wild Gemini queen and her distrustful warlock harem.

Bathed in the harsh electric light of this alien kitchen with its threatening appliances, so unlike the gentle witchlight and friendly stone hearths of my Unseelie palace, the silence seethes with the suspicions these warlocks yearn to whisper in my pointed ears. The air is loud with the accusations they burn to hurl at my moon-fucked head.

The dragon is the worst.

Maxim Grigoryevich Rasputin.

I've made it my business to learn their true names. If they should ever threaten me…

Well, I'm Unseelie.

They call us the Dark Fae for reasons. We're not exactly known for kindness and mercy, are we?

To defend myself and my bride, I will never flinch from doing what I must.

Maxim looms vigilant in the doorway, scowling ferociously at me and blocking my access to the rest of the house, to the rooms where my precious queen showers and prepares for her day. This dragon shifter mate of hers looks utterly disreputable, brooding barefoot in torn jeans and worn shirt, with his dragon eyes slitted and his hair twisted in a warrior's braid that bares his ruthless face. A barbed wire tattoo loops around one sinewy wrist.

Dressed impeccably in Academy uniform and chunky combat boots with vivid green soles, Vasili Nikolayevich Romanov lurks near the complicated device called *espresso machine*. He leans casually against the counter and watches me with poisonous eyes the treacherous hue of quicksilver, expertly rimmed with smoky liner under a shag of silver hair, while he sips in pointed silence from a tiny cup of that revolting mortal beverage whose acrid reek corrupts the morning air.

That one is dangerous.

So dangerous he makes my skin twitch and my nerves prickle.

I've known it since the night he killed my moon-cursed mother.

For that vast mercy, I owe him a debt.

For any Fae, a debt is no small thing. The obligation sits uneasily beside my wary respect for his powerful witchcraft and my bitter envy for his mating bonds with all of them—Zara, Ronin, even that timid Neo. All the hearts this one collects so casually.

Romanov is the one Zara calls her dominant alpha.

To me, he is a rival to be vanquished.

If not for the debt I owe him, I would have killed him already.

Neo Theodophilus Mercury presides capably over a sizzling skillet at the monstrous six-burner stove, where he has coaxed a pop of reluctant blue flame to sputter under the ancient-looking grate. He is frying up what appears to be an entire sow's worth of bacon. A jaunty apron tied neatly over his schoolboy uniform proclaims *Don't kiss the cook. Bend me over.*

From this one, I sense no danger.

Only sweetness.

Every time his bashful eyes meet mine, Zara's innocent fated mate blushes to his hairline.

Well.

When the time comes, I know exactly what to do with all that shy submission.

Soon, I'll have the lot of them safely installed with Zara in my royal bed.

I spare Neo a predatory grin and let my fangs peek out. He ducks his head, but his blush deepens.

And then there's Ronin.

My Ronin.

Ronin stands at the counter whisking eggs with his back turned pointedly to me. His powerful shoulders and lean hips look unreasonably sexual, encased in those leather pants and another man's button-down shirt, braced in a silent challenge I burn to master. His inky hair spills between his bunched shoulders in a sleek fall I long to wrap around my fist.

By the moon.

*Ronin.*

In the endless years we've spent apart, the graceful slimness of boyhood has vanished. That boy I loved to the point of hopeless despair—the boy I risked everything to win, the boy whose betrayal all but killed me—he has vanished.

Ronin Kilcannon Pendragon, scion of the powerful Leo clan, is a man now. A deadly one. One who harbors a lethal grudge.

Against me.

In the midst of this hostile crowd, I stand alone.

Same as always.

I stand sentinel in my armor behind the granite island that houses the deep kitchen sink, with an absurdly tiny cup of that vile mortal beverage called *espresso* cooling on the counter beside me.

I'd rather drink arsenic than this tar-like sludge.

But that is not the only reason I spurn it. When a Fae offers food and drink, it's a form of entrapment.

"I beg your pardon, Maxim." That old-fashioned courtesy belongs to the wolf, Lucius Aries, the headmaster of this residential college, who looms suddenly behind the dragon. The wolf places a hand at the dragon's waist in a way that whispers of all the intimacy this harem shares.

An intimacy from which I'm excluded.

"Lucius." Without shifting his gaze from me, Maxim rubs his whiskery jaw affectionately into the wolf's shoulder to scent him, then sidles to one side to let him pass.

Aries pads past the wary dragon into the kitchen, his rangy frame respectably attired in houndstooth trousers and a tweed coat with suede patches on the elbows, wild chestnut curls bound in a civilized knot around his scholarly face.

He is bearing a neat sprig of clipped leaves.

"Fresh mint from the garden," the wolf explains to my curious face, "for your herbal tea. I, er, understand the Fae don't care for coffee."

My nostrils flare to savor the welcome aroma of mint. In this one's expression, without the alluring complication of Zara looming between us, I see nothing but grave courtesy and a lively interest.

This is no entrapment.

This mortal world is… different.

This wolf means to offer me a gesture of genuine kindness.

My tense shoulders relax a notch. I incline my chin in a regal nod.

While Ronin joins Neo at the stove and starts frying eggs with a silent ferocity, the wolf calmly adds the sprig to a glass tea press, then pours boiling water from a kettle. The familiar tang of hibiscus flowers twines through the scents of coffee and aggression that perfume the pregnant air.

Lucius brings the tea press and a proper cup to me. I have laid aside my gauntlets, so I accept these offerings with the careful courtesy one gives these small rituals in Avalon.

Even an innocent cup of tea can be dangerous.

But it's true that I thirst.

Xhevith and I flew half the night through the portal at the standing stones—after I slew my loathsome cousin—in order to reach this place.

I study the tea flowers and mint leaves swirling in the slim glass cylinder of boiling water, then lean forward to give a wary sniff.

While everyone looks expectant, I survey the room—now wreathed in another weighted silence—with lifted brow.

Neo lowers his spatula and mouths, *Thank you.*

Ah yes.

Mortal manners.

In this world, I am not a king.

"Thank you," I tell the wolf stiffly. "For your hospitality."

"You're quite welcome, Your Radiance." The headmaster's alert face softens in a smile. His eyes are lovely, the color of warm sherry. They flicker over my wary frame and linger on the crossed blades that jut over my shoulders.

I'm far too guarded, in this ungodly land, to disarm.

"That tea needs a moment to steep. Do come and fill your plate from the stove," Lucius says kindly to my defensive face. "We don't stand on ceremony here. We all serve ourselves on school mornings."

"I do not dine without my bride," I say stiffly.

At this mention of Zara, a muscle flexes in the wolf's jaw. A wicked spark of red flares in his suddenly hostile gaze.

Near the door, the dragon bares his teeth in an unfriendly growl.

"Zara's… getting ready for school with the girls. As you may have gathered, we had some excitement here last night. They'll be along shortly," Lucius says with careful control. "Rest assured you've nothing to fear under my roof, Your Radiance. As long as you harm no one, then no one here will harm you. You have my word as your host."

Clearly this scholar knows something of Faerie custom. Still, he's no Fae to be bound by his sacred word.

Unlike the Fae, these men can lie.

Over his miniscule cup, Vasili Romanov utters a scornful snort. "Speak for yourself, Lucius. If that little pissant tries to whisk Zara away on his odious dragon like he did last time, I'll crush him like a cockroach."

"Vasili, my dear." The wolf gives him a reproachful look. "You're not helping."

I'm already bristling with offense. "I am not here to abduct my own queen. I told you I've come to crown her. I assure you, she'll come with me willingly."

"For fuck's sake, mate." Ronin drops the skillet to the stovetop with a noisy clatter and twists around to shoot me a thunderous scowl. "Are you blooming mental? She's got her own bloody royal crisis to manage here, hasn't she?"

Still looming threateningly in the doorway, the dragon growls a foreign word in his mother tongue. His shoulders flex under that ghoulish shock-rock shirt. His fists clench into white-knuckled knots that promise violence.

"Zara will go nowhere," the dragon bites out, "while she is breeding—"

"Ronin, Maxim, kindly let me handle this." The wolf levels me with a warning look. "As for you, Your Radiance…"

I begin to sense I'm treading on thin ice, even with this one who is more patient and shows me greater courtesy than the others.

Besides, I know well that if I spur them all to violence, Zara will not be pleased.

Already, I've angered my volatile queen with my long absence.

For her sake, I can see, even I must bend a little.

I pull in a long breath and reach for my forbearance. "You may address me by my common name. I am Zephyr."

This is a great concession on my part. In Avalon, it would be considered a rare honor. Yet I suspect these troublesome mates of hers will not view it in this light.

Besides, even to my own ears, I sound truculent.

"Very well, ah, Zephyr," Lucius says firmly. "We can discuss the future of your realm and this one—with Zara—*after* we've all eaten. Come now, surely you must be hungry."

"I am not—" I begin loftily.

My empty stomach chooses this untimely moment to voice a noisy rumble.

Vasili, the one Zara calls her snake, hisses rudely. "Sweet fuck. Just let him starve, Lucius."

The snake abandons his espresso and slithers to the stove. Instead of snatching a plate as I expect, then stuffing his hateful face before my hungry eyes to taunt me, he shoots an arm around Ronin's waist and pulls him into a hard fierce kiss.

Ronin's hand rises to cup the other man's cheek in a tender moment of contact that seems to steady them both.

Without breaking this consuming kiss, Ronin reaches behind him to pull Neo close. Neo snuggles in and hugs both of them (even that prickly snake, which seems to me the height of recklessness) and the three of them share a moment.

I wait for Vasili to push Neo violently away, this interloper who is getting between him and his precious Ronin.

To my surprise, I even find myself tensing to spring to that innocent boy's defense.

Instead, Romanov's arm twines around Neo's waist. The bookworm tucks trustingly into both of them with a happy murmur. The sight of those three, wrapped in each other's arms, makes my chest ache with a poignant sensation I find… unsettling.

Surely, this is not the ache of yearning.

Lucius Aries watches them with a quiet fierce love that holds nothing of envy.

Very clearly, they're together—all of them in this harem—precisely the way Zara always said. These warlocks of hers are more than bedmates or friends or even political allies. They're a true polycule.

They're deeply committed, not only to her, but also to each other.

They love each other.

Me? I'm alone and unloved on the outside.

Peering in.

Same as always.

A quick step in the doorway draws them apart. Awareness crackles through the room like a bolt of lightning. Everyone turns with alacrity as Zara appears on the threshold and loops her arms around Maxim's neck for a quick kiss, which he returns with a dragon's brooding intensity. Then she ducks into the kitchen.

She is not dressed for Avalon, which vexes me.

Clearly she means to make me wait.

I'm in no mood to idle and tarry on her doorstep like an addled suitor while Avalon seethes with rebellion, my spider of a cousin spins his web of deceit and betrayal, and my love—my Ash—holds my throne alone.

Still, at the sight of her, my heart lifts with pleasure.

My bride's fetching curves are on pleasing display in a short plaid skirt and smart emerald blazer—at least she is wearing my color—with the Academy logo stitched over her lush breast. Her teal curls stream over her shoulders in saucy pigtails she's tied with two snips of black ribbon. Black knit stockings encase her slim legs. A handspan of sleek bare thigh peeks between the tops of her stockings and the hem of her skirt. Beneath, she wears black-and-white saddle shoes.

"Mmmm, maple bacon." Zara ambles in as though we're not all teetering on the naked edge of violence. She shoots a warm look at her three mates snuggling near the stove and gives an appreciative sniff. "I'm *starving*."

"I'll fix a plate for you, Zara." Looking perfectly happy to perform this menial chore like a servant, Neo detaches from the huddle and fetches a clean plate.

"Thanks, baby." Her casual glance finds me standing alone and wary near the sink. "How about you leave those swords somewhere, Your Transcendence? There's not gonna be room for your whole medieval arsenal at the breakfast table."

Now I feel beset from all sides.

As my bride clearly senses, I don't feel comfortable disarming in this alien land. Nor do I wish to sit cozily bumping elbows over a rasher of greasy eggs and burnt sow with these rivals and enemies.

If I accept their hospitality in this way, if I disarm and eat and drink at their table, I myself will be bound by the sacred obligation a guest owes his host. I will be bound to harm none who dwell beneath this roof—

Unless they harm me first.

The quiet knowing look I'm receiving from the wolf tells me he too knows these ancient laws.

Perhaps he even senses my turmoil.

I feel my brow furrow. I itch to return with my bride to Avalon. It is for this reason alone I've come.

Now, all too clearly, I will not achieve my aim without patience. Perhaps it was churlish of me to arrive late and unannounced, then make my distrust of her mates so blatant.

Now I experience another emotion I do not often tolerate. My face heats with the awkward burn of embarrassment.

"Forgive me," I say stiffly, hands rising to the harness that straps my swords to my back. "I meant no offense. I will disarm."

"If you intend to disarm," Vasili Romanov fires back spitefully, "don't forget to remove the pole that's currently riding your royal Unseelie ass. There's no room for *that* at the breakfast table either."

Ronin snickers. His sullen face lights with a sudden grin. It's a mocking grin, to be certain.

But it pulverizes my heart.

Once I would do anything to see him smile.

"Okay, everyone grab a plate," Neo says with determined cheer, while he busily fills Zara's. "Your eggs are getting cold."

We do not mind cold food in Avalon. Our witchfire is not capable of a gas stove's sustained heat.

But apparently cold breakfast is a problem here.

Neo's comment prompts a general migration for plates and cutlery and an orderly procession of bodies past the heaping skillets.

While Zara fearlessly engages the hissing and grinding contraption of the espresso machine in some sort of struggle involving steam and milk—while she ignores me completely—I unbuckle my harness and prop my sheathed swords neatly against the wall.

Still, I keep them well within reach.

Covertly I watch her mates pile eggs and sow on their plates. Vasili holds himself apart and graces his plate sparingly with a tidy dollop of scrambled eggs and a token strip of sow. Ronin and Maxim tussle playfully over the sow, like two brothers instead of the intimate lovers they probably are, until Lucius intervenes to claim the lion's share of the sow with a wolfish growl.

At last, they've all tromped noisily out to the great room with their eggs and suspicion.

Leaving Zara and me blessedly alone.

By now, my wild Gemini appears to have compelled the infernal espresso machine to do her queenly bidding. She stands in a shaft of sunlight that streams through the open kitchen window, cradles a steaming Icarus Academy mug between her small hands, and eyes me with pensive periwinkle eyes while she sips her latte.

She seems to expect me to speak. But I am afraid to make matters worse.

As the silence stretches, her teal brows compress in a pucker of annoyance.

I yearn to vanquish this abominable distance between us, crush her delectable body in my arms, bend her backward under the force of my ardor, and ravage her sweet mouth with kisses.

But her expression is not inviting.

She does not appear to appreciate the sight of me standing rigidly in her kitchen with my swords and armor, before my untouched tea, brewed by my host with his own hands.

In the tight-stretched silence, with the savory aroma of eggs and meat thick in the air, my hollow stomach gives another undignified grumble.

At last, her expression of annoyance softens. She hides a small smile behind her mug.

"They left some for you, okay?" She sighs. "Plus the girls are coming down. Dez and Racetrack. They're my friends and they're part of my court, you should meet them."

"I am not opposed to meeting your court." This much I can say in all honesty. "They will be welcome in Avalon."

At the mention of Avalon, her expressive face hardens.

"Up to you whether you eat with the rest of us at the table—*minus* those swords—or standing alone in the kitchen." Now her voice too is hard. "But I'm not doing this with you unless we're with all of them too. All my guys. Right now, they don't trust you, and I don't blame 'em. So you gotta figure your shit out."

That's how my bride leaves me, in her strange and perilous electrified kitchen.

Standing alone.

Same as always.

# Chapter Fifteen
## Zara

There's a Dark Fae in our kitchen and a feral dragon in our yard.

Right now, they're both causing issues in our *domus* for totally different reasons.

"I don't mind about the rose trellis or the herb garden, cobber," Dez says timidly to the massive dragon who's sprawled across our peristyle courtyard, with his snout protruding through the open glass doors and filling half our great room, while his thick forked tail floats in the pool.

"I've never been much for roses, to be honest, what with the prickly bits. Bloody-minded buggers, they are. And I can always plant more herbs, yeah?" Looking schoolgirl-tidy in her Monday plaid and sable ponytail, Dez hesitates with one hand resting on the big guy's scaly muzzle.

Wistfully she glances at me standing next to her, nose-to-nose with Xhevith's monumental mass. "If he could just spare the orchids…?"

"He doesn't understand mortal speech," Zephyr says coolly from his place at our oversized table.

He's sitting, stiff as a fucking poker, with a gaping ring of empty space (super obvious) yawning between him and the rest of my guys.

Clearly, they're all barely tolerating his presence.

"How d'you tell him what to do then?" Dez's clear eyes are wide with fascination. Since we don't have complex mating shit lurking between us but just a solid friendship, she clearly feels free to satisfy her curiosity about our exotic guest in a way the others don't. "Tried telepathy with the big fella already, haven't I?"

"Avalon dragons *are* telepathic—but only with their riders."

Zephyr's gaze rests on his dragon and his cold face thaws into something resembling warmth. "Xhevith communicates with me alone, through images and emotions."

"Well, maybe you can give him the gist then, huh, flyboy." That's Racetrack, whose poor concussed head seems to have benefited quite a bit from the numbing potion Lucius doled out, but who still sounds cranky as fuck.

Wearing her own version of the school uni (accessorized with scuffed leather jacket and studded cuff), RT ambles in from the courtyard, where she's been checking out the rest of Xhevith, with her combat boots clumping on the flagstones.

"Looks like the big galoot managed to miss your orchids, hun," Racetrack reports to Dez. "Unless he rolls over or something. Maybe *someone* in this *domus*—like, I dunno, his *rider*—could tell him not to do that."

Dez looks hopefully at Zephyr, her olive eyes round with entreaty. To resist that look, you'd have to be a monster.

My Fae (if he is still mine, because the jury's still out on that one) inclines his regal chin, like, an inch.

But he does make that inward-looking face he gets when he's talking to Xhev.

The dragon chuffs out a surprised snort that blows my pigtails back in a gust of hot breath. His lips curl back from his fangy teeth in his version of a smile.

I figure that's him agreeing not to smush the orchids.

I grin up at him and give the sun-warmed scales over his nose a friendly rub. Under my palm, his well-oiled hide feels smooth as leather. Looks like he's totally recovered from our deadly adventures in Wonderland (a.k.a. Avalon) last term, and it's pretty obvi Zephyr takes really good care of him.

His rider might be on my shit list, but I missed Zephyr's pet dragon.

"The courtyard of this *domus* is no place for a dragon. That beast needs a proper lair," Max growls around his second heaping plateful of Ronin's eggs.

My dragon shifter eats with one arm wrapped protectively around his plate, so no one can steal his food (which is, like, a leftover habit from his fucked-up childhood) and one eye fixed warily on the rival dragon.

"Where would you advise he make that lair?" Zephyr's tone is wintry as he delicately navigates his own eggs.

At least he's eating at the table like a normal guy.

Plus he left his swords in the kitchen.

*Small steps, showgirl,* I tell my own inner dragon, who's been over-the-top excited and elated and wanting various forms of fucking (super distracting) ever since he showed up. *He's eating and not stabbing.*

"As for myself, when I am dragon…" Max pauses to engulf another big forkful of his second breakfast. In this one way—where his appetite is concerned—it's like being mated to a hobbit. After first period, to tide him over till lunch, he'll pack a sandwich and a big apple for elevenses.

"I sleep on the roof. Especially when it is sunny." Max gives the big green a warning scowl. "But that is my place. That dragon is not welcome there either."

"I'd actually prefer that *your* dragon find another place to sun himself as well, Mr. Rasputin." Lucius sips patiently at his coffee. "We've discussed this, have we not? The roof of this *domus* is no place for a three-ton dragon."

Our headmaster couldn't finish his grading last night, what with plunging into a mating rut and stuffing me and then Ronin with his first-ever knot, etc. So Lucius has been grading while he eats. Now he tucks a stack of neatly graded essays into his oxblood briefcase.

But he pauses long enough to give Max a stern look.

Honestly, right now you'd never know my headmaster spent a chunk of last night losing his mind with his thick dick buried down Max's throat. (I mean, if you weren't right in the middle of that shit, getting off on it yourself bigtime, the way I was.)

The sun-bronzed skin stretched over Max's Slavic cheekbones gets a little ruddy, which fascinates me.

Is Lucius actually making that dragon *blush*?

While Max mumbles something contrite and hunches over his plate, Vasili lounges back in his chair at the table's head, swings his punk-rock combat boots onto the table, and crosses his elegant legs.

That maneuver plants his vivid green soles right in Zephyr's face.

"Never mind about that acid-breathing dragon, darlings, *do,*" the Goblin King drawls. A glimmer of malice surfaces in his sly gaze. "Whatever shall we do about this trespassing Fae?"

Looking down his royal nose at V's intrusive boots, the Fae in question says tightly, "By the moon, I am no trespasser. Zara herself invited me here, many weeks ago. Else I could never have crossed the wolf's powerful wards that guard this house without triggering them."

"*Many weeks ago* being very much the relevant point." V bares his wicked fangs in a sneer.

For a warlock with shifter genes like him, that's an intimidation display.

Because normally he's kinda sensitive about showing those permanent fangs he can't retract like a pure shifter. Those incisors of his aren't tiny, and they make him self-conscious as fuck.

Apparently unmoved by all V's bullying, Zephyr unbends enough to polish off his eggs. Even though he deigned to accept that heap of scrambled eggs and what he disdainfully calls *sow* only after Ronin himself shoved the plate in front of him with a scowl.

Perched uncomfortably at our table in his dragonscale armor, with his savage face all wary behind his green eyepatch and his pretty pointed ears poking through the spill of his mossy hair, alternating between stretches of uncanny stillness and flashes of sudden movement, twitching at every unexpected sound—that Dark Fae is practically feral.

When Neo fired up the espresso machine a few minutes ago to steam an encore hit of milk for my latte, he practically launched Zephyr into orbit.

I'm afraid to even ask what that psycho did with his cousin's severed head.

I really hope it's not buried in Dez's garden.

Because, like, we eat from there.

Now that fucking axe murderer of a Fae eyes V's invasive boots on the table. His nostrils flare in annoyance.

"I've explained the delay, have I not?" Zephyr's frowning at the boots, but I know he's talking to me. "My throne is in mortal peril. While he serves as my regent, Ash is bare of back, without my strength to guard him. Every hour I linger here, his danger grows more acute. If my enemies manage to unseat him, they'll slaughter him without mercy."

Sweet Jesus. *Ash.*

My chest tightens in a straitjacket of worry.

My tummy nosedives in a spiral of dread.

Sure, Zephyr's been an ass since the literal minute he popped up here, after ghosting me for ten weeks, sporting that lofty and totally unapologetic *hi honey I'm home and aren't you lucky to see me* attitude.

I'll probably be waiting for an apology till the day I grow sea dragon gills like Cleo.

But that asshole just managed to put his royal finger on the part of that whole sitch back in Avalon that's bugging me most.

"Yeah, I hear you." Giving Xhev's friendly muzzle a final rub, I work off my nerves by pacing around the familiar comfort of our sun-splashed great room. There's not a ton of room between our big Renaissance sofa and Neo's book-stuffed study nook and that dragon's muzzle practically nudging the central hearth, but I manage.

"Ash is no slouch, but sounds like he's gonna need some backup, for real." I drum my restless fingers against my thigh. "The thing is, like I just explained, right now I can't leave here."

Over our breakfast, I filled in the awkward silence by walking Zephyr through this whole epic cluster about me being dethroned and Cleo moving right in on campus to seal the deal and me being the unofficial new head of the witching world resistance.

Zephyr's been bristling with tension—I mean, like, more than usual—ever since.

"That fucking Cleo. Can't wait to run into that bitch in the student commons." Ronin slants me a dark look over his toast and marmalade. "Don't care if her skinny arse *is* on the cover of *Vogue*. She's a new freshman at this Academy. You know what that means."

"Purgatory for the new girl?" Vasili gives a wicked snicker. "How delicious."

Ronin grunts in agreement. My Brit's sitting as far away from Zephyr as humanly possible, with Neo tucked up against him. Under the table, my bookworm's big palm is planted on Ronin's knee for reassurance. That's such a Neo thing to do—offering comfort—it makes me love the guy even more.

Ronin won't even look at Zephyr.

But Zephyr can't stop sneaking peeks at him.

My Fae's doing it again right now, with his narrow jaw tight and his jade gaze all shadowed.

"Purgatory, huh?" I drift up behind Ronin to sift my fingers through his silky ponytail. Zephyr watches us both like he's starving. "Guess I should feel bad about that. But I don't. At least this time it won't be *me* getting hazed."

"And I'll not stop at a few nasty pranks, will I?" Ronin grins up at me with his topaz eyes narrowed in menace.

"Hazing is a violation of the Academy Codex, Mr. Pendragon," Lucius says mildly, locking his briefcase with a whispered word. "I'm disappointed, if not surprised, with Mr. Romanov for condoning it. Rest assured, Zara will have her opportunity to prove herself against Ms. Ferrari—in a manner that's entirely sanctioned and safe—during finals over the next few days."

*"The next few days?"* Zephyr jolts straighter (if that's possible, because V was right about that pole riding the Fae's ass) and looks appalled. "The Faerie Ball occurs in two days' time."

"Faerie Ball, huh?" That's Racetrack, who's stealing Dez's bacon and eating standing up. "What the fuck's that?"

"The Faerie Ball is a magical event," Zephyr says with mounting impatience. "According to Dark Fae lore, the *fête* takes place in the Unseelie city on the night of the summer solstice—a night when powerful witchcraft can be woven. This makes Midsummer Night the most auspicious date for my queen's coronation ritual."

That's Mr. Self-Absorbed right there, adding his two cents from the cheap seats.

"Yeah, finals. How's that even supposed to work?" Ignoring Zephyr and that pole up his Unseelie ass, I duck into the kitchen to collect my latte, then give Lucius a rueful look. "You and all the profs have been closemouthed as fuck about finals."

I actually aim this grievance, not for the first time, at both Lucius and Vasili, because my snake's provisionally on the faculty, despite being simultaneously a graduating senior.

(Staffing shortage, don't ask, but Vasili's class is a reign of terror. Half his students already have PTSD from the experience.)

"Every year's magical challenge is unique, little queen." V smirks at my simmering impatience. "With the parameters of the examination established by the Dean herself. Surely you're not suggesting that *I* spill the tea? I'm still on a faculty improvement plan after our, shall we say, unauthorized vacay in Sin City on your behalf last winter."

"Oh, honestly." I roll my eyes at my snake, who's clearly having way too much fun with this. "I mean, what's the point of having a sexually inappropriate relationship with the faculty—a relationship that's currently front-page news across the whole witching world, by the way—when you don't even tell me this shit?"

"My dear, you mustn't blame Vasili. Or me, for that matter." Lucius gives me a wry look. "I certainly appreciate that the academic stakes have risen since Cleopatra Aquarius enrolled at this Academy. This late in the term, she'd typically not even commence her studies until the fall. All too clearly, she's making this exam an integral element of her succession strategy, to strengthen her claim to your throne."

"Exactly." I point at him with my cup. "She wants to prove it's not just some morality issue with me fucking all of you and liking it and getting caught on film by the paps—which shouldn't even be an issue for a poly queen, once everyone calms down from seeing my tits and your dick splashed all over *The Witching Inquisitor*."

Lucius clears his throat and shoots Dez and RT an embarrassed glance. But I figure those two are probably the only female students at this Academy—along with Mallory, who's too decent to peek—that *didn't* check out our headmaster's junk in that scandal sheet.

Neo pushes his glasses up his nose and looks worried. "Cleo wants to prove she's a stronger witch than you, babe. That's gotta be the reason she's taking the test. So she can prove you don't deserve to rule."

"Fuck me," Ronin mutters.

Zephyr voices a little snarl like the barely civilized Unseelie he is. Between his snarling lips, one sharp tiny fang peeks out.

I just can't tell whether it's the threat to my reign or the thought of fucking Ronin (or maybe both?) that's triggering him.

"Yup." I give my guys a tight nod. "Everyone at school knows my grades suck. Since the Dean posts 'em like the fucking sadist she clearly is. Hell, my whole transcript got leaked to *The Inquisitor*."

Vasili's dangerous eyes narrow and his smoky lids lower. His subtle reaction validates all my instincts and tells me I'm not being paranoid.

I'm being smart.

Smart like I need to be if I'm gonna win back my throne.

"Wow." Neo's earnest green eyes get big as dinner plates. "Do you think Cleo wants to be… First Girl on the Dean's List?"

"Oh, dear. Now it's *your* crown in danger, First Boy." Vasili smirks at our bookworm's worried face.

I give that snake one of my queen looks that tells him to stop terrorizing Neo and behave. "She'll settle for getting a better grade than me—which, let's face it, probably won't be hard—but yeah. Bet she thinks being First Girl at the Icarus Academy would definitely prove she'll make a better queen."

"Bollocks." With a sudden violence that makes everyone twitch, Ronin shoves to his feet and starts roughly clearing the table. I know it's because he can't sit still.

He's been simmering with nerves and guilt and anger since Zephyr showed up. My Brit's psychic barriers are usually airtight (when he wants that). But I can feel that shit like it's mine, because he's broadcasting on all telepathic channels.

Under that kinda barrage, my own issues feel tiny.

But they're still festering.

So I can't stay still either, I gotta pace.

I tap my fingers against my latte cup, violet sparks popping at the contact, and roam back over to Xhevith's big green snout.

"It's not like I'm even on the Dean's List," I remind the room at large without looking at anyone.

I know it's for *reason*s, not because I'm stupid, that my grades are in the crapper. But I'm feeling pretty judged and defensive and overall inadequate, in a way I'm definitely not used to, since my own predecessor spouted that shit on live TV about me being too wicked and unworthy to be queen.

Neo pops up from the table and hurries after me. "Yeah, babe, but that's only because you missed the whole first semester."

Which is true. I wouldn't even be here now if Lucius and Ronin hadn't kidnapped me right off a penthouse roof in Singapore last winter and dragged my ass through the wards.

Guess that's what you'd call a cute meet, right?

Yeah, not so much. At the time, I was pissed as fuck.

Now it looks like maybe they screwed up.

You know, pinning all their save-the-world queen hopes on me.

"One." I park my hip against Xhevith's snout and tick off my academic shortcomings on my glittery fingers. "I'm shaky in Witching

World History. Two, I've been struggling all quarter in Common Magics. Three, I'm barely passing Science of Witchcraft. If I don't pass my finals I'm, like, seriously at risk of failing the whole year."

"You'll pass your finals, Ms. Gemini, if I have anything to say about it. Don't forget you're acing your independent study with me," Lucius rumbles. That's his wolf lurking in his voice, because our turbulent independent study sessions in the Belfry are how the two of us first started fucking. "You're the strongest lightning witch the arcane races have known in decades—if not centuries. I truly believe we've only begun to explore the depths of your power."

"You are a fully manifested dragon shifter queen." Max pushes aside his empty plate and stares at me with broody eyes that smolder with heat. "And you are fertile. You and I will breed clutches of beautiful dragonets to restore our failing bloodline."

That's Mr. One Track Mind with the breeding kink weighing in right there.

"Plus you're a wicked telepath, love, thanks to that badass Valyrian pedigree you're rocking," Ronin calls from the kitchen over the gurgle of running water.

"*And* you levitate," Vasili purrs, "due to your delicious Mogadon DNA."

"Yeah, I know. My whole genetic code's like a tossed salad with mystery dressing on top. That's the whole reason the Senate voted me in as queen in waiting." I stand on tiptoe and stretch to give Xhevith a good scratch under his eye ridges.

The attention makes his inner lids lower over those golden orbs in lazy pleasure.

"Here's the thing," I say softly, because Xhev's getting sleepy and I don't wanna wake him up. "If I've got all these dormant recessives that keep popping up and manifesting as weird strains of witchcraft we didn't even know I have, who's to say Cleo doesn't have a few tricks up her own witchy sleeve? She's half Aquarius and half Fae. We already know she's a sea dragon shifter, and they're supposed to be extinct."

"Her Unseelie pedigree is no enigma," Zephyr says coolly from the table. "If this stray mortal you speak of truly is Messalina's lost daughter with my late uncle Oberon, that connection would make her my first cousin."

"Yeah, that's another part of what's fucking with my head." I groan and lean my forehead into Xhevith. "You two being cousins. And of course I boinked both of you. Think she's gonna cause problems for you too?"

"I do not." Zephyr's tone gets edgy. "Your queen Messalina irrevocably renounced her daughter's claim to my throne the day she stole the babe from Avalon." He pauses, and his voice turns diffident. "Still, the girl's Unseelie pedigree offers… insights… into the type of Faerie magic she's most likely to manifest. These are insights I'd be willing to share."

"And what will you demand in exchange?" Vasili sounds nothing but suspicious, and honestly I can't blame him. "The Unseelie offer nothing for free."

"Consider it a bridal gift," Zephyr says tightly. "I've been called a generous lover."

The clatter of crockery and a sudden curse drift from the kitchen.

Shit. I'd bet real money Ronin just dropped a plate in there.

Lucius murmurs Ronin's name and his chair scrapes back. I know he's going to check and make sure our guy's okay.

"Hear that? Zephyr's gonna help, we all are. It's gonna be okay, babe." Neo hovers anxiously in my periphery. "I know it."

I turn and pull him into me for mutual comfort.

"She was more than my bestie, okay?" I sigh into the side of my fated mate's neck. His soft purple curls tickle my face. "And I'm not even talking about us being friends with benefits. She was my accomplice in my burglar days—and she was wicked good. She's always been sneaky. *And* smart."

"You're smart too, Zara. Once we know the test questions, I'll help you study. You're gonna do great." My bookworm wraps his arms around my waist and tucks my head into his nice broad shoulder.

Gratefully I snuggle into his solid warmth and breathe in his clean soapy smell of sage and lavender. "I just feel like I need as much of a head start as possible to bone up for that fucking exam."

"There's no need to fret over the timing, my dear." Lucius emerges from the kitchen and calmly gathers a stack of plates for the sink. "I expect you'll find the examination announcement, with all the necessary details, posted in the student commons this morning."

Zephyr's still body fires into motion. He flows to his feet to loom over the table (which at least gets V's boots outta his royal face.)

"There is no time for Zara to visit this *student commons*," my Fae announces with a frown. "Has no one heard a word I've spoken? Zara must return now to Avalon with me."

Maxim passes over his plate to Lucius and gives our pain-in-the-ass houseguest a ferocious scowl. "Zara will go nowhere while she is breeding and multiple shifter males in this *domus* are in rut. Frankly speaking, even the commons is a stretch."

"Yeah, good luck with that, Godzilla." Racetrack snorts at Max and beelines for her backpack. "Z calls the shots about her own life, not you. She's got class and shit. Anyway, if you're gonna start talking about being all horny, Dez and I are outtie."

The two girls gather their books and papers, though Dez darts me an apologetic look over Neo's protective shoulder and mouths *Sorry!*

I wave goodbye with a wry grin.

The two slip out through our vestibule for their walk through the village to the deconsecrated church where our Academy classes go down. Lucius slips into his office to finish getting ready for class.

After a minute of shared comfort, I detach from Neo and give my fated mate a gentle nudge to help Ronin finish cleanup in the kitchen. With Zephyr lurking around this *domus* and the minefield of unexploded ordnance looming between those two, I don't want Ronin alone right now, and Neo's super comforting.

While I organize my backpack full of textbooks and grimoires and transfer my stiletto from my jacket to my pack, I'm uber-aware of the Dark Fae King lurking in my living room.

He's gone to stretch his lean sexy body casually against Xhev's big scary muzzle, while that dragon dozes off in a seesaw of rumbly snores.

As Zephyr cautiously sips a mug of what smells to my shifty senses like mint-and-hibiscus tea (because the guy can't stand coffee, it's a Fae thing), he broods at me with his inscrutable gaze.

"You better not be planning another snatch and grab," I tell him, just to be clear, while I muscle the zipper of my own straining backpack shut around my crapload of pre-exam schoolbooks. "No more of that Hades-Persephone shit. I mean it. Or else you and I are *not* gonna get along."

For the first time since he turned up on my doorstep, one corner of the Fae's mouth curls in a tiny smile. "Hades is your mythical god of the underworld, is he not? I am… flattered… by the comparison."

Oh, man.

That smile of his… does things to me.

Always has, because he doles them out so rarely.

Even now, when he's acting all standoffish and totally hasn't given me a real answer, my tummy gets all fluttery and my face heats up.

Suddenly I wonder if the reason he's all standoffish is because he's uncertain too. I mean, we haven't exactly rolled out the welcome wagon for the guy. The fact that he took a timeout and came through the portal at all, with a literal rebellion against his reign going down in Avalon, tells me I matter to him.

Even if he's shitty at saying it.

I unbend enough to give him a little grin back. "Don't let it go to your head, Your Radiance."

"Too late," he says softly. "Your Persephone fell in love with her terrible abductor, did she not? Thus, I am hopeful."

I'm contemplating the idea of actually going over there and seeing if maybe that hello kiss we still haven't shared might actually be in the cards when, from the table, Vasili utters a rude snort.

My Goblin King's still lounging with his combat boots on the breakfast table, sipping his coffee and watching both Zephyr and me intently. He looks deceptively relaxed, but that snake is never relaxed.

He's actually at his worst when he looks relaxed.

Despite what Max has been saying about shifty cycles, I totally don't expect Vasili to go into rut. He's always been adamantly anti-baby when it comes to his own little swimmers.

Still, V *has* been all intense and lurky (like the homicidal psychopath he is) since we started this whole breeding convo.

Then there's the fact that his dick barely left my vag all night. That snake was literally hogging my pussy.

All my other guys had to, like, work around him.

Of course Max should be getting ready for class himself. But he can't bring himself to leave me with a rival male. So he paces around the great room in his jeans instead.

"There is a rival queen on this island," Max announces. "One who will have allies we cannot guess or guard against. You should remain here in our *domus* where you are safe, my sovereign. I will remain at your side to protect you."

Zephyr's eye narrows to a dangerous slit. "She will be safest from mortal assassins in Avalon. Especially once she's crowned. When Zara comes into the full potency of her power—"

"Okay, guys." I've had enough of this shit, for real. "I'm standing right here. Let's all get a couple things straight."

Everyone looks at me attentively.

Lucius emerges from his office, briefcase in hand and tweed jacket folded neatly over his arm. Even Neo and Ronin crowd into the kitchen door, with Neo wearing his apron and Ronin toting a dishtowel, to listen.

"Look." I direct my first remarks at Zephyr. "I definitely appreciate that there's crap going down in Avalon. I get that Ash needs help. But he's also a BFD, like a literal Seelie Prince and a badass, so I hope he can hold his own for a minute till we get there."

A storm of protest gathers in the face of the Dark Fae King.

Typically he isn't the kinda guy you wanna piss off, he's *really* used to getting his way, and he's worried as fuck about Ash. Consequently, right now he looks fucking lethal.

But no one died and made him king on this side of the portal.

That means he's just gonna have to cope.

My gaze shifts to Lucius' alert face. "After what went down last night, I gotta show my face in the classroom this morning. I gotta. Plus I honestly do need to know ASAP what kinda fuckery the Dean's cooked up for our finals."

My headmaster gives me a careful nod, which reassures me he's on board with where I'm heading.

Finally I lock onto Max's intent and flaming stare.

"And we can't make any other, uh, big decisions till all that fate-of-the-world shit's resolved."

Max's chest rumbles with a subterranean growl of protest. Even my own inner dragon voices a chirp of indignation like the mouthy bitch she is.

I swallow down that sound and keep right on going.

"So here are my priorities." Squeezed by my mates' expectant silence, I count off on my fingers. "First, finals. I gotta pass 'em. And I gotta do better than Cleo on the test to save my crown. The witching world deserves, like, a queen who at least makes her people the priority rather than her next photo shoot."

Honestly speaking, I'm still not sure I'm all that. The witching world needs saving before we all go extinct, and that's the queen's major job.

But let's face it, I gotta be a better option than Messalina or my lying ex-BFF.

Right?

"*Then* we help Ash." I can't hide my uncertainty from my guys, and I really don't want to. But I use my queen voice for this little pep talk to brace everyone up, including myself. "We nail down Zephyr's grip on the Avalon throne. That relative of his doesn't sound like one of the good guys, and those Unseelie suffered enough under the curse we just broke."

I give Zephyr a sec to react to that, but my own personal Unseelie has retreated to his usual sphinxlike silence. Once you get past his downturned mouth and possessive stare, he actually looks lonely and kinda lost.

Now, as usual, my stupid heart goes all achy for the jerk.

God. I really wish I could read him like I do the rest of my guys.

While I'm talking, all three of my alphas have drifted close, pulled into me like magnets by the force of our bond. The mounting intensity of their need hums in my bones.

My divided attention hones in on them.

"Once we've got both realms sorted… and *only* then…" I pull in a breath to steady myself. "I guess the next thing on the to-do list could be, uh, babies."

Neo sucks in a gasp. Our mating bond floods with his excited sense of wonder.

Ronin slings an arm across Neo's broad shoulders and looks thoughtful, but his barriers are up and I'm not gonna pry. He'll let me in when he's ready.

At least there's no doubt where my shifters are coming from.

Lucius' wolf gives a sharp bark of triumph and his eyes burn crimson with hunger. Vasili hisses like the rattlesnake he is (but maybe that's a hiss of protest). Max lets rip with a dragonish snarl and lunges toward me.

I plant a warning palm between us to hold them all at bay.

"We only breed if it's safe for a kid of ours. That's a hard rule. And here's another one." My wary gaze follows the dangerous fault line in our cobbled-together polycule from Zephyr to Ronin to Vasili. Their tolerance for each other is brittle as shale. "We only take that plunge if we *all* agree."

# Chapter Sixteen
## Maxim

I am late for class.

Again.

Because I am dragon, self-taught in the lair, I do not navigate the tedious schedules and rigid routines and repetitive rhythms of a traditional schoolroom very well. I am at the bottom of my class, always somehow running late, never quite where I am supposed to be, according to the wobbly dictates of the schedule I have copied carefully into my notebook in my awkward script.

As for my homework, it is a hopeless snarl of assignments I have overlooked and deadlines I have missed.

For all these reasons, my grades plunge Lucius into a quiet despair. For this, I am very sorry. My dragon and I both hate to disappoint him.

But today is different.

Today I am late for a different reason.

I am late because I have guarded my deliciously fertile and soon-to-be-breeding mate through her shower and her breakfast and her walk to school to ensure she is never alone and vulnerable to that rival male.

The Dark Fae King.

I can scarcely believe he is here.

Once I entrust my precious queen safely to Witching World History under Lucius' protective eye, I race back to the *domus* to wash and don my detested uniform, which strangles my neck and makes my dragon chafe.

Finally, I gallop breathlessly back to campus to ensure I am waiting for my mate when the church bell rings at the end of first period.

In fact, I make such good time that I arrive well before the bell.

It is too bad this timing is not so good for me.

I slip into the classroom while Lucius' back is turned and he is simultaneously lecturing and inscribing neat lines of text on the chalkboard. I tiptoe inside and creep toward the back row (where I can watch the door and Zara without any impedance) as though I am a mouse and not a dragon.

This is because Lucius does not tolerate lateness in his classroom.

The instant I breathe in a lungful of Zara's alluring scent, I am lost.

By all the saints, I swear she is ovulating.

*Ours she is ours we will pump her full of our dragon seed—*

I veer toward the empty desk directly behind her. There, I can drink her in and savor her rich creamy spice and dream of tonight when I will fill her womb with my clutch. Saint Sergius guard me, my cock is already swelling behind my zipper. My barbs shoot out hopefully, already questing for her cunt.

Unfortunately, before I can sneak into my seat, Lucius' wolf smells my arrival and pounces.

"If it isn't the *delinquent* Mr. Rasputin." My headmaster's clipped tones bring me up short, midway down the sun-splashed aisle of the old-fashioned schoolroom with its high ceilings and worn floorboards. "How very good of you to join us."

Ignoring the ugly snickers of the Villa Tiberius crowd (they are members of our rival residential college, the ones who threw stones at me and beat me when I first enrolled, they have always hated me), I drop into my seat behind Zara, order my mating barbs to retract until they are needed, and swing my scuffed backpack to the floor.

"I am sorry to be late," I say meekly, once again, to Lucius' stern face.

Zara glances back at me and rolls her turquoise eyes.

She did not want me to walk her to class like she is five (her exact words). But I would not be dislodged.

Now I have annoyed both Zara and Lucius.

"It's a pity you've missed most of our final review session." Lucius looks both exasperated and annoyed. "A review whose assistance you, in particular, sorely required."

His irate tone makes me hang my head.

As he resumes his place behind the podium where he keeps his inexhaustible pile of lecture notes, Lucius' lovely whiskey gaze finds me drooping in my seat. His expression shifts from wrathful to reproachful.

Still, he is unyielding. "You can begin to redeem yourself, Mr. Rasputin, by summarizing for the class the three major periods of interracial relations in Faerie history."

My already flagging spirits sink to my shoes.

Truly, he might as well ask me to summarize the alchemical composition of gold, which is so difficult to master it is notorious. That is one of the subjects in Neo's Honors Alchemy course (into which I will never be admitted).

Even on the best of days, I am a slow learner.

Today, with the delicious creamy spice of my queen's mating scent (growing richer and more seductive by the hour, because she is definitely preparing to ovulate) filling my head and seeping from her skin and drenching the air in nectar, I am hopelessly distracted.

"Um." Awkward, I clear the thickness from my throat and try to focus.

If we were alone, I would drop to my knees before Lucius—who is now my alpha, to my amazement and delight—and I would rub my face into his thighs and groin until he reeked of my scent and I reeked of his. Then I would unbutton his fly and take his thick-veined cock between my contrite lips and let him fuck my mouth until he forgave me.

Just the thought of this electrifying new state of affairs between myself and my headmaster, whom I have idolized from afar for so long, is a heady one.

Last night he let me suck him.

He let me suck him until he exploded in my mouth with a primal bellow that was raw with pleasure—

"No answer?" Lucius' disappointed face penetrates my fantasy (which is not what I want him to penetrate) and makes me long to crawl under my desk and hide in shame. "What a pity. Perhaps Ms. McSnicker can shed some light on the subject."

Before I can unknot my hunched shoulders and release my held breath, Lucius' wrathful tone lashes me like a whip. "I'd suggest you take *copious* notes, Mr. Rasputin. I expect to see a ten-page essay from you on this subject waiting on my desk by this time tomorrow. If you're a minute late, the length of that assignment doubles."

I barely manage to swallow a groan of dismay.

The only thing worse than being asked to recite long lists of historical facts I can never seem to master is being required to coax an encyclopedic essay from the ancient manual typewriter, with its stubborn carriage and sticking keys, in our *domus* library.

I especially cannot manage this task while I am simultaneously guarding my irresistible Zara and her fertile womb from that rival male Zephyr and his dragon.

I give Lucius a look of mute entreaty.

But it is no use. He has already turned the scalpel of his attention to Mallory McSnicker, who is sitting quietly next to Zara.

Mallory too gives me an apologetic look and a grimace of sympathy. She feels sorry for my discomfort.

She is a nice girl. She is a good friend to Zara.

But she is, in the classroom, the female equivalent of our bookworm Neo.

Deftly she tosses her copper braid over one skinny shoulder and recites, "The three periods of interracial relations between the Dark and the Light Fae are the Discord, the Sundering, and the Exile. Some scholars claim the Faerie races are starting a fourth period in their history, called the Renaissance. But this is controversial because there's so little scholarship on the lost Unseelie race—"

"Very thorough as always, Ms. McSnicker. Thank you." Lucius gives Zara and Ronin and me—the only members of our polycule who have him this period—an inscrutable look. "I'd advise all of you to take careful note. This year in particular, Faerie History will very likely play a prominent role in the Dean's examination."

Sitting on Zara's other side, Ronin props a foot against his desk, slaps a notebook against his thigh, and scribbles a careless bullet.

Ronin is also my mate, so we are closely attuned. This is why I notice that his powerful body moves with less than his usual grace. And it is not only because of the way he engulfed Lucius' formidable knot last night and rode that wolf's cock like a stripper on a pole.

It is obvious to me that Ronin is… distracted. He fiddles with his pencil and drums restless fingers against his desk.

I wonder if, with his powerful clairsentience, he can sense the nearness of that rival male and his worrisome dragon.

*Zephyr.*

The very thought of my rival—and that devil's bargain I made with Vasili weeks ago, a debt which is now coming due—makes my hackles rise. My dragon grumbles a warning. His heavy coils slither inside my skin.

An ominous growl rises from my chest.

This disturbance stirs a ripple of covert glances and sly whispers from my classmates.

"Now then," Lucius says briskly, choosing to ignore my latest disruption. He pads around his lectern and advances down the aisle with his silent tread. "Who can tell us about the Discord? Let's hear from you, Ms. Gemini."

He is fooling no one.

No one is deceived by his careful formality toward Zara.

The entire school knows they are fucking.

Just as the entire school knows that, despite our latest glaring breach of decorum and those shocking photos splashed across the pages of *The Witching Inquisitor*, the Dean has not fired him.

Perhaps this is because Lucius is so strict with Zara in the classroom.

Even now, when his wolf is in rut and he is looming over her desk as though he can barely refrain from bending her over and lifting her skirt and shredding her schoolgirl panties so he can knot her again—

"Um, okay, the Discord." Zara squirms in her seat under his heated gaze and sits up straighter. Because I have bitten her, I can sense the force of her concentration through our mating bond. She is determined to pass her exams.

In truth, I can sense everything she is feeling. Especially the warm ache of need that pulses and throbs in her divine pussy.

My sovereign's fertile body is preparing her to breed.

*Ours she is ours we will fill her with our seed she will ripen with our clutch—*

Through the restless rumble of my rutting dragon against my inner ear, Zara's lively voice floats through my inflamed senses.

"So, the Discord is the period when, you know, the Dark Fae and the Light Fae lived together with each other and all the races in the regular witching world and sang *kumbaya*." Zara's dutiful tone turns wry. "Only that didn't go so great. That's because the Fae made war on the other arcane races—"

"In point of fact," a cool voice sneers from the doorway, "it was the other arcane races that made war on *us*."

Suddenly our doorway is commanded by a slim green figure who is both familiar and strange. The intruder's olive slacks and blazer, buttoned over a tight waist and narrow hips, bracket a trendy shirt with oversized cuffs and a slender stripe of tie. This classic attire looks exotic and unsettling when it is coupled with a curtain of moss-green hair, a pair of pointed ears, an eyepatch, and a heartless expression.

Undeceived by his conventional clothing, I recognize at once the hated form of my rival.

I push back my chair with a noisy scrape and shoot to my feet with a snarl.

Lucius gives me a quelling look that commands me—very clearly—to remain where I am. While I hover reluctantly and quiver with tension, Lucius turns courteously toward the door.

"Excellent," my headmaster says to our staring class. "Here's our guest speaker now. Zephyr, King of the Dark Fae, Your Moon-Dazzled Radiance, you are welcome."

Lucius speaks with the deliberate heft of witchcraft being woven. As his words fade, the tingle of common magic ripples over my hide. This is the feel of the protective ward he has placed on this classroom to protect our precious queen.

Parting to allow my enemy inside.

"Oh, bloody hell," Ronin mutters in a tone of absolute disgust. He shoves his notebook aside and plants his feet on the floor with dangerous intent—a breath away from violence.

My dragon trembles with the need to explode from my skin.

That is an instinct that would demolish this classroom, injure my mates, and get me expelled.

Narrow and assessing, Zephyr's jade gaze slides over me—the most immediate threat. Then his eye skips over Ronin, as though he flinches from the heat of that blazing glare, and settles on Zara's riveted face.

With her usual candor, she says what we are all thinking.

"What the fuck?" No one lobs the F bomb like my Zara. "Lu—uh, Master Aries, why is that Fae suddenly standing in our history class?

Lucius is a stickler for old-fashioned courtesy, which is what happens when you are strictly raised in a gloomy old castle with a gruesome history by an aristocratic Hungarian grandsire.

Now my headmaster's brow furrows in a repressive frown. "I should think it quite obvious—"

"I was invited." The Unseelie's smooth voice ripples like water running over rock. "To deliver the capstone lecture for your Faerie history lesson. The Discord is where your history books begin. But our noble race is far older than that."

By now this creature has prowled right into our classroom like the predator he is. His otherworldly scent of burnt amber twines through the dusty classroom smells of chalk and parchment like a magical miasma.

If my enemy dares to come anywhere near my breeding queen, I swear I will lunge for his throat.

Instead he flows toward the blackboard with that uncanny liquid grace, feet soundless as mist on our creaking floorboards, hair spilling like ivy down his straight back.

Deftly Zephyr captures a stick of chalk and writes in a flowing hand that is like calligraphy.

*Prejudice. Jealousy. Greed.*

The entire class, even those bullies from Villa Tiberius, is riveted.

"This is where our tale rightly begins. With the whole world's hatred." Zephyr pivots smoothly on his heel, hair swirling around his shoulders. He spurns Lucius' podium and hops lightly to sit on Lucius' desk instead, legs folding over each other like a lotus, fingers tenting under his narrow jaw.

My classmates stare at him. Clearly, they are enraptured.

The fools.

Aware of Lucius' irate frown at my threatening stance, I subside warily back to my seat.

"We Fae were here first," Zephyr murmurs, so softly we all lean forward to hear, "dwelling in harmony with nature and the childlike mortals who worshipped us. The other arcane races… your honored ancestors of ever-so-sainted memory… they came later."

His tone turns cruel and his face turns mocking.

"Your ancestors despised and envied mine," he hisses. "They distrusted our differences and they feared our power. So they set out to slaughter us down to the last babe. They drove us into hiding and stole our ancestral homes and profaned our sacred spaces with their churches and the stink of incense. Just as upstart peoples have always slaughtered and stolen from those they deem to be *lesser*. The embattled Fae fought to protect their lives, their homes, their children. *That* is the truth of the Discord you will never read in your histories."

As he settles into his story, he loosens his tie with an impatient tug. Truly, I cannot imagine where he has found that clothing. Or how he has even managed to arrange his tie, which is very unlike anything in his homeland, in that confident twist.

But I darkly suspect Neo (who is supposed to be in Honors Alchemy this period).

My Neo has always harbored a soft spot in his tender heart for this deceptive and terrible creature.

"As our sacred spaces diminished and our numbers dwindled," the creature says, "the Seelie and Unseelie cast blame upon each other. They began to squabble among themselves over the scraps. Those squabbles led to bloodshed and then—inevitably—to a bitter and brutal civil war. Fae against Fae. The Dark against the Light. In the end, my people—the Unseelie—withdrew from the mortal world entirely. They passed through the portal into Avalon where they would be safe."

His ruthless mouth twists in a mocking grin. "Or so they imagined."

Ronin utters a rude snort they can surely hear in the hallway. "Skipped over a bit there, haven't you, mate? You glossed over that ghastly bit where your Unseelie ancestors sacrificed a thousand of your Seelie kin to open the portal."

The class sucks in a collective breath of horror.

"A footnote to the text." The Fae's shoulder flexes in a shrug. "If you expect me to deny it, by the moon, I will not. Unlike the flotsam and scrum of your arcane races, the Fae alone cannot lie." His sleek ribbon of voice goes thin. "I never claimed we were nice, Ronin."

"Too right." Ronin pushes back in his chair and scowls.

"Let's return to the lesson, shall we?" Lucius is leaning against the podium, watching his guest lecture with a degree of fascination I find concerning. "What of the Light Fae who survived the, ah, incident? What became of them?"

"Well." Zephyr presses the tips of his tented fingers to his lips. "The Seelie survivors remained here, of course, while the Unseelie vanished into the depths of our secret world for our thousand-year Exile. Traumatized by their ordeal, the Seelie chose to conceal their origins. They wove a powerful glamor to disguise their most distinctive feature— their wings. The better to hide among the common folk, yes?"

His gaze drifts across the scatter of curious and (in my case) hostile faces. His stare pauses on Ronin, who is seething in a silent fury, then on Zara whose face I cannot see (but whose blend of annoyance and fascination pulses through our mating bond with an intensity that is very alarming). Then Zephyr pauses on Mallory, who is unremarkable in all ways except for her commendable loyalty to Zara.

At last, his glacial gaze finds my bristling frame and narrows.

My dragon senses this silent confrontation and roars his defiance. A spark of fire flares in Zephyr's commanding stare.

I am no telepath and neither is he. But, in that moment, that Dark Fae leans forward with a sudden fierce focus. A silent message hums between us like an electrical current.

This dragonrider king is… challenging me.

He is challenging my dragon.

My beast spreads his wings and all but splits my skin. If he rises now, this upstart will roast.

"Sucks to be Seelie, I guess, huh?" my Zara says. Her tone is casual, but she twists in her seat to give me a thoughtful look. Clearly she is sensing my turmoil through our mating bond.

Zephyr draws his slim knees to his chest and perches his chin. "'Tis worth stating that the ancient war between our Faerie races is over. That period is, as they say, history." A small secret smile curls his lips. "These days, we Unseelie quite like our Seelie kin."

Now, surprisingly, it is Mallory McSnicker who snorts. "Doesn't sound like the Seelie return the favor, mister. Maybe they're not that quick to forgive?"

"Oh, that depends on the Seelie." Zephyr looks like a cat licking cream from his whiskers. I know this is because Zephyr and Ash, the Seelie Prince he abducted, are lovers.

Mallory whispers something under her breath that even I, with my shifter senses, cannot catch. No doubt this is because I am distracted by another powerful whiff of Zara's delicious scent as my sovereign shifts in her seat.

She too is thinking about Ash and Zephyr.

And her thoughts, all too plainly, are arousing.

"The Exile was clearly an ordeal for both Faerie races," Lucius says in a guttural voice. He too is affected by our queen's arousal, but he is determined not to show it. "My question for you, Your Radiance, is a simple one. Now that the portal between your world and ours lies open once more, what comes next for the Dark Fae?"

Zephyr wraps his arms around his updrawn legs and pulls in a slow breath. Truly, he lectures like no other professor—visiting or otherwise—that I have ever seen.

"Some say this new era will herald our return. 'Tis why the scholars are calling this time, under my reign, our Renaissance." Zephyr's cold face turns toward Zara and darkens with a brooding intensity. "But that will depend on my queen."

As if on cue, the deep gong of the church bell resonates through the ancient walls.

All around me, chairs scrape and pages rustle as my classmates snatch their belongings and rush eagerly to their feet.

"Don't forget to stop by the student commons before next period." Lucius raises his voice to be heard above the clamor. "Final examination announcements from the Dean are now posted."

"Oh, fuck," Zara mutters, scooping up her backpack and shoving to her feet. "Guess that's where I'm headed."

Already Ronin looms at her side, with his back turned pointedly to Zephyr. My mate's tawny face is set in a thunderous scowl and his topaz eyes are murderous.

Needless to say, I plant myself to stand shoulder to shoulder beside him.

Still, I keep a wary eye trained on the Dark Fae, who is conversing with an intrigued-looking Lucius near the podium, but whose assessing gaze is narrowed on *us*.

Clearly, for the moment, my rival male must wait.

Now that Zara's own rival for the witching world throne has come to the Icarus Academy to challenge her, the student commons is where we will find Cleopatra Aquarius.

# Chapter Seventeen
## Zara

"I feel like I'm gonna hurl," I mutter.

I know, I know. That's the kinda TMI my guys probably don't need right now.

But it's how I fucking feel. I'm standing in the doorway of the deconsecrated church that's our student commons, with Ronin and Max looming protectively at my shoulder, all of us staring at a wall of turned backs. A bunch of my classmates huddle intently around the old-fashioned bulletin board in a spill of colorful sunlight under an arch of stained-glass window.

Fuck.

"If you are queasy," Max says hopefully, "could that mean you are pregnant?"

Ronin snorts with laughter and gives Max a friendly nudge. "Bollocks, that's like a comic obsession with you, love. Whenever Zara's got a pea in the pod, pretty sure she'll not tell us in the commons."

Max says with heat, "It is easy for you to joke—"

"Cheese on toast, will the two of you knock it off. I'm not pregnant." I divide an exasperated look between them.

Ronin's still snickering, topaz eyes alight with mischief. But, shit, Max looks crushed. The big guy's been all hangdog, head droopy and shoulders slumped, ever since Lucius came down on him in class like a dropped anvil.

School is hard for my dragon.

This mating rut is hard on him.

And me being all cagey and skittish about popping out little Zaras (which, like, the world probably doesn't need more of right now, just one of me seems like enough to handle) is the hardest.

For Max's sake, I make a real effort to soften my tone. "I'm queasy because I'm nervous about our finals, okay?"

Apparently for good reason.

Ronin's wicked smirk vanishes. Max growls low and deep in his chest.

When my guys finally fall silent, I hone in on the echoey specifics of my classmates' speculative murmurs, bouncing off the stone walls and marble floors, from halfway across the commons.

"*Mon Dieu*, I thought it was lost for good! That artifact has not been seen since, when, the last Witching World War…?"

"Guess that rules me out from a shot at the Dean's List, mates. Counting on those finals to boost my marks, wasn't I? With a challenge like that, be lucky if I don't fail outright and have the whole year be a do-over. Me mum won't be happy."

The unhappy mumbles of Mallory's Villa Hadrian housemates (who are the Icarus equivalent of Hufflepuffs and mostly harmless) are drowned out by a spiteful rill of laughter from one of those Villa Tiberius bitches in the Aquarius clique.

They're the opposite of harmless.

"Well, well, witches. *Someone*'s been polishing the Dean's apple. Looks like Deanie's playing favorites in the succession scrimmage after all."

Those ominous words finally unlock my frozen muscles and unstick my saddle shoes, which feel glued to the cathedral floor (a form of common magic I wouldn't put past those Tiberius witches, except no one's noticed me standing here yet).

I tilt my chin and swank into the church like I'm Vasili and I own the place because one, appearances matter, and two, I've already confirmed Cleo's a no-show. My ex-BFF likes to sleep in and probably won't show her celebrity face till noon, after she's caffeinated. If she's feeling splurgy, she'll allow herself the caloric indulgence of an organic açaí yogurt smoothie (the exact thing I used to blender for her the morning after a wild night of clubbing or a big heist) and then not eat again all day. That way, she doesn't risk her famous figure or her ability to walk the runway next Paris Fashion Week.

I wonder how that whole supermodel It Girl thing she's rocking in

New York and Milan and Paris is even gonna work if she's also queening it here in the witching world?

Not that I'll give her that chance.

My guys fall in behind me and we saunter through the commons, past clusters of arranged couches and a row of study carrells where the confessionals used to be. Our footfalls echo off the soaring walls.

Disturbed by our passage, an explosion of pale feathers erupts from a vacant carrell with a violence that jams my heart against my sternum. My pulse hammers in my throat as a dove flutters wildly past, so close a wing brushes my hair.

The bird streaks into the shadows of the church's vaulted ceiling and settles safely on a high beam.

Max growls after the poor dove with his dragon eyes flaming. Ronin rests a steadying hand against my lower back.

"Easy, loves," my Brit murmurs. "You're both torqued so tight you're making *me* twitchy."

Super aware of all those Tiberius eyes watching me for any sign of weakness, I give a hard nod and pick up the pace.

To camouflage my nerves and project the proper attitude, I sway my ass with Gemini sass.

That shit works, because the wall of students parts before me like the Red Sea before Moses (mostly). Except for that trio of Tiberius bitches, who eye me and my guys with mocking grins they wouldn't have dared a day ago, before I got my supposed comeuppance on live TV.

I especially don't like the sleazy speculation in the way their stares slide over Max and Ronin. I mean, sure, Ronin was Mr. One and Done till I came along and he's pretty much shagged everyone at this Academy. The whole school (all genders) knows what he's got under the hood.

But Max's unique peen got a closeup below the fold in his debut press appearance. So thanks for that, *Witching Inquisitor*.

"Oh, look," one of the witches says brightly, eyeing Max's junk in a way that makes me want to punch her in the face. "It's Captain Hook."

"Did you see his *scars*? His whole back is gross." The queen bee (as in bitch) flashes her pearly whites in a grin that's pure poison. "No wonder he won't take his shirt off at the beach."

Max is self-conscious as fuck about those scars. Plus he's an abuse survivor and he doesn't deserve this shit.

I suck in my breath to roast the bitch.

"You lot had best sod off, unless you fancy a row." Ronin shoves up beside me and flashes the mean girls his own ugly grin. "Max is a bloke you'll not like when he's pissed. And Zara's still the baddest bitch on this rock, isn't she?"

"Thanks, Adam. But I can take out my own trash. Right, Scarlet?" I lock onto the HBIC of the bunch, she's clan Scorpio and some kinda distant cousin of Vasili's, though she's way beneath the Goblin King's notice.

"It's *Skyler*, you mingey cunt." The brunette Barbie tosses her moussed-up mane and gives me a sulky pout. "This time, even Deanie's turned against you. Looks like you'll finally get what's coming to you."

That's a level of aggression I don't usually get around here, I mean, not since I survived Purgatory my first quarter and claimed my power.

Looks like I might actually have to assert myself to defend my terrain.

Dean or no Dean.

"That is a vile insult to my queen and sovereign. She is not mingey. Her cunt is very bare. And she is glorious." Bristling with violence (and clearly taking that whole hairy pussy slur super literally), Max does the asserting for me and pushes up beside me.

That shit takes courage when I know he's still shriveling up inside from shame over the whole world seeing his poor scarred back.

*Easy there, big guy. Let me handle this, okay?* I send the silent reassurance through our mating bond to hold him in check. He's all rutty and protective, so it's hard for him.

His dragon grumbles at me, but at least he listens.

Because, clearly, I gotta nip this bitchy Aquarius attitude in the bud myself.

"That'll be you giving it to me, will you, Scarlet?" I snap my glittery fingers at the other girl in a crackle of violet sparks.

I won't summon actual lightning in the building, but my little lightning's a problem these Tiberius bitches have learned to respect. Fear flickers in this one's surly stare.

"You're a slutty little nobody. A trashy casino whore—just like your trashy mother!" Skyler flounces out of my way and cedes the bulletin board with a huff. "Read it and weep, Gemini."

Under normal circumstances, to pay back that insult to my mom and especially because she made Max feel bad, I'd do a whole lot more to assert my dominance.

But I'm not actually a bully (unlike half the guys in my harem).

Anyway, I've finally got access to the bulletin board. Which was the whole point of coming over here in the first place.

"Thanks for nothing, witch." I swagger up to the curling parchment tacked to the corkboard. The official-looking paper is blazoned with the handsome cobalt-and-gold Academy crest and the Dean's scrolling script.

"Icarus Academy Final Examination: Dean's Challenge," Ronin reads aloud for Max's benefit, since our dragon's guarding my back and scowling possessively at the bystanders. "Retrieve the Horn of Ceres from its watery shrine."

"Horn of Sarees?" I repeat phonetically to get the pronunciation down. "What the fuck's that?"

"The Horn of Ceres is a mythical treasure." Max looms suddenly over my shoulder, his Slavic face sharp and slitted pupils blown wide with interest. Any sort of treasure fascinates the guy, it's a dragon thing. "Ceres was the Roman goddess of agriculture, childbirth, and fertility. The Horn is the symbol of her power, yes?"

"A fucking *horn*? Like, a cow horn?" For me, this factoid does not compute.

Maybe it's because that F word Max just dropped goes off in my head like a hand grenade.

*Fertility.*

"It is, how do you say, a… cornucopia?" Max produces the word triumphantly, because his labored English has been getting so much better.

"Look at you then." Ronin gives him an impressed-sounding murmur and an admiring look. He's generous like that with Max. "That's a ten-pence word, that is."

My dragon looks happy at the praise, which he totally deserves, because he tries really hard, even when his grades don't show it.

But I'm fixated on that shit he just said.

"So it's a horn of plenty?" I press.

"Erm, sort of. Magical artifact." Ronin wraps a possessive arm around my waist and nuzzles Max's ear. "Vasili mentioned it once. Learnt about it in Senior Seminar."

"Oh, great. Bet it's a fertility object, right?" I snort. "Since Ceres is a fertility goddess. With a thing like that at large, maybe *that's* why half the island's pregnant."

Meaning maybe it isn't me and my queenly magic after all that's sabotaging my classmates' BC and knocking everyone up.

I honestly don't know how to feel about that.

"Supposed to be locked in the Academy Vault, though, innit?" Ronin's arm tightens around me. "Bet that's where it's been till now. Guess that watery shrine bit's the challenge. Got to be underwater somewhere round the island, hasn't it?"

"And Cleo's a sea dragon." I sigh. Now I get what that bitch Skyler meant about the Dean taking sides. "Groovy. Now even the Dean's turned against me."

"No, she hasn't." Neo pops up like a helpful genie at my side, with his uniform tidy and his purple curls mussed and his big eyes all earnest behind his specs. "I know she's kinda distant, but she's always been fair. There's always more to these challenges than the obvious." He hesitates. "Still, something's up with the Dean, that's for sure."

My guys both welcome him with possessive scenting (Max) and a hard hug (Ronin) while I snuggle up for a bookworm kiss from his soft warm lips.

"Hmmm." I sigh into his kiss. "What's up with the Dean, baby?"

Neo surfaces from our cuddles and kisses and straightens his glasses.

"She just missed our Honors Alchemy class and sent Mistress Aggie to sub instead. Even though Aggie's an awful alchemist." Now my fated mate looks apologetic for throwing shade at our prof. "Aggie couldn't really manage our final review sesh. So she gave us a bonus lesson on Witchcraft in the Kitchen instead. We made floating brownies."

"Brownies?" Max (who's always hungry and probably wants his elevenses by now) gives a rumble of interest and looks hopeful. Neo grins tolerantly at him and roots around for one in his backpack.

But I'm focused on the other thing Neo just said.

"The Dean's still sick? That's not good." I frown.

Sure, she's like a million years old and a total recluse, but she's been a source of stability and a firm hand on the tiller here for a really long time. I'm pretty sure her being a no-show on the yacht last night is one of the reasons that whole shitshow went down.

"According to Aggie, the Dean's got company." Neo lowers his voice and glances around. Most of the students have scattered for class by now, but that Tiberius clique is lurking near the coffee station and watching us like lions stalking a watering hole.

"I, uh, think it's Vasili's dad," Neo whispers. "Holed up with the Dean right now."

My mouth falls open. "Shut. The fuck. Up. Nikolai Romanov is *here*?"

Ronin bites out a vicious curse.

Because he knows how the intel on this close encounter—even if Vasili's dad doesn't seek V out, maybe especially if he doesn't—is gonna fuck with our snake's head.

Silently I add the challenge of Vasili, already hating on Zephyr and now getting all emo and pissy over his estranged asshole dad, to our growing list of problems.

Caught in mid-brownie and cupping his treat in both hands so it doesn't float away, Max's slitted eyes turn narrow and crafty, the way only a dragon's can. "Nikolai Romanov is the director of the AIB. And that man is always working. Why would he come to Icarus now?"

The AIB is like the witching world equivalent of the FBI.

So I get why Max is asking.

"We bloody well know the bastard's not here for Vasili." Ronin jams his hands in his trouser pockets and starts to pace. "Think it's about this succession cockup?"

"What else?" I give the bulletin board a gloomy look. "Listen, we gotta focus on these finals. We gotta. They start tomorrow. Like, how are the mechanics even supposed to work? If there's only one prize and forty-some students?"

Neo nudges his glasses up his nose and gives me a serious look. "It's a group assignment. We work in teams. Final exams are designed to synthesize everything we've learned over the semester and probe the power and limits of our witchcraft. We're supposed to build teams that capitalize on each other's strengths and compensate for each other's weaknesses."

"We do the test as a team?" On the one hand, that makes me feel way better, because obvi my warlocks and my court and me, we're the bomb. We're the BFD on campus.

On the other hand, this Academy can be lethal.

If the Dean really is throwing her weight behind Cleo, my guys and Dez and RT could be in actual danger.

Just for teaming with me.

"Bugger me." Alerted by my telepathic leakage, Ronin swings toward me and levels a warning finger at my chest. "Don't even think about trying to ghost us and pop off alone on the sly after that artifact. We're a proper team, love."

"Well, except for Lucius." Neo's picking up my thoughts too, because fated mate. Now he too is starting to look and feel worried. "He has to proctor the test, so he'll have to be neutral. And Vasili's a graduating senior, so he's not allowed to intervene. He'll do qualifying exams this summer instead."

Welp, there go my two strongest warlock allies.

Plus Max has performance anxiety and gets all up in his head over any kind of academic test.

Except I'm not gonna say that out loud.

And I'm definitely not gonna bring up the wild card.

Zephyr.

He's not even a student here. Him getting involved at all would be against the rules. I'm pretty sure accepting outside help of any kind would be considered cheating. We'd all get disqualified and fail the test.

Now I just need to explain that to Zephyr.

I level a look at all three of them—Ronin, Max, and Neo. "Guess it's the four of us then. Plus Dez and Racetrack. We'll kick ass and take prisoners. And Lucius will make sure no one cheats. Right?"

Maybe it won't matter that much if the Goblin King sits this one out. Maybe it'll give him the space he needs to work through all the shit his dad's drive-by visit is sure to dredge up.

While I'm trying to convince myself on this front, and trying to convince myself that Zephyr will wait patiently like a model citizen on the sidelines while we're all testing and not cause problems (like trying to kidnap me again), Neo frowns at the bulletin board. He's reading the fine print—the exam instructions.

"This is more than a race," our bookworm says softly. "It's a mortal combat."

"What's that then, love?" Ronin saunters over to hover at his shoulder and slides an arm around our bookworm's waist.

Neo snuggles into him with a pensive sigh. "What I mean is, to ace the test, we need to be more than the first team to find the Horn of Ceres. We also need to be the team that fights off the other competitors—who can get kinda violent—and the team that returns the artifact safely back to the Academy Vault where it belongs."

Except maybe that Horn doesn't belong in the Vault at all anymore. I mean, it's a fertility object, right? And the witching world needs witches.

But I figure I'll keep that sedition shit to myself for now.

At least till I kick Cleo's ass.

Besides, I can't just go around collecting magical artifacts. I'm already toting the witching world crown around in my backpack because I'm afraid to leave it behind at the *domus* with my thievish ex-bestie at large.

I slice a hard look across the commons at the Tiberius clique. They're all #TeamAquarius, natch, I bet they'll *all* compete with Cleo. They're badass witches in their own right. Plus they're the biggest residential college at Icarus, like three times our size, because Lucius is really finicky about who he lets into our *domus*.

Which gives Cleo all kinds of advantages.

Max follows my gaze and the direction of my thoughts and scowls at our rival house. "They will be the favorites, will they not?"

"Yeah, pretty much." To project a degree of confidence I'm definitely not feeling, I force a stiff shrug and summon up my queen voice. "Guess the witching world betting pool at the Double Gem in Vegas is gonna go wild over this one. We're definitely the underdogs."

"Same as always," Ronin mutters dourly. "Bollocks."

# Chapter Eighteen
## Lucius

I unlock the door with a whispered word and slip into my office in the crypt with an audible sigh of relief.

Between the looming threat of this Academy's frequently lethal examinations and the ongoing angst of the succession struggle, there's so much tension and youthful drama ricocheting through these halls that I'm experiencing a migraine.

With the aid of my wolfish senses, I pad through the darkness, moving gently to avoid jostling my aching skull. From memory, I skirt the ancient sarcophagus that holds the moldering bones of the headmaster who preceded me (mine being a post that comes with internment privileges as a job benefit). While my wolf whines in sympathy, I lower my briefcase to my desk and ease my rump into the creaking chair.

Hunching my shoulders protectively around my tender cranium, I clutch my temples with a heartfelt groan.

From the shadowy depths of the sofa directly before me, the sudden scrape and flare of a match nearly makes me leap from my skin.

I shoot to my feet with a snarl of alarm. My fangs punch down to fill my mouth.

Regrettably, my violent recoil creates a gust of air that blows out the fragile flame.

"There's no cause for alarm, Professor Aries." The voice that ripples through the darkness is very nearly Vasili's. A tenor like butterscotch silk strokes my senses, edged with the rolling R's and sibilant S's of the Russian tongue.

But Vasili, to my sustained annoyance, never addresses me as *Professor*.

"The devil there isn't," I growl through my fangs.

I'm crouching on my desk, palms lowered to grip the ancient wood, claws sprouting from my fingers. In short, I'm a breath away from leaping for the stranger's throat.

My office is protected with powerful wards this intruder has apparently disarmed with ease, so I already know he's a powerful warlock.

My nostrils flare to sniff the air.

His scent too is Vasili's, the dark spice of vetiver with an underlying note of birchwood. Clearly, this is why it failed to rouse my wolf.

As it happens, Vasili bent me over that same sofa yesterday and pounded into me so hard we overturned the lamp. Consequently, that sofa reeks of my alpha's essence (as well as mine).

With a soft sigh, the trespasser strikes another match.

He may smell like my alpha and sound like my alpha, but the ruthless face that appears above the dancing flame, as my tall intruder bends to light a candle, is older and harder. A smooth wing of mahogany hair, streaked with silver at the temples, falls over a craggy brow to frame eyes dark and potent as espresso, flecked with shimmering gold.

In the flickering candlelight, those eyes glimmer with secrets.

This man is easy on the eyes, if you like them older, and if you like the Mads Mikkelsen type. Still, he has none of his son's lethal prettiness and none of his flirtatious charm. Vasili must have inherited those traits from his mother.

We've never met, but the sudden swell of certainty about who this creature must be nearly shatters my skull.

Truly, this damnable complication is the very last thing we need.

"Nikolai Romanov," I say warily.

"In the flesh," he murmurs. "Rather unfortunately for you, Lucius Aries."

Down the back of my neck, my hackles ripple and rise with danger.

Inside my skin, my wolf mutters and paces.

Moving with care to avoid inflaming my migraine, I climb down from my desk (keeping its protective expanse between us, because I'd still like to lunge for his throat). I dip my tortured head with a courtesy I'm far from feeling.

Nikolai Romanov is the mighty prince of the Scorpio clan, one of the great witching families. Not to mention the fellow is also a trustee and patron of this Academy—all honors that demand my respect.

Then there's his day job.

As much as I'd like to, I can't simply eject this menacing newcomer from my office by the scruff of his neck like an erring student.

Far from it.

I clear my throat and light my desk lamp to banish the unholy ambience. The shadows creep back to the corner behind the sarcophagus. Nicolai Romanov emerges fully from the gloom.

He towers over my desk, tall and slim as the White Witch of Narnia in a conservative Brooks Brothers suit, features coldly composed above his crisp collar and perfectly knotted silk tie. The gleaming links of an old-fashioned pocket watch—a magical artifact that hums with enchantment—loop neatly from his breast pocket.

All perfectly civilized.

After all, this man is known for that.

Under his directorship, the vast and faceless bureaucracy of the witching world's notorious spy agency has become a reign of terror.

But he rarely bloodies his own hands.

"There's no need to lurk in my crypt like a vampire." I swallow down my misgivings and give this unwelcome arrival a wry look. "There's a perfectly habitable guest suite for visiting trustees in the Dean's Tower."

"Yes, I'm already occupying it," the man says briskly. His Russian accent is sharper than Vasili's, who's been immersed in my English-speaking *domus* for years. "The Dean and I have been in conference all morning."

This news is concerning, but I manage to conceal my unease. All too clearly, this visit is no casual drive-by. We've barely spoken, yet the master spy has already threatened me twice.

Now it appears the infernal fellow plans to stay on.

Probably, if I had to guess, we'll be stuck with him until Zara and Cleo compete in the Dean's Challenge. Until the royal succession is settled. Until the flame of rebellion sparking from Zara's incendiary defiance is quenched.

Dear God. How I dread his effect on Vasili.

My student-slash-colleague-slash-alpha is already dangerously disturbed over the unsettling arrival of the Dark Fae King. For Vasili, his estranged father's prolonged presence is enough to render him actively homicidal.

"I see." Swallowing a grimace, I gesture my unwelcome guest toward the sofa with a reluctant hand and settle warily back to my chair. "You should be aware these are my office hours, so various students are likely to turn up with tardy assignments and examination jitters at any time."

Ideally, they won't find me lying dead down here in a pool of my own blood. Murdered by the vengeful parent of the student I've ruined.

Even if my downfall would be considered a just fate.

The director of the AIB merely lifts a cold brow that disdains my concern.

My migraine pings in my temples. Deliberately, I unclench my jaw and summon a stiff smile that bares my still-extended canines.

"That said," I growl, guttural with warning, "how can I assist the mighty Arcane Investigative Bureau?"

"I'm not here on the AIB's behalf. Nor even as a trustee of the school." Nikolai Romanov folds his elegant frame onto my couch (thankfully, he seems to have no idea what level of depravity routinely occurs there) and steeples his fingers before his thoughtful face. "I'm here as a concerned parent."

I eye him with a skepticism I scarcely manage to conceal.

Indeed, it's all I can manage not to utter a rude snort.

You'd never know it to look at him, but this affluent spymaster began life as a penniless aristocrat. (When it comes to old blood, it takes one to know one). Nikolai made his millions, like other Russian oligarchs, in the rubble of the old Soviet empire. Everything he owns—his hotel in Monte Carlo, his *dacha* in the Crimea, his megayacht in the Seychelles, all his ill-gotten gains—this man has earned through the toil of his clever brain, the application of his ruthless instincts, and an utter lack of scruples.

"You're here about Vasili?" I wait for his nod, although I'm perfectly aware he has no other offspring.

"With all due respect, Mr. Romanov." My voice hardens. "If you ever intended to express concern for your son's welfare—or, God forbid, his happiness—that ship sailed into the sunset years ago. Since the day you booted him off your yacht and abandoned him on our doorstep for the so-called *sin* of being gay, Vasili has more than survived. He's thrived. That traumatized child you abandoned has matured into a formidable warlock with a blistering intellect and staggering powers."

Barely perceptible, those clever eyes narrow. "I'm very well aware of his strengths, Professor Aries—"

"I highly doubt that." In fact, I'd bet my grandsire's castle this man has no clue who his son is or what he's become.

But the man is a trustee. I'm merely the faculty, and mine is a position I cherish.

With considerable difficulty, I bite my tongue, order my wolf to subside, and will my wicked canines to retract.

Clearly discerning my silent war with my beast, Nikolai Romanov tilts his head. "At the least, Professor Aries, I'm reliably informed my son is the holy terror of this institution."

"You raised him to be a bully and so he is one," I say with deliberate lightness. In truth, his father raised him to be practically psychotic. "However, he's also a graduating senior and our adjunct professor of Mogadon Magics. Assuming he survives his qualifying exams this summer, Vasili will begin fall term as the youngest tenured professor in this Academy's storied history. So, as you see, there's no need to worry."

One corner of that ruthless mouth lifts in a chilly smile. "You're protective of him. Of course, I've been fully aware of the unusual nature of your… relations… with my son, even before *The Witching Inquisitor* published its distasteful exposé."

An uncomfortable heat climbs in my face.

Saints above, am I blushing?

Aware of the spymaster's keen gaze on my ruddy face, I busy myself unlocking my briefcase and extracting a sheaf of freshly penned essays on the Fae Sundering that are in urgent need of grading.

"Our relationship may be unconventional," I concede, addressing the essays, as my blush subsides, "but I'm still Vasili's headmaster, an arrangement fully sanctioned by the Dean. Academically speaking, I've no cause for complaint. He scarcely bothers to complete his homework, of course, but that's mainly because it bores him. I fully expect Vasili to excel at his quals."

"Ah, but my concerns are not academic in nature." Romanov

dispenses another small cold smile. The man may be posing as a concerned parent, but he's a cold fish—and a cunning spider.

Whatever he might claim, I seriously doubt Nikolai Romanov harbors a particle of genuine concern for his son's academic success or his moral welfare.

This man is spinning a web of lies.

Lies he intends to trap me.

Try though he might, I have no intention of being ensnared.

Clearly sensing my suspicion, the spymaster leans back on the couch in a posture of casual ease. (Merciful Christ, he's sitting precisely where his son first rimmed me and then railed me until my wolf nearly shredded the leather.) Nikolai crosses one deliberate ankle over his knee, flashing an inch of charcoal silk sock. His thoughtful fingers remain tented before his lips.

"I seem to have made a series of… errors in judgment… regarding my son," he says quietly. "Errors in judgment which are, for me, far from typical. In my own defense, the discovery of Vasili's homosexuality— and the *manner* of its discovery— came as a considerable shock and a public embarrassment. Rather than showing a flicker of sympathy for the appalling political dilemma he'd dumped in my lap, he rubbed my face in it with obnoxious glee."

"Well, that certainly sounds like Vasili," I murmur, hunting through my desk for a red pen.

*Like father, like son. He learned his utter lack of compassion from you.*

Romanov taps a pensive finger against his lips. "If I'd known then that he is capable of tolerating a woman in his bed—even experiencing passion for one, as he clearly does for the Gemini claimant—I would never have sent him away. You see, I harbored… certain plans… for his future."

I bristle at his turn of phrase.

Zara is no mere *claimant*.

The Senate voted her in, damn it, to succeed our childless current queen. A vote which has yet to be overturned. For that to occur, that timid constellation of nervous politicians—masterfully managed by Theo Mercury—will await the outcome of the Dean's Challenge.

To see if she survives.

If Zara wins, I'm certain, they won't budge. Neo's father will tell Cleopatra Aquarius to pound sand.

Only then will Zara's crown be safe.

But my feelings for Zara are an exposed flank I dare not reveal to the perceptive villain currently lurking in my crypt.

Besides, we're speaking of Vasili.

"I understand you planned to marry your son to Maxim Rasputin's rather odious sister. That would have been a disaster." I draw the stack of essays toward me in pointed hint. I'm in desperate need of a numbing potion for my migraine, but I don't dare reveal weakness before this spider with his envenomed bite—

Without any warning, my office door bursts violently open and slams into the stone wall, as though it's been smashed with a telekinetic hammer.

I startle and my talons shoot out. Nikolai Romanov twitches.

Abruptly Vasili's tall frame commands the doorway. "Lucius, I—"

His gaze lands on his father, who rises sharply to his feet.

Under the protective patina of his skillfully applied foundation, my most troublesome student goes white.

In an arrested silence that hums with tension, the two Romanovs eye each other across the width of my office. The distance between them yawns wider than the Great Rift Valley.

"Oh, dear fuck. It's *you*." Recovering swiftly, Vasili speaks first, with a brittle contempt that shreds any scrap of sentiment.

"*Privyet,* Vasya,*"* his father says quietly. "You're looking well."

"Don't you mean I'm looking *gay*?" My alpha gestures in an exaggerated way that encompasses his black-painted fingernails, his gilded shag of punk-rock hair, his trendy Duran Duran spin on the Academy uniform, and his tastefully applied cosmetics.

A muscle flexes in Nikolai Romanov's jaw. "Apparently not. Judging by the photographic evidence of you and that Gemini girl displayed on every newsstand in the witching world—"

"Well, darling, don't get your hopes up." Rudely Vasili cuts him off. "I assure you, I didn't suddenly wake up straight. I still adore a thick dick and a tight hole."

Now it's Nikolai's turn to whiten. (I sympathize.)

My breath hitches and my own hole clenches. My alpha shoots me a mischievous look.

"Vasili, er, Mr. Romanov," I say in a strangled voice. They both look alertly at me. "A bit more respect, if you please."

After all, it's *my* hole he's talking about. In front of his own father!

The spymaster rebounds swiftly. "I'm well aware of your eccentricities, Vasya…"

"Oh, never mind all that." Vasili strikes a pose in the doorway like a runway model and pouts. "Finding you lurking here in the crypt, *papachka*, is like living in a Shakespeare play. Only I can't quite decide whether you're trying to reprise the role of Macbeth's bloodthirsty wife or the ghost of Hamlet's father." Vasili smirks at me, but his smile is strained. "How tedious."

"Why are *you* here?" I ask Vasili pointedly. "You're supposed to be teaching Mogadon Magics this period. Is something the matter?" My gaze flickers toward Nikolai. "Ah, aside from the obvious?"

"Well, pet, since you ask." Every trace of my student's petty spite vanishes in a blink. Vasili's pretty face hardens to a mask of menace. "I tried reaching you telepathically, Lucius, but I couldn't—not through these horrid wards you insist upon in here." He pauses. "Take a numbing potion for that head first, *do*. You'll need it."

Of course he's familiar with my migraines, and he's sensing my pain through our mating bond.

In his own fierce way, he's protective of me.

Conceding to my alpha, I dip a hand under my desktop for the potion. But my beast is already crouching and baring his teeth in alarm. My palate tingles under the press of my fangs.

"After the potion, what then?" I growl, gruff with wolf.

Nikolai listens closely to our exchange, no doubt cataloging every nuance of our complex dynamic in his coldly analytical brain. But he too is poised on the razor's edge of violence.

"*Then* they need you—and your wolf—in the commons, darling," Vasili says briefly. "Zara and Cleo are fighting."

# Chapter Nineteen
## Zara

"Truly, Zara, you should have stayed away."

My ex-BFF is totally the villain in this situation.

Obviously.

Yet, somehow, as she stands there posing in the big arched doorway of the student commons—looking like she just stepped out of a Burberry ad in her plaid skirt and knee socks, with her Academy blazer hooked casually over one shoulder—and commanding every eye without effort like the celebrity she is, Cleo manages to make her sigh sound all put-upon and tragic.

"Well, that's a bummer. Sorry to disappoint?" Despite the nerves fizzing like seltzer in my gut and the heartbreak burning like ground glass in my chest, I plant a hand on my hip and whip up some Gemini sass. "Maybe the fate of the witching world is, like, more important than a little personal inconvenience. Just a thought."

Never mind that I'm standing awkwardly in the middle of the nave, exposed and conspicuous, right under the big oculus window with my heavy backpack slung over one shoulder.

Plus I'm all alone, natch.

That's because I made my warlocks (even Max, *especially* Max who's failing half his classes but still in rut and grumbly about leaving me), go wherever they're all supposed to be for second period.

Me?

*I'm* supposed to be up in the choir loft library for study hall, boning up on the Horn of Ceres and cramming for that freaking final.

Now it doesn't look like I'm gonna get that chance.

"Oh, Zara." My ex-BFF tosses the glossy rope of her merlot braid over one shoulder and gives me an exasperated look. "You could have fled. You could have hidden. You could even have supported me, which would save us all a great deal of trouble. But I told him you wouldn't."

My gaze flickers to Xiao.

My ex-fuck toy is lurking in the Gothic doorway at Cleo's heels like a pet poodle (same as always). So I assume he's the *him* she's talking about.

In his spiffy new Academy slacks and blazer, with his moussed-up black hair and his smoldery glare, he's the other half of that Burberry ad she's rocking.

Except his arm's in a sling (an apparent souvenir of his scuffle with Lucius' wolf). That's a good look on him.

Now his sulky expression makes me smirk. I pop my hip out and fold my arms across my chest.

"Lemme get this straight." I muse. "You two waltz into my birthday party without an invite, physically attack me *and* my warlocks, literally try to shoot me and knife Ronin, plan to steal *my* fucking crown on live TV, then expect me to just accept that shit and skulk off with my tail between my legs?"

I nail Cleo with my own version of the Romanov eyebrow. "Keep dreaming, Sunshine."

That's my old nickname for her (an ironic one, because she's all stormy and pouty, especially early in the a.m.) I'm actually kinda proud of myself for saying it without flinching.

My ex's long lashes fall over her violet eyes. Under a slick of nude lipstick from one of the high-end brands she pimps, her full lips tighten.

For a sec, I wonder if maybe being mortal enemies and vicious rivals for the same throne is as painful for her as it is for me.

Then her bony shoulders straighten. Her lashes lift and her eyes flash. Her gaze shoots straight to the backpack I'm schlepping.

The same backpack that holds the witching world crown V lifted right off her mom's head last night.

Her lips part with what looks like surprise.

Deliberately she saunters into the commons with her long-legged runway stride. Xiao slinks in after her like a jackal.

The heavy church door swings shut behind them with a thud.

*"Cavolo,"* Cleo murmurs. "I suppose we do this the hard way."

Sweet Jesus.

Do not even tell me that bitch is clairsentient.

I scramble to recall the Aquarius genetics from my Science of Witchcraft class and whether she's got Valyrian telepathy (as well as Dark Fae and, apparently, sea dragon shifter) in her witchy DNA.

At the same time, I ease away from the study carrels to give myself maneuvering space and scope out the commons to see who my allies are. I deliberately sent my guys away (because one, they have classes, and two, I don't need their hovery closeness setting off my superheat, that's literally the *last* thing we need right now). Dez is off with a grouchy RT in the clinic, getting the status of Racetrack's concussion checked.

Which means I'm pretty much alone in here except for a cluster of worried Hadrians, all friends of the absent Mallory, near the coffee nook.

Plus Skyler and her Villa Tiberius clique (who were leaving till Cleo showed up) just circled back to watch the show.

Cheese on toast.

Guess we're doing this now.

Anticipation tightens my chest and crackles along my skin. I narrow my gaze on my approaching ex-bestie, measure the cadence of her unhurried footfalls in the suddenly silent church, and hum in the back of my throat. The echoey rumble of the lightning voice lifts my hair from my shoulders and flutters my skirt against my thigh-highs.

"Don't touch her, Cleo," Skyler calls. "The bitch is electrified."

*"Grazie.* I'm well aware." With the dismissive flick of a manicured hand, Cleo gestures Xiao toward the spiral staircase that leads to the choir loft.

He peels right off to do her evil bidding, natch.

That move puts him between me and my power place. Maybe she knows if I'm gonna summon actual lightning, the best place to do that is up in the belfry.

Cleo angles her approach to keep herself between me and the door that opens on the big piazza outside the church, which is the other easy place I could summon from.

Plus she's still coming.

She's coming for my crown.

My heart beats in my throat and my skin tingles with anticipation.

Skyler and her minions have blocked the interior passage that leads to the classrooms in the rear cloister, so I'm pretty much trapped.

My only remaining escape route (if I needed one, which I don't) is the shadowy stairway that plunges through the floor into the crypt. That's where they keep the Academy Vault, which is supposed to be off limits to students.

More important, the crypt is where Lucius has his office. Given the time of day, he's probably down there now, doing office hours. Vasili has an office down there too, but he complains about the dismal aesthetics and hardly ever uses it.

Knowing at least one of my alphas is close if I need him clears my head and steadies my jitters.

Still, I wanna handle this shit on my own.

If I'm being totally honest, that's the real reason I sent my guys away. I need to prove my queenly mettle to all the doubters and the haters in the witching world.

Well, here's my chance.

I swing my backpack securely across my shoulders and drop my hands to my sides. Purple sparks arc between my fingers and dance across my knuckles.

"One warning's all you get," I tell my ex softly, with lightning humming in my throat.

Fuck. Despite everything she's done, I still don't wanna hurt her.

But it doesn't look like she's leaving me much choice.

She drops her blazer carelessly on a couch and keeps on coming. Across the narrowing space between us, her shimmering violet gaze locks with mine.

"Don't force my hand, *bella,*" she whispers in Italian—the love language for our *ménage*. My chest clenches with old grief. "Not while he's here. You're not the only one in this situation who is running short on choices, *si*?"

My brow furrows. I don't know what kinda game she thinks she's playing.

Xiao's vanished up the stairs to the choir loft, which is an issue. I wouldn't put it past my light-fingered ex-boyfriend to hoover up all the Horn of Ceres intel he can find up there, then vamoose with the books I need myself (which aren't supposed to leave the library) for our finals.

"You want my crown?" I say. The air around me turns lavender as psi fire spills from my eyes. "Then you're gonna have to take it."

*"Bene."* The bitch sighs like I'm breaking her heart. "Skyler."

From the corner of my eye, a dark object tumbles toward me through the air. I barely fling up an arm in time to deflect the heavy brass-bound book that's sailing toward me under the steam of Mogadon magic. Instead of hurtling into my head, the thing slams into my shoulder.

As the heavy book drops to the floor with a thud, a red wash of pain spreads through my deltoid region.

Fucking Scorpio telekinetics.

"Ow." I spear that witch Skyler with a murderous glare, because that's gonna leave a bruise. Worse, seeing that mark's gonna make my warlocks lose their minds. "Shit, Scarlet. You can't treat an old book like that."

Skyler tosses her long dark mane like she's filming a shampoo commercial and shoots me a triumphant look. "How do you plan to stop me, Gemini?"

Before I can answer, another heavy book flies out of a study carrel and hurtles toward me. I manage to duck-and-dive this one, because that shit hurts when it connects. My shoulder's still throbbing from the last hit.

A flicker of motion from the side tells me Cleo's circling around behind me while I'm distracted. Clearly she's got her eye on the prize.

The crown in my backpack.

With a mental apology for the ancient artifact, I swing my pack off my shoulders and sling it down the shadowy staircase into the crypt.

*Lucius,* I send through our mating bond, because keeping that crown safe from Cleo's grabby hands is way more important than my pride. *Delivery for you on the stairs.*

I wait for the familiar solid warmth of my alpha's bond to lock into place.

But, alarmingly, there's nothing. Takes me a sec to remember those magical wards around his office—

Something slams into the back of my head like a kettlebell. The impact sends me staggering and almost knocks me down. I fling out a hand wildly to grab the rail and barely manage to avoid tumbling down the long stone stair (which would leave me with way more damage than a few bruises).

Fuck. Another flying book. I didn't even see that one coming.

Pain pours through my battered scalp. A trickle of heat spills down the back of my neck. My vision is fuzzy and it feels like I'm bleeding.

Dizzy, I spin around to put my back to the stairs, because protecting that crown's the hill I'll die on.

The steaming pot from the coffee nook whizzes toward me, with ribbons of scalding coffee streaming in its wake. Still woozy, I swear and lurch out of the way, tucking my aching body into a clumsy somersault that makes my bruised shoulder scream in protest.

Droplets of boiling coffee splatter painfully across one hand and my bare leg as the object sails over me.

But I manage to avoid the worst. Like third degree burns.

I come up snarling and slam both fists into the floor. A purple crackle of electricity spreads outward in all directions from my crouching form. My little lightning takes the poor Hadrians down like ninepins (ugh) but also knocks Skyler's besties off their feet. (Bullseye.)

But not Skyler, who scrambles onto a nearby table in a flurry of plaid skirts and swirling hair to avoid getting juiced by the voltage. Without her hand on the helm (so to speak), the flying coffeepot plummets to the floor and shatters.

I also miss Cleo. That's because my ex-BFF springs like an Avenger, a good eight feet in the air, to land with inhuman grace on top of a study carrel.

"What the fuck?" I yelp, peering up at her.

She's always been graceful (because supermodel), but that was some Zephyr-like agility. She scrambles nimbly toward me across the row of little peaked roofs like Scarlett Johannsen in that *Black Widow* flick. I'm starting to believe my ex really is half-Fae, so maybe Messalina wasn't lying about that piece of her history.

And speaking of Zephyr…

*Hey, guys?* I decide to adjust my solo strategy and broadcast to my warlocks on all psychic channels. *I, uh, think I fucked up. I could maybe use a little backup in the commons.*

Again with the nothing.

Shit.

Either Cleo or Xiao must still be carrying that nullifying object. Which means I really am on my own. We really gotta get that item off the gameboard.

I dash to the head of the crypt stairs to cut off my ex-bestie and stay between her and my crown, lying somewhere in the darkness below. Then I scowl up at her, balanced effortlessly on the peaked roof of a study carrel like the supervillain she apparently is.

"You're not getting past me, Sunshine." Even though I'm bruised and bleeding, I crank up the bravado. "I'm not even breaking a sweat down here. But you keep this shit up and someone's gonna get hurt."

Skyler's venomous voice snakes toward me from the side. "We're not trying to get past you, cunt. We're going to slice right *through* you."

A shower of glass shards from the shattered coffee pot lifts from the floor and knifes through the air—straight toward me. That Scorpio precision Skyler's rocking with her telekinesis is deadly. Which means I gotta stop holding back. If I'm not picky about the collateral damage, I could summon a bolt of lightning right through the oculus window.

But if I do that, I'll kill her.

Besides, Skyler's smart enough to attack me from right in the middle of that huddle of spell-stunned Hadrian kids, all still in varying degrees of incapacitation and struggling to get back on their feet.

Nope.

Not doing that.

My lightning's caused enough of a body count.

Fortunately, I have other tricks up my Academy uniform sleeve.

I wait till that incoming broadside of jagged glass is too close for Skyler to redirect. Then I launch into the air like Tinkerbell, let the glass slice past beneath me, and zip straight toward Cleo with murder in my heart.

I'm getting better at this levitation shit. She's got about two seconds max to get her arms up in self-defense before I slam into her and sweep her off her feet. We crash into the ancient stone wall behind her, with Cleo taking the brunt of the hit. Her sleek merlot head smacks into the wall with a good solid thunk.

Not gonna lie. That thud of impact feels satisfying as fuck.

At least I won't be the only one walking away from this catfight with bruises.

"Knock it off," I hiss into her stunned face. "Or I'm gonna stop playing nice."

I've barely found my footing on the sloping carrel roof, gripping her shoulders to hold both of us upright, before she twists free of my hold.

Her knees bend, her torso drops, and her shoulder shoves into my diaphragm hard enough to spill my breath and shift my balance.

What the fuck. That's a combat move. A skill I never even knew she had.

All too clearly, I never really knew her.

At all.

Still locked together, the two of us stagger on the tricky footing across the carrels. I'm dizzy from getting conked on the noggin by Skyler, and the familiar perfume of Turkish rose and ylang-ylang rising from Cleo's skin and hair makes it worse. Mindful of the nasty drop behind me, I wrap a hand around my ex's flying braid and twist, hard enough to make her cry out.

She retaliates by sucker-punching me—right in the throat.

Lucky for me the angle's bad and her aim is off, but that punch is plenty strong enough to bruise my voice box (which is where the lightning voice lives. If I can't talk, I can't summon.) I cough and gasp and my eyes water, but I manage to keep my grip on her braid and deliver a left hook to her famous face that stings my burned knuckles but wrings a good Italian curse out of my nemesis.

Blood trickles from her cut lip. The bitch claws for my eyes. I sweep her hand away, follow up with a jab that bloodies her nose, and pull her braid till she screams in pain and fury.

We're still grappling when the monumental crash of shattering glass rips through the church.

Cleo and I spin in unison toward the oculus window as the huge circle of stained glass explodes inward around the spiked head and extended forelegs of a massive green dragon.

With a deafening bellow of rage, Xhevith soars through a spray of colorful glass into the church with wings tucked tight against his scaly body and a lithe green-haired figure clinging to his back.

Suddenly, the student commons is full of angry dragon.

With a powerful backwing that sends chairs flying and dazed students scrambling in all directions, Xhev settles to a landing amid the wreckage in a crunch of shattered glass.

Shit. What a mess.

I'm gonna end up in detention again over all this, I just know it. Even though it's totally not my fault.

Xhevith's long neck twists toward Cleo and me, both momentarily frozen on the carrel and gaping. His golden eyes slit at Cleo and his muzzle peels back in a menacing snarl that bares every one of his pointy teeth.

"By the moon," Zephyr says coldly into the sudden silence from his lordly perch in the dragon saddle. "This rancid creature who stinks of roses and fear is, I presume, the usurper."

That's one point for him and his apparently discerning nose.

Cleo stands so still beside me, I don't even think she's breathing. Blood drips from her nose to splatter her crisp white blouse.

I clear my bruised throat, blink the tears from my eyes, and croak in a raspy voice, "Yep."

Clearly picking up my pain even though he's no telepath, Zephyr's single green eye narrows in a way that's fucking terrifying. (The eyepatch adds to the overall effect.)

His lips curl in a feral smile. "Shall I end her pathetic life for you, my queen, and give you her head as a bridal gift?"

A soft spill of breath from Cleo's parted lips, too quiet for anyone else to hear, is kinda gratifying.

Even with all the unresolved shit lurking between the Dark Fae King and me, plus another aggravating reference to our supposed nuptials, I gotta admit I'm not too unhappy to see him. My Unseelie has never looked more impressive than he does right now astride the menace of his snarling dragon, with one hand wrapped around the reins in casual command and plenty of fang showing in his bloodthirsty grin.

He's a vicious little savage, but he's mine.

He really is.

Still, he probably shouldn't make a habit out of gifting me with the severed heads of our enemies. (Granted, this is only the second one, but clearly there's a pattern emerging here.)

I'm about to say so when a calm voice with a Russian accent intervenes. "That's certainly one option, Your Moon-Dazzled Radiance. But if you have any care at all for the health of your queen's harem, I'd advise against it."

I wrap Cleo's braid a little tighter around my fist to keep her tethered and in check (because I've had enough of her shit today, for real). Then I crane to see past Xhevith's big obstructive body.

What I find down there jams my heart all the way into my battered throat.

Standing at the head of the crypt stairs looms a tall aristocratic guy with a tailored suit and a ruthless face who looks like a cross between Mads Mikkelsen in *Casino Royale* and a conservative Wall Street broker version of Vasili. In one hand, the stranger's gripping my backpack with the crown. Which sucks, but right now it's a minor issue.

The major issue is his other arm, wrapped tight around a stiffly immobile Lucius.

This new guy's holding a wicked stiletto jammed right up against Lucius' throat.

# Chapter Twenty
## Vasili

My hands are cold with terror.

But my vision is red with rage.

As I stand—spellbound and sidelined—in the blackness of the crypt, while my abominable father upstairs threatens to destroy everything I love, it occurs to me I've been waiting years for some obliging person to come along and kill him.

Now, with toxic fear for Lucius spreading through my paralyzed limbs like poison, I resolve on a bone-deep level that today will be everyone's lucky day.

No more waiting around for someone else to step up and do the deed.

It will be my absolute delight to kill my own father.

As soon as I manage to wrench free of this reprehensible Compulsion spell.

That spell of his froze me, like an insect in amber, at the foot of the crypt stairs the instant my wretched sire dropped a charmed amulet around my neck and whispered my full name in my ear.

Unable to move or speak, I watched the bastard slink silently up the stairs after an unsuspecting Lucius with his horrid stiletto in hand and black rage filling my murderous heart.

*"Lucius."* Zara's horrified voice drifts down the stairs where I stand, helpless and fuming in the dark.

Hearing the terror in my darling's voice, I clench my casting hand in a fist of rage. This much movement I can still barely manage—but to zero effect.

My powerful telekinesis lies dormant under the spell.

Why on earth did I allow myself to be distracted, even for a heartbeat, by the Shakespearean drama unfolding between Zara and Cleo up there?

A heartbeat was all the opportunity Nikolai Romanov needed to destroy all our lives.

"I'm afraid you oblige me to issue a warning, Mr. Romanov." Lucius' controlled tone echoes down the stairs. From this vantage, I can barely see him, standing with his back to me, with my father lurking behind him like the trained assassin he is.

Still, somehow, despite the knife pressed to his throat, my headmaster manages to sound like he's chiding a misbehaving student.

"Threatening a faculty member is a violation of the Academy Codex," Lucius warns my father sternly.

Despite the drumbeat of terror for my lover roaring in my ears and the adrenaline rush of violence pounding through every vein, I quiver with a sudden, wildly inappropriate urge to laugh.

Leave it to Lucius to cite the Academy Codex while someone's holding a damn knife to his throat.

"Well, mister, you certainly got my attention," Zara drawls, deceptively casual, at my odious parent. I can't see my little queen from down here, but lightning lurks in her voice. "And given the mood I'm in? My attention might not be what you want, Le Chiffre."

I need a moment to place the cultural reference. When the memory slots into place, a snort slips past my grimly set lips. Zara's just compared my vicious bloodthirsty prick of a father to the poker-playing James Bond villain in *Casino Royale*.

"What I want is actually quite simple," my father says calmly. (He never laughs, so humor is wasted on him.) "Release Ms. Ferrari now, and I'll let your wolf live. Threaten her life or mine and the wolf dies."

My brief flicker of levity is swept away and obliterated in a thundering avalanche of rage.

He's threatening my Lucius.

Triggering every alpha instinct I possess.

My casting hand trembles, but I can't summon. My heels rise from the floor, but I can't levitate.

*Fuck.*

"Well, here's the thing." Zara still sounds casual, and I can't read her telepathically, not with that wretched nullifying object obviously still in play.

But I know her.

I know seeing Lucius in danger makes her murderous. To protect any one of our warlocks or anyone else she loves, Zara Gemini is more than capable of manslaughter.

"I can't really trust you," she says to my father (quite accurately), "or anyone else in Messalina's gang. I mean, like, that ship sailed when that shit went down on the yacht, you feel me? The way I see it, you putting that knife away's gonna be your best shot—pretty much your only shot—at walking outta this joint in one piece."

Now the Aquarius bitch with her faux Eurotrash accent, whom I also can't see from down here, tosses in her two kopecks. "For pity's sake, Zara, don't be a fool! Threatening him of all men, it's the worst move you can make." She pauses. "Surely you must know who he is, yes?"

"Yeah, sure. He looks like the Goblin King. I'm guessing he's Nikolai Romanov, the AIB guy, right?" I visualize my sassy darling's delicious shrug. "Yay for you. Guess that puts the spy service in your corner."

Of course, my queen sounds completely unimpressed. I bare my teeth in a malicious grin I'm certain must look homicidal.

Too bad there's no one else down here in the dungeon with me to appreciate the effect.

Cleo Ferrari might be a household name. But, clearly, she doesn't know how to read the room.

"*Cavolo!* You still don't see it, do you, *bella*?" the bitch exclaims. "I *am* the AIB. He's my mentor—"

"Yeah, that's enough outta you, Sunshine. No one asked you to talk." Whatever Zara does next wrings a yelp out of that Aquarius bitch.

Sounds like a hair pull to me.

The sound of that brief violent scuffle makes me tense. I strain against the spell that holds me until I nearly burst a blood vessel.

But it's useless.

I can move enough to breathe, but I can't cast or levitate. Clearly, this amulet is bespelled against all forms of Mogadon magic.

Above me on the stairs, watching the encounter unfold, Lucius and my father both go rigid. But Nikolai Romanov is famous (or infamous) for having nerves of steel and a cool head in a crisis.

"Shift and I'll slit your throat," my father mutters in Lucius' ear, so quiet I can barely hear. "I'm already tempted, Professor Aries. Of all the students in your care, how dare you seduce *my son*?"

*Oh, for fuck's sake.* I barely swallow a groan of disgust. *I'm the one who seduced Lucius, you homophobic idiot.*

Lucius, of course, feels responsible for ruining me. Even with his back to me, I've seen the expression so often I can visualize the guilt written all over his agonized face.

"I won't shift unless you threaten her," Lucius says roughly, with a wolfish growl he can't subdue. "Or Vasili."

Clearly, he's realized I've been taken (momentarily) off the board. Still, I don't like that knife pressed to his throat.

Truly, I won't abide the danger to him much longer. The alpha in me won't tolerate it. My father might have temporarily contained my Mogadon witchcraft, but there's at least one magical card I still have to play.

Another cry from Cleo rings out.

Zephyr's dragon, who was previously silent (for a dragon), rumbles out a brassy warning.

Dear fuck, I'll just have to trust that Dark Fae (eight words I never thought I'd say) to hold that feral beast of his in check until Lucius is free.

My father twitches at the rumble and Lucius gasps. The faint metallic tang of spilled blood hits my enhanced senses like a freight train.

Sweet fuck. My father's infamously steady hand must have slipped.

Only the fact that Lucius is still standing, and not in visible physical distress, keeps me from losing my homicidal shit.

But I swear to myself Nikolai Romanov will regret every drop of precious blood he's just spilled.

Even if he spilled it by accident.

"Okay." Zara sounds a bit breathless from whatever futile struggle she's clearly just subdued. But bless her witchy heart, she's hard as nails when she needs to be. "Sorry about the hair loss there, Sunshine. Now we got *that* outta the way, here's how this is gonna go down. You listening, Le Chiffre?"

"If you're referring to *me*, Ms. Gemini," my father says, sounding testy, because he seems to feel protective over that Aquarius bitch and besides, Zara can get under anyone's skin, "I'm addressed as Director Romanov. Now I'd advise you to release Ms. Ferrari, before you do something we'll all regret—starting with Professor Aries. This is my final warning. You yourself are in no position to issue orders."

Another rumble from that green monstrosity of Zephyr's is followed by the heavy slither of scales over stone.

"Oh, but *I* am," the silver trickle of a different voice croons. "In fact, I was born to give orders."

Oh, lovely. Apparently, that fucking Fae has decided to join the fun.

Now Zephyr's tone turns to stone. "Go ahead and slay the wolf if it pleases you. For me, he's nothing more than a rival suitor. Gladly shall I add his head to my collection."

An electric current of shock makes me hiss.

"Whoa." That's my Zara, finally losing her cool. "Zephyr, what the fuck? This isn't helping. It's literally the opposite of helping. You and Xhev both need to back off and let me handle this shit."

"Oh, but why should I, my bride?" the Dark Fae bastard murmurs, in that voice that's like silk sliding over stone. "My sole interest lies in removing every obstacle that stands between me and your presence, seated in your throne at my side, at the Faerie Ball. The wolf is my rival and the girl is yours. Why should I not command Xhevith's breath to boil the flesh from both their bones?"

"Because Lucius is my *mate* and I'm fucking telling you not to, that's why!" A crash of thunder rattles the church windows, but Zara's lightning voice is built to carry. "You stay outta this, Your Radiance. I mean it."

Lucius, despite having a knife pressed to his throat and an acid-breathing dragon towering over him, tries to intervene. "Let's all take a deep breath—er, except for you, Xhevith."

"Alas." Zephyr sighs like the high-functioning sociopath he clearly is. In fact, he's *so* over-the-top sociopathic I dare to hope he might be bluffing. Whoever says *alas* in this day and age, for Christ's sake?

Besides, he gave his slippery but binding Dark Fae word to Zara. Didn't he?

"Xhevith follows no man's orders except mine," the twisted fuck murmurs now. "Is that not so, my dear?"

A massive clawed foreleg, sheathed in scales of emerald green, descends heavily into my limited vantage. Now that damn dragon is looming directly over the stairs.

Even my father, peering up at the beast, wavers on his feet. He sways as though he'd really like to retreat down here.

Of course Nikolai Romanov is smart enough to grasp that he won't be able to clear the death trap of these stairs tunneling down through stone, whether he frees Lucius first or not, before Xhevith exhales and showers all of us (myself included, given where I'm standing, assuming the Fae's *not* bluffing) with a spray of flesh-eating acid.

"Zephyr, what the actual *fuck*?" Zara cries. This time, the accompanying crash of thunder makes the stone tremble under my combat boots. "You swore not to hurt him—or any of my guys. You gave me your fucking *word*."

"I swore not to harm any under your roof, my bride," that slinking sly fox of a Fae says softly. "That is an oath I kept, to the last syllable, while we remained within your *domus*. As you can see, we no longer reside there."

A violent shaft of realization spears through my chest like a cocktail skewer through an olive.

Of course, I never for a moment made the mistake of trusting that twisty bastard. But I did rather assume he'd mind his Ps and Qs until he could entice Zara back to Avalon.

Apparently, my belief in his patience was misplaced.

"You shall have my eternal gratitude for your sacrifice, Lucius Aries," Zephyr says in a formal tone. "You may be my rival, but I'm not unaware of my bride's… affection for you. Or, for that matter, her lingering affection for the girl. Even Director Romanov here shall benefit from my royal benevolence. Xhevith will ensure any anguish the three of you experience will be… mercifully brief."

He's barely finished speaking before the frozen silence fills with the coughing rumble of that green monster, who's getting ready to spray his flesh-eating acid.

So, clearly, he's not bluffing.

Needless to say, his little plan is simply *not* happening.

Trembling with the need for violence, I fling my head back as far as this accused amulet will permit and summon the only witchcraft I possess that isn't Mogadon.

I have shifter recessives on my mother's side, a distant genetic legacy held in contempt by my father, that I'm betting the xenophobic bastard didn't care to acknowledge when he bespelled this amulet.

Under the force of my witchcraft, a blinding blaze of light obliterates the darkness. My spine lengthens and my jaw elongates. My neck thickens and the chain of the amulet snaps. My hands sweep up and wings sprout from my arms.

I explode from my human skin into the coiling serpentine form of my shifted shape.

All around me, the stone chute of the staircase cracks and splinters under my rapidly expanding mass. I catch a crooked glimpse of Lucius breaking free from my father, both of them sprinting left and right out of my path. Lucius is bellowing for Zara and anyone else who's up there to clear the commons before the floor caves in.

In mid-command, his voice unravels and stretches into the deep-throated howl of his wolf.

As the crypt walls shatter around me, I erupt from the stairs into the commons in the twining form of my wrathful dragon, with a teakettle hiss that screams *rage*.

# Chapter Twenty-One
## Zara

I'm summoning lightning. Even if I kill with it.

That's something I swore I'd never do again. Lose my shit. Kill with lightning. Let my deadly witchcraft slip the leash.

Under normal circumstances, I'm no killer.

But I'll do anything to save Lucius.

Including manslaughter.

My fingertips crackle with voltage. That fatal hum rises in my throat. The air turns thick and staticky with the metallic tang of ozone.

That's when the floor caves in.

The glittering silver scroll of Vasili's snaky dragon uncoils through a shower of falling rubble and explodes into the student commons with a rattling hiss. Iridescent wings, glinting with cobalt and emerald, launch his thrashing body airborne with a scream of rage.

Lucius' wolf, howling with alarm, bounds across the collapsing floor toward the huddle of spell-stunned Hadrian kids who are about to become the innocent victims of this clusterfuck. Cleo's sidekick Skyler scrambles off the table where she's been crouching and dives for the choir loft stairs.

That's smart, because it's a tight passage where dragons can't follow. But it's good for me too, because Skyler can't levitate, so she and Xiao (the small fry) are now contained up there.

Nikolai Romanov (who's definitely large fry, if there is such a thing, especially with my backpack slung over his shoulder) veers right across the commons and vanishes into the narrow passage that leads to the cloister. Which is another place dragons can't follow.

This time the scream of rage is mine.

*That fucker just stole my crown.*

I suck in a breath to hurl lightning right through the open door after him. That's when a hard punch slams into my diaphragm.

My breath spills out with a winded *"Oof!"*

The impact empties the air from my lungs before I can let loose with the lightning voice.

The crackling electric charge in the air fizzles out. My balance shifts. I stagger back to stay on my feet. But I lose my grip on Cleo.

That's when the slippery bitch twists out of my hold and shoves me hard in the direction I'm already heading.

Which is backwards.

Right off the treacherous sloping surface of the study carrel roof.

I've got a heartbeat to grasp that I'm falling. The flagstone floor rushes toward me with bone-breaking speed, while Cleo sprints across the carrels toward the cloister and her mentor.

Then a taloned foreleg closes around me and snatches me right out of the air.

The world swings upside down and the blood rushes to my head. I flail around with a yell. Before I can summon any kinda witchcraft, hard hands encased in green leather gauntlets grip my flailing arms and drag me into the dragon saddle.

I scramble behind a gilded leather pommel worked in green and gold like something from a jousting match at the Renaissance Faire, tug my plaid skirt down over my thighs, and fight furiously free of Zephyr's hold.

That homicidal Dark Fae maniac lurks right behind me in the saddle.

"What do you think you're doing, you crazy fuck?" I shout over the earsplitting crack and grind of the settling floor and Xhevith's trumpeting bellow. "Telling Xhev to *boil* Lucius—?"

"No time," Zephyr says tightly, arms closing hard around me (again) to snatch his discarded reins. "Watch the girl."

My gaze veers toward the carrels to see Cleo launch into a flying cartwheel that morphs into a catlike twist. She can't fly, but it's pretty obvi she's been trained in freerunning or *parkour* or some shit (one more secret she's been hiding). She pushes off from the carrel roof, uses her outstretched hands to bound away from a flying buttress, and hits the floor in a tight roll that absorbs the impact.

Hissing with menace, Vasili's flying serpent twists in a tight loop and flows through the air to get between Cleo and the enclosed maze her mentor just vanished into. V's silver mane streams in the wind and his pretty blue eyes narrow in rage. His long muzzle splits and a flurry of snow and ice streams through his gaping jaws.

Cleo pivots in mid-stride to avoid his icy breath and darts into the narthex that connects the church to the piazza. She slams the door hard behind her.

Yeah, no. That's stopping no one.

Vasili veers to overfly Lucius' wolf, who's herding the shocky Hadrian kids and Skyler's abandoned besties toward the same exit. Our headmaster's growling and snapping to make them run faster, like he's a massive German Shepherd.

With a sinister hiss, the Goblin King flows through the broken oculus window and soars into the open sky.

I tense and lean out, all ready to levitate from the saddle and launch right after him and probably shift myself. But Zephyr's gauntleted arm wraps tight around my waist and drags me against his supple strength. With a powerful bunch of the massive scaled body between my knees, Xhevith roars and launches into the air after the Goblin King.

Le Chiffre, I mean Nikolai, is temporarily outta reach.

Which has to mean we're all going after Cleo.

I catch a flashing glimpse of Lucius and my classmates scrambling to safety through the same exit Cleo just took. Then Xhev tucks his wings tight and sails through the broken oculus into the hot blue blaze of the summer sky.

As the church's slanted roof drops away beneath us, a brisk wind, briny with sea salt, whips through my pigtails and flutters my skirt around my thighs. If I'm gonna ride like this, I really need my catsuit or, better yet, the nifty dragonscale armor Zephyr had made for me in Avalon, and not my school uni. Right now, I'm barely decent.

Then again, it's not like the whole witching world hasn't already seen me naked.

Thanks for that, *Witching Inquisitor*.

A powerful beat of Xhev's vast green wings tilts us sideways. We chase Vasili's glittering silver scroll as he twists lithely through the air. We plummet from the sky with the wind screaming in our ears and soar across the piazza's cobblestone expanse. My own inner dragon (who doesn't like it when someone else takes the wheel while we're airborne) bugles in alarm.

Sweet Jesus.

I'm not even wearing the fighting straps that are supposed to harness you into a dragon saddle. But I know Zephyr (whatever his other shortcomings, which are major) won't let me fall.

I lean way out to see around Xhevith's scaly green shoulder so I can get eyes on Cleo.

Takes me a tick to find her, already halfway across the piazza and making excellent time, pelting with her light-footed Fae grace for the harbor and the turquoise dazzle of the sea like she's Usain Bolt nailing the forty-yard dash.

Vasili's dragon hisses in fury and arrows in her wake, eating up the distance between them. The tinny scent of snow floods the air—that's him revving up another round of his Asian dragon cloud breath. A direct hit of that shit will encase her in ice and freeze her right to the cobblestones.

Which I don't think she'll survive.

My pulse roars in my ears. My heart shoves up against my throat.

I don't normally get airsick, like, *at all.* Still, I feel like I'm gonna hurl.

*Get your shit together, showgirl.* I give my skittish conscience a bracing pep talk. *She just punched you in the throat and pushed you off a roof, remember?*

*Yeah,* my conscience whispers back. *But she didn't really wanna kill you. She knows you can fly.*

Xhevith roars like a tyrannosaur in *Jurassic Park* and labors to close the distance between him and Vasili. With a powerful beat of his scaly wings, we pull up alongside my snake. The big green rumbles under my legs as flesh-eating acid fills his gullet. His massive ribs expand like a bellows.

Of course, that dragon's linked telepathically with his rider.

And I know the Dark Fae King really wants to be the one who brings me Cleo's head.

*"Don't kill her,"* I scream at everyone, shoving the command through my mating bond with my snake for good measure. "Just grab her."

If we've got Cleo, Nikolai having my crown won't be such a show-stopper. Because there won't be a rival claimant who can wear it. If we're lucky, he and Messalina might even be willing to trade that crown for Cleo's royal half-Unseelie ass.

Of course, neither one of my guys likes this command. V's dragon, who doesn't have limbs to do the requisite grabbing (because snake), swings his long toothy muzzle toward me and screams in protest. Zephyr's arm clenches hard around my waist.

"Don't be a softhearted fool, my bride," the Dark Fae hisses in my ear. "The girl is your enemy. She deserves to die."

"For fuck's sake, Zephyr. She's your long-lost cousin, right? Just grab her." I crouch in the saddle so I don't slide off and catapult that order at both my guys, both out loud and through my bond with V. "I mean it."

My snake lets loose with a teakettle scream of frustration and fury.

Xhev roars like blazes in response. But he angles his wings and dives, soaring low behind Cleo's sprinting form with forelegs extended.

I'm not bonded to this dragon, so obvi his rider's told him to do what I want.

For once.

Yeah. Zephyr and me, we've got some shit to discuss once we handle this immediate sitch.

And it's a nick of time kinda thing, for real, because Cleo's almost reached the boat dock and the refuge of the open sea.

We're soaring right behind her fleeing form, with her burgundy hair streaming in her wake (because I've pretty much destroyed her schoolgirl braid). We're all ready to do the snatch-and-grab when my ex-bestie glances over her shoulder.

Her face fires with alarm. With a cry, her arm sweeps wide.

A curling wall of water rears up from the harbor like a tsunami. The tidal wave crashes over V and engulfs his thrashing form to drag him out of the sky.

Riveted to the saddle by shock and horror, I scream his name in the lightning voice. A deafening crash of thunder shakes the sky. Purple lightning forks and flashes.

Zephyr snarls and reins Xhevith violently away from the looming wave. From Cleo's racing form on the dock below, a blinding blaze of light sears my retinas and practically fries my optic nerve.

When my dazzled vision clears, we're winging over an empty dock. Fuck my life.

I barely glimpse the coiling slap of a forked merlot tail as Cleo's sea dragon dives into the drink and vanishes.

"Elemental Faerie magic," Zephyr growls in my ear as we soar fruitlessly over the empty sea. "Clearly, your rival possesses it. My element is air, but hers is water."

While Xhevith circles helplessly and croons in dismay, the airborne curl of water showers down into the sea. An awful stillness settles over the harbor.

"Goblin King?" I whisper through a bone-dry throat. Through our bond, I reach for him, groping for his lurky, snaky vibe.

What if—?

Vasili's silver snake explodes from the depths with his mane drenched and water streaming from his jaws. Half-drowned, he coughs to expel a torrent of water from his lungs. My snake's new to shifting, just like me, and he's flying pretty erratically (though he'll never admit it).

Under the awful hack of V's retching, the sea's blue expanse settles into stillness.

Cheese on toast. Cleo's gone deep.

And I already know Nikolai's gone too.

That bastard has my crown.

I'm linked up with Lucius, who's still in wolf form. Now that he's gotten his students to safety, my headmaster's using his shifty senses to hunt the cloister for Le Chiffre. Judging by his vibe, my wolf's pretty frustrated.

Nothing gets past his nose. Plus we already know from last night that Messalina's gang includes some Mogadon witch or warlock who teleports.

That has to be how Nikolai's slipping through the wards.

The slender spear of the harbor lighthouse, sooty and black with burn marks, looms dead ahead. I use that landmark for target practice when I'm hurling lightning, so I know it's abandoned.

I shoot a worried look at Vasili's uncertain flight, while my snake hacks and heaves.

Time to make an executive decision.

"Meet up at the lighthouse," I tell everyone I can reach through our mating bond, while Zephyr gets the downlow out loud. "Lucius, we better find Neo and Ronin. Make sure they're okay. Bring 'em out here with you in the dive boat. Goblin King, you get that pretty ass of yours outta the sky, like, now."

Normally I wouldn't be able to get away with bullying my alpha like that. But he just almost drowned. V twists his long neck to give me a horrible hiss, but he spirals shakily down to the rocky breakwater that holds the lighthouse and settles clumsily on the stone pier.

He's barely down before he shifts, with a weak flicker of light that's barely visible, into his hunched human form. While Xhevith wheels overhead, I eye my alpha's huddled body, naked and miserable and still weakly coughing.

Then I add for Lucius, *Better bring Vasili some clothes, okay, Teach? And maybe some bottled water. He's looking kinda rough.*

Lucius can't project human speech while he's wolfing out, he's pretty primal like that, but his instant surge of concern for our alpha floods through our bond.

I know he'll be here ASAP. That knowledge settles me down too.

"Okay, Your Radiance," I announce out loud for Zephyr without looking at him (because even the sight of him pisses me off). "You too. Get your ass down there. And you better not even look crosswise at my warlocks. You're on the last of your nine lives in this harem."

His gauntlet fists around the reins. In response, Xhevith tilts into a lazy descent toward the breakwater.

"You're angry with me," my Unseelie observes, after a long beat of silence.

I shrug off the lean warmth of his body pressed against mine. "You think?"

He leans in till his breath teases my ear and his scent of burnt amber tickles my nose. "Concerning the wolf—"

"Lucius," I remind him tightly. "He has a name. He's one of my mates."

"Zara." Zephyr sighs into the wind. "At the church. I was bluffing."

I twist around to glare into his single eye. "Yeah, right. You can't bluff."

One corner of his mouth tilts into a wry grin.

"I assure you I can. Wordcraft is an infamous Dark Fae gift. 'Tis merely that I cannot *lie*." He leans his forehead against mine. "I was buying you time to act, Zara. I never actually said I'd slay him."

"Word games and semantics." I snort and jerk my head away, then whip around to face blindly forward before I can fixate on how close he is to me.

The closest he's been in ten whole weeks.

At times like this, I suddenly remember he isn't human. He's not a witching race. He's Fae. To hear him tell it in class, they were here way before us.

All I know is, his twisty Unseelie logic makes my head spin.

Xhevith's slow circling descent makes my own inner dragon chafe and fret. But if I let that genie out of the bottle and shift myself, I'll be nakey.

Right now, I don't wanna be that exposed.

"Zara the Moon-Blessed. Lady of Lightning. Queen of Dragons." Zephyr's silvery whisper singsongs in my ear. "You're my bride. That means you command me. Not through your power, although that is formidable indeed. You command me through your love."

My chest clenches and my tummy flutters. Him and me, we haven't said the L word yet.

Now doesn't feel like the time or place.

Even when Zephyr's warm lips graze the piercings that rim my earlobe. Or when his hot breath fills my ear. Still, I shiver and his breath hitches.

Damn.

I missed him.

Even now, it's really hard to ignore the lithe press of his lean strength against my back, the supple slide of his dragonscale against the backs of my thighs, and especially the hard jut of his codpiece nestled against my ass.

Heat pools low in my belly. Moisture gathers under my gusset.

But I'm a witch on a mission. I really am.

That's why I ease away from the major physical distraction of a sexed-up Fae pressed against my back. That's why I wait till Xhev settles to the sea-washed jumble of rocks below the lighthouse.

Then I scowl up at the lightning-scorched landmark towering over us and shake my head. "Here's the thing, Your Radiance. I don't feel like I can trust you."

His breath rushes in on a hiss.

"Zarina Selene Gemini," he grits through his teeth, fierce with heat. "You know I cannot lie. That makes me the *only* man in your bed you can truly trust—"

"Nope." I pop the P hard on that shit. "One, you're not in my bed right now. Two, Vasili hates you. Three, Max feels threatened by you— God, not to mention, just hearing your name's enough to make Ronin a hot mess. And fuck knows how Lucius is gonna feel after that stunt you just pulled on him in the commons."

I swing my leg forward over the pommel and jump down to the pier before Zephyr can try to help. Then I spin around to face him, tilt my head back to glare at him while he looms over me on dragonback, and plant my hands on my hips.

Still seated in the saddle like an emperor on his throne in his dragonscale armor and gauntlets, with his ever-present swords crossed over his back, the Dark Fae King frowns down his royal nose at my belligerent stance. His eyebrow lifts and his moss-green hair streams behind him in the ocean breeze. With his tiny fangs and his pointy ears, the eyepatch slanting across his face just makes him more savage, like a sky pirate.

"Zara," he murmurs, in that silky ribbon of voice that strokes my senses like a finger.

Under my Academy blazer, goosebumps rise along my forearms. Heat licks along my skin.

But fuck that shit.

I'm still pissed at him for, like, so many reasons. I can't even articulate all the reasons.

Next to me, his dragon noses gently at Vasili, who's finally stopped coughing and stretched out like a cat to dry on the pier in the summer sun, with all that sleek skin pulled taut over the yummy long lines of his sinewy body and his pretty cock on shameless display. Oblivious to his whole effect, my snake is wringing seawater from his dripping hair with a look of utter disgust.

Now he stops fussing long enough to shove the inquisitive dragon irritably away.

Xhev really doesn't wanna go. His hopeful muzzle hovers over the Goblin King. The dragon's nostrils flare wide with interest to breathe in the scent of caramel and vetiver and Mogadon aggression.

Rudely Vasili shoves that interested muzzle aside, more roughly this time, with a huff.

The knot of worry in my gut unclenches in a rush of relief.

*He's fine, showgirl,* I tell my own fretful and restless inner dragon. *Peace out. Our snake is fine. No thanks to this guy.*

I swing back around to confront the waiting Zephyr—who's also watching the naked Vasili with a singular intensity, his dragonrider gaze smoking with heat, a blazing smolder in his feral face.

Yowsa. Talk about distraction.

Like I just said, V hates his guts. Even more now than he did before. Plus those two guys are both dommy as fuck. If Zephyr's gonna start lusting after my alpha, that'll definitely make things in this harem, uh, *interesting.*

I resist the urge to fan myself, but I do clear my throat. Zephyr's alert gaze veers back to me.

"You still want me to go with you to Avalon, right?" I wanna hear him say it, on account of that whole *no lying* thing.

"Indeed I do. Ash needs us." His fist clenches hard on the reins. "My kingdom—*our* kingdom—is where you belong, my bride. The seat of your strength. At the Faerie Ball in Avalon, you'll come fully into your power."

I wish.

Wish I could put Ash first, the way that sweetheart Seelie Prince Charming of mine deserves.

Wish I could trust Zephyr.

At times like this, I've never felt less trusting. Or more powerless.

"Yeah, well, the Faerie Ball sounds like a fairy tale to me." I sigh. "Plus you're got major ulterior motives, Your Radiance. It's not only about Ash. Am I right?"

When he stays silent (because he can't deny that shit), I nail him with a look of challenge. "Right. Before we go anywhere, you're gonna need to convince me—convince all of us, and that includes Ronin—that you're someone we can trust."

# Chapter Twenty-Two
## Ronin

When we pitch up at the lighthouse in the dive boat in a muck sweat—I mean Lucius and Neo and me—Vasili's having a nice leisurely sunbathe on the pier.

Without a scrap of clothes on.

Apparently half my polycule (including him) just almost got their tickets punched in the commons. Now here he is having a lie-about.

My boyfriend's lounging flat on his back with a languid arm draped over his eyes and one knee coyly raised to cover his junk (barely). Like he's on blooming holiday on a nude beach in the Greek Isles.

I swear he makes me mental.

Only it's not really him setting me off, is it?

As I maneuver the dive boat up alongside the pier under Lucius' anxious guidance, then kill the engine to coast the last few ticks, Zara pops up from that solitary brood she's having on a jumble of rocks. She knows her way round a boat, my girl does, so she scrambles to catch the mooring line tossed by a worried Neo.

She is, very pointedly, ignoring the green dragon draped on his belly over the breakwater. Xhevith's sunning himself in the Mediterranean heat with his eyelids lowered and his tail in the water.

And Zara's definitely ignoring that sinuous Dark Fae dragonrider propped against the curve of Xhev's neck, simultaneously sharpening his swords on a handy ledge of rock—and having a look-see at my naked boyfriend.

Just the sight of that bloody-minded Fae, brooding over someone else who's mine, is enough to flip my switch.

Again.

My heart starts tripping like I'm defibrillating and my gut goes to butterflies.

Bollocks.

"Oh my gosh, babe, we've all been worried sick." That's Neo, scrambling over the gunwale before we've even moored to engulf our girl in one of his smothery hugs. (He's generous with the PDA, our Red is, and we all love him for it.)

"I'm fine, baby. We're all fine." Zara stops snuggling into Neo long enough to shoot a glare at Zephyr. "No thanks to that guy."

My Unseelie ex stops sharpening his sword long enough to give my girl an inscrutable look. Then his gaze shifts to me. Slowly his stare wanders over me, barely in compliance with the dress code in my take on the Monday uni, with my blazer left behind in Genetics of Witchcraft class, the inky black flames of my dragon tattoo creeping up my neck, and my green-striped tie tugged loose and crooked in the June heat.

Under that smoldery stare Zeph's rocking, my whole body heats up like he's just tossed me in the skillet and turned on the hob.

While Zara gives Neo all kinds of reassurance and Lucius ties us off at the jetty, I grab the knapsack I've stuffed with fresh duds for Vasili (who's going to need a new Monday uni after he shifted in the old one). Then I leap off the boat to the pier.

Zara unwinds from Neo to fling an arm round my neck. Simultaneously, she pulls Lucius into a hard snog that feels desperate.

A bit like her vibe in our bond.

"God, Lucius," she mumbles against his mouth, while she clings tight to both of us. "He could've killed you."

"My dear, I was never in any real danger," Lucius rumbles. "In the commons, I was merely a bit of leverage. Nikolai Romanov does nothing by impulse."

Zara pulls back long enough to aim her incandescent glare at Zephyr. "I meant *him*."

I bare my teeth in an ugly grin that's sparked by a nasty sense of glee. I mean, come on. Zeph's given me the cold shoulder for ages, after he made me choose between loving him and protecting my own twin sis. He let me think I'd murdered him. Left me to flounder in the quicksand of my own guilt. Left Gwen and me to grieve and suffer and mourn his so-called passing.

That fuckery might not be the actual reason Gwen hanged herself. She was bullied to death. But all that Zephyr-related drama in her rearview mirror didn't help.

So if Zeph's in the doghouse, I definitely don't mind the turnabout.

"Too right. Bloody little savage, he is." I wrap an arm round Zara's tiny waist and bend to give my girl's lush mouth the quick ravage she's begging for.

Her hot curves fit into my arms like she's spoiling for a fuck. Her lips part on a breathy moan that tastes like sweet vanilla and mating heat. The creamy scent of roses seeps from her overheated skin.

That's her mating scent, that is. Just a whiff makes my head spin and my dick hard.

I wrap my palm round her succulent arse and haul her up on tiptoe against my boner.

"Ronin." She licks into my mouth and pulls Lucius closer. "You feel so nice, Adam."

"Same, love. Care for a shag?" I slide an arm round Lucius so he's included. Even though I know we've not got the time for the proper rogering I'd like to give both of them, a rousing fuck would clear everyone's head.

"No thank you, Mr. Pendragon," Lucius says, all growly with alpha firmness. "You have class in an hour."

Neo wraps round us too, his big hand rubbing my back to console me for the turn-down, while he tucks his face into Zara's neck.

While I breathe in our bookworm's wholesome scent of soap and sage and enjoy our cuddle pile, my skin's tingling under the stalky heat of Zephyr's stare.

Safe to say I don't mind that prick getting a gander at what I've got and he doesn't.

"Where's Max?" Zara wiggles away from my rampant dick and divides a worried look among all of us. "I thought he'd be the first guy here. I can't even find him in our bond."

"Maxim is quite unable to concentrate on his studies at present," Lucius says gently. "That became apparent to me this morning. To channel all that energy, I've given him a hall pass and assigned his dragon to patrol duty. He's opted to overfly the island—including the portal to Avalon. Consequently, he's out of range at the moment."

Lucius pauses and eyes Zara's flushed face. "I'm afraid he's going to become increasingly difficult to handle. He's, ah, very close to full shifter rut."

"Right." Zara bites her lip and looks adorably contrite. "Guess that's my fault, huh."

While Lucius reassures her that it's not, I snort and roll my eyes—and it's not over the comic visual of Max's big black dragon toting a hall pass. I'm snorting because Lucius has been in full shifter rut himself since Zara started that bit about making babies last night.

Even Vasili, who's only got shifter recessives to deal with, has gone a bit rutty.

Speaking of.

I detach gently from our kiss-and-cuddle, hitch my knapsack over my shoulder, and amble over to V, who's still having a full-on sunbathe with an arm draped over his eyes.

He's playing it up casual for our Unseelie viewing audience. So I follow his lead and drop the knapsack carelessly at his feet.

"Best have a care, love," I say lightly. "You've getting a bit sunburnt."

"Darling, I'm working on my tan." V lowers his arm and sits up to sulk. "Took you long enough."

His high cheekbones are flushed with sun, he has the palest sprinkle of freckles coming out across his nose like fairy dust, and his petulant pout's too yummy to resist. I hunker down and run a rough palm over his damp hair.

Ah. He's sticky with salt, that's what's got him all pouty.

"Had to round up Xiao and Skyler, didn't we?" I remind him. "Left that lot in detention with Aggie in the crypt. Between them, Cleo and her crew have crushed half the rules in the Codex to rubble. Your sweet cousin Skyler's looking at suspension for attacking our girl on Academy grounds. Could be Sky will miss her finals and have to take a do-over for the term."

"Too bad." That little nugget sparks my beau's malicious grin in a way that shows off his pretty fangs. "It appears Cleopatra doesn't trouble her head over the academic welfare of her minions."

My reply's lost when he winds an arm round my neck and pulls me close for one of his snakebite kisses.

Now that's what I'm talking about.

His lips taste like salt, but his fist clenches in my hair with a ruthless insistence and his tongue licks into my mouth with a hunger that makes me forget all our troubles. Makes me forget everything, in fact, except the consuming need to climb on top of him and straddle his hips and dry-hump him till he spills all over my uniform trousers. Till I paint his sleek chest and smooth abs with a load of my own spunk.

Of course we're linked, same as always. So he's got the filthy fantasy from my mind in a blink. He hums with approval and cups my still rampant and quite interested boner through my trousers.

So much for him being half-drowned.

"Thought it was a blooming crisis," I grumble, though I'm not really whingeing. "Lucius yanked me out of class for this, you know."

"Poor you," he purrs against my lips. Even after his immersion, he smells like vetiver and he tastes like vodka. I'm getting sozzled just kissing him. "And, for your information, I nearly *did* drown. Now I need conditioning rinse and a hair dryer on an emergency basis."

I grin and nudge the knapsack closer with my foot. "I've brought your duds and a few other bits and bobs."

"Hmm." That's his way of saying thanks. But he's distracted, and what he says next proves it. "Truly, we really must do something about this plague of Faerie magic running amuck at our fair Academy."

"Uh huh." I navigate his deadly fangs (not that I'd mind getting nicked, but he's self-conscious about his fangs and he'd be bloody appalled) so I can deepen our snog.

Of course, knowing Zeph's watching gives the whole experience an edge that's keen enough to cut. That royal prick's definitely not immune to the sight of me getting some from my pretty boyfriend, who happens to be sunning in the nude.

And Zeph's not immune to me either.

I was his first.

Just like he was mine.

That shit gets under a bloke's skin.

Not to mention, he's always been territorial and possessive as fuck.

"Okay, guys, listen up." Zara's insistent voice breaks our kiss and swings us all round to where she's sitting on the dive boat gunwale with her stockinged legs swinging like a Hollywood pinup girl. She's swigging from a bottle of water to rehydrate and flashing a good handspan of suntanned thigh, with Neo tucked up tight at her side.

When we all look at her with appreciation for that naughty schoolgirl vibe she's giving off in her plaid skirt and teal pigtails, she grins at us and waves a hand toward our headmaster. He's lurking nearby, clearly drawn to her pending fertility, but fighting like blazes to keep his rut in hand.

"Lucius has something to say," she tells us.

Obediently, we all look toward Lucius. He's rocking that vibe Zara calls his Gary Oldman look, still sporting his silk tie and seersucker suit, with his eyes hidden behind violet-tinted specs. The harbor wind's tugged his mane of chestnut curls loose from their tidy knot to spill down his back.

Of course, I've sensed him holding something back.

But it's telepath manners not to pry.

Now Lucius slips off his shades to give us all a sober look. "Thank you, Ms. Gemini. Here's the reason I was late arriving at the dive shop. I was summoned by the Dean to account for this morning's unfortunate altercation."

"Fuck. Me," Zara groans. "The Dean. Same Dean who just handed the Horn of Ceres to Cleo's sea dragon, right?"

Lucius slips out his Old World handkerchief and frowns as he polishes the seaspray from his glasses. "I assure you, the Dean is a neutral party, both in the succession struggle and as the creative force behind your finals. But she's under a great deal of pressure from the school board. Not to mention, she'll now be obliged to announce a tuition hike. This morning's damage to the student commons will be rather expensive to repair."

"She should send the bill to my father," Vasili says coldly. "He's the one who tried foolishly to confine me in the crypt while he threatened to slit your throat."

Clearly done with his lie-about, my boyfriend gestures imperiously for the knapsack I've brought him. I nudge it obligingly toward him and he pillages it like a naked pirate.

"Well, in fact…" Lucius hesitates. "Your father has precipitated the Dean's latest dilemma. He's phoned in, from wherever on the mainland he's now lurking, to file a grievance—on Cleo's behalf."

"A *grievance*?" Zara nearly chokes on her H2O. "She thinks *she's* got a grievance? That bitchy witch and her clique attacked *me*, remember?"

"Skyler attacked you, yes, and she'll be held accountable." Lucius stops polishing his specs and looks grim. "But you attacked Cleopatra first, my dear. There were multiple witnesses from her villa—witnesses whose loyalties lie with Messalina rather than you—to substantiate the allegation. With Nikolai Romanov a trustee on the board, the Dean clearly felt she had no choice."

Unease ricochets from mate to mate in my polycule like a bleeding pinball machine.

"Uh oh," Neo says softly, eyes worried behind his glasses. "What has Deanie done, Lucius?"

Lucius clears his threat. "She's, ah, suspended both Zara and Vasili. In his case, the offense is wanton destruction of school property, thanks to that catastrophic shifting incident."

"Oh, dear, suspended again. Well, cry me a river." Impatient, V pulls the silky black tee shirt I've brought him over his pretty head and reaches for his black lace panties, the sight of which (I can't help noticing) makes Zephyr lean forward with interest.

"It's unfortunate, Mr. Romanov." Lucius gives V's antics a repressive frown, because you can take the prof out of the schoolroom, but you can't take the schoolroom out of the prof. "You've only just been removed from probation after your last offense."

"Blooming Dean. That old throttlebottom." I sneer. "How long are they out for, then? For this suspension?"

Lucius replaces his specs with a sigh. "Two days."

Zephyr's watching V slither into those boy-cut briefs that cup his pert ass like a pair of hands. Now Zeph's gaze veers toward Lucius with a sudden narrowed focus that makes my pulse skip.

*"Two days?"* Zara jumps down from the gunwale and plants her hands on her hips.

"That was the bare minimum penalty she could assign under the Codex." Lucius eyes our girl's militant stance. "I'll say it again. The Dean's not working against you, Zara. She could have expelled you outright, but she didn't."

"Yeah, well, thanks for that." Zara's glittery fingertips drum with agitation. "Finals start tomorrow, Lucius."

I've been a bit distracted myself by all that energy humming under the surface between Zephyr (whose non-human mind I can never read) and Vasili (who's definitely aware of his scrutiny, but pointedly ignoring it). Not to mention that potent tension zipping between Zeph and me, which is palpable enough to taste.

Now I zoom in on what's being said with a curse.

"Bollocks." I give in to my nerves and start pacing. "Gives that rotter Cleo and her lot a full day's head start on finding the Horn of Ceres, doesn't it?"

"Not like she needs one," Zara grumbles. "She's a sea dragon, and we already know the Horn's in a watery place."

Zephyr unfolds from his sinewy recline against Xhevith's neck and flows to his feet. Under that supple green dragonscale I used to fantasize about peeling off him with my teeth, every drum-tight muscle and tendon in his lethal body is alert and twitching with suppressed passion.

"Your punishment can be turned to your advantage, my bride," he breathes.

"Oh, yeah? How do you figure?" Zara shoots him a suspicious look that makes the air crackle. Clearly, after that rubbish went down in the commons, he's First Boy on her shit list.

Vasili's already on his feet, working a pair of black glitter jeans I love on him over his supple thighs. Now his gilded head jerks up with a hiss. He knows where this is going, we all do.

Fuck.

Undeterred by the hostile looks he's getting, Zephyr scrambles over his sleeping dragon's foreleg and prowls toward our girl like the predator he is.

"Since it seems you're not permitted to attend class for the time being," he says softly, "nor to commence your examinations, 'tis naught to prevent you from attending the Faerie Ball and taking your throne at my side."

Ever since he pitched up at Icarus, I've been a smoldering volcano of suppressed emotion. Now, without a tick of warning, that volcano erupts in a cataclysm of molten rage.

"Bloody hell, Zeph, are you daft?" I burst. "She doesn't *trust* you. None of us trust you! And for damn good reason—"

"No, wait," Neo says quietly. "Please let him finish, okay, Ronin?"

It's so rare for our Red to interrupt anyone that I slam on the verbal brakes and we all stare. Our bookworm gives me a look of total understanding through those big green eyes of his, then hops down from the gunwale and reaches for Zara's hand.

She's crackling with static, but she dials down the voltage and lets Neo take her hand.

Zeph, who's no fool, gives him a careful nod. "I sense that you grasp the essence of the matter. Will you not speak for me, friend?"

"Babe, you need allies," Neo tells our girl gently, but he's talking to me too. "You need a crown. You basically need as much power right now as you can grab. Plus you're already conflicted about leaving Ash to fend for himself back in Avalon. Even though you don't wanna admit it. So I think you should listen to Zephyr."

Vasili, finally dressed but still barefoot, zips his fly ferociously and glares at poor Red like a basilisk. "No one asked you to weigh in here, Mercury. If you want to help Zara find allies, I suggest you start by recruiting your senatorial father to the Gemini cause."

I expect Neo to feel hurt at getting verbally kicked in the nuts like that. But he gives V the sweetest look. "Dad's on his way back to the Senate, where he can help Zara the most. We talked on the landline this morning. But that won't be enough and we all know it."

To my alarm, Lucius gives a slow nod like he's actually buying this load of codswallop.

Meanwhile, Zeph's gotten with touching distance of Zara, but he knows better than to touch her while she's all pissed and bristly with her hair floating around her shoulders and the electric charge of lightning crackling in the air.

She tilts her chin to lock onto his stare with her own look of challenge. Which is how I realize he's actually a hair shorter than her.

He's not physically a big guy, but you tend to forget that because the whole Dark Fae King vibe he projects is so intense.

"What Neo Theodophilus Mercury says is the truth." Zephyr speaks so softly I can barely hear over the slap of the sea on the rocks, so I sidle closer for a listen. "I shall give you a crown no mortal witch or warlock can steal. I shall give you power the like of which these mortals can scarcely dream."

Zara nibbles her lush lower lip in a way that makes me want to bite it for her. But the look she gives him through her big Betty Boop eyes is brimming with a blend of challenge and vulnerability that makes my chest ache.

"What about your heart, Your Radiance?" she breathes. "Aren't you gonna tell me you'll give me *that*?"

"That you have already." His silvery whisper turns husky. "Do you not know?"

Her thick lashes flutter and her voice gets tight. "Yeah, I thought I did. But ten weeks is a long time to ghost a girl, you feel me?"

A furrow digs between Zeph's green brows.

"I have explained my absence. Although it grieved me to be so long apart from you." His hand twitches like he's aching to touch her.

But Red gives a little head shake that tells Zeph to wait.

Very clearly, our bookworm's on his side.

Wisely Zephyr hesitates, then clasps his hands behind his back instead. "Also, there is Ash. If you will not aid him for his own sake, my bride, aid him to add a Seelie Prince to your list of allies."

Instant annoyance flashes in Zara's turquoise stare.

"Look, I don't need a political reason to help Ash, okay? I'm gonna do that anyway." She taps her toes on the rock and frowns. "If I'm sidelined here anyway, maybe now's that time. Just a quick in and out. Go to the Ball, get my crown, make sure Ash is okay, and get out. Just in time to nab the Horn of Ceres and put Cleo back in her place."

"Dear fuck." Vasili's hunkered down to lace his combat boots. Now he looks up in patent disbelief. "Am I hallucinating in this tiresome heat, or are you actually considering this Unseelie moron's absurd proposition?"

"Right, it's not like popping down to the pub for a pint, is it?" I agree with mounting heat. "We'd be starting after the Horn *at least* a day late, and it could be a lot longer. Just look what happened the last time you followed this prick to fairyland."

Zephyr shoots me a blazing look that nearly sets me on fire and pulls in a harsh breath. My own breath roughens and a rush of adrenaline lights me up like a Beltane fire.

Yeah, mate, bring it on. Every cell in my body rises to meet his silent challenge.

But Zara raises a cautionary finger to silence the lot of us before all hell breaks loose.

"Like I said before," she says firmly, "I'm not going anywhere unless we all agree. We'd only stay for the Ball. And this time, you'd all have to come with—including you, Lucius. I know you're supposed to be proctoring finals, but—"

"It seems I too am suspended," Lucius announces wryly, "for my unfortunate involvement in this morning's incident. Without pay, I might add. So it appears I too am relieved of my academic duties, at least for the next two days."

While I stare with my jaw gaping in indignation at every single aspect of this pronouncement (Lucius didn't do a thing wrong!), our headmaster turns to Zeph with a slight smile. "Besides, I've been… quite curious… to visit the Avalon Academy."

"Lucius Laszlo Aries, you would be most welcome," my ex says formally, inclining his head in a kingly nod. "I shall arrange a guest lecture for you as a visiting professor in the student kiva."

Great.

Crisis or no crisis, our headmaster looks pleased as fuck at that prospect.

Clearly Zeph knows the way to Lucius' heart.

And our bookworm's already on board. Just like Vasili's been warning all along would happen if my poisonous ex ever turned back up.

That Unseelie bastard's splitting our found family right down the center.

Feeling powerless to stop what's clearly about to happen—which is Zara flying off to fairyland again with my deceitful, unreliable, untrustworthy ex-boyfriend—I look desperately to my current boyfriend for help.

"Aren't you forgetting someone, little queen?" Vasili says rudely, rearing up between Zara and Zephyr like the adder he is. "Let me offer you a little hint. He's big and black and breathes fire when he's angry, and he has a forked dick—"

"Well, of course we gotta find Max first." Nothing about any of this is remotely funny, but Zara looks at V like she's fighting a smile. "What with him being in rut and my BC giving up the ghost, he'll obviously wanna come with. Anyway, I'd want you all to have equal access to my uterus—I mean, uh, assuming you'd all want that."

Now she's leaning around V's tall obstructive body to look at *me*, because I'm pretty much the only guy in our polycule who hasn't been queuing to knock her up.

Of course Vasili claims he's not. But he had his dick in her continuously all last night. Literally would not be dislodged. We all sort of fucked around him.

So I don't trust him on this one.

"Ronin?" Zara prods gently. "We're not doing this without you. Are you in?"

"Don't look at me like that, love," I mutter, sounding sullen even to my own ears. "If you fancy jaunting off to Avalon with this untrustworthy arse, you bloody well know I'm coming with you."

Sure, I'm no shifter and I'm not in rut. Too young to be a dad, if you ask me. I'm just a blooming sophomore. I'm not desperate to make her preggo.

But I'll not hold her back on my account.

And fuck if she's leaving me behind.

# Chapter Twenty-Three
## Zara

Very clearly, Ronin's pissed as fuck that we're here.

But he's right about one thing.

Getting in and out of the parallel world of Avalon is, like, a major ordeal.

First there's the magical portal over the Icarus Island standing stones that turns your guts inside out in that mindfuck transit between our two realms.

Then you gotta avoid those massive flights of feral dragons flying amuck all over Avalon Island. Those dragons are, one, carnivorous hunters that literally eat random Fae for breakfast and, two, maniacally drawn to my dragon when she's in heat in a way we definitely don't wanna encourage.

Having my own guys in rut is more than sufficient to knock me up. I mean, if we decide for sure we want that.

Finally, there's apparently this whole Dark Fae insurrection bubbling under the political surface that Zephyr and Ash between them are barely keeping in check.

Long story short?

By the time my guys and I come winging into view over the goblin city (that's what I call the Dark Fae capital, kinda an inside joke, because *Labyrinth*), we've been flying for hours.

My warlocks and me, we're all pretty rough.

Insurrection or no, we arrive on the wing (which is a power move) because I figure this is one of those times when you don't hide your light under a basket.

Besides, even if I felt like being sneaky, Zephyr's too proud to come slinking into his own city like a thief in the night. This is a guy who shows up with fanfare and the blowing of trumpets to hail His Moon-Dazzled Radiance.

And Vasili never lets anyone dim his sparkle.

So I soar over the Unseelie city at sunset like the dragon queen I am, my teal wings spread wide like sails to catch the downdraft, while the swollen red orb of the setting sun paints the sea indigo and bathes the shining spires and pale walls of Zephyr's fairytale castle in a wash of crimson. The shadowy bulk of the Avalon volcano—now dormant since the two of us broke the curse that was dooming this whole island—looms in shades of mauve and lilac against the magenta sky.

A balmy summer wind washes over me, laced with the spicy fruit of jasmine and the voluptuous sweetness of tuberose. I breathe in deep to fill my cavernous lungs with that half-forgotten scent—a heady aphrodisiac to my shifty senses—and my six-chambered heart beats harder.

I've grown to think of Icarus as home, mostly because that's where my warlocks are. This place... Avalon... exudes all the seductive enchantment of fairyland.

But that seduction is deceptive as fuck.

We're not safe.

We've finally left the ferals behind, and only royals ride on dragonback in Avalon. That means we have the sky to ourselves.

So I arrow boldly over the dizzying jumble of twisting streets and sloping rooftops, while wary citizens scatter and bolt from the streets in a panic (because dragon) and startled faces pop into view in the tall arched windows. I bellow in the brassy rumble of my lightning voice to announce our arrival.

Behind me, the deep rumble of Max's dragon cleaves the air, punctuated by Xhevith's nails-on-chalkboard scream and Vasili's rattling hiss. Then we all plummet straight down from cruising altitude in a daredevil descent. Ronin's gleeful yell, where he and Neo are strapped to Max's back in a riding harness my clever bookworm rigged for both of them, is like the coda of our soundtrack.

No doubt about it, we're coming in hot.

Even if poor Lucius, whose wolf clearly does *not* like flying, has been clinging green-faced and grimly silent behind Zephyr in the dragon saddle all day.

As the shining spikes on the castle turrets rush toward us, I spin in a tight spiral to clear my six (that's because dragons have a major blind spot behind us). Then I dive for the broad stone ledge of Xhevith's lair, alight and snap my wings in tight to make room for my guys, and surrender to my shift in a blinding flash of heat and light.

My bare human feet have hardly hit the ledge before Xhev's big green bulk settles heavily beside me.

That's when the scream of literal trumpets nearly makes me jump out of my human skin.

"Cheese on toast!" I yell as Zephyr unbuckles his fighting straps, swings a leg over, and scrambles nimbly down Xhev's helpful foreleg to alight beside me. "What is that, a doorbell?"

"Royal accolade." Calmly he twists back to unbuckle Lucius, whose face is pale as milk as he sits stiffly in the unfamiliar saddle. "You will grow accustomed. After all, you are now our queen."

"Think I'd rather have a blast of something a little more… today? Like maybe some K-pop?" That's me trying to joke.

Of course, this Unseelie mate of mine has a cultural gap big enough to drive a Mack truck through. So he tilts his head quizzically and gets that little furrow between his green brows that happens when he's perplexed.

"K-pop." Carefully he tries out the word. "I shall instruct the minstrels."

I snicker and reach for my gorgeous dragonscale leathers, custom-made in my teal and his green to fit my royal posterior and still hanging on the peg where I left my gear weeks ago (because of course I'm all nakey after my shift). I'm pulling the pants up my legs, commando style, when my eye catches a flash of green and silver.

That's a forked banner—a massive one—being winched up a flagpole by unseen hands on the peak of the highest tower looming over us.

"King in residence," Zephyr explains briefly to my probably startled face. "That banner is the Unseelie equivalent of a witching world news broadcast. The next will be yours."

Sure enough, a teal banner follows his up the flagpole. My banner's as big and splendid as his. Seeing it makes my chest glow with a sudden warmth I don't expect.

That's the warmth of belonging. The warmth of feeling welcomed.

"Queen in residence, huh?" I say softly.

Zephyr inclines his head in a regal nod. Confronted with whatever must be written on my face, the hint of a smile softens his cold Fae features.

It's not like I need validation. But considering what's going down with my crown in the witching world right now?

I kinda appreciate this level of acceptance.

While I'm feeling all the feels, Zephyr extends a courteous gauntlet to help Lucius (who looks like he needs it) down from the saddle.

"Thank you, Your Radiance," my headmaster says faintly. "With any luck, we'll not be obliged to do *that* again in a hurry."

My wolf is fully human at the mo, but he's got the bipedal equivalent of a tail tucked between his legs. His hands look unsteady as he unbuckles his oxblood briefcase and vintage satchel, then slides an old-fashioned Mary Poppins umbrella from behind the saddle.

(To be fair, it does look like rain.)

"Hey, Lucius. You okay?" Hastily I pull the dragonscale catsuit over my shoulders, zip that shit up so I don't flash my tits at the staff, and hurry over to help him. Especially considering half the clothes in that satchel are actually mine.

Lucius summons a wan smile and hands me the umbrella to carry. "The less said about how I'm currently feeling, the better."

Maxim's massive black dragon settles beside us on the ledge with a powerful backwing, then fills the air with a deafening bellow that almost blows us all over.

Among this island's population of scrawny ferals, Max is the dominant male. Clearly, his dragon wants all our enemies—both known and unknown—to know he's here.

Being in rut with a permanent boner just makes him worse.

Ronin unbuckles from the harness and leaps down to the ledge with a whoop. He might not be happy about our visit to fairyland (like, *at all*), but my psycho Brit loves flying. He looks wicked in his leather pants and shitkickers, with the inky flames of his tattoo sneaking past the collar of his heavy metal tee. His golden eyes are fiery and his tawny face is alight in a savage grin.

"You see Max flame at those ferals?" He gives Max's scaly black shoulder a hearty thump. "He's a proper badass, he is."

Max twists his long neck around and rumbles affectionately at Ronin, his round dragon orbs lidded and glowing with pleasure.

Meanwhile Neo unbuckles his harness and clambers down Max's foreleg under his own steam, though my fated mate feels kinda wobbly in our bond. Flying's definitely not a bookworm thing, but he's gotten used to it, and overall he's looking a whole lot better than Lucius.

Ronin reaches back to swing the hiker's pack Neo's toting over his own strong shoulder, then throws an arm around our bookworm's neck to give him a rough hug of encouragement.

"Good job in the air, love," Ronin murmurs. "I'm proud of you."

Neo blushes with happiness and snuggles into him, then turns his soft smile on me.

Ronin turns to watch Zephyr coax his dragon into the lair to make room on the landing ledge for Vasili, who's still circling the dragon-haunted city in a way that's gotta upset the locals.

My Unseelie King's got staff these days, the kind he hand-picks for loyalty, so a couple of capable-looking Dark Fae stable hands are already mucking around with Xhev's saddle and bridle and a jar of that oil the dragon likes getting rubbed down with, you know, to moisturize. (Otherwise, Zephyr says, a non-shifting dragon's scales get itchy.)

The Dark Fae King divides his attention between dragon care and the interior stair that twists down to the palace. Clearly he's worried about Ash, who should've come charging up those stairs like a linebacker to welcome us home.

A ping of worry tightens my gut and quickens my breath. Now that I'm here, I wanna know Ash is okay, like, immediately.

While Zephyr fulminates around his dragon with his mouth tight and his movements twitchy in a way that clearly makes his staff nervous, and while Ronin pretends not to watch, a coil of glittering silver lands on the ledge with a flash of iridescent wings that sparkle in the setting sun.

Vasili's barely down before he shifts. He's already reaching impatiently for Ronin's backpack (which holds his flashy clothes) before he's settled fully into his human shape.

Maxim shifts back last, which tells me he's on edge and probably still high on endorphins and testosterone from bullying the ferals.

Max is easily the most disreputable of my guys, with his scarred back and the twin barbells through his nipples and that barbed wire manacle tattooed around his wrist. Under my appreciative eye, he rakes a hand through his long blond hair and twists it into a warrior's braid (in case we need to fight). Then he dips into Ronin's pack and pulls one of Ronin's silky button-downs around his scarred shoulders.

Poor Max. He's more sensitive about covering his scars than he is about covering his dick.

Meanwhile, his suspicious slitted eyes dart everywhere. The skittish stable hands give him a wide berth.

"You must wear whatever pleases you, of course." Zephyr casts a cool eye over my windblown harem. "However, I've commanded suitable attire and guest chambers made ready for your entire harem, my bride."

"Yeah, we'll all get cleaned up in a sec." I swipe a worried hand through my own messy curls. "We gonna look for Ash first or what?"

A frown shadows Zephyr's wary gaze.

"In truth, he should be here already. At this hour, our home is his accustomed place, and the Seelie Prince is very much a creature of habit." He pauses. "But Ash is regent in my absence, and those duties demand odd hours. Perhaps he's merely… asleep."

"Huh." I shoot a dubious look at the setting sun. "He'd be a pretty late riser—or early sleeper—if he is."

"'Tis possible." Zephyr's gaze narrows on the high tower. "No matter. If he's indeed in residence, I know precisely where to find him."

My Unseelie's already stalking for the stairs, swords crossed over his shoulders and green hair streaming in the wind. Now we stream after him (in various states of undress) like chicks after a hen.

Xhevith is slurping water from his big trough in the lair, and I know he'll fly out later to hunt. When I scurry past, he lifts his dripping muzzle to croon at me. Under his possessive stare, my dragon queen gives him a flirty chirp and preens like the diva she is.

We all pile into the twisting stone stairwell, lit by pale glowing crystals stuck in the walls like torches that generate the cool illumination the Fae call witchlight. I'm used to the spectacle by now, but Lucius gazes around in rapt fascination.

"Your guest chambers await on the lower level. I trust you'll find the accommodations to your satisfaction," Zephyr says coolly to the collective, then turns to me. "Of course, my queen shares the royal chambers in the tower with me."

My mouth pops open in shock.

Oh, hell to the no with that shit.

But Ronin beats me to the punch with a rude snort. "Yeah, good luck with that, mate."

"Um, no." I give Zephyr the stink-eye. "We talked about this on Day One, remember? My guys and me, we're a package deal. If we're too much for you to handle? Houston, we have a problem."

Zephyr's clearly chafing to find his missing mate, but he breathes out strongly through his nostrils and visibly strains for patience.

"I have indeed agreed to accept your other males in our bed to please you, my bride. You need only choose the one you desire to join us this night." Zephyr looks nowhere in particular while my mates crowd around us in the stairwell, but I can feel the tension humming between him and Ronin like a live wire.

"Looks like *someone's* failed his Basics of Polyamory exam." Vasili slips one arm around my waist, one arm around Ronin's, and sneers at our prickly host. "Haven't you been reading your why-choose romance, darling? Zara doesn't have to *choose*. In this polycule, we're all together. If you can't manage the math… or the biology… you and the winged wonder will be occupying that royal bed of yours alone."

V's not a lightning witch, but fuck if this stairwell doesn't crackle with electricity.

Max lets loose with a possessive growl and his lean hot body crowds up against my back. Like the peacemaker he is, Neo hovers between the warring parties, but nibbles his lip and looks anxious. Even my patient Lucius is glaring at our obnoxious host, wolf eyes pulsing red in the witchlight. Ronin leans in to nuzzle V's ear, but my Brit's amber gaze smolders at Zephyr the whole time.

"Very well," Zephyr says curtly under the weight of our hostile stares. "By the moon, follow me or do not. I thought to give us all time to grow accustomed to this… novel arrangement. If you are so eager to warm the king's bed without delay, the lot of you are welcome there in your entirety."

Half my guys are still wrapping their heads around all that, and bristling over the irritating parts, when my Unseelie pivots away and darts through the little door that leads to the high tower above the lair. He's a fast mover, but I sprint right after him, now that he's not actively trying to separate me from my warlocks.

"Want me to push him off the roof again?" Ronin mutters behind me. "Forgot how pissy the bloke can be."

Despite the tension sparking in the air and my mounting concern over the absent Ash, I'm relieved Ronin can crack a joke (even a tiny one) over their effed-up history.

"Cut him a break, okay, Ronin?" Neo says softly as they all crowd into the snug spiral stair behind me. "He's really worried about Ash, and so is Zara."

I swear our bookworm is sweeter than any of us deserves.

Ronin grumbles as he climbs. Max can't seem to stop growling, low and deep in his chest. Lucius' wolf whines as our headmaster brings up the rear—guarding everyone's back. And Vasili's skulking silence is downright sinister.

But this uneasy state of affairs is probably as good as it's gonna get in this harem. I mean, at least until we all fuck (if that's even in the cards).

"Not if I have anything to say about it," Vasili murmurs in response to my thought, his tone sharp with spite.

I sigh and switch off the psychic leakage, then power up the stairs behind Zephyr's lithe scramble. A sudden gust of wind fills the stairwell and the door at the top blows open before Zeph even touches it, because his elemental Fae magic is wind.

He shoots through the doorway with me right on his heels. The room beyond opens around me. I jolt to a stop and stare in amazement.

This entire tower was closed off during my earlier visit, so I've never seen this joint.

And man, was I missing out.

I'm standing in a perfectly octagonal jewel of a room that's like an eagle's aerie, all high ceiling and sunken floor and leaded-glass windows all around. A wooden ledge like a window seat rims the space, piled with colorful cushions in some places and rows of vintage books and exotic artifacts in others.

Otherwise, this whole joint is basically one huge round bed, soft and squishy, gleaming with the feathery pastel iridescence of Faerie blankeys. I take one look and wanna sink right down into those deep soft depths with all my guys. Especially with accessories like fur-lined leather cuffs chained to the wall, a cushioned spanking bench parked against one window, and Zephyr's impressive collection of immaculately kept floggers, crops, and whips lovingly displayed on the walls.

Sweet Jesus.

The guy's even got a high-end dildo collection I've somehow missed getting acquainted with, I mean, until now.

Now he's not even hiding that shit.

This whole space is dimly lit by an impressive jumble of glowing violet crystals hanging from the ceiling, plus an ebbing sliver of ruby sunset over the flat expanse of orchid sea. Faint pinprick stars wink into view against the purple sky.

I'm still gaping at the spectacle when the guys pile into the room behind me. Like me, they stop and stare.

"Oh, crap," Neo whispers.

But he doesn't sound freaked out. He sounds… awed and reverent.

I sneak a peek at my fated mate and find him gazing at the elegant St. Andrew's Cross suspended over the bed. His lips are parted and his glasses are steaming.

Yowsa. That's gonna be something worth exploring.

But not now.

Zephyr slices one look across the empty room with its intriguing array of sexual options, then pivots and darts through one of two doors that bracket the one we just came through. I peek past the open door not chosen—clearly some kinda ultra-luxe bathroom sitch I totally wanna check out later, but it's empty.

Then I follow my fleet-footed Unseelie down a couple of stairs into a crescent-shaped den.

These digs are totally different, more like an Old World library done in weathered seadrift wood, piled high with shelves upon shelves of books that soar all the way to the shadowy ceiling. Complete with a rolling stair, a cluster of high-backed chairs and ottomans around a fireplace, the dangling complexity of an orrery with planets and moons and shit, then a massive desk backed up against a pair of stained-glass doors and a balcony.

It's obvi to me this is a well-loved and lived-in space, the desk cluttered with open books and curling papers and a witchlight orb for a reading lamp. Lavender witchfire crackles from a jumble of crystals in the hearth.

But this room too is empty.

Even though the still air is haunted by the bracing ocean-and-citrus aroma that says Ash to me.

"Ash," I say softly to Zephyr's still frame. He's standing totally still before the desk, staring at it intently, like he really hoped to find our guy there and now he's trying to will his Seelie lover into appearing. "Where is he?"

Slowly Zephyr turns to face me, his face all stark and drawn. Under the green slash of his eyepatch, his olive skin stretches tight. His throat ripples as he swallows.

"Where is he?" I ask again in a tiny voice, because now I'm afraid to hear the answer.

My Unseelie pulls in a slow breath. The soft sound fills the heavy silence.

Quietly he tells me, "I do not know."

# Chapter Twenty-Four
## Neo

"That's bullshit," my Zara says, in a hard voice that's meant to downplay how freaked out she is, just so we don't worry about her. "If Ash is supposed to be here and he's not, that means there's a major problem. We gotta find him. Like, *now*."

I'm worried about the Seelie Prince too.

I mean, it's not like Ash and I are lovers or anything (yet) because things are really complicated between Ronin and Zephyr (and don't even get me started on Zephyr and Vasili). So we've all been taking it really slow when it comes to integrating Zara's Fae *ménage* with the rest of our polycule.

But Ash is just really decent. He's always been super nice to me.

Plus my fated mate's in love with him.

Zara falls fast and hard. I think it's a queen thing and her Gemini instincts tell her when someone's right for us.

At least, that's the way she's been with all us guys. She falls in love like a woman falling off a cliff.

But we're always there to catch her.

Lucius lowers his briefcase and satchel to the floor and studies the endless rows of fascinating-looking books lining the king's den with wistful eyes.

Then my headmaster turns away from all that literary temptation with a determined sigh. "We'll gladly assist you in the search for Asher Aurelius, Your Radiance. Only I'm not certain how much help those of us who are new to Avalon will be in locating your lost prince—"

"No point searching for Ash in Avalon." Zephyr gives an impatient headshake and rushes over to a bookcase, where he starts scanning the titles on the spines like all our lives depend on it.

Vasili sneers horribly at our host's averted back, then strolls over to the desk and drops into the ornate royal chair parked behind it (which is clearly some kind of throne and not where he's supposed to be sitting). Totally undaunted, V drapes his long legs in his glitter jeans across the desk and props his combat boots with their violet soles right on a pile of important-looking papers.

"Well, if we're not going to bother searching for the winged wonder," V says coolly, examining his black-painted fingernails, "I could use a manicure before tomorrow's Ball. My cuticles are getting ragged. Does this kingdom of yours have a beauty salon? Or better yet, a day spa?"

"No. But if Ash is missing, I know where to find him." Zephyr drags a massive brass-bound book off the shelf with a soft exclamation, rushes over to thunk it down on the desk, then gives V's elegant sprawl a narrow look. "That chair is an Unseelie relic and a royal throne, Vasili Romanov. It is rightly mine."

"Apparently, I'm the Unseelie King's consort." Vasili frowns over his fingernails. "If you don't want me sitting in this chair, darling, where exactly *do* you want me?"

Ronin's drifted over to check out the massive orrery suspended from the ceiling that dominates the back corner. There's even a little staircase with a landing he's climbed to get a better look at a ringed planet. The moons and plants in that orrery are actually revolving around a bronze sun, and the whole fascinating assemblage definitely draws the eye.

But Ronin looks away from that so he can eyeball the unfolding Goblin King vs. Unseelie King dynamic. In a few seconds, it'll be like Godzilla vs. Mothra in here (I mean, if the monsters fucked while they fought).

Ronin snickers into the suddenly loaded silence.

I guess I'm not the only one who noticed the way Zephyr was ogling V in his black lace panties back at the lighthouse.

Zephyr's been flipping through the big illustrated book and poring over the heavy volume in a barely controlled frenzy. He's in such a rush I'm seriously worried he might tear one of those gorgeous hand-painted pages.

Now, hearing V's loaded challenge, he pauses in his frantic rummage to glance sharply at Vasili.

"If you're asking where I'll have you later," the Unseelie murmurs darkly, "I suspect the St. Andrew's Cross above my bed will do nicely. For now, get out of my chair."

Holy cow.

The charged silence that electrifies this room leaves me breathless. There's literally enough amperage crackling through the dim gloom of this room at twilight (despite them not having electricity in Avalon) to make my skin tingle and my hair rise.

Oh my gosh, the thought of V on that cross…

Vasili shatters the impasse with an eye roll and a rude snort.

"Keep dreaming, little king, *do,*" that snake hisses. "I'm the dominant alpha in this polycule. If anyone in this harem's getting spreadeagled over that cross with a dildo planted balls-deep in his derrière—beyond our First Boy, who's clearly already considering it—that person is going to be *you.*"

I'm so startled to hear my secret fantasy dragged into the open like that, I almost swallow my tongue.

I let out a mortified little moan that makes Max (who's pacing the perimeter of this room like a predator) pivot toward me with a hungry growl.

Zephyr gazes up at V in astonishment, then blinks and returns to his reading. "By the moon. At least you are now willing to concede that I belong in the harem. Now get out of my chair."

Deliberately Vasili leans back in the forbidden chair and closes his eyes with a look of total boredom that makes even me want to smack him. "What do you imagine you'll do if I don't?"

"Do you truly wish to know?" Zephyr breathes, in a voice that smokes with danger.

"Wow. Okay." Zara sounds breathless, and I totally don't blame her. There's enough testosterone swirling in here for me to grow a third testicle just from proximity to those two. "Let's not get distracted. We need to find Ash PDQ, guys."

"'Tis precisely that task I intend to accomplish," Zephyr mutters, turning pages in a frenzy. *"Ah."*

He stills like a fox who's just spotted a mouse. I mean, he's crouched over that book so intensely he's almost quivering.

At times like this, I remember what Zara always says about how the Dark Fae King's not actually human and we can't expect him to behave like one. The Fae aren't a witching race, they're a whole other thing. I'm betting that's why Zara didn't totally lose her shit when he brought her the severed head of his enemy as a bridal gift. Kind of like a cat leaving dead mice on your doorstep.

Anyway.

Zephyr's crouched over that open book like a feral animal.

Lucius pads across to peer deferentially over his shoulder. Zara grips my hand to draw me with her and pushes up against Zephyr's other side to look too. The Unseelie slips an absent arm around her little waist that makes me so happy, because those two need to touch more and interact more, until Zara forgives him for ghosting her.

Even V edges his combat boots casually to one side to get a peek at the book that's getting all this attention.

"Is this an Unseelie spellbook or what?" Zara looks up at Zephyr with her pretty eyes all round. "Cuz I can't read it."

"'Tis written in Ancient Fae," Zephyr says, clearly distracted, one finger gliding over the esoteric-looking glyphs and sigils inscribed in a rusty red ink that's all faded and flaking. "If you wish to read the Old Tongue, I'll teach you."

"Merciful Christ," Lucius murmurs, sounding deeply intrigued. "Is that volume… a demonology?"

"Yes." Zephyr leans in to peer at a faded line of text. "Written in mortal blood and bound in mortal skin."

*"Eeeew."* Zara recoils from the thing and from Zephyr with a shiver, and I swallow a quiet sigh of regret. So much for those two kissing and making up. "What the fuck, Your Radiance?"

The whole time we've been parked here, Ronin's been pretending to check out the orrery while Max paces the room like, well, a chained dragon. Now Ronin curses and swings over the brass rail to drop lithely from the viewing platform to the floor. He and Max both converge rapidly at the desk and crowd in close to get a look.

Vasili lowers his combat boots to the floor and leans over to see too.

Zephyr adjusts his eyepatch with a slight grimace like the thing bothers him, which it probably does. I've literally never seen him without it, he's probably self-conscious about the disfigurement. Now he presses the tips of his fingers to the bridge of his narrow nose and squeezes.

"If Ash is not in his accustomed place," the Dark Fae sighs, "that assuredly means my enemy must have him. I think perhaps 'tis time and more to speak to you of my cousin Mordred. He is the one whose brother's head I buried in your garden."

Yikes.

"Is *that* what you did with it? You buried that head in my garden?" I squeak like a mouse, which isn't a great sound for me. I clear my throat and dial it down an octave. "Um, no offense, Zephyr, but I hope you didn't bury it with the veggies. We eat from that garden."

"What kind of primitive do you take me for?" He lowers his hand and spares me a short exasperated look.

"Don't answer that," Ronin mutters to the room in general.

"If you must know," Zephyr says stiffly, "I interred him under the rose trellis in your *domus* courtyard, which is more honor than he deserves."

"Dez's roses." Ronin hovers behind him and looks like he's trying not to laugh. "She's been whingeing they're not thriving. They'll probably grow like bonkers now."

"I think we're all getting off topic," Zara mutters, peering warily over the Dark Fae's shoulder at the book. "You were talking about your cousin, uh, Mordred, right? Geez, I know you said before that he's demonic. But I didn't think you meant that shit, like, literally. I mean, you're not a demon yourself, right?"

"Of course not. He's merely a second cousin once removed," Zephyr says repressively. "Our bond of kinship is not close. But, yes, Mordred is half-Unseelie and half-demon. When he is not making my life hellish here in Avalon or tormenting those foolish mortals in your realm who dare to summon him, he resides in the demonical plane. Wherever he resides, if I wish to compel him to speak with me, then I too must summon him."

Whoa.

Actual, old-fashioned demon-summoning.

I didn't even know demons were a real thing.

Under normal circumstances, the Dark Fae King isn't exactly forthcoming. He's actually kinda taciturn. But when he isn't all clammed up, he's really worth listening to.

For example, there's so much information packed in that last reveal he just uncovered I don't even know where to start digging.

"Are you really going to summon Mordred from the demonical plane like Beelzebub?" I venture, peering at the book. "Is that even safe? I mean, even with chanting and candles and a pentagram, like that one right here in this book, for protection?"

Everyone pushes in closer to see what I'm pointing at.

We're all staring down in varying degrees of horror and fascination at the page blazoned with an inverted pentagram (apparently drawn in human blood on a skin page, which is really awful all on its own) when a sudden breeze from the open stained-glass door behind the desk brushes my skin.

At the exact same moment, a fresh whiff of ocean air and citrus hits my nose.

"No need to go summoning that little shit on my account," a craggy voice says wryly from the balcony. "Besides, Mordred's been kickin' up plenty of ruckus right here in Avalon since you lit outta here, Sparrow."

Both Zara's teal head and Zephyr's green one jerk up from poring over that awful book like they're marionettes and someone just tugged their strings in unison.

Behind his eyepatch, Zephyr's ruthless face ignites.

The stained-glass door swings wide under the thrust of a brawny male arm. I can't see much from this angle, just a big hand and a leather-cuffed forearm and a dark thorny vine with drops of crimson blood inked around a really impressive biceps.

But that's a tattoo I recognize.

My wonderful fated mate lights up like a Christmas tree and rushes around the desk toward the balcony. "Oh, thank fuck. *Ash.*"

# Chapter Twenty-Five
## Zara

"Sweet Jesus, Ash," I mumble into my Light Fae's consuming kiss. "Where've you *been*? You scared the living piss out of us."

But I sound more breathless with happiness than cranky.

I've *missed* this guy, like honest-to-God missed him—for months—and kissing him's a headrush. It really is.

"Sorry 'bout that, princess." He chuckles at my enthusiasm and engulfs my ass in his two big hands to ease me into the fortress of his body.

Ash is the biggest guy in my harem by a long shot, just a massive hunk of male, especially when his muscled frame's all on display in the slate doeskin pants and vest that fit his beefcake body like he's Conan the Destroyer, with his gorgeous pewter angel wings fully extended from colossal shoulders so the feathers caress my arms when I hug him. Laced tight behind that doeskin, and currently nudging me in the belly, is literally the biggest cock I've ever had.

He's so tall he towers over me.

He's so thick my arms barely span the tight column of solid muscle at his waist.

He's so big he could tighten his arms and snap me in two like a matchstick.

But he won't.

Ash would never, ever hurt me.

He's more than the biggest guy in my harem. He's also one of the gentlest. His brawny arms engulf me like I'm his precious treasure. His smooth fair skin smells bracing like ocean air and his kiss tastes tangy like Florida grapefruit.

I surface with a gasp from that monumental kiss and rise high on tiptoe to thread my fingers through his spiky pewter hair (which I can only do because he bends low to allow it). My touch skims over the tips of his pointy ears, that's an erogenous zone on a Fae. His silver eyes lock on mine and crinkle in a smile that creases his rugged face.

He's got some years on him, my Seelie does. But he wears them *really* well.

"Ash," I breathe.

I'm honestly so relieved and so happy to see him, my eyes blur and overflow with a sudden spill of tears.

Fuck.

"Howdy, princess," he rumbles deep in his chest. "Guess ya missed me, huh?"

"We thought you were stolen by demons or something." I blink fast to keep the tears back, but that just makes them spill over. "I mean, *demons*. How is that even a thing?"

"Welcome to Avalon, honey." He cups my chin in his big weathered palm and thumbs my tears away. "Demons from this particular legion— I mean Mordred and his brother—they're demi-royalty over here. Just born on the wrong side of the blanket."

"*Ash,*" Zephyr breathes, appearing suddenly at my side. His voice quivers with barely suppressed intensity. "You are never to do that again."

"Well, that's debatable. I'll do what I gotta. Hasn't exactly been a picnic here without ya." Ash opens his arms to gather in our Unseelie mate. "Hiya, Sparrowhawk."

And suddenly it's the three of us again, this Fae *ménage* I fell for, back when I was lost and drifting in the enchanted magic of an Avalon spring.

Zephyr's wiry arm shoots around my waist and drags me close. Simultaneously, he rises on tiptoe to give our Seelie Prince a hard claiming kiss that makes my pussy weep.

Ash's massive wings close around both of us to enfold us in a dark cocoon of warmth. Suddenly we're enveloped in eiderdown softness.

"Mmmm, that's what I'm talking about," I sigh blissfully into Ash's soft doeskin vest.

"Never again," Zephyr whispers into Ash's kiss, so soft only I can hear it. "You swore never to leave me. I was prepared to summon the very kraken to free you, my heart."

"Kraken, huh?" I turn my face into the silky spill of Zephyr's moss-green hair and breathe in his burnt amber spice. My lips brush his pointy ear in a way that makes him gasp. "First I'm hearing of that."

"You mustn't expect me to spill all my secrets." My Unseelie twists like a cat.

And suddenly his mouth is scorching mine.

The sweet spice of cloves and nutmeg—his distinctive aphrodisiac taste—sweeps over my tongue and floods my senses. This is the first time we've kissed since Zephyr turned back up. Kissing the Dark Fae King is like falling through a wardrobe into the enchanted land of Narnia. The hot slick of his tongue plunders mine with a consuming demand that tightens my nipples and roughens my breath. His tiny fierce incisors prick my lip.

A lick of heat sweeps through me like a bonfire and makes my hair rise and swirl. Under the gusset of my dragonscale catsuit, my cunt softens and opens for him like a night-blooming flower.

"My bride," Zephyr moans into my mouth. One hand closes around the back of my head to deepen our kiss. Pretty soon, he'll be tonguing my tonsils.

I moan into his mouth to encourage him.

"How I've longed for you… these weary weeks," he breathes against my lips between fiery kisses. "Tonight I shall make you mine… so completely… you will never again… doubt me."

Hell to the yeah for that shit.

That's what I'm talking about.

Xhevith's distant bugle rises from the lair, now somewhere below us in the purple twilight, under this balcony suspended high over the faerie sea. The haunting sweetness of lotus drenches the soft night air.

"Oh, God, Zephyr." Head spinning with need, clit aching with hunger, I grip a fistful of supple dragonscale and a fistful of doeskin and pull them both into me.

Both my guys.

Plus Xhev, who's linked up telepathically with his rider, in kinda this daisy-chain effect.

This is the way we're all meant to be.

Almost.

From the open balcony doors behind me, an ominous subterranean growl rolls out. That's Max's dragon, deeply in rut, responding to Xhevith's distant challenge.

"It's okay, Max." I emerge from the warm cocoon of Ash's wings and reach a hand back for my dragon. "I'm right here, big guy."

At least he knows Ash, so there's no need for intros. But Max is rutty as fuck, so he engulfs my hand in his hot grip and pulls me back possessively against his lean frame. While a crescent moon floats like a canoe over the night-dark sea, I wind an arm around Max's narrow waist and tuck a hand into the rear pocket of his ripped jeans to squeeze a palmful of taut dragon ass.

This dragon shifter of mine needs to put on weight, for real.

He's always been lean, he was half-starved growing up, plus he burns a ton of calories shifting and fucking.

Now he rubs his bristly jaw into my neck to scent me and rumbles a grumpy warning at both Fae to keep their distance.

My inner dragon croons to reassure him, and his dragon grumbles back at her. The thing he really needs right now (more than reassurance) is pussy, and ideally a clutch of his dragon eggs filling my uterus.

But for that, he's gonna have to wait.

And then share.

I wonder if I'm gonna have a problem with him tonight.

Ash steps back from all of us with a gentle sigh and lets his wings retract. They fold up against his back and rustle under the cut of his vest that's designed to accommodate. Underneath, I know, those wings will dwindle and melt into the ornate angel's wing tattoo that spreads across his broad shoulders and down the powerful column of his spine.

"For moon's sake," Zephyr murmurs at him with a frown, "where were you?"

"Teaching a Potions class," Ash says dryly. "More or less. Mordred's been plenty busy while you were gone, kid. Haven't seen his pissant brother though."

"That's because I killed him," Zephyr says offhandedly. "Lothian the Proud is no more."

"Huh." Ash grunts. "Well, he was always the lesser of two evils. With Mordred stirring the pot, whole Academy's turning into a hotbed of sedition. Figgered I'd give your students someone else to listen to about the politics for once."

"Ah, the legendary Avalon Academy for Promising Royals of the Faerie Court," Lucius says with interest from the balcony doorway. "Zara tells me you're a professor there."

"Yeah, mostly Potions and Healing Magic." Ash shrugs. "Just the standard Light Fae stuff. I'm the resident Seelie in this joint. I don't do the deportment and the arts shit on the core curriculum."

"Fascinating," Lucius says fervently, studying Ash with keen attention.

At least one of my alphas isn't growling.

My wolf's doing better than Max at handling his rut, but he can't tolerate being very far from me right now either. I reach back to lace my fingers through Lucius' callused grip and draw him outside with me, which pretty much fills the balcony.

"You're Lucius Aries, ain'tcha?" Ash gives him a respectful nod. "I knew your grandpa Laszlo. Long time ago now, but you look a lot like him."

While those two guys of mine swap their *hi how are ya's* (both reassuringly calm and cordial, clearly interested in each other's academic shit, but these aren't the two I'm worried about), Zephyr herds us all back into the library and closes the glass doors against the encroaching night.

Neo rushes over to say an enthusiastic hello, because he knows Ash and likes him. Needless to say, the feeling's mutual.

Everyone likes Neo. That's literally his bookworm superpower.

While Zephyr deploys this *Downton Abbey* manual bellpull thingie and orders up dinner for eight (eight of us now in this polycule!) to be schlepped up to the library, Ash ruffles Neo's purple curls and asks him about his studies, which my bookworm is sweetly eager to tell him.

Vasili's not openly nasty the way he easily can be, he's holding his fire in reserve. But he's still aloof as fuck and acerbic as vinegar, because he's Vasili. Ash swats aside V's stinging verbal zingers about his long absence with what looks like good-humored patience.

But Ash knows better than to trust him.

In fact, there's an edgy awareness sparking between those two that has us all twitchy.

But nothing can blunt the edge between Ash and Ronin.

Ash takes one look at Zephyr's first love, the guy who took Zephyr's eye and pushed him off a roof, then pins my Brit with a steely gaze that makes me genuinely afraid to leave the two of them alone and unsupervised in a room together.

Like, ever.

Ash doesn't say much to him (which is unusual all on its own, he's normally a friendly guy). But the way he's eyeing Ronin, I'm seriously afraid he's gonna unsheathe that hunting knife strapped to his corded thigh and bury it between Ronin's shoulder blades the second my warlock's back is turned.

Shit.

As for Ronin, he meets that Seelie's hostile stare with a nasty scowl that bristles with his own aggression. Then my Brit clams up and skulks off to check out the orrery.

That's a silent exchange that worries Lucius and upsets Neo.

Vasili gives Zephyr a venomous look like the whole steaming mess is his fault, then slithers off to join his boyfriend. Those two huddle on the viewing platform among the circling moons and planets, whispering and shooting suspicious looks at any Fae who strays too close.

Max hovers possessively at my side on the ottoman near the cool witchfire, his hand planted firmly on my thigh the whole time, and keeps a wary eye fixed on the balcony doors. Every time Xhevith's distant bellows seep through the glass (that dragon's restless tonight, so he's vocal), Max's slitted pupils narrow and he snarls at the rival dragon.

Long story short?

By the time an orderly queue of Zephyr's Unseelie servants file into the room bearing the covered dishes that contain our dinner, there's so much tension filling this study, the air in here's practically too thick to breathe.

Once Zephyr dismisses the servants with a regal nod, I can barely coax Vasili and Ronin to the big driftwood table where we all gather to eat. Even when I do manage to entice them over, those two warlocks range themselves as far from the two Fae as possible. Neo hurries over and snuggles up tightly against Ronin in a futile attempt to offer comfort.

That arrangement just makes the yawning abyss between my old guys on that side of the table, and my new ones on this side, more painfully obvious.

In addition, that fucked-up dynamic leaves a distracted Lucius and me, along with my very suspicious alpha dragon, to converse with Ash and Zephyr.

"You've implied you're the only Light Fae in Avalon," Lucius says to Ash with keen interest. My wolf's wielding the Fae's bone-handled cutlery with Old World elegance to navigate the rich game fowl, stewed in violet apples and pink pears, that came out of the big domed serving dish onto his plate.

Zephyr served Lucius and Max and me himself, which I know is a pretty major concession from a Fae royal, and Lucius was vocal in his appreciation. But Zephyr won't go anywhere near Vasili's side of the table. And Ash has his big shoulder turned in a way that very pointedly excludes Ronin on the end from the whole convo.

"Yup," Ash says now in response to Lucius, passing him the loaf of nutty bread we're all using to sop up the rich sauce. "I got nabbed by this guy and dragged through the portal to Avalon a long time ago. Ain't that right, Sparrow?"

Ash's eyes crinkle at Zephyr.

"'Tis what we Unseelie do," Zephyr murmurs. Briefly, his gaze flickers to Ronin, who's listening to this with a face like stone. Then, with a sigh, Zephyr turns back to Ash. "What an Unseelie covets for himself, he steals. Besides, as you've reminded me many times, you barely put up a token struggle."

Ash runs a gentle hand over the Dark Fae King's green hair and messes him up in a way no one else would ever dare.

"Yeah, well, like I said," Ash says tolerantly to Lucius, "I got nabbed, kinda like the princess here. But that's water under the bridge now. It's my choice to stay."

I know Ash isn't criticizing me for *not* staying, for going back to Icarus instead, which is my royal realm the same way Avalon is Zephyr's. Criticizing isn't the way Ash rolls. But next to me, Max stiffens right up. A potent hit of his bristly Russian aggression floods through our mating bond.

Under the table, I lay a hand on my dragon's sinewy thigh and squeeze gently to settle him down.

Shit. He's quivering with rut and territoriality.

Even before his hand closes over mine and wraps my fingers over the straining bulge behind his zipper.

Yowsa.

A pulse of my own mating heat lights up my pussy like a fireplace. Lucius' gaze locks with mine and his eyes glow red.

Still, my headmaster minds his manners. He clears his throat, retracts his fangs, and takes a genteel sip from the pewter goblet that holds his wine.

"I have so many questions about the Seelie race," Lucius says earnestly to Ash. I'm probably the only one who notices the hint of ruddy color (because he's hard and doesn't want anyone to know it) riding his high cheekbones above his goatee. "In the mortal world, they've grown exceedingly rare."

Ash swallows a bite of fowl and gives Lucius an unreadable look. "Not as rare as you think. We're just real good at hiding."

Which suddenly makes me wonder if maybe we've got some kinda Seelie hiding right under our noses at Icarus.

I give Max's thick dick a squeeze through his jeans, then ease my hand out (reluctantly, because he's not the only one at this table who's horny) from under the table to pour us both more wine. His dragon eyes smolder at me in a way that makes me wonder how long it's polite to wait before some of us—or, if I get my way, all of us—climb into Zephyr's big round bed.

"Oh, really?" Lucius leans forward and looks alert. "Your Seelie kin would be welcome at the Icarus Academy and in my *domus* at Villa Augustus. Truly, they would find no need to hide. You have my word on that as headmaster."

"Old habit." Ash shrugs. "That's how we survived the Sundering, you feel me? We learned to keep our wings under wraps and just fly under the radar."

By now, Lucius is totally intrigued. "But how would I know one if I saw—?"

"Never mind the medieval history lesson, *do*." From where he's holding court at the foot of the table, Vasili slices into this comfy convo like a jungle guide with a machete. "Let's not get distracted by shiny objects, darlings. We seem to have found the missing Seelie. Zara claims her crown tomorrow at the Faerie Ball—assuming we trust our Unseelie host. All that's needed now is to ensure this insurrectionist demon stays well out of our way for the next, oh, twenty-fourish hours. Then we fly straight back to Icarus—and make that bitch Cleo Ferrari wish she was never born."

My snake is clearheaded and coldblooded as fuck (same as always).

But I agree with most of that—except that part about abandoning Zephyr and Ash to deal with a possible insurrection alone.

I figure we'll cross that bridge when we come to it.

Max grunts with agreement for V's plan, then engulfs what looks like half a loaf of bread dripping with juices in a single bite, because that dragon's never met a meal he can't finish.

Seriously, that bite's so big he practically has to unhinge his jaw like a python swallows a rabbit.

"Too right." Ronin gives V's pronouncement an approving nod. "What we should be going on about is this blooming demon. Mordred."

"That does seem relevant," Neo says gently, with an apologetic look at Lucius, who clearly wants to dig into how to find hidden Seelie at Icarus. "We don't even study demons in our curriculum back home. It would definitely help to know something about their strengths and weaknesses."

Zephyr gives Vasili a narrow look, then shifts his gaze to meet Neo's big earnest eyes. "In their realm, they are legion. But a demon's strengths on this plane depend very much on the demon. This one— Mordred—is both helped and hindered by his Unseelie blood."

Neo tucks up against our broody Ronin and gives Zephyr an encouraging nod. "How so?"

"Once he's summoned—unlike a pure demon—no common pentacle can hold him," Zephyr says grimly. "He can appear in dreams and materialize in the flesh. He can disappear at will. He can travel great distances with a thought. He can bear with him any person or object he happens to be holding at the time. Moreover, he wields the elemental witchcraft of his Dark Fae bloodline in full wicked measure. But to enter this plane, he must first be summoned from the demonical realm—a curse which can only be cast at Samhain. Even so, 'tis no easy witchcraft for my rivals here to accomplish. Suffice it to say, I was… surprised… to find him skulking in Avalon a few weeks ago."

"Sounds like a fun guy." I take a hefty swig of the fruity golden wine in my cup to clear out the bad taste all this is leaving in my mouth. "So how do you get rid of him?"

"To the demonical realm," Zephyr says, "he can also be banished."

Lucius murmurs with respectful interest. Neo pushes up his glasses and his writing hand twitches like he's longing for a notebook.

"Guess that's our play then," I say casually. "Lure him to appear wherever we need him to be. Then just banish him back to the, uh, demonical realm. You know how to do that, right?"

Zephyr hesitates. "In a manner of speaking."

"Okay then." Shit, I'm actually starting to like this idea. "Once he's gone, sounds like he'll be stuck there till Halloween at minimum. By then, we can do whatever we need to do so these rivals of yours don't summon him out again."

"*We* will do nothing of the kind." Vasili homes in on my choice of pronouns and stings like a hornet. "*We* are already joining the party at Icarus a full day late. *We* are missing the start of our finals. The Horn of Ceres isn't going to stay hidden forever, you know. If you want Cleo's airbrushed ass out of your throne, little queen, *we* need to keep our priorities straight."

"He isn't wrong," Max mutters around another big bite. He's already emptied his plate twice and shows no sign of stopping.

Now he and V exchange a sneaky look across the table that gets my Spidey-senses tingling. I swear, those two are in cahoots over something. Probably some kinda anti-Zephyr campaign, and I'm not gonna put up with it.

But V's right about one thing.

I need to pick my battles.

"Okay, okay, no need to get snarky. We'll get my crown, head for home, find the Horn, pass our finals, and deal with Cleo." I tick off the priorities on my glittery fingers, but it's a growing list. I'm gonna need both hands. "Then we come back here and kick some demon butt. You don't need to come with, Goblin King, if you don't wanna."

"Yeah, some of you kids should probably stay home," Ash says casually. His silver eyes flick over Ronin, lounging disreputably across the table with his plate shoved away and his face all broody behind a curtain of inky hair. "Fewer backs to watch when we're hip-deep in demon shit."

Ronin sweeps his hair back and his tiger eyes turn menacing. Slowly he leans forward. "Hope you're not implying someone here needs to watch our backs like we're all lads in nappies."

"Naw, not implying that at all," Ash drawls. "But I'd rather focus both eyes on Mordred than keep one eye on you and your loose knife hand, Pendragon."

"My *what*?" Ronin pushes back from the table and shoves to his feet with a scowl. "The fuck's your problem with me, Aurelius? You've been giving me the stink-eye all night."

Ash's baritone voice drops multiple octaves to a rumbly bass. "Yeah, well I'm the one who patched up Sparrow after you knifed him in the face. Hell, you might as well have knifed him in the chest. You gutted him that night, Pendragon."

"Ash," Zephyr says tightly, shoulders hunching. *"Don't."*

Ronin's fists clench at his sides. "Not that I owe you any explanations, Aurelius. But I was *defending my sister*, you wing-tailed wanker."

"Defending your sister?" Now Zephyr shoots to his feet and incinerates Ronin with an incandescent glare. "Now that is absolute rubbish. I meant her no harm. I never in my life laid a finger on Gwendolyn Pendragon and you know it."

"But you were *stealing* her!" Ronin's face convulses in a rictus of pain that makes my chest ache. "That's what you do, you just said it yourself. Supposed to be an arranged marriage, so she'd no choice, had she? She never wanted you. You scared the piss out of her. Yet you snuck into our home in the middle of the night to steal my fucking sister for a wedding she didn't want."

"You pure, asinine, unmitigated *fool*," Zephyr breathes into the strained silence. "I did not creep into Pendragon Tower at midnight to steal your frail, fearful, uninteresting nitwit of a sister. I came to steal *you.*"

Ronin staggers, literally staggers, back a step and almost falls.

Vasili shoots to his feet to support him, but Ronin waves him wildly off.

My Brit's eyes are riveted on Zephyr with pupils blown wide. "W-what? But I—I thought—"

"For moon's sake," Zephyr hisses. "It was you I wanted. It was always you. The same way it was you and not Gwendolyn I chose for a lover at the Beltane fire. Ronin Kilcannon Pendragon, by my own Unseelie word—for you know I cannot lie!—I was coming to steal *you.*"

For a sec, I really wonder if Ronin's gonna keel over.

Under his tawny skin, his face goes white as paper. His spreading shock ripples through our bond like an earthquake.

I'm not even sure he's breathing.

Neo stares at this whole awful scene with his mouth open. Lucius presses his fingers to his lips and closes his eyes. Max senses his mate's distress through his bond with Ronin and starts growling, but I grip his arm hard to keep him in his seat. Ash studies Ronin with his brow furrowed in disbelief. Vasili smolders at Zephyr, nostrils flared and eyes venomous, as though he'd like nothing more than to drench this inconvenient ex from Ronin's troubled past in kerosene and light him on fire. (I honestly wouldn't put it past him.)

"Okay… wow… this is a lot," I whisper.

No one even looks at me. The entire table is riveted on Ronin and Zephyr.

Well, shit.

This is one convo that definitely does not need an audience. So I clear my throat and get up too. "Everyone out except Ronin and Zephyr."

When no one budges, I use my queen voice. "I mean it. Everyone out. Except you two. You really need to talk. It's, like, years overdue. Don't come out till you're done."

# Chapter Twenty-Six
## Zephyr

My lost eye pains me like hellfire.

This happens when I am under strain. But the hellish pain in my eye is naught compared to the volcano of heartbreak and outrage erupting in my heart.

Although the Avalon night is summer-warm, I crouch on my heels before the witchfire hearth and hug my knees for comfort.

At the edge of sight from my remaining eye, I can just discern Ronin, huddled wretchedly at the table over the messy remnants of our abandoned supper. He remains precisely where he has lingered since Zara cleared the room for this long-delayed encounter.

My former lover's face is buried in his hands, midnight hair streaming over his fingers and pooling on the table before him like inky tears. His white-knuckled fingers dig cruelly into his face. As though he would peel off his own skin to escape this ruin of all that is left of our love.

In fact, he's digging those digits into his own skin so harshly he'll surely do himself an injury.

Not that I would care, for my own sake.

But Zara will not thank me if her warlock is damaged under my watch.

With a reluctant sigh, I adjust my eyepatch over my empty socket, straighten my stiff and aching body, and tread toward the table with leaden feet.

My approach is not silent. But he—this consummate hunter and killer of men—he betrays no sign that he hears.

I clear the residue of old rage that clogs my throat. Swallow down the bitter bile of old regret.

"Ronin," I say gruffly.

"How can you even stand to look at me?" His muffled voice barely seeps through his palms. "I ruined your face for nothing. Spurned your love for nothing. Halfway *blinded* you—for nothing. And Gwen, she… died anyway. She always felt guilty that I—killed my own lover—for her sake."

His voice splinters and his shoulders shake. I am no mind-reader, not like he is. But I require no telepathy to know he is weeping.

A perverse and terrible ache of tenderness—for *him*, this treacherous mortal lover who betrayed me—seeps through my frozen heart.

"Stop scrubbing at your face," I say roughly. "It won't bring her back. Besides, if you damage yourself, Zara will have my very head on a serving platter. One whiff of physical pain through that bond you share, and our queen will descend on this chamber like a Valkyrie."

Ronin huffs out a harsh breath that acknowledges this truth. But at least his shoulders stop shaking.

Zara is a safer subject for him than Gwendolyn.

Safer for both of us.

"Word to the wise. You'll not get the shifters off her tonight," he mumbles through a raspy throat. "She's almost fertile, and they're in full rut. All three of them. Even Vasili, though he hides it better than the rest of that lot. Denies it, even to himself. But he's pissy with rut."

This sounds more like the Ronin I knew.

"'Tis a useful insight. Though if Zara wishes to open her womb in this realm, she need only drink enchanted moon tea or wine to conceive. This I have told her before. A certain herb, mixed with either, will open any womb in Avalon." I unbend enough to splash common wine from the pitcher into his long-dry goblet. "Fortunately, I have never opposed the notion of sharing her. We Unseelie royals have long been polyamorous."

He grunts and lapses back into brooding silence.

But at least he's stopped tearing at his own face.

I fortify myself with a long swallow from my own cup and savor the fruity bite of Avalon apple laced with pomegranate. A poor antidote to the bitter brew of rage I've been quaffing by the dram since the night took my eye.

"Let us speak plainly," I say at last, frowning down at his lowered head, "if speak we must. Ronin… how… for moon's sake, how could you possibly *ever* imagine I meant to steal your sister?"

His hands drop at last to reveal his ravaged face. His amber eyes are reddened and his lashes spiky with tears.

Damnation.

My unruly heart twists like a wrung cloth.

Ever since we were boys, striking up our unlikely friendship, playing at kings-and-castles near the standing stone portal on his Welsh estate, I've never been able to abide his tears.

"Bollocks. How could I think anything else?" His voice scrapes, raw with disbelief, through a throat thick with grief. "Your mum and my dad arranged that blasted betrothal between you and Gwen before we could toddle. Always looming over us, wasn't it?"

"Indeed, it was." Under the cutting strap of my eyepatch, my brow furrows. "But then there was *you*. My secret friend, my would-be brother, and then… in time… more." Harshly I clear an obstruction from my throat. "After that night—after we came together at the Beltane fire—I knew I would never take any other Pendragon to my bed."

His topaz eyes fire with mutiny. "Yet you pitched up for Gwen anyway, right on the blooming night that contract called for—"

I lower my cup to glare. "I 'pitched up' to repudiate that moon-cursed contract and steal you instead."

"Left it a bit late then, didn't you?" he demands with mounting heat. "My poor sister was in hysterics. She bloody begged me not to let you drag her off."

The vast extent of his incomprehension is truly hopeless. For too long, he has doubted me.

For too long, he has hated me.

My hands lift in a gesture of utter futility.

"My mother, Queen Maeve, was not… an easy woman," I say carefully. This is so clearly a gross understatement that my Unseelie throat, which is physically incapable of uttering an untruth, nearly closes around the words.

I hack through the obstruction with the ruthless sword of truth. "That infernal contract was purely Maeve's doing. I—needed every minute of that time—to persuade her to undo it."

"But you're the la-dee-dah Dark Fae King. The omnipotent almighty tyrant of the Unseelie realm. You're bloody King Henry the Eighth, only there's physically less of you." He looks me over, in all the militant splendor of my dragonscale armor, with a blatant disbelief that drips with scorn and mockery. "Nothing happens here except by your command."

"In those days, believe me, Maeve wielded far more power than I did." I meet his skepticism with my own exasperated grimace. "As you can surely appreciate, Ronin Pendragon, 'twould serve me no purpose to steal you away to the Faerie realm, only for my wrathful royal parent to send you straight back!"

In truth, my monstrous mother—with her carnal appetites—would have been equally likely to snatch up an exotic morsel like Ronin, with his beauty and power, and make him her own slave and concubine.

That abomination, I could never have borne.

My own wrath is rising and my patience slipping. After all, am I not the wronged party in this hellish mess? That Ronin lost his sister is none of my doing. But it is, most assuredly, his fault that I lost an eye.

"By all that is right and proper," I grit, "it should be I who condemn you for having so little faith in me. So little trust in our love."

The harder I fight for control, the swifter it slips like sand through my fingers. I lean forward, grip the table's edge until my nails leave crescents in the wood, and glare at this bedamned creature who stole my tender heart, then valued it so cheaply.

"That night…" I breathe deeply "…the night we finally came together… that night meant *everything* to me. Yet to you, very clearly, it meant nothing—"

"Nothing?" Ever the warrior, he shoves to his feet and glares right back. "For fuck's sake, Zeph! When you turned up trespassing on my roof—at the same damn hour the contract said you'd come for Gwen— even then, I only meant to throw the knife to warn you."

"Pity your hand slipped," I say tightly.

"You moved just as I threw." By the moon, he even dares to sound indignant.

I've heard this from him before. Amidst a blinding snowstorm on a night without moon or stars, chaos reigned on that roof.

But he is mortal.

He can lie.

And I've clung to my grievance against him far too long to relinquish it so easily.

He frowns at my stubborn silence. "Bollocks, how'd you even survive the fall? I—searched the rocks under Pendragon Tower straightaway, I searched till dawn, but you were nowhere. I… assumed the tide took you."

These are memories I scarcely care to revisit. The forced recollection clips my syllables and abrades my courtesy.

"I was barely conscious. I can scarcely recall. But Xhevith plucked me from the sea—and brought me straight to Ash." My fists clench and unclench. "'Tis fortunate for you I didn't tear down that tower around your ears and seed your farmer's soil with acid in wrathful retribution. Believe me, I was tempted."

Ronin folds his arms across his chest and scowls.

For a breath, I'm utterly distracted by his furious beauty. His decadent mane of midnight hair spills in a wind-whipped tangle down his back, his golden skin is flushed with passion, and the mortal witchery called psi fire makes golden flames dance in his eyes. The inky fire of his tattoo—an adornment that is new, in the years since I traced and tasted every handspan of his skin with my tongue—that tattoo wicks above his collar to lick along his neck.

What's more, he still wears those damnable leather pants that encase his narrow hips and sinewy thighs like a glove. In proper dragonscale, he would look truly wicked. For he *is* a dragonrider. He rides that behemoth Maxim without a trace of fear, by all appearances he glories in dragon flight, and I hold utterly no doubt my Xhevith too would tolerate him.

If Ronin were ever my consort, he would have that right. To share my dragon, to wear my colors, to warm my bed—

"So what happens now?" he says abruptly. "An eye for an eye?"

Rudely interrupted in my ogling and musing, I release the table and fall back in shock. Mine is a reaction I'm far too startled and too appalled to hide.

In earnest truth, no matter what's passed between us, I'd rather take my own remaining eye than ever wield my blade against him.

No doubt he can read these thoughts—and the others too—in my face. Where I'm concerned, he was always far too perceptive.

It occurs to me that I'm tempted to ask him what he would *like* to happen.

Most of all, what he would like to happen between the two of us.

But I'm nowhere near prepared to hear him answer.

"Now…" In desperate search of some safer inspiration than these unruly musings about my unresolved feelings for my former flame, I glance toward the closed door that leads to the royal bedchamber.

Beyond that door, the hushed murmur of my queen and her harem—*our* harem, if I can ever manage to win them—beckons me.

Yet the deep baritone rumble of my own Seelie consort is (uncharacteristically) silent.

"Now," I sigh, "I must somehow persuade Ash not to challenge you to lethal combat to avenge my lost eye and shattered heart. I fear that persuasion will be no easy feat."

# Chapter Twenty-Seven
## Zara

By the time Ronin finally stops shaking with grief and shock, it's after midnight.

Not that I'm wearing my dive watch or anything, because that battery-powered shit doesn't work in Avalon. But Lucius packed an antique pocket watch that winds with an old-fashioned key, so we can keep track of the passing time here (because finals).

Anyway.

Ronin.

I've got him tucked up behind me in the soaking tub in Zephyr's luxe Unseelie bathroom. Ronin and I are immersed to the chest and floating in piped-in water from the hot springs under this volcanically active island. Pale lotus petals cover the tub's steamy surface and obstruct the view down under.

But I can feel that my warlock's finally stopped trembling against my back.

Thank fuck.

I tilt my head back against Ronin's slick chest and lift my gaze from the sea-green frescoes of mermen and krakens swirling over the walls so I can check out the dome overhead. Through the ripple of thick volcanic glass, strange constellations revolve through an indigo sky, sliced by a sickle moon.

"Feeling a little better now?" I say softly.

"Gods, I dunno." Ronin still sounds raw, but he loops his arms around my waist, settles me more comfortably between his corded thighs, and rests his chin on top of my head. "It's a lot to wrap my head round. I took his eye for nothing. Be lucky if that Seelie bloke of his doesn't knife me in the face tonight while I'm down for a kip."

"Ash would never do that," I say as firmly as I can. "He'd never attack someone—especially one of us—while we're sleeping."

Even though there's no hiding from a telepath like Ronin that (at least in this specific case) I'm not one hundred percent sure.

Zephyr and Ash have been gone for hours, working through all this shit (I hope). Ronin filled in the blanks from his convo with Zephyr for the rest of us. My other warlocks are holed up in the royal bedroom next door. Judging by the cadence of Lucius' patient murmurs and Max's halting replies, my headmaster's quizzing my dragon to help him prep for the written part of our finals.

Their words are too muffled to make out, but the whiplash crack of Vasili's biting intervention makes me wince. Neo's soothing murmur in reply makes me smile.

Thank fuck for Neo.

Tonight we're all on edge.

We could all use a little sweet bookworm love.

"Hardly blame him if he does." Still stuck on the subject of the vengeful Ash, Ronin heaves a sigh that makes the water quiver. "Fuck me. Can't believe Zeph's even letting me stay. If not for you, love, and all this succession rot, I'd be tossed out of Avalon on my arse. And I'd bloody well deserve it."

I'm totally limp and boneless in the heat, muscles and sinews *al dente*, like overcooked spaghetti. But Ronin has a warrior's survival sense, and I trust his instincts.

Hearing his misgivings, I stir in the slippery tub with a twinge of unease. "Zephyr knows the truth now about what happened. You both do. I'm hoping you'll find some way to forgive each other. Or at least, you know, tolerate each other."

Now it's my turn to heave a worried sigh.

I really *don't* want one polycule in Icarus and a totally separate Fae *ménage* here in Avalon.

I don't want two warring bands of warlocks hating and distrusting and sniping at each other across the miles.

I want all of us together.

That's what I've always wanted.

For tonight, I guess, I'll have to settle for no one getting knifed in their sleep.

The bathroom door swings open with a creak. Because the new arrival doesn't bother knocking or asking if maybe we want privacy, I'm not surprised when the cool hiss of my snake's stealthy approach slithers through our mating bond.

"Maybe knock next time first, bad boy," I murmur, because it's never too late to learn basic manners. "Ronin or I coulda been peeing in here."

Vasili spares a scornful look for the quaint gravity-flush toilet in the corner that makes Ronin snicker.

"I certainly knew Ronin wasn't." V sneers. "He pisses with the door wide open."

This is true, and an unfortunate reality of living with multiple guys is that half of them don't bother closing the door when they pee. I've had to lay down some pretty firm boundaries to stop those guys from barging in on me or Neo or Lucius (the modest ones in this harem) while we're doing our business.

"Knock first next time, okay?" I repeat. Just because you're sociopathic doesn't mean you can't learn basic bathroom etiquette. "But c'mon in now, I guess."

I mean, since he's already in anyway.

"Thank fuck." V closes the door pointedly on Max's struggling recital of the timeline of the two Witching World Wars. That's the last time the Horn of Ceres was at large—in some private Nazi art collection—before the witching world magicked it back. Then the artifact vanished into the Academy Vault.

Now, apparently, it's out again.

"I literally can't tolerate another syllable of that tedious Witching World History," Vasili pouts, "without turning actively homicidal."

"Poor love." Ronin gives him the affirmation he's looking for, even when V's being a pissy prick who's been mocking Max all night.

"Hmm." Vasili still looks cross. "Well, if you don't like having me in here, you can blame Lucius. He practically ordered me out of the bedroom. Says Max doesn't do well with me listening."

"Can't imagine why," I murmur. Poor Max.

"Nah, we don't mind. Let's have a kiss," Ronin suggests easily. "Been missing you."

The Goblin King hums and prowls over the swirling vortex of the maelstrom mosaic floor without a single apparent shit for the ancient fae artistry of our surroundings. He rears over the tub to peer down on us. He's carrying an open wine bottle without a label carelessly by the neck.

When he reaches the tub, he lifts the bottle for a casual sip, then swipes his tongue over his glistening lips.

Simultaneously, he takes one look at my pierced tits bobbing among the lotus petals and purrs at the sight.

Just the sound of that purr makes my nipples tighten.

"Hiya, bad boy," I breathe.

My gaze and Ronin's drift over our mate in unison. V's long lean body looks scrumptious in the silky sleep pants and lace cami he lounges around in at night. He's like a male ballet dancer, sculpted and sleek—and already hard. His impatient length juts against the thin fabric in a way that makes my heart pound and my skin heat. Under his tousled punk-rock shag of silver hair, he's all dewy-faced from the moisturizing goop that's part of his bedtime beauty routine.

I lick my dry lips and reach for that wine bottle he's toting. His eyes, blue as glaciers, lock with mine.

"Gimme," I say softly.

His lips part and one fang slips into view. He hisses in a breath and passes me the bottle. Without breaking his shimmering stare, I lift the bottle to my lips and take a swig.

I swear to fuck, the Fae make the best wine. V's already drunk half of it, but this vintage tastes like honeysuckle and wildflowers and something tart like blackberry. It's fizzy and fermented and more like medieval mead than modern wine.

I lick the potent fizz from my lips and take another slow swallow.

Ronin reaches for Vasili's hand and gives a playful tug.

*"Darling."* Our snake swoops down to give Ronin the kiss he's demanded, all domination and hunger and an electrifying flash of tongue. That's his way of taking care of Ronin and soothing his grieving heart.

Ronin wraps an arm around V's neck and gives a throaty moan that vibrates with raw need.

I tilt back the bottle again, because this honeysuckle wine is addictive, and let the vintage slip down my throat. Faerie wine is potent shit, so I'm already feeling warm and floaty.

Then I turn my head lazily against the curve of Ronin's arm to watch.

Up close and personal, the caramel-and-vetiver wallop of my snake's Mogadon mating scent—laced with fuck-me-now pheromones—hits my already-intoxicated senses like a freight train. Vasili's tall supple frame radiates heat like the *domus* furnace (I mean, when it's working). His high cheekbones are flushed and his glacial eyes glitter like that iceberg must've done in the moonlight right before the *Titanic* went down.

Long story short?

Our Goblin King's not really rooted in his clever coldblooded mind tonight.

He's sexed way the fuck up.

And even though this Avalon moon isn't full enough to boost me into full-blown mating heat, I am *here* for it.

V has one hand braced on the tub for balance and one hand fisted in Ronin's man-bun thingy that our mate rigged to keep his hair out of the water. (Because there aren't any blow-dryers in fairyland. And long hair takes forever to air-dry.)

This choreography gives me all the leeway I need to prop the wine bottle on the floor, slip my fingers under the hem of Vasili's cami, and start peeling the creamy carnation-pink lace up the supple length of his torso.

Ronin helps me while those two deepen their kiss, and V helps too (for once) by slipping his sleep pants down his narrow hips. His long pretty cock pops into view, flushed and twitching and *very* erect in the pearly moonlight that's our only source of light. Silver steam twines from the tub and beads all those sleek inches with tiny glittering jewels of moisture.

Fuck. Me. Sideways.

Just the sight of that cock.

It's shifter dick. It's *his* dick.

That first glimpse of Goblin King dick makes my greedy pussy clench right up.

I reach for another swallow of wine, then lean forward to lick a slow cool stripe up his shaft from his balls to his tip.

V's breath spills out on a gasp. His hand clenches hard in the careless knot I've twisted my curls into. His other hand grips his shaft, gives himself a leisurely pump, then feeds me his length.

"Better get your pretty ass in this tub, Goblin King," I breathe against his cockhead, not giving him what he wants, but tonguing his slit to tease out a few drops of precum. "I want you to fuck my face. But we're doing this my way."

"Oh, fuck yeah." Ronin leans forward intently to cradle my tits and thumb my nipples, already tight and tingly from the foreplay. "This shit's just what I need tonight. Take my mind off things a bit, yeah?"

"Hmmm. The two of you seem to forget who gives the orders," Vasili breathes. "And contrary to popular belief, it's *not* that pointy-eared tyrant with the dragon. But I like where you're taking this, so I'll allow you the privilege this once."

Graceful as a ballerina, V smirks at me and lifts one leg into the tub.

I can barely hold off long enough to let his foot find purchase between my entwined legs and Ronin's before I'm on him. My hands wrap around V's tight little ass. My mouth seals around his cock.

Then, I swear, I go down on him like a cheerleader on prom night.

His hard shaft fills my mouth and his delicious musky spice spreads over my tongue. He waxes like a stripper, so I can bury my face in the smooth vee of his Adonis belt and breathe in his spicy mating scent. I hollow my cheeks and suck up and down his shaft till his breathless moans bounce off the walls. He grips my head and bucks into my mouth and it's amazing he doesn't fall right into the tub.

But, you know, he's Vasili.

When he nudges the back of my throat, I wrestle my gag reflex into submission and swallow him down. Then I back off his glistening length and do it again. I give all those inches he's packing a real throat massage.

"Oh, little queen, I swear," he breathes on a velvety moan, "you give the most delicious head."

Ronin curses and tips a trickle of cool wine down the side of my neck, then leans in to lick it off. He mouths his way down my neck and shoulder with slow sucking kisses that send tingles racing down my spine.

I can feel the play of his lips and tongue all the way down to my clit.

When he finds the twin punctures of Lucius' mating bite, nestled in the junction where my neck meets my shoulder, Ronin sucks hard enough to make me whimper, because my scars are super sensitive.

Meanwhile, Ronin slides a hand down my tummy between my thighs to explore my slippery folds. I part my knees wider and wiggle impatiently till he finds the hard nub of my aching clit. When Ronin hits exactly that right spot, I cry out around V's cock.

Ronin lets out a sound somewhere between a winded chuckle and a starving groan.

While he runs slow teasing circles against my happy button, his rapidly thickening boner nudges into the crack of my ass.

This is a promising development, because this water's slick with bath oil. The scent of lotus and sex perfumes the steamy air. While I massage the throbbing underside of Vasili's shaft with my tongue and tease his perineum with my fingers, I writhe under Ronin's touch and notch his rock-hard dick right up against my pucker.

"Bloody hell," Ronin groans through gritted teeth.

In the background, the soothing drone of Max's history lesson abruptly switches off.

Vaguely I realize we must be getting kinda loud.

"Hush, darlings, *do*." V sneers around a genteel sip of wine. "You'll disturb Maxim's history tutorial. God knows, he needs it."

Sad to say, I'm already too far gone to focus on Max's academic needs right now. Besides, our growing arousal ricochets through our mating bond in a way all our mates have to be feeling.

*Um, babe?* Neo whispers through our bond, sweet as fuck. *Lucius' fangs are out and Max is half-shifted out here. Would you three mind, like, company?*

Vasili picks this right up, because he's bitten Neo and they're bonded.

*You should know there's a queue for her cunt,* my snake volleys right back at him. *And I'm first.*

He's so awful Ronin starts laughing. It's the wild unhinged kinda laugh that's the reason half the school calls him a psycho.

But I'm so thankful to hear Ronin laugh (even like a psycho) after the shit he's been through tonight. I disengage from V's cock with a *pop!* and give my horrible alpha a coy upward look.

Vasili gazes down at me through hooded lids. His pupils are all dilated to swallow the cool blue of his irises. A hectic flush rides his elegant cheekbones.

"Don't be a brat, Goblin King," I warn him with a wink that makes him snarl. "Better hurry if you want first pussy."

In a blink, this tub (which really wasn't built for three) is full of slippery punk-rock warlock. My alpha's crouching between my legs with water splashing around his thighs and lotus petals clinging to his tummy. I lean in to tongue the neat punctures of Lucius' mating scars on his sinewy inner thigh.

"Naughty queen," he growls. "Don't tease."

Then the velvet fist of V's telekinetic witchcraft plucks my dripping body right out of the water and—holy fuck—impales my needy pussy balls-deep on his dick.

Whoa.

Vasili's normally a foreplay-first kinda guy. He likes to sample and nibble and graze before he feasts.

But tonight, somehow, he's starving.

His possessive arms close hard around me. He shoots to his feet with me spitted on his dick and fused to his body by the force of his witchy gift. I yell and wrap my limbs around his slippery frame to find some kinda leverage. My cunt clamps around his cock and pulses with hunger for all those eager inches. His face hardens with ruthless intent and his mouth opens on a feral growl.

He lunges for my kiss. My mouth fuses with his honeyed heat. I lap the taste of Faerie wine off those sexy fangs he's always hated.

Vasili snarls and grips my ass and pumps into me, setting a hard desperate rhythm that makes me see stars. The tiles echo with the slosh of water and the carnal slap of flesh on flesh.

Behind me, Ronin coils to his feet. His hot feral body winds around both of us. His impatient dick rides the crack of my ass, the smooth ring of his Prince Albert slick with oil. I'm really slippery back there, and he's both skilled and motivated. He works his way around Vasili who's currently hogging me, our snake's hands simultaneously engulfing my ass and spreading me wide.

"Mine," Vasili growls at both of us. "This is mine."

"Yeah, I know, love," Ronin moans. "We're both yours. Not gonna challenge you for her cunt while you're rutty."

Cheese on toast. Is *that* what's happening?

Is this my cool, aloof, inscrutable alpha—the guy whose only shifter genes are recessive, who literally needed the biochemical hit of Lucius' bite to trigger his first shift?

Is Vasili going into rut?

V's eyes open and he gives me a sly look. "If I am, darling, then lucky you."

Well, shit.

That's all three of my shifter guys in rut.

Clearly, Ronin knows how to placate a rutting alpha. Vasili subsides into short slow thrusts while Ronin fits his pierced dick against my pucker and starts working his way in, inch by tortuous inch.

His mouth meets Vasili's over my shoulder in a scorching kiss.

I like ass play and I get lots of it in this harem. But I still whine at the burning pressure of Ronin's cock filling my ass. My head falls back on a gasp. Vasili wraps his telekinesis around our abandoned bottle and drizzles a trickle of honeysuckle wine between my breathless lips. I gulp and swallow the cool fizz.

When Ronin bottoms out deep inside me, we all moan and shiver. Now I'm the bacon in a warlock sandwich, pinned between their hot slippery bodies, filled to bursting with warlock dick in all the best ways.

"Sweet Jesus," I whisper. "I love you guys."

These two together. They've always been lethal.

Lethal to my self-control.

Even more lethal to my heart.

Vasili's savage stare locks on mine. "Say it again. Just for me."

I know what he needs to hear. "I love you, Vasili. You're mine."

He shudders hard all over, then pumps into me deeper.

"*Fuck,*" Ronin groans from the heart. "Gods, love, I can feel that. He's so hard. And you're so tight."

"Uh huh." I twine my arms around Vasili's neck and our tongues meet in a slow hot glide. V's eyes are closed and his brow is furrowed. His cock pulses against my core.

He's barely holding off his big O. But I want him to spill inside me.

Then my Brit rocks inside me, which drags his Prince Albert against Vasili's shaft through the thin membrane that separates these two dicks inside me.

And V… he… loses it.

An animal howl tears from his throat. His dick pulses inside me and heat spurts against my inner walls. He pumps into me fiercely, Ronin matching his pace, their two dicks pistoning into me fore and aft in a relentless rhythm that makes hot cum leak past V's still-erect cock and trickle down my thighs.

Under this kinda attention, my magic moment shoots me into the stratosphere like a goddamn rocket.

I scream in a vibrato that makes a fork of purple lightning zigzag past the glass dome.

Ronin grips my hips and buries himself deep in my ass with a shuddery groan like I'm killing him. When his dick kicks and jets inside me, he slays all three of us.

Pinned limp and twitching between them, all of us trembling and slick with sweat and oil, I'm shattered.

They're both still pumping me through the aftershocks when the bathroom door flies violently open. Max shoulders in, with a feral-looking Lucius and a wide-eyed Neo crowding in behind.

Max peels his shirt off with one arm and leaps halfway across the room in two bounds, with the other two right behind him. Then he stops sharp—so sharp the other two pile right into the back of him.

"Hi, guys," I gasp with a loopy grin.

I'm high on endorphins and shifter biochemicals from Vasili's jizz injection. I'm drunk on Faerie wine and the potent spice of my own mating scent.

But I've still got enough left in the tank to give all my guys a ride tonight.

Max gives the air a hard suspicious sniff. His slitted pupils telescope wide.

"Saint Sergius guard us," Max growls. "Vasili. You are fertile."

"What's that, love?" Ronin slips his spent dick out of my pucker and nuzzles a satisfied kiss into the side of my neck.

"I said, Vasili. He is fertile," Max grates in his gravelly voice. "He is… ready to be filled with eggs."

"Well, darling, *that* would be a bit difficult," Vasili pants, smirking into my muddled gaze. "Since, the last time I checked, I don't seem to have a uterus. Have a peek under my nonexistent skirt, why don't you, and see for yourself."

"Not in this form." Max is so guttural I can barely make out the words. "As warlock, you are male. But your dragon is… both. Sometimes, in your shifted form, you are female."

My head and Ronin's snap toward Max in unison.

"Merciful Christ." Looming at Max's shoulder, Lucius' fangs drop and he literally falls to all fours like a dog.

His wolf will be out any second.

"Oh my gosh," Neo breathes, eyes huge behind his glasses. He clutches Max's hand and almost vibrates with excitement. "Max. Are you saying V's dragon is, like, non-binary?"

"Don't be ridiculous," V says shortly.

"That is what I am saying." Max draws his free hand across his mouth. I wonder if maybe he's drooling.

"Wow, V!" Neo grins at all of us with his eyes shining. "Why didn't you tell us? That's so awesome."

"Hold on a sec. I'm not sure I'm tracking." Carefully I start to wiggle off my snake's still impressive boner so I can think.

But V hisses and tightens his grip on my ass. Clearly, he's not finished. Definitely a rut situation going down with him (in addition to whatever else). And I'm certainly not opposed to accommodating.

Okay then.

While Ronin sinks down into the tub like his rubbery legs won't hold him up, then folds his arms over the rim and stares at Max, I wrap an agreeable arm around V's neck and look expectantly toward our dragon.

"You were saying?" I prompt.

"In his human form, Vasili is very male." Max's fangs (which are bigger than Lucius') drop prominently into view. The orbs of his dragon eyes pulse with fiery heat. "But his dragon form… is both. Both male and female. I have always known this."

My brain expands to wrap around this whole concept. I'm not turned off by any of my guys expressing every aspect of their identity. The concept of a gender fluid dragon in the polycule doesn't seem to faze my dragon queen either.

So far, V's flying snake has always presented to my dragon as male. But I feel like maybe my dragon's open to other options.

And, Jesus, the thought of V and Max together like that…

"Wow," I say, low and husky.

Vasili is silent, but I'm guessing it's occurred to him before that his shifted form is polygender. But he's still wrapping his complicated Goblin King head around it. It's totally his private thing to share (or not) when he's ready.

It's the other piece of what Max just said that's hitting him so hard.

"Explain yourself… if you can," V says shortly. "About the *eggs*. Lucius, pet, I can barely hear him over your growling."

Lucius sits back on his haunches with an apologetic look. But he manages to throttle back his wolf's lusty rumbles.

Guess I'm not the only one who's having a reaction to the thought of a gender fluid Vasili—even if he's only non-binary in dragon form— in our harem.

"If your dragon rises tonight," Max says slowly into the resulting silence, "in that form, Vasili, you are fertile. You can carry eggs. I can smell it. Sweetheart… my God… will you let me—?"

"No," V snaps. Color floods into his face. "Are you insane? *Obviously*, no. Dear fuck. The last thing this harem needs is me coiled up in a nest somewhere for months *incubating*, with you in dragon form brooding over me."

"Zara will be with us in the nest," Max says darkly, giving me a look that smokes with purpose. "I will breed her first. You will both carry my dragonets."

My tummy flutters and my cunt clenches.

It shocks the fuck out of me to realize I'm not totally opposed, for my own self, to this whole breeding and nesting scenario. Max and Lucius have both wanted this forever (except, in Lucius' case, his fantasy leans toward dens and packs and wolf pups).

Either way, we've got Cleo and Messalina and maybe even this insurrectionist demon Mordred to deal with first.

"Well, you can leave me out of *that* little fantasy." Vasili sniffs with absolute disdain. "Now you just come over here, Maxim Rasputin, and feed that impregnating dick of yours to Zara."

# Chapter Twenty-Eight
## Maxim

My impregnating dick is fully on board.

Since my sovereign has now abandoned that maddening regimen of shots and hormones she deployed to prevent us from breeding, her mating scent has been changing. She smells sweeter. More enticing. More erotic.

In a word, her scent is… riper.

Her body is hotter.

Her lips and breasts are lusher.

Her skin glows with all the tiny biochemical changes occurring inside her body.

My Zara smells and tastes like a ripe peach drizzled with honey.

Now my Vasili too is entering his fertile time, with a deep note of birchwood threading through his caramel-and-vetiver scent that is new.

My dragon is already wild with rut.

Seeing my two mates entwined in the bath, with his possessive hands gripping her ass, his dick buried inside her, and his copious spend dripping down her thighs, my self-control shatters.

I growl, pop the button of my jeans, and drag down my zipper to release my weeping shaft.

"Wait," Lucius says roughly. His taloned hands flex around my naked hips.

My dragon snarls at the restraint.

But this is Lucius.

I trust him.

For my headmaster's sake, I push out a harsh breath and lace my fingers through his savage grip.

"I will… share her with you," I promise. Christ, my voice is gravel. Already I am half-shifted. "I will share Vasili too—if he will have us. But, for all that is holy, I *cannot* wait."

"I'm merely saying let's take this to the bedroom." Even half-shifted, Lucius is a steadying presence against my back. Still fully clad, he rubs his whiskery muzzle into the side of my neck to scent me. "We'll all be more comfortable in a proper bed. That will be better for Zara."

That is the one thing he could say that my raging dragon will accept.

"Go," I say harshly to Vasili. "Take her. We will follow."

I know Vasili will not relinquish his claim on her delicious pussy. He is in rut, but his dragon is also fertile. He is a treacherous landmine of yo-yoing hormones and mating instinct.

Rather than climb from the tub, Vasili levitates.

His witchcraft lifts them both effortlessly, entwined and dripping, into the air. Zara gives a throaty laugh and an approving murmur. She is impressed with his control.

I too am impressed.

But his ego is not the part of him I intend to stroke.

My Neo is casting aside his own clothing left and right, but he rushes back to hold the door. With Zara wrapped tightly around his body, Vasili sails past me through the air, with a sort of imperial majesty and a sidelong smirk at my exposed dick.

"You're not coming near me with that dragon dick of yours tonight," he murmurs as they float past. "Where I'm concerned, you can forget about fucking."

"Sweetheart, I intend to fuck you senseless," I vow with a dragonish rumble. "And I swear you will like it."

"Unlikely," V snipes over his shoulder. He zips into the bedroom with Zara and vanishes.

"That does not mean impossible," I mutter.

"Bloody hell, love, sign me up for that." Ronin scrambles out of the tub, collects the bottle of wine they are sharing, and gives me an appreciative grin. His swept-back hair bares the savage lines of his face.

I cannot breed Ronin, but I can surely fuck him. The twin barbs in my randy cock quiver with anticipation.

But Ronin too stalks past me. He heads straight for a hopeful-looking Neo.

Those two are not in rut, but they are beautiful. Ronin with his broad shoulders and tight ass and sleek golden skin glistening with oil. Neo with his fair skin flushed and his purple curls tousled and his eyes shining and eager behind his glasses.

"Love you, Red. You're so fucking sweet, you slay me." Gently Ronin plucks off our bookworm's steamy glasses and leans in to kiss him. It is a slow sensual kiss that makes Neo blush.

"I love you so much, Ronin." Neo sighs happily. "I just love all of you so much."

These days, our Neo is easy to please. He is bitten and claimed and bonded. We are giving him everything he needs. In truth, we all spoil him.

Still, seeing him so happy makes my chest ache with love.

Ronin snickers at whatever besotted look I am wearing on my face, then nudges Neo into the bedroom with wicked purpose.

Lucius utters a wolfish growl and pulls me with him after our mates.

It is strange to me, this soft yielding I feel for my alpha. His wolf is no match for my dragon. I am the Sagittarius prince. Yet I yield to the pull of Lucius' hand and follow obediently where he leads me.

The Unseelie's octagon bedroom with its glass walls is awash in stars and moonlight. The round bed shimmers, rose and violet, in this eagle's nest that crowns the high tower. The X-shaped silhouette of the St. Andrew's Cross divides the vast horizon of the Avalon sea.

Neo is already eyeing that cross with a bashful interest that makes my balls clench and my dick jolt.

But it would not be proper to use Zephyr's toys without his consent. And the Dark Fae King—Vasili's deadly rival, and therefore mine, even if Zara does not know it—he and the winged Seelie remain absent.

While Ronin whispers filthy things to Neo between more of those slow hot kisses that make our bookworm blush and shiver, my gaze shoots past them to my sovereign.

Zara is kneeling on the bed with her hands on the glass, peering through the window at the endless sea. She is, just barely, levitating. The air around her shimmers with mating heat. Her teal curls—lustrous and shining with fertility—have fallen from their restraint to spill down her back and graze her tiny waist. The flare of her hips beckons me like a siren song.

Every curving line of her succulent body speaks of *longing*. All too clearly, she is searching for the dragonrider and the winged one. She is longing for them. For her two Fae lovers. She is longing for them to join us.

But she is mine tonight.

She is *mine*.

As for Vasili (who is also mine), he has temporarily vacated her delicious cunt. He is rampaging, twitchy with impatience, through an assortment of jars and potions that clearly belong to Zephyr. Just as he opened and consumed Zephyr's wine without asking. In short, he is causing chaos in Zephyr's orderly home.

Vasili will never admit this behavior is occurring because he is nervous.

In the end, I am what will soothe him. But he is prickly with rut and he is wary.

Because of the eggs.

If I try for him now, he is more likely to slap my face for my impertinence (which he has done before when I offend him) than to welcome me.

He wields a vicious backhand. Just the memory of that backhand makes my eyes water.

Clearly, for now, breeding him must wait.

Tonight all of me is for Zara.

"My queen," Lucius growls, with his wolf in his voice.

My headmaster pushes me into the bed with a roughness that ignites me, then scrambles in himself with lupine ease. His clawed hands tear the shirt from his shoulders with an impatience that shreds the cloth.

He is unleashed.

I snarl through my fangs at him.

I love Lucius. I love him. He is my mate, he is my teacher, he is the father I never had. But in this moment, he is a rival alpha for my female.

He bares his fangs in response to my threat. His eyes pulse wicked red in warning.

Zara's head turns toward us. Her wild mermaid hair swirls around her shoulders. Purple fire spills from her eyes. In the starlight, her glowing orbs burn like pinwheels.

"C'mon over here, Teach," she says in her throaty sex voice. "You too, big guy. You've been waiting for this."

She means that we have waited to breed her.

Trapped in the shell of my human skin, my dragon spreads his wings and bugles.

I cannot shift here or I will injure my mates. But I drag my jeans roughly down my legs so I am naked. Then I leap across the bed and launch myself at her—*my mate, my sovereign, mine*—while my beast mutters and paces in the prison of my skin.

My hands lock around the lush swell of Zara's hips. My lips find her succulent mouth. Her taste is drenched with honeyed sweetness from the wine. Her skin is silky and burning with heat. She exudes that velvety note of peaches that is so new in her creamy mating scent.

I swear, I am drunk with her. My senses are swirling and my head is spinning.

My barbs are flaring and my dick is dripping.

Every cell in my body is consumed with need.

I will not waste a single drop of my seed. I will spill inside her or I will burn.

The feral scent of wolf and alpha invades my senses. My scarred back is vulnerable. I can abide no one behind me. My nostrils flare and my dragon snakes around to peer at this intruder with suspicion.

At my side (where I do not mind him), Lucius is lurking. He is watching. He is protective.

But he is always so careful not to trigger me.

He is relentless. But he is also patient.

With infinite care—so careful I can take no offense—his tender claws sift through my braid until my hair spills loose around my shoulders. Tenderly Lucius nuzzles my cheek, his goatee rasping against my stubble. Soothed, my dragon rumbles at him.

Lucius swigs wine from our shared bottle, then leans past me to claim Zara's smiling mouth in a savage kiss.

"Mmmm." She moans with pleasure and reaches for the bottle herself. "Can't believe we haven't finished that yet."

"Well, you see, the bottle is enchanted." Lucius passes her the wine and shucks his trousers at ferocious speed. But he pauses long enough to lecture. "Faerie wine never runs dry until those who savor it have drunk their fill."

A furrow appears and vanishes between Zara's teal brows. There is something she is thinking. But she tilts the bottle back and drinks deep.

As for myself, I have no patience tonight for talk or lectures, even from Lucius. I hover impatiently at Zara's back and barely wait until she has satisfied her thirst before I am reaching between her legs.

Saints of the northern steppes defend me.

Ronin and Vasili.

Of course, they have both already had her.

Ronin's ambergris musk lurks in my nostrils. His milky spend still trickles between the pert rosy globes of her ass. Meanwhile, her thighs are sticky and her pussy is slick with Vasili's seed.

The hot suck of her cunt closing around my fingers nearly makes me spill all over her.

"Yeah, V got in here before you," she breathes, arching her back and spreading her thighs to welcome me deeper. "But there's plenty of me to go around, Max. You gonna give me that thick dragon dick?"

*"Yes."* My lips skim back from my fangs. "I will fill you and breed you, my Zara, until you carry my dragonets."

"Not sure the shot's worn off." Now, surely, she is teasing.

If she is not already fertile, judging by the erotic richness and spice of her mating scent, she will be fertile very soon.

When I withdraw my fingers from her cunt with a snarl, Lucius is waiting. He pounces on my drenched hand like the wolf he is, wraps his hot mouth around my fingers, and sucks my queen's juices and Vasili's cum from my fingers.

Now, truly, I am destroyed.

While Lucius moans and mouths my fingers (the way I hope he will one day mouth my cock), I fumble one-handed to fit my swollen dick against Zara's dripping core.

Her hot slippery folds envelop my cockhead with an audible suck that is heaven. I sink deep into her slick heat on a ragged groan.

Zara whimpers and yields, inch by inch, to my invasion. Her alluring pussy clenches hard around my shaft and pulses. "Oh, fuck, Max. That's so good. Need you to fill me up with your dragon spunk—"

Deep in her core, my twin barbs shoot out and engage. She breaks off on a shuddery gasp. Now we are locked together and she cannot escape me.

She is *mine*.

I flex my hips, ass clenching, and pump into her with a dragonish bellow. My beast roars in primal triumph.

*Ours our mate she is ours we will breed—*

As I pound into her in a frenzy, Zara fumbles to grip the ledge below the window and knocks over the wine. The green glass bottle tips over with a *thunk!* A torrent of golden wine spills out—far more wine than any bottle should hold. The vintage splashes over our legs and drenches the air in potent fruit.

Lucius fumbles to right the bottle (which it seems is still not empty). Then he watches us fuck, with his corded thighs spread and one fist wrapped around his ruddy dick. Sinew flexes in his arm and shoulder as he pumps. His face is savage with intent, brows thick and lowered, jaw elongating toward a muzzle. His knot swells and flushes purple against the dark thatch of his pubes.

Later, he will knot her. And I—I will yield her cunt to him.

Later.

But only because he is Lucius.

Now it is my turn.

Already my balls are drawing tight to my body and the base of my spine is tingling. Braced on hands and knees with her head hanging low, Zara is pushing into my cock, meeting and matching my every thrust. Violet light spills from her eyes, purple lightning forks in the sky, and lavender shadows writhe around us. I am grunting with effort, surging into her divine heat, my hips slamming into her sweet ass with every thrust, barely holding my dragon at bay.

Later, when we nest, I will have her and Vasili both like that. As dragons. Nothing can prevent this. We will breed and we will nest.

We are already linked, my queen and I, so she is sharing these thoughts.

Now, lost in the grip of our shared fantasy, Zara flings back her head and cries out. My climax rears up and blazes through me like dragonfire. I roar and spurt deep inside her, giving way to spasm after spasm of trembling release.

I fill her sweet pussy full with gout after gout of my potent seed.

My thick fork bottles every drop safe inside her.

Kneeling beside us, Lucius arches his back and bays at the moon. He pumps himself so roughly I fear he will do himself damage. His creamy seed splashes Zara's hips and thighs. A few hot jets splash over me, which prolongs my own pleasure.

With this tribute, he honors me.

I am deeply, ferociously pleased.

Behind us, Ronin is doing something that makes Neo moan and plead, while Ronin voices a husky chuckle. Both my non-shifter mates are well pleased and their pleasure too satisfies me.

Vasili is lurking somewhere, keeping himself well out of my reach, but he is here.

Now, suddenly, the stairwell door flies open. A cool wind that reeks of dragon rushes through the heated musk of our mating chamber, followed by the sharp hiss of an indrawn breath.

"By the moon." Zephyr's startled voice pierces the sex-drenched night. "Why in the world are you all drunk and swimming in enchanted moon wine?"

# Chapter Twenty-Nine
## Zara

As Zephyr's words ring through the pulsing heat of this fuck palace he's built, that loaded phrase hits the surface of my sex-drenched thoughts like a stone skipping across a pond.

Spreading consequences in its wake.

*Moon wine.*

That's the magic potion a Fae girl chugs when she wants to hang a flashing sign on her uterus that reads *vacancy: inquire within.*

When she wants to get knocked up.

A ripple of awareness spreads through my sex-drunk body. I'm still coming down from the massive endorphin rush of fucking Max and half my guys. My own fuck-me pheromones, mingled with Vasili's potent hit of caramel and Max's acrid brimstone mating scent, flood the night air like hallucinogens.

So the cogs in my brain are turning at, like, half their normal speed.

Still, I'm cognizant enough to realize one thing about that moon wine.

*I already knew.*

I knew, at least on a subconscious level, the minute Lucius said that wine was enchanted.

I knew.

I knew and I kept drinking anyway.

Then I let Max fuck me, even after I knew.

So it seems kinda pointless to act all shocked and freaked out now.

"Yeah." I clear my throat and wade into the pregnant silence. "Guess I just decided to go for it. The witching world needs a Gemini kid. A Gemini butt in the throne after mine to keep Cleo's ass out of it and keep the good times rolling. Plus a fertile queen has magical and symbolic value for all the witching races. That's what's gonna save us from going extinct, remember? And that shit's more important than me not getting tied down."

I tilt my head back to get a look at Vasili, whose tall slim silhouette looms over me like a guillotine, inked against the silver expanse of the Avalon sea. With the sickle moon floating behind him, rimming his silver hair like a crown, and all his psychic barriers locked down tight, he's even harder than usual to read.

"Sorry if I caught you off guard, bad boy," I tell my terrible snake of an alpha softly. "I kinda made up my mind before you fucked me. But I honestly think I've known for a while. The witching world needs this… and I finally feel like we're ready. What with all the shit going down in this harem, I didn't have a chance to talk to you."

He doesn't even hum in acknowledgment.

Which isn't exactly the ringing endorsement I'm hoping for.

But he doesn't strike back either.

Anyway, he certainly knows I'm off the shots, and he still opted to fuck me bare. He coulda used a condom.

I just don't know if that's the vast mindless instinct of his rut making the calls. Or if Vasili actual is piloting his own battleship and his fiendishly clever brain is still calling the shots.

I twist to peer over my shoulder at Max, who's still hovering possessively over me with his impregnating dick locked tight inside me. After literally months of nonstop campaigning to fill my uterus with a clutch of dragonets, my alpha dragon looks ferociously pleased with himself. He's actually really cute like that.

My heart swells and softens at the sight.

I give my satisfied alpha an affectionate smile, then crane past him to see the door.

Zephyr's not a big guy, but he manages to dominate the space. The scabbard with his crossed swords dangles from one hand and his green dragonscale armor is unzipped to the waist. This fashion choice exposes the smooth expanse of the Dark Fae King's olive-skinned chest and the taut ripple of his abs. His green hair is windblown, his sharp-edged face is flushed, and his jade-green gaze is fey and feral.

Yowsa.

That's the way he looks after he's been fucking.

"That's a pretty big decision you just made, princess. Better be sure you're makin' it for the right reasons," Ash rumbles from the stairs.

Gently he nudges Zephyr into the bedroom, angles his wide Seelie shoulders to sidle through the narrow Unseelie door himself, and pulls the door closed to give us all privacy.

"You sure?" Ash finishes softly. He pushes a hand through the rumpled spikes of his pewter hair. He's looking disheveled too, with his doeskin vest gaping open around the impressive width of his chest and his leather Conan breeches half-unlaced over the impressive bulge of his cock.

But his keen silver stare searches my face. "Sure you're ready for all that?"

"No." I push out a chuckle. "I don't feel ready at all. But I do feel committed to you guys. I'm committed as fuck—to all seven of you. Some of these guys have been wanting kids for a while. The others aren't opposed." With the possible exception of Vasili, but I'm not going down that road in front of Zephyr. "I've been the big holdout. And I'm not just changing my mind because Messalina said I'm all wicked on live TV."

"Good," Neo says stoutly. He reaches to pull a pillow over his naked hips, with a bashful look at the two Fae he's not fucking (yet). "Because you're not wicked. You're *good*. And we want what you want."

"Thank you, baby." I was never really worried about Neo raising hell, but I'm not taking him for granted either, even if he is my fated mate. His warm acceptance and devotion flood through our bond. I wrap myself in that feeling like a blanket.

"The point is," I sigh, "I *am* the queen. And if I wanna keep the gig, I gotta start acting like one. The witching world needs me fertile and breeding to reverse our own decline. So I know we'll figure it out. Together."

I add this last part with a searching look at Ronin, who's been crouched between the thighs of a spreadeagled Neo and looking all savage and guarded at the Fae.

Looks like Zephyr and Ash interrupted those two in mid-blowjob. Judging by the loopy half-smile that lingers on Neo's face, Ronin must've just managed to finish him off before the interruption.

Zephyr pulls in a slow breath. His gaze drifts from me to Vasili, who's lurking in the shadows like a rattlesnake about to strike, then to Neo and Ronin.

When his stare locks on the watchful Ronin, something in Zephyr's face ignites.

"If 'tis truly the case, my bride," my Dark Fae murmurs, his voice unspooling like a ribbon of gray silk through the sex-soaked night, "I'm certainly prepared to do my part. Your mortal queendom is not the only royal realm that requires an heir. Preferably, in my case, a daughter with royal blood. My Unseelie have grown… accustomed to a female sovereign."

For weeks now, I've been pushing back when he calls me his bride, because it's always implied something he shares with me that excludes the others (except for Ash).

Now, for the first time, I feel like it doesn't.

Plus Zephyr's just hopped on the baby bus.

A fragile bubble swells in my chest. More ephemeral and fleeting than a soap bubble. But that shining bubble of hope feels a lot like happiness.

*Slow down, showgirl,* I tell myself sternly, before my optimism spirals out of hand. *That happiness shit's, like, premature. We've still got issues in this harem. Major issues.*

"*That's* putting it mildly, little queen," Vasili says under his breath, in a tone like acid.

But, for him, that's a mild reaction. Plus he's the worst of my warlocks (by far) and the one who's the most opposed to adding Zephyr to the harem.

Although V definitely does have designs on Ash.

That's been obvi (at least to me) since those two met cute last spring.

To be honest, they met when V abducted Ash at spearpoint.

But Ash seems to be kinda into that. Seems to be standard courting behavior in fairyland.

"Okay." I sigh and give an experimental wiggle around Max's dick. My dragon's softened up inside me (kinda) since he came, though his barbs are still engaged.

But I haven't been fucking him all these months without paying attention.

"It's okay, big guy." I snuggle my back into my alpha dragon's front and coax him to roll over with me so we're both lying on our sides. "You filled me up with dragon cum. You can do it again later. But right now? Mission accomplished. Time to make room in my hoochie for Lucius."

Lucius snarls in surprise.

My headmaster's shifted back to fully human. He's stationed himself between the Fae and non-Fae contingents in this bed, all ready to mediate the conflict, while we deal with Ash and Zephyr turning up.

Now the immediate prospect of getting inside my pussy pushes his inner diplomat into the background and switches Lucius' wolf side right back on again.

Lucius drops to all fours on Zephyr's big round bed and howls like the beast he is. His chestnut curls tumble down around his face, his thick knotted cock swells between his corded thighs, and his claws burrow into the shimmery Fae duvet hard enough to shred the thing.

Straight up? Lucius is impressive as fuck.

Plus he's the one guy in our polycule Max defers to.

Max grumbles and snorts a dragonish protest into the back of my neck. But, for Lucius' sake, his barbs soften enough for my dragon to work his forked dick obediently outta my snatch.

When he pulls out, a gush of warm spunk spills out to slick my thighs. With reverent fingers, he diligently pushes his spilled cum back into me (which is hot as fuck). Even though there's already a lot of him (and Vasili) still squishing inside me.

"I will yield for Lucius," Max mutters. "For now."

"Good dragon," I murmur.

Max nuzzles a possessive kiss into his mating scars on my shoulder that makes my inner dragon purr for him. Then he rolls away.

I can already feel the relentless focus of his breeding kink shifting to V, who's gonna have to fend for himself in this new situation. But he's the Goblin King and totally capable.

I mean, if all else fails, he can just backhand Max in the face again.

Knowing my snake, he might do that anyway, even if he's feeling receptive.

That's *his* standard courting behavior.

Me? I'm gonna have my hands full (along with various other parts of my anatomy) integrating those two Fae into our polycule.

My gaze shifts to my wolf king, who's eyeing me from halfway across the bed, so ready to pounce that he's trembling.

"Lucius," I say softly. "Come."

"Your wish," he growls through his fangs. "My command."

He bounds across the bed in a feral scramble that has Ronin diving out of his way with a laugh. If he were Max, he'd have me balls deep, face down, ass in the air and stuffed with dick before I could say *doggie style.*

But this is Lucius.

He knows how much I need to make this harem work—for all of us. Plus he's linked up with me pretty tight, so he knows exactly what I'm thinking.

He dives in to claim my mouth in a fangy kiss that ramps my vampire fetish right up. I moan appreciatively into his mouth and stroke his wild curls back from his tortured face.

"Hiya, Teach," I whisper against his kiss. "Wanna make some puppies?"

His breath breaks around his wrecked voice. "Christ. I have never wanted anything more."

He tucks up tenderly against my back, spooning me into his sheltering strength while we're both on our sides, and lifts my upper thigh to open me up. His hairy chest rubs against my shoulders and his pubes prickle against my well-ridden ass. From behind, his thick dick prods my soaked and well-stretched snatch, then slides inside with an audible squish.

I whimper with anticipation. He lets out a deep groan of need.

V and Max have already worked me open pretty good, but Lucius is a lot to handle.

Knot or no knot.

*Titanium pussy,* I remind my lady parts like a mantra. *You can take him.*

My pussy cooperates with a gush of girl juice to help me accommodate all that girth. Lucius fits himself in, stretching my inner walls and filling me so full of wolf cock my eyes cross. He fills me till the base of his knot nudges my pussy.

Then he takes a gentlemanly breather to let me get used to the stretch.

I mean, just until he knots me.

I gasp and undulate against him, working myself up and down all those inches like a stripper on a pole. My mating scars are tingling and my clit is swelling with a sweet ache for the imminent promise of that knot.

He growls and mouths my puncture scars and ruts gently into my pussy. I pulse and clench and quiver around him.

He's so fucking considerate, so deliberate and controlled, even when he's lost in the grip of a vicious mating rut, that grateful tears rush into my eyes.

"God, Lucius," I say on a shaky sigh. "I know I'm hormonal right now. It makes me weepy. But I swear to fuck, you're everything."

His wolf mutters, deep in his chest, a low velvet rumble of affection and pleasure.

Still linked tight through our bond, Lucius rolls onto his back and pulls me with him. Now I'm sprawled on my back too, with his bestial strength pressed into my spine. His thighs spread me wide so all our guys can see his ruddy shaft pushing ruthlessly in and out of my glistening folds. His hands, hard and callused from running through the woods on all fours, wrap around my tits and thumb my pierced nipples roughly.

A current of pleasure sweeps through me, sweet and sharp. Stars sparkle and burst before my half-mast eyes.

Or maybe that's my power rising.

The Avalon skies are alight with violet lightning.

My headmaster's offering me to anyone who wants me in a way that feels obscene but is so fucking hot. I let my head fall back against his chest and squirm against him, enjoying this sense of being spread and dicked and helpless, offered up to the whole room for fucking.

In a blink, Vasili coils between our spread thighs and rears over me with a hiss.

But he's not alone.

Zephyr, with his uncanny Fae speed, crowds right in next to him. Behind the green slash of his eyepatch, his wild face burns with smoldering purpose. His lips part to expose his tiny fangs and his hair spills over one shoulder in a silky green tangle.

At least, he's finally left his swords behind.

"Careful, Your Imperiousness," V sneers at him. "You're not the tyrannical king in this little harem. That distinction belongs to *me*. If you join, I'm your alpha."

Zephyr's smoldering gaze shifts from my spread and spitted form to drift slowly over the naked warlock lurking at his side.

"Vasili Nikolayevich Romanov," my Dark Fae breathes. "I'll not deny I have… certain designs… in mind for you. But I won't challenge you for her. Tonight I only wish to share. 'Tis what you do in this harem, is it not? Do you not share… everything?"

By now, Zephyr's stare has made its way over V's sleek abs and streamlined hips to my snake's pretty cock, which is once again erect and straining and ready for me.

Clearly I'm not all Zephyr wants a piece of.

Needless to say, I thoroughly approve. But Vasili's cagey and tricky as fuck to woo. Poor Max has been trying for months.

So I decide to lend our Unseelie a hand.

"The two of you can start by sharing me," I say huskily. I clutch the rumpled blankets in both fists and writhe on Lucius' cock as he pistons slowly in and out of me, working me wider for his knot. "Lucius won't mind a little extra attention either. Will you, Teach?"

"No," Lucius rasps, thick and guttural. "I won't mind a bit."

"Hmmmm." Vasili still sounds highly skeptical. But his gaze sneaks back to where I'm joined to Lucius. My cunt clenches under his predatory interest and my clit pulses with heat.

But Zephyr seizes the opening I've given him. His wicked hands skate up my inner thighs to spread me wider.

With a moan, I release my death grip on the bedding and reach for my aching clit.

"I'll have none of that." V darts in to catch my straying hands and pins them to the bedding on either side. "I *own* that delectable cunt of yours, darling. Our Lucius is, of course, a welcome guest."

He doesn't say a single word about Zephyr.

But at least V's not actively pushing him away

Now I feel even more exposed with the three of them surrounding me: Lucius fucking me, Zephyr spreading me, Vasili pinning me to the mattress. When Ash looms suddenly behind Zephyr, shrugging out of his vest to expose his colossal chest and the flex of his six-pack abs, that feeling of exposure gets even more intense.

Sweet Jesus. These guys of mine.

My need is spiraling like a corkscrew coaster. I swear to fuck I'd cream all over the four of them—if I could just get a hand on my clit.

While I writhe and moan against them, Zephyr leans in to press his hot lips to my inner knee. I never even realized (till right this second) that's an erogenous zone. Then he mouths his way up my inner thigh with tortuous slowness.

Ash leans in to gather Zephyr's loose hair in a gentle fist so we can all see what he's doing.

"Not fair," I gasp on a laugh that's almost a sob. "All four of you ganging up on me."

"Whoever said love was fair." Zephyr's silky whisper tickles the sensitive crease where my thigh joins my crotch.

Ash huffs out a chuckle and squeezes Zephyr's neck in a tender clasp.

Good thing I'm not really opposed.

For the first time ever, I've got all seven of these guys in the same bed. There are still fissures between them. Ash is still wearing pants and barely participating, Vasili's barely tolerating Zephyr, and Ronin's definitely hanging back and watching (but he's got Max and Neo all over him—my adorable bookworm, who always knows exactly how to help, is distracting both of them so sweetly.)

So it's a start.

It's actually a pretty fucking awesome start. You better believe I'll take it.

Not that I'm being given the choice to do anything else.

By now, Zephyr has his mouth right over where Lucius' cock is tunneling into my pussy. At the first taste of our mingled essence, my Fae gives an appreciative murmur.

Lucius gasps out what sounds like a Hungarian curse that makes me grin.

Now that skilled Unseelie tongue is stroking both of us, Lucius' pistoning shaft and my eager snatch, lapping up Max's jizz and V's spunk and some of Lucius' precum with every swipe. I know that shit's getting to Vasili (who likes a little cream pie himself) because the Goblin King's intense interest in this entire proceeding is snaking through our mating bond.

Every purposeful swipe of Zephyr's tongue around Lucius' cock and my pussy lips stokes me higher, because I *really* want some clitoral stim, and Zephyr's the closest thing right now to providing it. And, with Zephyr mouthing persistently over my wolf's swollen knot, Lucius is finally losing his grip on all that ironclad self-control.

"Merciful Christ." Lucius sounds like he's dying. *"Your Radiance—"*

The Dark Fae King huffs out a laugh against Lucius' knot and my slickness. "Oh, I dare say you can now call me Zephyr, Lucius. Rest assured I'm nowhere near finished with you either."

Under the extra lube of that Unseelie tongue, plus Lucius' increasingly frenzied fucking and all the other action going down in Pussytown, that wolfish knot stretches me wide and finally seats inside me with a *pop!*

"Cheese on toast," I yelp. "That's one tight fucking fit. Oh, sweet Jesus, Lucius…"

Rigid and trembling with effort against my back, Lucius howls to the heavens with triumph.

Zephyr (who's got an up-close-and-personal VIP seat for all this) moans like he's just been knifed (again). Vasili pins my flailing hands harder to the bedding and swoops in to capture my shrill cry with a snakebite kiss that burns with the honeyed potency of enchanted moon wine.

I'm barely aware, from the supple brush of dragonscale against my inner thighs, that Ash is peeling Zephyr out of the rest of his armor.

So that's one more guy in my bed who's nakey.

Clearly my Seelie Prince is only playing wingman right now.

But at least he's playing.

He hasn't turned on Ronin. And Ronin isn't running away—

Then the fiery inferno of Zephyr's diabolically skilled mouth closes over my aching clit in a hard sucking pull that launches me right into orbit.

My orgasm slams through me like six G's of gravity, pressing my skin to my bones and making this whole tower vibrate with intensity.

I arch into Vasili's kiss, clench tight around Lucius' knot and the fierce piston of his cock, and tumble spinning into the night sky blazing with stars all around us. Lucius bays at the sickle moon and flies with me, the hard kick and spurt of his climax flooding my basement, the thick bulge of his knot bottling all that potent wolf seed inside my fertile pussy.

I'm still blind and gasping and shuddering with climax when Vasili (who hasn't exactly been #TeamPlaypen during this whole breeding debate so far) leans over to snatch up the moon wine and tip a generous pour of potent tartness into my open mouth.

I guzzle that shit down my parched throat like it's the desert and I'm dying of thirst.

"In for a penny, in for a pound," Vasili whispers. His glacier-blue eyes burn down at me. "Are you certain about the Unseelie, darling? Really, truly certain?"

Zephyr's mouth lifts from my clit, which is exactly the right thing because I'm super sensitive after just coming like that, so he can listen in.

I meet the Dark Fae King's single eye, suddenly wide with apprehension, and wonder if he's ever gonna feel comfy enough in my bed to take off that eyepatch. I can tell it chafes him to sleep wearing the thing, but it's like a permanent part of his armor. I've never seen him without it.

"I am," I pant into the sudden, trembling silence, broken only by Lucius' labored breaths. "I really am. You're one of us, Zephyr. Ash is too. Whatever happens now, whoever knocks me up, we're all in this together."

Ash studies my face with his level gaze, then gives me a slow nod.

"Gonna take me a little time to get used to… some of this." His keen silver stare flickers toward Ronin, then he fixes on Zephyr with a furrowed brow. "But assuming Sparrow here's game? You can count me in, princess."

"My word on it." Zephyr crawls up my body like a cat, dragging his supple olive-skinned frame right up against V's tall pale length. His Unseelie scent of burnt amber and dragonscale perfumes the night air. His cock rears from a lick of moss-green pubic hair that tickles my tummy. The contact leaves a slick of precum in his wake.

"My word," the Unseelie repeats intently, head turning to lock on V's suspicious stare. "Your enemies are my enemies. Your allies are my allies. All your offspring, from any sire, I shall protect and champion as mine own. Whatever you love, I too shall love—with every fiber that remains intact in my twisted and damaged soul.

"If…" Zephyr pauses, his face fractures, and my heart nearly stops. "If, that is to say, you are willing to accept me, with all my… flaws… and Ash alongside me, into this harem. If that is so, then we are—both of us—yours."

Now he's asking me about his eye.

About whether it matters to me that he's disfigured (which is the way he sees it).

I don't give a single shit about the eye, except for the damage its loss has clearly caused to both Zephyr and Ronin. So I suck in a breath to jump right on that offer. (I mean, two Fae for the price of one? That's like a blue light special in the fun department.)

But before I can answer, my snake pounces.

"Do you expect someone to give you a medal, darling?" Vasili's lashes, slicked with mascara in cobalt blue, drop over his dangerous stare. "So you're damaged goods like the rest of us. Don't expect anyone here to be impressed. Let's just hope that fabled Fae word of yours is worth the hype."

Too quickly for anyone to react, V shoots out an arm to wrap around Zephyr's tousled green head, then dives in to seal the promise.

The Goblin King fuses the Dark Fae King's alluringly cum-stained lips with his in a fierce claiming kiss.

# Chapter Thirty
## Ash

So you probably wanna know what went down in our bed after that Romanov snake (a guy I still don't totally trust) laid a liplock on Zephyr.

Well, sorry to bust anyone's bubble, but that story's gonna have to wait. The eight of us in this polycule can't just fuck all the time.

Not when we got a ball to attend and a demon to trap.

I roll out of the sack at first light. Light Fae like me, we're early risers. We like to say howdy to the sun. So I'm the first one up.

Plus I didn't just spend half the night fucking like Sparrow and those shifters in rut with our fertile princess.

Yeah, I mighta joined the royal harem.

But I'm a wait-and-see kinda guy.

So I still haven't dipped my wick in one of these full group encounters. Dick's still dry, and gonna stay that way till I trust these guys.

Same way I trust Sparrow and the princess.

While I lace up my britches and pull my vest over my shoulders in the early morning hush, the first burning sliver of morning sun peeks over the horizon to paint the sea red. Sure hope that's not some kinda omen, considering the shindig tonight. A finger of sunlight stretches through the ripply volcanic glass to graze the tangle of naked bodies piled in our bed.

Our princess, she's right in the middle of that puppy pile.

Her curvy little body's barely even visible under the possessive sprawl of the wolf and the dragon and my Sparrow. (Sure, Sparrow's not fucking her other guys yet—only her—but I don't need a crystal ball to know that shit's coming.) Zara's teal curls and his green mane spill together like a color explosion across that rumpled pillow they're sharing.

That's a sight that makes my chest ache, for real. My guy deserves to be happy. With her, I figure he's got a real shot.

Zara deserves to be happy too. Not just be queen popping out kids for the kingdom.

She deserves actual happiness.

Assuming we can figure out how to banish that fucker Mordred back to the demonical realm before he causes any more trouble.

Speaking of trouble.

That snake Vasili's spread over the sleep heap like a python—or maybe a big saltwater croc—drowsing in the morning sun. He's got one arm thrown over Zara's hips (no surprise after he fucked her into a goddamn sex coma last night) and one hand wrapped around Sparrow's ankle like a manacle.

I'm kinda surprised Sparrowhawk's willing to tolerate the snake being that close to him. But, I mean, surprised not surprised. Lotta sexual tension crackling under the surface in this new polycule we just hooked up with.

Long story short? Those two guys—Sparrow and the snake—are just gonna have to fuck it out.

While I toe into my boots and buckle my knife around my thigh, my gaze shifts to *him*.

Pendragon.

That guy I've been swearing for years I'd make pay in blood for every ounce of pain and tears and heartbreak he wrung outta my Sparrow.

Now Sparrow wants me to hold my fire? Wants me to try and make nice with his asshole ex? Even though he knows I'll never forgive the guy for what went down the night Sparrow lost his eye.

Geez, what a monumental fuckup.

Right now, Pendragon's sleeping face down at the edge of the heap, with the wolf's arm wrapped possessively around his waist and his face hidden in the snake's neck. I'm kinda amazed the snake—I mean Vasili, gotta get used to using his name—lets a rabid dog like Ronin Pendragon anywhere inside his paranoid guard. Vasili's throat has literally been exposed to the guy's teeth all night.

Pretty safe bet those two are more than just allies or even lovers.

They're close.

Real close.

Better keep an eye on him… that pissy Russian alpha whose tongue stings like a hornet… if I need to take his boyfriend down.

Under a blanket of inky hair, Ronin's broad shoulders are all nakey, that traffic-stopping ass is on full display…

And his back's exposed.

My skin sings with the drive to bury my knife in my enemy's back.

My shoulders ripple and my wings emerge, feathers mantling and ready for combat.

But I tamp that shit right down.

My back tingles with warmth and witchcraft. But my wings melt reluctantly back into my tattooed skin.

Promised Sparrow I wouldn't off the fucker in his sleep, didn't I? Not to mention the princess won't be any too keen if I knife her boy toy warlock the way I wanna.

Doesn't change the fact Pendragon slept on one side of the heap and I slept on the other last night. Bed still wasn't big enough for the two of us.

I'm turning away from the pile, all bitter and grumpy as fuck, when my eye falls on Neo. He's half-smothered in sleeping dragon, but his bleary green eyes blink warily up at me.

He's watching me watch Pendragon.

Without his glasses, the Mercury kid looks even younger. Shoot, they're all kids compared to me. I'm robbing the cradle with this crew, for real. Except maybe for the prof—Lucius Aries—they're all way too young for me. Even Sparrow used to be my student.

Knew what I was getting into, though, didn't I? Didn't stop me from falling toes over teakettle for Zara.

"Hiya, kid," I say softly to Neo, so I don't wake anyone else. "Don't get up."

"Don't go," Neo whispers.

Well, hell. The tangled knot of anger and worry in my heart softens right up.

This kid's blinking up at me, all drowsy and sweet as fuck, through a swath of the sleeping dragon's blond hair.

Carefully I stroke back Maxim Rasputin's hair, soft as butter. The scent of brimstone rises from the dragon's suntanned skin and tickles my nose. First time I've touched that dragon shifter. Under my gentle touch, he mutters something fretful—sounds like Russian—in his sleep.

Clearly, this guy's had a hard life. He's all skin pulled over sinew, like he missed a few meals, and his long back's a tortured canvas of old scars that make my gut clench. I've noticed the way he tries to hide the damage, like it's somehow his fault some asshole flogged the shit outta him, not once but a bunch of times.

So I steer clear of his back, and he doesn't pull away from my careful touch.

Even though shifters are notoriously twitchy, this one tolerates me stroking his hair without waking.

For some crazy reason, that little thing makes me happy.

Although this dragon's still in la la land, I get a glimpse of how it could be. Me hooking up with this harem.

"Not goin' far," I breathe, turning away from Maxim and cupping Neo's square jaw. I look down into the kid's open, trusting face and rub my thumb over the soft curve of his lower lip. "I got a thing I do at sunrise. Plus I gotta rustle up some kinda breakfast for you all."

"I mean it, Ash," Neo mumbles, ducking his curly head to nuzzle my palm. "You need to come right back, okay? Zara needs you. We all do."

Well, hell.

"I'm comin' back." I sigh, because I know it's true. "I'm in this thing up to my eyeballs now, ain't I?"

"You promise?" His worried eyes search my face.

"Yeah. I promise." I lean in to kiss his furrowed brow, and he leans trustingly into my touch. "Go back to sleep, kid."

He settles back with a sweet sigh that, I swear, busts my old guy ticker wide open in my chest. The kid's eyes drift closed.

All messed up in my noggin from my interactions with those two, I finally duck outta there and schlep downstairs to give the kitchen crew their marching orders. Sparrow's got a lotta servants these days, on account of him being the only ruling royal. But today's a holiday. Summer solstice. Lotta folks are off getting ready for the Faerie Ball tonight.

Sparrow's made this one—the shindig tonight when he crowns his queen—a command appearance.

So we only got a skeleton crew on kitchen duty. The unlucky few that drew the short straw and couldn't get time off. They ain't exactly thrilled about cooking for eight instead of two. But I'm the king's consort, so no one gives me any lip.

Then I hightail it to the tower roof for my sun salutations.

Yeah, I do yoga. It's a Seelie thing.

Who do you think the mortals learned it from?

Being up there in the morning air, watching the sun ease fully into view over the sea while I do my forward bends and downward dogs? With my boots and vest shucked off and my wings out to feel the wind in my feathers? My soothing morning ritual helps me regain some balance.

Maybe I can tolerate sharing a bed and a table and a roof with Ronin Pendragon.

Maybe.

If he makes Sparrow happy.

But if he hurts Sparrow again—in *any* way—I'm gonna go *Game of Thrones* on that Pendragon's ass. I'll castrate that fucker and feed his balls to Xhevith.

On that happy little note, I finish my sun salute, then do my breath-with-sound thing while I'm hunkered down in child pose (not so easy anymore on the old knees, but I get through it).

Now that I've got my priorities straight and my shit together, I leg it back to the bedroom. The yeasty scent of baking bread and the greasy sizzle of cave eggs greet me on the stairs, and my gut gives an appreciative rumble. At least the sulky kitchen crew's doing their thing.

In our bedroom, the princess and her guys are waking up.

First thing I see is Vasili Romanov, stretched like a cat on the ledge in the morning sun, naked and unconcerned, with some kinda sparkly gel beauty mask draped over his eyes.

"Is that you, Ash?" he murmurs without stirring. "You're causing a dreadful draft. Close the door, darling, *do.*"

The sight of him naked's bad enough for my composure. Him giving me orders to boot? When he's that good at giving them, and Goddess knows, I love to take 'em.

It's early in the day to get a hard-on.

But fuck if he hasn't managed to give me one.

"Sorry about that, beautiful." I dredge up a snort and nudge the door shut with my foot. "You might wanna put something on. I mean, something more than an eye mask. Breakfast'll be up in a few ticks."

"Hmmm." Without lifting his eye mask, Romanov twitches a fold of the sheet indifferently over his pretty dick. Even that much, he's obviously just doing to humor me.

If I wait for him to thank me for organizing his breakfast, I'll be standing here till the cows come home. And we don't have cows in Avalon.

With an effort, I manage to look away.

Next my gaze shifts to *him*.

Pendragon.

He's still shirtless but standing, sunlight dancing over all that golden skin and the flaming dragon tattoo inked in black across his chest. He's pulling his leather pants over his lean hips while Sparrow—who's curled next to Zara in this lazily contented way—watches his ex suit up with that smoldery look my guy gets when he's horny.

But Pendragon is watching me.

Not gonna lie. That Brit's a looker. Sexy as heck. Another time and place, I'd be all over a guy like him.

Here, now, with our history? It's all I can manage to give Pendragon a short nod.

His tiger eyes narrow. But his chin dips, microscopically, in a stiff howdy-doody.

Through the open door behind him, I catch a glimpse of Lucius, already fully dressed, browsing through our rare Fae book collection in the den. That wolf's rapt with fascination. I'm guessing we could leave him in there all day and he'd be happy.

Behind me, the trickle of the gravity shower floats from the john. I'm guessing that's where Maxim is. He and that forked dragon dick of his got a lotta action last night.

But Zara's the star of this show.

She's sitting up naked against a heap of pillows, stroking Neo's tousled curls as the kid lies blissfully with his head in her lap, and rubbing the sleep outta her pretty turquoise eyes.

Despite every distraction, my ticker gives a ping and a hard thump at the sight of her.

Damn. Just damn.

Zara Gemini. Queen of the witching world.

Fucked six ways to Sunday last night. And she still glows with vitality and power like a goddess.

She looks so comfy and trusting and *right* in my bed… our bed… the bed we all share now, I guess. I sure fell toes over nose for that gal. Haven't seen her for months and I'm still under her spell.

"Hiya, princess." I lean over Sparrow, run a hand over his messy green hair to greet him, then wrap my big hand around Zara's jaw and pull her in for a deep slow kiss.

She sighs my name and melts right into me.

She's like a sleepy punk-rock version of Marilyn Monroe with her lush lips and her dreamy eyes and her pretty titties with their silver rings. My palms itch to explore every inch of her. Relearn what makes her shiver and gasp and moan. The way Sparrow and me learned her together last spring.

But if I get into all that now, I'm never gonna get outta this bed. We got shit to do today.

And if I fuck her now the way I want, I won't be able to keep my eye on Pendragon.

So I keep my hands off her tits and my dick in my pants. "How'd you sleep, honey?"

"Dreams," Zara mumbles against my lips. She still tastes tart and sweet like moon wine, but her voice is fretful. "Dreams of… drowning. And, uh, fucking."

I pull back to eye her slightly anxious face.

"Which one of us?" Vasili smirks behind his eye mask. "Or was it more than one?"

Her teal brows draw together. "*Not* one of you. That's the thing." She hesitates. "Think I was fucking the shit out of someone with, uh, tentacles."

I'm still leaning over the bed, so I can feel the way Sparrow stiffens right up.

I ease back so he can sit up the way he wants. He adjusts his eyepatch with a pained grimace (he shouldn't sleep wearing the thing, for real) and looks for his swords, still propped against the wall where he left his gear last night.

"Tentacles, huh?" I keep my tone easy, because there's no reason to get anyone all worked up before we gotta. "Like an alien or something?"

"No, something more… aquatic." Frowning, Zara bundles her hair in a messy twist. A few colorful curls spill around her troubled face. "Like a kraken?"

Yikes.

I sidle back so Sparrow can scramble outta the sack. I toss him his dragonscale armor, which he immediately starts wrestling his way into. "Easy, Sparrowhawk. All these shifters in rut and these Mogadon pheromones smelling up the joint? Could be just a sex dream."

"You know 'tis not," my guy says tightly, the way I knew he would. "Our return last night from the mortal realm was hardly subtle. All of Avalon knows I crown my queen tonight. And by now, he's very likely aware that his brother is dead. It's *him*."

A frisson of tension ripples through the room. Romanov slips off his eye mask and sits up. Pendragon stops rummaging around for a clean shirt and looks dangerous.

Next door, the gravity shower shuts off. Simultaneously, Lucius Aries appears in the library doorway with an open book in hand.

*"Him."* Zara's head tilts to look up at us. "You wanna elaborate on that, Your Radiance?"

Zephyr drags his armor over his legs with an irritated hiss. "I mean Mordred, of course. Like any infernal being, the half-demon commands dreams. In his demonic form, he is kraken."

I wait through a fraught silence while they all absorb this newsflash. Vasili's pale eyes narrow, and Ronin tosses the guy some pants with a soft curse.

"A kraken," Lucius murmurs. His face kindles with a scholar's keen interest. "How remarkable. A mythical monster brought to the surface… as it were."

Zara draws her knees to her chest and perches her cute chin on top. "Uh, well, the thing is, it wasn't exactly a hostile dream. I mean, I don't know if it was *him*, obviously. And it's not like I have a tentacle fetish or anything, uh, normally."

A revealing wash of color rises in her face. "But that dream guy was sexy as fuck."

Uh oh.

"That's him all right." I heave a sigh and exchange a grim look with Sparrow, who's still fighting furiously into his armor. "His Pops is an incubus. So Mordred is too. Him sexing you up in your sleep? That's just his way of checking you out."

Maxim Rasputin bursts out of the john, dripping wet and growling, with his dragon eyes flaming and a towel wrapped carelessly around his hips. "Who threatens my mate!"

"Oh, dear fuck." Vasili rolls his eyes over the drama. He's sliding his long legs into a pair of hot pink lace panties that I think belong to Zara. (Apparently those two swap lingerie, but I'm not gonna get distracted here.)

"Take it easy, big guy," Zara says patiently to Max. "We're just talking about the whole demon thing. Go dry off and get some clothes on, okay? We got some planning to do."

Maxim gives Zephyr and me a suspicious look. I slouch down and try my damnedest to look harmless despite my size. The dragon grunts and ducks back into the head, followed by the vigorous sound of toweling.

"So he knows I'm here," Zara announces to the room. "So he's interested. We can use that."

"My dear, how precisely do you mean?" Drawn to our girl like a magnet, looking cautious but intrigued and still clutching his book, Lucius comes in to loom over the bed.

"Indeed, darling." Calmly Vasili buttons his sparkly jeans over the hot pink lace that sheathes his junk. "*Do* tell."

"I mean," Zara says in her steely queen voice, "we use his interest in me to lure him in. Then we trap him. Zephyr already said he knows how to banish him. That means we just need to catch him."

"Hmmm." That snake of hers looks thoughtful. He exchanges a silent glance with Pendragon, who just looks dangerous.

Neo parks his glasses on his nose, then tucks up next to her and takes her hand. The kid looks worried but trusting.

"'Tis easier said than done, believe me. Else I would have banished the kraken already." Sparrow zips up his dragonscale with a single fierce pull and reaches impatiently for his swords.

I pass him his gear and figure I better grab mine before he's on the wing without me.

Curtly my guy warns, "Mordred thrives on unpredictability. His dead brother pursued me like a stalker. That obsession gave me the advantage. But Mordred is far more wary and clever. Thus, he has kept his distance."

Zara leans forward, stubborn as heck. "Well, it's a safe bet he shows up at the ball tonight, right? In, like, his Fae form? We can predict that much."

"Yeah, if you wanna call that safe," I mutter.

The loose curls start floating around our girl's shoulders and her eyes light up with ultraviolet fire.

"So we trap that fucker in front of the entire Unseelie population. We flush out his allies and snuff out this whole insurrection against Zephyr's reign on the spot. Once and for all. We do it at the ball, where he knows I'm gonna be, where he knows he'll have his audience."

"Geez Louise, princess," I breathe. "For someone who doesn't even know the guy, that's one gutsy call you're making."

Her eyes lock on mine. "Yep."

She even pops the P.

The balls on this girl.

Just in case I needed one more reminder why I fell for her.

Xhevith's trumpeting bellow floats through the open window. Sure, he's projecting what he picks up empathically from Sparrow.

But it's clear as day she's got that dragon wrapped around her glittery finger.

My girl's determined gaze ricochets from face to face, every one of us circling her gravitational pull like planets around a sun. Her incandescent stare encompasses all of us and pulls us in. She makes us all part of the half-baked plan this wild princess of ours just cooked up before she's even had her breakfast.

Even Maxim, who's just hauled ass back in here, now wearing his jeans but still looking kinda damp, doesn't say anything beyond a shifty growl of protest and a suspicious look out the window toward Xhev's lair.

"There's no time to fuck around. We gotta take care of this shit tonight," our girl proclaims like the queen she is. "I mean it. So we better get started. Because tomorrow we've got finals back at Icarus. That Horn of Ceres won't wait. And neither will Cleo."

# Chapter Thirty-One
## Zara

I've been a lotta things in my short but scandalous life.

Runaway kid.

Cat burglar.

Student witch.

Rebel queen.

But I've never been a fairy princess. That's a new one.

Despite all my badassery, which I've been really leaning into all day to keep myself and my whole group in the right headspace, my heart thunders like a kettledrum under my dragonscale party dress as Xhevith descends from cruising altitude and wings in for a landing over Party Central.

The Faerie Ball.

In a moonless night (which is a totally different phase than the moon at Icarus), under the light of a thousand stars arranged in constellations no mortal eye will ever see, Xhev circles the tall shining spires of the Avalon Academy for Promising Royals of the Faerie Court like he's a predator owl circling a porcupine.

I'm supposed to do an exchange program with the Avalon Academy—like a semester abroad—one of these terms.

You know, assuming we ever settle all that succession shit back home and now this demonic insurrection thing over here?

Right now, looking down on the total ruin of the roofless kiva where Zephyr's psycho mom and I duked it out last spring—the crystal dome still shattered from me busting outta there in dragon form—the sight of all that leftover carnage just unsettles me worse.

"Do we really have to do this *here*?" I say grimly (even though I know the answer). I pitch my voice under the whistle of the wind and the steady beat of Xhevith's wings.

That way, the wind carries my words back to Zephyr, who's gripping the reins in the dragon saddle behind me, and to Lucius who's buckled in behind him.

"'Tis the traditional setting for a coronation," my Dark Fae King murmurs. The brush of his lips against the studded rim of my ear makes me shiver like I'm spiking a fever. "'Tis where we Unseelie have always crowned our royals. Admittedly, this open-air arrangement is a novelty. The dome has resisted all repair. Be thankful at least we banished eternal winter when we shattered the curse."

"Yay. At least we won't freeze to death." I lean way over Xhev's scaly green shoulder to get another gander at the Faerie Ball.

And, you know, that demon we're trying to lure.

The dome over the kiva used to be shaped like a tulip. Huge stabs of crystal petal, broken away from the alabaster stem, lie scattered but mostly intact around the jagged circle of open space that used to hold the queen's lecture hall.

Inside, the circular rings of student desks and seating and the prof's lectern are all gone. On the podium, two tall empty thrones stand rigid on tiptoe in a flaming circle of witchlight torches. On the terraced lower tiers that surround the stage, the kiva seethes with sudden flurries of inhumanly fast Fae movement. They're dancing down there (sorta). But they dance like the vamps move in *True Blood* or something, all graceful glides, punctuated with spurts of frenzy that come close to violence.

Looks like the entire Unseelie population's assembled, decked out in their exotic finest—which for them means bone antler jewelry, tooth-and-claw necklaces, and other gothic accessories, because these are Dark Fae and they're not, like, nice.

They're bloodthirsty little savages and they're practically feral.

The Unseelie horde is mingling over wine and canapés under the eerie arpeggio of music from an Unseelie war-harp that's taller than I am. Not to mention, the thing looks like it's playing itself—with no musician in sight. The fermented honey of moon wine twines through the air, mingled with the briny tang of ocean and the musky spice of dragon.

All those Unseelie.

Assembled by royal command.

All summoned to see me get what I've got coming.

A massive shadow plummets from above and slices across the festive scene, black wings blotting out the starlight. Even though the summer night is balmy, that sudden sweep of shadow makes me break out in goosebumps all over.

*Steady, showgirl*, I tell my thundering heart. *That's just Max showing off.*

Max's bellow of domination splits the night. His tyrannosaur roar is echoed by a lusty war whoop from Ronin, who's strapped to that dragon's back, his powerful frame glittering in ice-white dragonscale that clings to every muscle, his raven hair streaming in the wind. In that getup, every delectable inch of him looks like a Dark Fae dragonrider.

Even Neo, who's plastered behind Ronin gamely clutching his waist (but who still hates flying) manages a dutiful yell.

That bookworm yell makes me smile. Despite the strain we're all under.

Yeah, I know. Maybe demon-hunting on my coronation night isn't the best idea I ever came up with.

But if not now, when?

We've all got finals back at Icarus tomorrow.

We can't leave this rebellion festering behind us.

Now it's Xhevith's turn to sound off. The green dragon splits the sky with his nails-on-chalkboard scream. Between my thighs, his scaly ribs expand and vibrate with challenge.

Max might be the dominant dragon on this island. He's definitely the biggest and (unlike Xhev) he breathes fire. But that doesn't mean Xhevith—who's the dominant dragon whenever Max isn't around—has to like it.

Lucius flings back his head and howls at the moon like the wolf king he is. It's a full-throated bay that's extra impressive coming from a human throat. My headmaster's really hoping he knocked me up last night—him and that knot he's rocking—so he's been quivering with tightly contained exhilaration and desperate hope all day.

Then Vasili's steam kettle hiss makes the giant crystal petals tremble and knocks small rocks from the rubble to tumble downhill till they plop into the sea. My silver snake spirals through the night like a diamond javelin, eyes burning cobalt, platinum mane rippling in the wind.

On the wing, V's definitely keeping a lotta distance from Max. That's been glaringly obvi, in a totally understandable but still awkward way, since the second we took off.

I can't exactly check under that snake's skirt (because V's junk hides coyly in a slit when he's shifted). But I'd pay good money that my alpha, in this form, is currently female.

And fertile.

If a dragon fucks Vasili like that, my snake could literally carry eggs.

Just one more damn thing to keep track of.

As we all spiral over the enchanted bubble of the Faerie Ball—my guys and me, all eight of us united (more or less) at last—Ash's winged form sweeps over the kiva in a low recon. The Seelie Prince is stunning in the moonlight with his pewter wings spread wide, his regular doeskin swapped out for an ivory dragonscale version of his vest and breeches, scales flashing with facets of Zephyr's royal green and my signature teal.

Ash glides low over the gathering, pivots in a lazy spiral to retrace his path, then soars into yet another pass. My Eagle of the Air (as he's called) has the sharpest eyesight of any of us.

Plus he knows what he's looking for.

And my shifter guys and I don't.

"Once, twice, thrice," Zephyr whispers on the wind like a spell.

That's the recon pattern we agreed to (because the Fae aren't telepaths, so we have to plan this shit in advance). Three passes for Ash to signal the all-clear for my guys and me.

Wherever that demon Mordred is lurking, he's not visible in the crowd.

Not even to Ash's eagle eye.

I push out a breath and roll my shoulders to loosen the tension.

Not that it helps.

Zephyr leans hard into the reins, his supple form straining against my back, because reining a dragon into a tight turn takes real muscle. Xhevith's big body tilts into the turn and sweeps toward the kiva's broken rim, with my guys arrowing right behind, all hot on our tail.

My gaze shifts to the night-dark sea, foaming white against the ancient bones of the Unseelie city rushing toward us.

Maybe that demon's waiting and watching in the deep.

In, like, his kraken form.

An electric flash of last night's dream, *way* more vivid and disturbingly tactile than a normal dream has any right to be, sears through me like a bolt of lightning.

The supple flex and suck of tentacles soft as suede gripping my limbs.

A swirl of indigo hair like spilled ink caressing my skin.

The rigid prod of a mighty cock parting my thighs.

Only there was something… different… about that particular boner—

Fuck.

If that was him… Mordred… then fuck.

I don't even want my warlocks knowing I came, much less how *hard* I came, during that dream fuck. I never consented to that shit—

"Sure we're good, mate?" Ronin shouts through the wind. He's finally talking in a strained but civil way to Ash, at least.

"Yeah, far's I can see? Demon's a no-show. So far." That's Ash, finally shouting back, also strained but civil.

We've all been civil all day (except V, who's been his usual pissy self, only worse, but he's hormonal) while we planned out this gig.

Now we settle on the kiva rim in unison, me and my warlocks, with Xhevith ahead of the rest. As his cruel claws curl and flex around the rim, my eye zooms in on a tall skinny pillar that rises between those thrones on stage. Perched on top, under a shimmery dome that looks like some kinda protective forcefield, a jeweled circlet sparkles in the moonlight.

Then it croons my name.

*Zara. Zara. Zaaaarrraaaaa.*

Sweet Jesus. Well, hello there, crown.

*Zarina Selene Gemini. Queen of dragons. Lady of lightning.* A silvery voice shimmers through me. *If I cede you my power, showgirl, how then will you wield me?*

I swallow hard under the cold caress of that tinkling inner voice. Last time I saw that crown, Zephyr's mom was wearing it.

At least then, that crown was silent.

Now it's all chatty Cathy.

I tilt my chin and eye the suddenly vocal bling across the kiva. *Well,*

*I won't be a homicidal psycho like Queen Maeve, that's for sure. Hope that doesn't disappoint?*

When my snark doesn't trigger a comeback, I clear the chalky taste of nerves out of my mouth and unbuckle my fighting straps. Meanwhile, Zephyr (who disdains the harness like a child's safety seat and never uses it himself) scrambles nimbly down Xhev's foreleg.

The Dark Fae King's regal as fuck tonight, with his lithe sinewy frame encased in diamond dragonscale, winking with facets of teal and emerald. His moss-green hair spills down his back under a circlet of charmed silver (*much* less flashy than the queen's crown). Twin spikes of silver cap the tips of his pointed ears. The narrow slash of his green eyepatch divides the cold beauty of his cruel face.

He doesn't even need the crossed swords rearing over his narrow back or the snarling dragon at his command to make him lethal.

I lean back to help Lucius with his buckles, because my headmaster's hands shake when he's on dragonback. (Another nervous flyer in my harem, poor wolf.)

So I aim my remark at Zephyr. "What kinda power do we think we're looking at, Your Radiance? I mean, once I'm crowned."

Yeah, I've asked before. And he's told me.

Now that I'm within reach of that Dark Fae crown and the thing's all talky and shit, I need to hear the intel again.

"'Tis difficult to be certain." Zephyr adjusts his swords and leaps to help Neo (who's also wearing the royal dragonscale and looks cute as fuck) climb down and almost fall off Max.

"The Unseelie crown," Zephyr says, patiently steadying Neo on his feet, "amplifies and magnifies the powers, both physical and arcane, of any queen who wears it. You may, perchance, develop the ability to assume other forms, above and beyond your dragon. Or more of your witching world recessives—genes that are yet unknown—may be triggered."

Yeah, I need the power.

But I still don't like hearing that shit.

"Maybe you'll be able summon earthquakes like me, babe," Neo suggests hopefully, pushing his glasses up his nose. "Because you have Kryll DNA you're totally not using."

"I think one of us making the earth shake's enough, baby," I say gently. My sweet fated mate summoning earthquakes is one thing, but the thought of having that kinda power myself is not exactly comfortable. Hurling lightning is bad enough. "Maybe I'll start transmuting lead into gold like you, though. You might not be alone anymore in Honors Alchemy."

"Then I could tutor you," Neo says happily. Clearly nothing would make him happier.

Zephyr turns toward Ronin to help him off Max, but my Brit's already unbuckled and jumped down on his own. Ronin lands in an Avenger-like crouch on the kiva rim just as Zephyr turns toward him.

For a breath, all action on the rim freezes.

Max, who's twisted around sniffing with hopeful interest at Vasili's genital slit, rumbles a warning at Zephyr.

Vasili, who's baring those sharp fangy teeth and snapping at Max, lets rip with a sinister hiss.

Lucius stiffens in the saddle behind me. "Zephyr, don't—"

Undaunted by all the hostility, Zephyr gives my guys a narrow look, then reaches a gauntleted hand to pull Ronin easily to his feet. Ronin unfolds to tower over him…

But neither guy releases his grip.

"You are a natural, Ronin Kilcannon Pendragon," the Dark Fae King says quietly, "on dragonback. 'Tis as though you were always meant to fly."

"Always wanted to." Ronin looks down into Zephyr's upturned face, a blazing flash of eye contact that crackles with suppressed emotion, then clears his throat, unhands his ex, and looks away. "Talking about Zara's new powers, weren't you?"

"Indeed I was." Zephyr turns toward me with a small secret smile. "There is one power all Unseelie queens have in common. All our queens, once crowned, acquire an… attractive aura. A magnetic energy that draws armies of amorous would-be suitors."

"Yeah, no. That's one power I can definitely do without. I, uh, don't seem to have a problem *attracting suitors*." I snort and hop down from the saddle on my own, because Zephyr knows I don't want an assist. "Anyway, I've already got my army with the seven of you."

As we're all very well aware, even for a poly queen like me, both my hands and my bed are, like, extremely full.

A blinding flash of light announces V's shift back to his male warlock form. A heartbeat later, Max shifts after him, with another nuclear flash that leaves white spots dancing in my vision.

"Surely you don't imagine you're *finished* collecting amorous warlocks, do you, little queen?" V needles me, sharp as a wasp. "You can be certain none of the rest of us are making that assumption."

This definitely isn't anyplace I'm ready to go right now.

And thanks to the party going down right on top of us, I don't need to.

I turn away to let V and Max have their primping time, shimmying into their party duds from the saddlebag behind the privacy of Xhevith's lifted wing, while I take a sec to adjust my own getup.

Because the last thing I need tonight—as in, the *very* last—is a wardrobe malfunction.

Fortunately, a dragonrider's coronation gown is designed for… wait for it… dragon riding, so I don't have much to fix. Just an ice-white gown, strapless and fitted and slit high up the thigh, with supple dragonscale elbow gloves and dominatrix boots. Every time I move, emerald and teal flash in the witchlight like I'm encased in sequins. My hair's twisted in a braid that wraps around my head like Leia the rebel princess in *The Empire Strikes Back* (equally practical for dragon flight or saving the ice world of Hoth from Imperial attack).

Plus the getup leaves just enough leeway to strap my stiletto to my thigh.

So I'm good.

Actually, I'm more than good.

Ronin, Neo, Zephyr, Max, and Ash all glitter tonight like they're encased in ice. Like they've all been dipped in diamonds, with accents in my teal and Zephyr's royal green. Thanks to my Unseelie's generosity, we all look like we belong together. Like we're fitting consorts for a dragonrider king. Even Lucius, who's opted for his vintage tux and ascot with chestnut curls flowing loose down his back, fits right in with the enchanted ball theme.

And, sweet Jesus, Vasili.

When my horrible alpha finally emerges from the screen of Xhev's modestly lifted wing, V looks *so* Hollywood A-list celebrity in his narrow white tux and punk-rock silver hair, with a swipe of teal glitter across his eyelids and a pop of emerald sparkle at his cuffs, that I wanna ask for his autograph.

That magical war-harp is still plinking away, filling the balmy night with its uncanny melody. Couples and throuples and quartets of various genders are linking hands and whirling in circles around the kiva like they've been charmed to dance till they drop dead.

In a place like Avalon, honestly, I wouldn't rule it out.

But the minute Zephyr takes my arm like the king he is, grips Ash's elbow (because Ash is his other acknowledged consort), and squires the three of us onto the stairs, a militant blast of trumpets carves through the night like a cleaver.

The harp quivers into stillness.

All movement stops like someone flipped the off switch.

Under graceful falls of lavender and cornflower and sea-green hair, garlanded with spiky black flowers or loops of nightshade, a scattered sea of cold Fae faces turns across the kiva to track our approach.

My warlocks fall in behind us, all my shifters right on my tail, Ronin bringing up the rear and keeping a wary eye on our six. All around, I see heads bowing, hands pressed to hearts—and more than a few Dark Fae whose homage looks sullen and token at best.

Very clearly, Mordred's been making mischief.

Then the familiar chords from the trumpets (more invisible musicians) pluck at my nonexistent sleeve for attention.

"Royal accolade?" I shoot a sidelong look at Zephyr.

Behind his coldly regal face, a smile hides at the corners of his mouth.

"Cheese on toast. Is that… K-pop?"

"'Tis what you requested, is it not?" My Unseelie guides the three of us down the corkscrew stairs with their tricky footing into the kiva like he does it twelve times a day.

"Yeah, but we've been kinda busy today, Your Radiance," I point out. "Planning to trap your demon and all. So I'm impressed."

Zephyr says nothing, but his hidden smile deepens.

The minute we clear the stairs, he beelines for the platform.

Where the thrones—and the crown—are waiting.

*Zaraaaaa,* the damn thing breathes as we approach. *I hold the power you seek. But you claim me at a great cost.*

Zephyr's hand tightens around my arm. Clearly I'm not the only one hearing this. But he's the Dark Fae King. Maybe that crown's always spoken to him.

*Once I am yours,* that tinkling voice whispers like the chime of silver bells, *I can never be renounced. I will become your destiny—and your doom.*

"Fuck me," Ronin mutters from the rear. "You lot hearing this shit?"

"Every word," Vasili murmurs. "It's like surround sound. However *does* one turn it off?"

"I wish you good fortune with that," Zephyr says briefly.

Okay, so I guess my guys are all picking this up, one way or another.

*Once I am yours, Gemini queen,* the crown purrs, *your precious freedom is no more. Perhaps, after all, 'tis better to yield to the demon.*

Ash's wings unfurl and spread wide in menace.

"Not about me," I mutter, loud enough so all my guys can hear. "It's not about my freedom anymore. What we're doing is, like, way bigger than me. Bigger than any of us. If I wanna save the arcane races before we all go extinct, I gotta ascend. And for that, we need that crown."

Fired with purpose, Zephyr leaps onto the platform. I scramble up with him (a maneuver my slitted skirt barely allows, and I practically flash the whole room my thong in the process).

With a single downstroke of his mighty wings, Ash alights beside us.

Vasili, never one to be outdone, levitates onto the stage in his *Saturday Night Fever* tux, then drapes himself right over one of the thrones like his Goblin King namesake in *Labyrinth.*

I wait for Zephyr to tell V to get out of his chair, like he did yesterday in the study when those two almost came to blows.

Instead, Zephyr levels him with a look and mutters, "It suits you." Then he swoops in to lay claim to Vasili with a blazing kiss.

I swear to fuck, I almost burst into flames. For real.

That kiss just about sets my thong on fire.

While those two get to know each other better, my other guys claim the stage and range themselves around me. Max all protective and growly with rut, Lucius grave and serious, Neo excited and happy.

V's hand snakes around Zephyr's head and fists in his hair, so he's the one controlling the kiss. Zephyr grips the arms of the throne to fence

Vasili in. Ronin lurks at my side and stares at the two of them with amber eyes smoldering like he's seriously thinking about crawling onto that throne between them.

But Ash is watching the crowd.

He's watching for the demon.

*Where the fuck are you, Mordred?* I shift my gaze to the impenetrable depths of the midnight sea. *Cuz this is about the time we figured you'd show yourself.*

I can practically hear the low rumble of demonic laughter.

Meanwhile, Zephyr finally emerges from kissing the shit out of Vasili (though I can't tell whether Zephyr breaks free or my snake pushes him away or both). Anyway, Zephyr sorta staggers back from V and straightens. Smirking, V fishes his silver compact out of his tuxedo pocket and touches up his lip gloss while he sprawls elegantly over Zephyr's throne. Looking kinda dazed, my Unseelie draws a hand across his mouth.

Then Zephyr reaches to lace my fingers through his, draws me in close for my own slow kiss—a leisurely claiming of my mouth with his that makes my pussy melt—then turns to face the silent stares of our viewing audience.

I mean, I guess with him, they've seen it all by now.

But written like headlines over that sea of cold, unfeeling Dark Fae faces, I read astonishment, outrage, and smoldering anger at the sight of an impudent mortal warlock coolly fixing his lip gloss on the Unseelie throne.

Great.

V's, like, ten times more elegant and royal than I am.

Just wait'll they get a load of my Gemini ass parked on their throne.

Zephyr's fingers tighten around mine, like he can sense my trepidation, even if he can't read my mind. Gracefully he lifts my hand to his mouth and presses a kiss to my gloved knuckles.

"Here is the essence of the matter," Zephyr announces to the staring multitudes. He doesn't even need to raise his voice, because kiva magic does the projecting for him. "Tonight I crown this powerful Gemini witch, the first of her kind, as my most worthy and beloved queen."

A spark of warmth kindles in my chest and swells. That warmth spreads outward through my whole body till even my fingertips are tingling.

Of course, Zephyr never actually said he's in love with me. He didn't exactly spell out the letters just now either. But, hell, I didn't just fall off the turnip truck.

He loves me.

The King of the Dark Fae loves my aerobicized mortal witching world ass. And it feels freaking amazing to hear him say it out loud to his whole kingdom.

"Tonight, as well," he goes on calmly, "I claim my beloved queen's warlocks—all of them—as mine own consorts."

My heart gives a huge leap. I gasp and turn to gape. He's watching the murmuring crowd, but his hand tightens around mine in a warm clasp.

"I trust you'll enjoy your wedding gift, my bride," he whispers under the crowd's restive rustle. "All seven of your warlocks fucking in one bed for your pleasure."

Oh, that effing Fae.

He's been planning this.

My entire body tingles with anticipation and excitement.

"Whoa," Neo whispers beside me, eyes shining behind his glasses. "I can't believe it. Am I really a king's consort?"

"That's right, baby." I literally feel like my heart's gonna explode. I link my free hand with his. "Believe it. He's claiming you. *All* of you."

I desperately wanna sneak a peek at Ronin, whose emotions through our bond are really turbulent. Telepathically, he's all over the map. But physically, he's not in my direct line of sight.

Besides, Zephyr isn't finished.

"The Unseelie crown is hers." Zephyr's cool voice hardens to rock. "And the Unseelie throne is, most emphatically, *mine*. If any here dare oppose me, know that you do so at your utmost peril."

Every soft Unseelie syllable falls on those staring heads like stones. "Be warned."

Unexpectedly, my Dark Fae turns to me. Gracefully, gauntlet glittering in the witchlight, he gestures toward the pillar.

"My queen," he says gently, "'tis time to claim your crown."

I blink in surprise and my mouth falls open.

Somehow, I assumed he was gonna crown me himself. I mean, I'm not even Unseelie. It's not like I was born to wear that thing.

But fuck if I'm gonna make him tell me twice.

I close my mouth, release my mates' hands, raise my chin, and walk through my guys into the danger zone. Close up, that witchlight dome hums like it's electrified. Static races across my skin and sparks across my fingers, and I haven't even touched it.

Vasili lowers his feet from the arm of Zephyr's throne to the floor and leans forward, his sharp gaze intent on my face.

"Be careful, little queen, *do*," my snake whispers. "We really don't know what that forcefield can do."

But this isn't something he or any other of my guys—not even Zephyr—can do for me.

I'm either the queen or I'm not.

I brace myself, feet spread, and suck in my breath. Across the kiva, an awful silence descends.

In that stretch of nail-biting stillness, under the pressure of a thousand staring eyes, all my old misgivings come clamoring back. The babble of spiteful gossip and stinging criticism—every hurtful word stored up in my memory—makes my ears ring.

Maybe it's all a mistake.

Maybe I'm not worthy to be queen.

Maybe I'm selfish and self-centered and wicked.

A wicked Gemini who will never be queen.

"Cheese on toast," I whisper. God, I hate that my voice is shaking. "Not to be Captain Obvious. But there's literally one way to find out."

I steel myself for anything (not that steeling myself's gonna help if this crown is a trap or a curse). Then I plunge my dragonscale-sheathed hands deep into the sparkling dome. The forcefield wavers and hisses and sprays ultraviolet sparks like a blowtorch at a construction site.

Vasili exclaims and leaps to his feet. But I glare into his violently alarmed face and shake my head fiercely to warn him away. His narrow hands clench into fists and he hisses with frustration.

But, thank fuck, he follows my lead.

I just have this really strong sense that it's not safe for anyone else to touch the thing. And I'm gonna listen to my gut.

After all, I'm a fucking lightning witch.

I mean, honestly, I've handled worse.

My hands close carefully around the menace of glittery spikes, every one sharp enough to cut, and lift the crown from the surface. For such a major piece of bling, it's surprisingly light. Gripped carefully in my hands, it passes out through the witchfire dome like water.

*Will you claim me?* that silver voice chimes, so loud now it makes my skull ring like a bell. *Do you dare?*

Jesus. Now my own goddamn crown is daring me.

"Yeah, I claim you," I announce in a voice that rings to the heavens (and not only due to kiva magic, because queen voice). "I'm Zara fucking Gemini. And you better believe I dare."

Staring straight ahead and silently daring *anyone* (especially that demon) to stop me, surrounded and supported by all seven of my warlocks, I lift the crown, crackling with electrical energy, high before a thousand wide eyes.

From the rim, Xhevith stretches his long neck toward the heavens and bugles in triumph.

While his bellow fills the sky, I plant the Unseelie crown firmly in place on my head.

# Chapter Thirty-Two
## Vasili

If I'm being honest, my first Faerie Ball has proven to be a bit of a disappointment.

I mean, after darling Zara claimed her crown, I was certainly expecting at least a little homicide (if not regicide) with that demonic kraken surging from the sea like the leviathan in *Clash of the Titans* to tear down the kiva and claim Zara for his watery bed and (with any luck) hurl that aggravating Dark Fae tyrant with his smoldering looks and searing kisses into the sea.

At the very least, I expected some old crone in the crowd to rise up screaming "Boo!" and calling Zara the Queen of Putrescence, as in Buttercup's nightmare of marrying Prince Humperdinck in *The Princess Bride*.

Not that I'm complaining, of course.

But the fact that none of this has happened (yet), after all our well-laid plans to trap that demon and banish him back to the fiery abyss, *is* a bit… anticlimactic.

On the positive side, Zara certainly seems to be having a celebrity moment with these Unseelie. Since the instant they saw the crown accept her, instead of frying her to a crisp (which was apparently a distinct possibility, one Zephyr kept conveniently to himself), Zara Gemini has become the new It Girl of the Dark Fae court.

"Sorry, but no, she *won't* have this dance," I announce coldly, for at least the tenth time, to the latest hopeful suitor trying to butt in on *my* dance with Zara. "The queen's dance card is completely full—as is her bed, just in case you were wondering—for… oh… approximately the next fifty years. Don't bother coming back before then."

Zara manages to maintain her queenly composure until I've whirled her away from her disappointed suitor. Then she dissolves in my arms in a fit of slightly hysterical giggles.

"Don't be so horrible to my peeps, Goblin King. I gotta build some trust with these guys. Woo them over." Her Hollywood face alight with mischief, she grins up at me under the sparkly white-and-green dazzle of the Dark Fae crown. That crown certainly suits her, and she knows it. She hasn't taken it off once since she claimed it.

I do wonder if she's planning to wear it later while we're fucking.

Up close, her new bauble is charmed silver, twisted into vines and leaves cleverly crafted to mimic thorny smilax. Which is, fittingly, a poisonous plant. Every dazzling chip of diamond is a thorn sharp enough to cut.

How utterly charming.

In short, that crown is far more sinister than her innocent homecoming queen tiara in the witching world (which, in case you've lost track, is still in the clutches of my vile funnel web spider of a father).

"For pity's sake, don't talk to me about wooing these people over." I tuck my girl's delicious curves, sheathed in dragonscale like a domme in latex, possessively against my body and glare at the bystanders writ large as we whirl past. "Your new subjects would cheerfully have watched you fry if that demon had his way. They should be wooing *you*, little queen. They should be licking your boots."

Deftly I pivot to steer us safely past another determined-looking Fae who's clearly on an intercept course for Zara. I can waltz like a Bridgerton (one of my many hidden talents), even to that war-harp's tripped-out tunes.

Needless to say, I haven't let anyone outside our harem lay a finger on Zara all night.

"Well, I definitely think they're trying." My girl tilts her head toward a particularly lovesick trio—two lords and a lady—all of whom I've already given the brush off—who stare longingly at Zara as I whirl her briskly past.

"Power of attraction," my girl adds wryly, lifting one hand from my shoulder to adjust the crown over her teal hair on a rather jaunty angle. "That bennie certainly kicked in promptly. Let's hope whatever other superpowers I've just added to my repertoire manifest PDQ. Because we're gonna need 'em tomorrow to find the Horn of Ceres and pass our finals."

Her brows draw together. Her eyes darken to storm-cloud blue. "That's assuming Cleo the sea dragon hasn't already found it."

"Hmmm." I don't disagree, but I'm not ready to pivot quite so quickly from the current threat.

By all appearances, the coronation certainly seems to have gone off stunningly. Zephyr is enduring a dreary succession of tedious congratulatory toasts from his nobles while they all kiss the ring, with Ash looming protectively at one shoulder and (I'm quite interested to see) Ronin lingering at the other.

Max is slow-dancing with Neo, a sensual bump-and-grind that's definitely drawing Zara's attention and making our girl's breath quicken. Neo's trusting head is resting against Max's, and the dragon has a tender hand threaded through our bookworm's magenta curls.

Yet Max is watching Zara and me with his oblong dragon pupils narrowed to slits. Very clearly, he's fantasizing with obsessive focus about sticking his impregnating dick in both of us. The blazing heat in his smoldering face sharpens my own state of alert.

On the surface, this night is an absolute triumph.

But something is, nonetheless, very wrong.

With me.

My Armani tux is perfectly tailored to fit every inch of my scrumptious self to perfection. Yet somehow, despite my tailor's impeccable skill, my *haute couture* is chafing. Beneath, my skin stretches tight and hot against my bones. I've been struggling with temperature spikes and sudden sweats since that infernal dragon spilled my secret and dropped his bombshell about my newfound ability to *carry eggs* (like a hen!) last night. An inferno burns under my skin that makes my shirt cling to my back.

In fact, I'm perspiring so heavily I've already had to repair my cosmetics twice.

Now, with Zara's fuckable little body tucked up against my hips and thighs, this persistent boner I've been sporting all day is achieving truly epic proportions.

Until I know my mate is incubating a little Goblin Prince or Princess in her deliciously fertile body, I'll simply have to fuck both of us through this mating rut.

The fact that I'm simultaneously in heat, and (apparently) ready to incubate eggs myself, is an intolerable complication.

I don't want this. The eggs. *Obviously.*

Yet my snake is demanding the immediate sexual service of Max's dragon with a savagery that's both intense and alarming.

Well, she's simply not going to get what she wants.

As a result of all this, I'm fretful.

Anxious.

Not feeling at all like my usual horrid self.

The knowledge that I'm helpless to control what's happening in my own body stings like a wasp. Infuriated by the entire ridiculous mess, I lash out at the closest target I can reach and glare at Zara.

"You do realize, I trust, that Zephyr's demon is only biding his time?" I snap. "Clearly, Mordred wanted the crown to reject you in front of the whole Unseelie realm. Now that it hasn't, he'll move on to Plan B."

Sweet fuck, I sound positively shrewish. Truly, it's not a flattering effect.

Zara's lovely eyes narrow dangerously at my tone. "Pretty clear on that, yeah. Just not as clear on how we can trap him inside a summoning circle in, like, the next twelve hours if he won't come on his own. You have any ideas on *that*, bad boy?"

The best idea I have is one I have no intention of voicing. But I'm distracted by my rut, her fertility (how soon can we know if she's pregnant?), and my own mounting heat.

Consequently, she lifts the thought I'll never voice from our bond before I can block it.

"Put myself out there all alone… no ball, no crowd, no warlocks… as bait?" Zara tilts her head in thought. To my considerable alarm, I realize she's already contemplated the unpalatable notion herself. "Yeah. It's an idea I'm not opposed to. I actually suggested it to Zephyr while you were getting your facial this morning."

"Dear fuck." I stare at her, appalled. "Did it never occur to you to consult me?"

"No point." She shrugs. "It didn't go well when I raised it with the others. Total non-starter for the whole harem. But especially Lucius and Max. Guess those two are hormonally incapable of peeling off and leaving me exposed to danger while they're in rut."

"They're not the only ones," I say shortly.

Zara's stubborn face softens and her lush lips curve. "Yeah, I kinda figured that, Goblin King. How are you doing with all this anyway? I mean, you being non-binary and able to carry eggs in dragon form, plus being in rut for me and in heat for Max at the same time, then Zephyr and Ronin kinda making up, and the demon and everything else that's going down? It's… like… a lot."

I'm opening my mouth to assure her I'm in complete command of the entire situation when Lucius appears unexpectedly at our side.

He's still impeccable in his vintage tux and ascot with his delicious Renaissance curls spilling down his back. But my sharp eyes detect a flush along my pet's high cheekbones and a tinge of red in his whiskey gaze. With the creamy sweetness of Zara's intoxicating pheromones perfuming the air—with that addictive new note to her scent like ripe peaches that tells every shifter in sniffing range she's fertile—plus the lethal threat of that demon hanging over her head…

Lucius Aries is clinging to his aristocratic Old World civility by a thread.

"You've monopolized our queen long enough, Mr. Romanov," our headmaster says mildly. "I believe I'll take over for a time, if you don't mind."

Privately I'm amazed he's managed to give me this much time alone with her. Our three alphas (including Max) have been maneuvering delicately through the landmine of possessiveness, violence, and aggression that are defining characteristics of male shifters gripped in the biological and emotional crisis of a mating rut. For that reason—and because he's Lucius, and there's nothing I won't do for him—I command my reluctant hands to loosen their hold on Zara and entrust my darling girl to our wolf's eager arms.

Zara snuggles into Lucius' hungry embrace with an upward look that brims with so much mischief his fangs drop. He growls and drags her against his powerful body with a savagery that turns heads.

"To be continued," Zara calls over her shoulder, laughing, as Lucius whirls her away. "I seriously wanna talk about what's going down with you, Goblin King. Okay?"

Another couple spins between us and breaks our eye contact, which gives me the perfect excuse not to answer.

I pivot away from my mates and fight my way to the fringes of the pressing crowd. By this point, I've passed beyond any sort of genteel perspiration into a disgusting muck sweat. I'm a literal inferno of heat and hormones.

If I could only escape this crowd of alien Fae I dare not trust. Escape into the open air and *breathe*.

Desperately I wrestle open the sparkly bow tie that's strangling my throat and peel out of my smothering jacket. I glimpse the spiral stairs climbing to the kiva rim and twist through the crowd toward freedom.

I'm barely halfway to my objective when my snake uncoils and writhes inside the hot tight prison of my skin.

*Vasili, we rise,* she hisses, fierce with need. *We rise now. I burn!!*

Dear fuck.

This is happening. Whether I want it or not.

My mating flight.

My only conceivable option is to put as much distance as humanly possible between me and the male dragons at this fucking ball. Before I lose every shred of my sanity in this uncontrollable need to breed.

I abandon all restraint and bolt for the stairs, discarding my priceless designer jacket in my wake as I flee. Helped along here and there by an ungentle telekinetic shove from yours truly, Fae scatter left and right, yelping in alarm and cursing me for my rudeness.

With zero apology, I shove roughly through their ranks. Leaving chaos and bruises in my wake.

By the time I reach the stairs, I've torn my shirt open—buttons flying everywhere—and ripped the sweat-soaked garment viciously from my shoulders. My long legs devour the stairs three at a time, fingers wrenching open my fly with a violence that will surely make my tailor weep.

Halfway across the kiva, as I rise above the crowd, Maxim's eyes lock with mine.

He takes one look at my desperate face. Then his own predatory face ignites with triumph—and hunger. With truly alarming speed, he lunges for the stairs, ripping his Zephyr-provided dragonscale from his chest and shoulders as he charges after me.

Oh, fuck. Fuck!

In an uncharacteristic panic, I explode onto the rim and drag my trousers down my legs. The clothes tangle with my shoes—Italian leather, it would be a crime to spoil them—as I struggle desperately to rid myself of the lot.

Unexpectedly Xhevith rears before me, wings extended, head snaking down for a good sniff. One whiff of my heat makes his nostrils flare. He rumbles, long and low, with intense interest.

"Zephyr!" I shout without turning, frantically kicking free of my trousers. "For fuck's sake, control your fucking dragon!"

Dear God, *why* did I have to drink that magical moon wine?

Bitterly I curse the moment I found that innocuous bottle, standing innocently beside Zephyr's bed, and let my petty impulse to provoke him (by drinking his precious wine without asking) overcome my wits.

I'm smarter than that. I should've guessed—or at least suspected— it was moon wine. Laced with enchanted herbs to ensure fertility.

That moon wine is the entire reason I'm fertile.

I've barely gotten naked when the shift sweeps through me in a holocaust of heat and light.

I twist away from Xhevith and launch into the air, in my flying serpent form, with a teakettle scream of rage.

Behind me, the skies light up with a second shift. I don't waste time looking back. My wings churn the air for speed and altitude. I stretch my sleek form for maximum aerodynamics and minimum drag.

Xhevith's nails-on-chalkboard scream tears the air, echoed by Max's tyrannosaur bellow.

I entertain the brief uncharitable hope that those two male dragons will fight each other senseless in a testosterone-fueled frenzy for claiming rights to my genital slit, while I slip away from both of them and vanish in the night. Desperately I chart a course for the volcano, where numerous small caves offer countless hidden nooks and crannies where I can hide.

Until this abominable heat passes.

But all the while, as I'm far too keenly aware, my fertile female dragon—with her consuming need to breed—harbors other intentions.

# Chapter Thirty-Three
## Zara

"Yeah, so, that was sudden," I murmur to my remaining warlocks, not for the first time, as we file in a line up the steep tower stairs to Zephyr's royal bedroom. "Really hope V doesn't hole up somewhere all night and brood. He's definitely flown way beyond any range I can sense him. You?"

I direct this question over my shoulder at Ronin, who's still flushed and windblown from flying back in a rush with Zephyr and me on Xhevith, right after V and Max took off in their mating flight. After we did what we needed to (minus the whole demon thing) at the Faerie Ball.

With my two most vicious alphas sidelined in a mating flight and that elusive demon still at large, my remaining guys wanted me here, in the relative safety of the Unseelie palace.

"Same." Ronin's hands flex around my waist, because he's kinda hugging me for comfort as we climb. "When V lit out like a blooming house on fire and I lost the link, that snake of his was sexed up as fuck."

"I trust, if Maxim does manage to catch up, our dragon's better angels will prevail." Lucius sounds kinda winded from running back here through the streets in wolf form, because we don't have enough dragons (with Max gone) for everyone to fly. "He simply *must* control his dragon. If Vasili's serpent truly is biologically capable of incubating—carrying eggs that are fertilized by another male dragon—Maxim must allow that to be Vasili's choice."

"Max bloody well better." Ronin snorts. "Or we'll have a whole new set of problems in this harem, won't we?"

"I believe in Max," Neo pipes up stoutly, "and his better angels. No one gives him enough credit. He's not a jerk. He really isn't. He's just really nice and decent."

Speaking of nice and decent.

Neo's back there with Lucius, carrying my dominatrix boots and gloves that I've already peeled out of. Just having him with me, and so totally calm about whatever monumental thing's going down with V and Max, is a definite comfort.

The reason our bookworm sounds breathless is because Ash just carried him back from the Faerie Ball on the wing. It was a super sweet thing to do, Ash carrying him like Superman with Lois Lane. The whole dynamic makes me hopeful that Ash might actually be courting our bookworm.

Ash has already split downstairs to check the doors and locks, the same way Lucius does at the *domus*. But it's gonna be interesting to see how my Seelie Prince acts with Neo tonight.

I've definitely been tracking that Ash has been hanging back in the sack. He still hasn't fucked any of us (except Zephyr on the side) since I came back to Avalon.

But Neo's the gentlest point of entry into our whole polycule.

If our Seelie Prince makes any kinda overture tonight (which I'm definitely hoping for), Neo will be totally welcoming.

We climb past a tall arched window that opens over a shimmering expanse of starlit sea. I pause to peer out, but there's nothing to see. Under a moonless sky that glitters with a million stars, the ocean is flat and impenetrable as a sheet of hammered steel.

Though I do wonder if anything that might be lurking in the water (like our missing kraken) is peering back.

A delicate shiver races down my spine and makes my scalp prickle.

Oh, hell to the no.

I really hope that's just nerves, and not my erratic dash of Valyrian foresight acting up. Foresight is one of my recessives (I mean, until now).

Unless that's one of the genes my new crown switched on.

I reach up to touch the Unseelie crown, just to confirm it hasn't floated off my head, because that big pointy Evil Queen coronet feels light as thistledown.

Yep. Still there.

I'll definitely be showing up for finals at the Icarus Academy tomorrow as the Unseelie Queen.

And Cleo can kiss my royal ass.

I fucking dare that bitch—*and* V's Mads Mikkelsen doppelgänger of a dad—to try and take this crown.

"Well, shit, Goblin King. None of us expected what went down tonight, did we?" I frown at the empty sky (no snake, no dragon), then glance over my shoulder at my warlocks. "Did I make the wrong call? You guys think we shoulda gone after those two?"

"Vasili emphatically wished to be left alone. That much, he and his serpent made quite clear. Nor would Maxim's dragon have welcomed our intervention. A shifter's need to breed is a biological imperative." Lucius gives us all a patient nudge to keep us climbing after Zephyr, who's leading the way to the bedroom.

"Yeah. Guess those two are gonna need to work through it. Hopefully before we fly home in the morning for finals." I reach behind me to lace my fingers through Ronin's hot Leo grip.

Together, my guys and I keep climbing.

"Well, we all know V's… complicated," Neo says tactfully. "I mean, there's stuff he wants that he's not comfy asking for. He just needs space to explore that and make his own choices."

"If you imagine Maxim's dragon will give Vasili any sort of choice, you clearly don't understand the breeding frenzy that consumes a rutting dragon." Zephyr's strained voice drifts down from the head of the stairs.

We're finally at the top of the tower facing our closed bedroom door. Now my Unseelie sweeps an impatient arm outward. A violent gust of wind whips past us to blow the door open, so fierce the hinges almost splinter.

"Easy, love," Ronin murmurs. Takes me a sec to realize he's actually talking to Zephyr.

He's talking to Zephyr the way he talks to us.

His mates.

A little bud of hope for those two has taken root in my chest. That hope has been growing all day while I watched them interact. Now, hearing the gruff affection in Ronin's voice, that little bud unfurls and flowers.

Clearly Zephyr hears it too.

The Dark Fae King glances back, his eye startled and wary.

I come right up behind Zephyr and slip my arms around his waist. I'm still holding Ronin's hand, so he's half-pulled into the hug too.

Behind me, Ronin's breath hitches.

He's waiting for Zephyr. To see how he reacts.

Under our hands, under all supple strength sheathed in dragonscale, the Dark Fae King's strung so tight he's almost trembling. When our snake launched into that mating flight, it took everything Zephyr had to keep Xhevith from rising.

This dragonrider mate of mine basically had to cock-block his own dragon.

Even now, with Vasili way out of range, Xhev's sexual frustration has to be a lot for his empathically linked rider to handle.

I lean forward to graze the pointed tip of Zephyr's ear with my lips. "You okay, Your Radiance?"

"Xhevith craves your snake." His tense whisper spills out on a shuddery breath as I trigger his Fae erogenous zone. "My own… attraction… to the warlock is a complicating factor. Xhev wants him so badly, I fear, because I'm rather drawn to your Vasili myself."

"Think he's your Vasili now too." Ronin leans forward with a low murmur so he's embracing both of us. Now I'm pressed between Zephyr's lean back and Ronin's broad chest in a really good way.

Ronin laces both hands through mine so we're both touching Zephyr's taut waist.

"Go on in, love," Ronin breathes. "Let's give that dragon of yours something else to crave."

That little flower of hope in my heart blossoms.

When Zephyr pulls in a long breath under our fingers, then closes his hands over ours, a thrill of happiness skitters through me.

These two finding their way back into each other's hearts is gonna heal a major fissure in our polycule. We all need that.

To be healed.

"Are you certain?" Zephyr whispers, soft as a baby's breath. "Nothing we do will ever bring back your sister Gwendolyn."

"What happened to Gwen wasn't your fault." Ronin's voice thickens. "Wasn't mine either. It was those bullies who hazed her. Damien and Cybelle. Those rotters got what was coming to them, didn't they? They're both toes-up."

In the trembling silence, no one moves.

We all know what this moment means to Ronin, who's been tormented by misplaced guilt over Gwen's tragic end the whole time I've known him.

"So, yeah." Ronin lets out a long sigh that feels like a mountain of anger sliding off his shoulders. "I'm… okay. I mean, I'll always miss her. But I think I'm finally okay."

Under our linked hands, Zephyr's breath spills out in a ragged exhale.

Then my Dark Fae fires into action and drags us both into the bedroom. Neo tumbles in breathlessly after us, with Lucius right on his heels.

"Don't lock the door," I manage to get out. "Ash is still coming—"

Then Zephyr twists under my hands so he's facing me. With me pinned tight between my two guys, his mouth collides with Ronin's in a blazing kiss.

It's awkward and fierce and joyful. I wrap my arms tight around Zephyr's waist and laugh.

Behind me, Neo tucks up against Ronin's back. Our bookworm starts unzipping and working Ronin out of his dragonscale like a helpful house elf.

I turn my face into the hot column of Zephyr's neck, pull in a lungful of burnt amber and dragon musk, and work my Dark Fae's zipper open all the way past his navel. I'm totally not above copping a feel of his sleek chest and tight abs. Or dipping a hand inside his Avenger suit to find his taut cock jutting from a lick of green pubes.

"My bride. This is all your doing." Zephyr surfaces from Ronin's kiss like a drowning man surfacing for a gasp of air. His mouth fuses with mine in a kiss that tastes like cloves and nutmeg. His tiny fangs press into my lower lip in a stinging suck.

I stroke his hard cock, already so hungry he's pulsing. While he gasps and arches into my touch, I spread the first eager spurt of precum all down his shaft to get him good and ready.

Because I know this isn't gonna take long.

Neither one of these guys is in any mood to wait.

Both my guys are writhing against me and feeling me up, we're a hot tangle of hands and mouths and moaning.

Especially when I grab Ronin's hand and wrap his fingers around Zephyr's dick.

Both guys groan like I'm torturing them.

Laughter sparkles and bubbles up inside me in a geyser of joy.

I love this so much.

Having those two finally together and happy.

This moment has been such a long time coming.

"Fuck me, love," Ronin whispers into my ear. "He's blooming right, you know? You made this happen for all of us."

"You deserve it," I whisper back, leaning into him. "You both deserve to be happy."

Ronin's already hard and straining under all that dragonscale.

And I am *here* for that shit.

Muscle flexes in his arm. He's relearning the feel of Dark Fae dick he hasn't touched in years. Still smiling, I work a hand under Ronin's pumping fist to cup the tight silky bulge of my Unseelie's balls.

Zephyr swears at the moon and explodes in a frenzy of action, peeling out of his armor at lightning speed.

Ronin's process is more complicated because he's never done it before—peeling out of dragonscale—even with Neo doggedly tugging the Avenger suit down Ronin's torso.

Ronin twists and struggles to help him. "Bugger this armor—"

"I'd advise you to get used to it." Zephyr unzips me in a single pull and pushes my own dragonscale roughly off my shoulders. "'Tis what a king's consort wears in Avalon. I intend the entire Unseelie race to know you're mine."

My Unseelie's hands cup my tits and his tone darkens. "That intention applies to all of you. You are, all of you, mine."

I'm still kinda giggly, but his purposeful touch plus that dark declaration of intent makes my knees melt. For a guy who's never been with any other girl except me, and who's only been fucking me for a little while, he's a really fast learner. Zephyr's clever fingers tease my nipples and tug my rings. Then his mouth closes over my nipple in a hot suck that shoots straight to my clit.

I moan long and loud. Cradled in my hand, his balls clench tight.

"Oh my gosh, that's so hot," Neo sighs. "Ronin, stop trying to help and let me just pull this off you, okay?"

While we all strip each other down between kisses and strokes and plenty of bump-and-grind, I find a good strong lock with Lucius in our bond.

My headmaster's definitely watching, but he's not actively joining. He's shed his tie and jacket to get comfy, but that knot he's packing is still tucked behind his zipper. He's prowling barefoot, like the beast he is, along the wide window ledge that circles the room.

His wolf is close to surfacing.

*This is their time with you, my queen,* Lucius whispers through our bond. *Their time to be with each other. Tonight I'll stand watch and keep you all safe.*

"You're the best, Teach," I say on a smile. "You make me feel safe just by being here. Join in whenever you want, okay?"

"I'll take that under advisement," Lucius murmurs.

By now the rest of us are naked (Neo too, because him being nakey and snuggly is never a bad thing, even when he's trying to give Ronin and Zephyr their space).

I enjoy the fuck outta having Ronin buck-naked and flexing against my back, with one hand wrapped around Zephyr's cock and his other palm pressed against my clit to give me plenty of friction to grind against. And I love the way Zephyr devours my tits and bites a searing path down my neck and trades desperate kisses between me and Ronin like he legit can't get enough of either one of us.

When I feel like the moment's right, I squirm out from between the two of them.

For a sec, the whole scene freezes.

Those two are like two wild animals that just stumbled on each other in the forest. Zephyr's lean and streamlined like a lynx, feral features stark behind the green slash of his eyepatch, with Ronin's fist still wrapped around his dick. Ronin's like a panther with topaz eyes flaming, his tattooed chest powerful under a sleek spill of midnight hair.

"It's okay," I whisper. "You won't hurt each other."

Slowly, Ronin's hand drifts toward Zephyr's face. My Unseelie stands totally still, like he's not even breathing, while Ronin's hand lands gently against his cheek.

Very carefully, giving Zephyr plenty of space to pull away, Ronin strokes Zephyr's sharp cheekbone with a reverent thumb. At last, Ronin's thumb eases under the cruel press of the eyepatch Zephyr never removes.

Now even I'm not breathing.

Gently… so gently… Ronin eases the eyepatch aside.

Without it, Zephyr looks years younger.

Clearly Ash did a bang-up job healing him with his Seelie magic after the infamous accident. Just a slim pale scar crosses the silky eyelid that's closed over Zephyr's empty socket.

Zephyr's remaining eye closes and his green brows draw tight.

"Tell me the truth. Am I… hideous to look upon?" he breathes in a thread of voice.

"You're fucking beautiful." Ronin's voice breaks. "Inside and out. Oh, love. I'm so… so sorry… for hurting you."

He leans in to place the gentlest kiss on Zephyr's scarred eyelid. Then Ronin bows his head and presses his forehead to Zephyr's.

Zephyr's unsteady hands lift to cradle Ronin's face.

My Dark Fae doesn't make a sound. But he doesn't reach to replace the eyepatch either. That moment of acceptance is the sign Ronin's been yearning for.

The sign of Zephyr's forgiveness.

When their mouths drift closer and meet in a searching kiss, my eyes flood with a rush of grateful tears.

"Shoot, princess," Ash breathes in my ear. I jump a little, because geez, I never even heard him come in. "Guess you really are a goddess. You healed Sparrow in ways I didn't even think were possible."

"They're both healing," Neo says softly. "Ronin needs healing too, just as much."

Ash is silent, his massive frame still and thoughtful against my back. I turn away from the slow tender kiss Ronin and Zephyr are sharing and look up (way up) into the guarded cast of my Seelie's craggy face.

The starlight gilds his spiky pewter hair and turns his silver eyes to pools of mercury. I rise on tiptoe and reach up (way up) to thread my fingers through his hair.

His glowing eyes shift from Zephyr to me. Finally, his muscled shoulders ease and his face unclenches.

"Guess I'm all the way in the deep end of this polycule pool now, ain't I?" he rumbles, deep in his chest. "Same way Sparrow is."

"That's right, big man. You're one of us." I stroke the hard plane of Ash's cheek and trace his chiseled jaw. Then my hand drops to circle his thick throat and tightens in a way that makes him hiss.

"You gonna take good care of your queen tonight?" I croon.

I'm not often a domme, but that shit always turns my big Seelie into a sex puddle. Right on cue, he drops to his knees and stares up at me with his whole soul shining in his worshipful gaze.

"You just tell me how you want me, princess," he rasps.

"I want you up against the wall right here, in front of all our guys, with your thick dick buried so deep inside me I can taste you in my throat," I tell him, low and husky. "And I want Neo railing your ass until you wail. He's been such a sweet boy. He deserves a reward, don't you think?"

"Geez Louise," Ash almost whimpers. "Think the two of you together just might do me in."

Neo hovers behind him, flushed with excitement, eyes wide and shining behind his glasses. Gently his big hands settle over Ash's shoulders, tattooed with those Seelie angel wings.

"Don't worry about a thing, Ash," Neo says sweetly. "We'll both take really good care of you."

I'm already unlacing Ash's dragonscale Conan the Barbarian getup so Neo can slip the vest off his big shoulders. As soon as he does, I cup my hand under Ash's chin and lift him to his feet. Neo reaches around from behind to open his breeches. Ash's supersized cock springs free, ruddy and thick in a nest of pewter curls. The double row of silver studs from his Jacob's Ladder gleams down the underside of that proud dick I'm already wet for.

I need both hands to wrap around that shaft of his. But I know just how he likes it—gentle at first, till he's settled, my fingers gliding over his piercings and kneading his shaft.

Then he just wants to please me.

I look up into his anguished face, eyes closed, brow furrowed, lips parted with pleasure. Neo peeks around him to see my face, then reaches between Ash's thighs to cradle his balls and stroke his taint.

Sweat breaks out against Ash's brow and a low groan rips out of him.

I finally take pity on my poor Seelie Prince. "Okay, big man. Put me up against the wall."

Ash's silver eyes flash open. His pewter wings unfurl from his back and spread wide.

With a single flex of his massive biceps, he catches me under the thighs, hoists me effortlessly into the air, pins my back to the wall, and spreads me wide.

That's how my titanium pussy takes all that girth, with his big hands cupping my ass, my sweaty tits pressed to the hard flexing plane of his chest, and me gasping over every studded row of piercings as they ease into my slick and hungry hole.

When he finally works himself in to the hilt and gives a few gentle pumps to get me used to him, my gasps build to cries of need. That's when he kisses me. A deep consuming kiss that immerses me in the bright warmth of sunlight and the sweet tang of Florida grapefruit and the bracing bite of ocean air.

My cunt squeezes him tight and my hips ride his shaft. His wings beat gently with every thrust. Neo takes his time with him, working his dick into Ash's ass, so sweet and careful, he keeps checking with Ash to make sure he's not hurting him (even though Ash totally wouldn't mind).

And while I'm pinned to the wall and clinging to Ash's mighty shoulders and writhing with pleasure as the three of us find our rhythm, I've got a bird's-eye view of Ronin and Zephyr wrapped in each other's arms. When they topple together into our bed, their tender rain of kisses turns fierce and desperate.

When they finally fuck, their bodies join face to face, with Ronin flat on his back, hands cradling Zephyr's savage face, tears glittering in his amber eyes. Zephyr licks and kisses his tears away and whispers to Ronin, intimate words meant just for the two of them.

Ronin's intense joy in this mating hums through our bond and permeates the whole tower. With a telepath like him, we all share his cresting pleasure and his sense of wonder to be reunited with this special first love.

To forgive and be forgiven at last.

Afterward, we're all wrecked.

Pretty sure Neo's still buried inside Ash when those two finally conk out face down in the big round bed. Neo's never dommed anyone before, so the whole experience of having a big guy like Ash trembling and breathless and hanging on Neo's tentative commands is a heady experience for my sweet wide-eyed bookworm to process.

Zephyr crashes in a hot mess, sprawled half over Ronin and half over me, with his green hair wildly disheveled, his eyepatch abandoned on the windowsill, and his bare face peaceful and dreaming in the starlight.

Lucius lets his wolf out and stretches across the doorway, so no one can get in without waking him. The familiar susurrus of his snuffling snores normally sends me straight to dreamland. Especially when my entire body is sex-drunk and sluggish and sated from my sexy reunion with Ash.

But I can't sleep.

Not with two of my warlocks still MIA.

My body still hums with restless energy. I'm quivering like a plucked harp.

Rather than disturb the others, I wiggle carefully out from the middle of the sleep heap, grab Lucius' discarded button-down (which falls to my thighs) and my new Dark Fae crown, then pad out to the shadowy stillness of the adjoining den. Softly I close the door behind me so I don't wake anyone up.

After all that fucking, my guys need their sleep.

The balcony doors are locked with some complicated twist of silver but, hello, I'm a cat burglar. Even working by touch in the dark, I'm out there in no time.

Standing barefoot on the balcony, I button Lucius' shirt closed against the cool breeze blowing from the sea. The crown I park firmly on my head.

Right where it belongs.

I've only had this thing a little while. But I've already fucked in it. Wearing it feels, I dunno, deeply and profoundly *right*.

I shake my head just to enjoy the sensual feel of my tumbled curls whispering around my shoulders and brushing against my back. My thighs are still damp from Ash's copious cum, one of Neo's sweet little love nips tingles against the swell of my tit, and my greedy pussy feels stretched and finally satiated.

Over the past day or so, they've all had me.

All seven of my guys.

If I'm gonna get pregnant, they've all had a shot.

I rest my hands on the balustrade and pull in a deep breath of the Avalon night. The briny scent of ocean and the haunting sweetness of night-blooming lotus seep through my senses.

The slow rhythm of Xhevith's snores rumbles from his lair, somewhere under my feet, because that dragon's totally sex-drunk (since he gets off when Zephyr does) and they're both finally sleeping.

I scan the empty skies for any sign of my missing guys, which is an exercise in complete futility. I'd know if they were anywhere close. Finally, not ready to give up, I close my eyes and extend my other senses.

A turbulent rush of emotion, distant but potent as fuck, floods through our mating bond.

No doubt about it, Vasili's given Max a real chase. Like, for hours. Because that's how long they've both been gone.

But Max is a dragon on a mission. He's been hunting Vasili, one way or another, for a really long time. Now our determined dragon's finally tracked our wily snake to ground.

Those two mates of mine, they're together.

And they're… blissful.

Both of them.

Whatever that looks like when we all get back, whether those two manage to fertilize a clutch of dragon eggs together or not, whether that means Vasili has to hole up somewhere in a nest till they hatch or however it works (because this is totally uncharted terrain for me, plus Vasili is Vasili and he literally never behaves the way he's supposed to)… however this thing goes down, we're all gonna figure out the features of that new landscape.

Together.

Same way we always do.

What's more, I can *see* exactly where those two are. Like they're a painting dashed in lurid strokes of black and red and silver against the canvas of my closed lids.

V's been hiding out like a bandit in the little cave with the hot spring and the cave art Neo and Max found together last spring. That hideaway's near where my guys are fucking now in dragon form, locked together and spiraling through the open air under the looming shadow of that dormant volcano, with V's silver coils wrapped tight around Max's black bulk, my snake's fanged jaws buried deep in Max's throat to totally dominate him in a brutal mating bite (the first bite Max has ever taken)—and Max's forked dragon dick locked deep and pulsing in V's genital slit.

And the fact that I can physically see that shit, painted in hectic streaks of color, like a Fauvist expressionist painting you'd find hanging in the Met?

I'm manifesting a totally new arcane power we studied with Mistress Aggie in Science of Witchcraft class. It's a form of witchcraft that's linked to my Valyrian DNA. So I guess that's the gene my new crown just switched on.

The gene that encodes for clairvoyance.

Now all I need to do is *think* about Icarus Island—and I can see that shit. In fact, my brain lights up like a pinball machine. I can *see* the Horn of Ceres, glowing and pulsing with magical power, which I recognize from a pic Neo drew for us. Technically, that thing's not even underwater. The artifact is resting on a ledge in this sea cave grotto that I actually know.

In fact, I've dived that site more than once. I'm a certified diver, and that shimmering blue grotto's one of my favorite boat dives.

Maybe Nikolai Romanov, as a trustee on the school board, pressured the Dean to choose an aquatic site that's supposed to help Cleo win the Dean's Challenge.

But the site the Dean chose tells me she hasn't totally turned against me after all.

In fact, the Dean might actually be my secret ally.

Against the screen of my closed lids, Cleo's psychic presence pulses like a ruby sun. Yeah, she's hunting for the artifact. For her, the Dean's Challenge has already started. Xiao and Nikolai—V's dad—they're hunting with her (even though they're not supposed to). But she's nowhere close.

She's hunting in the wrong place.

I'm off my academic suspension and free to join the hunt at noon tomorrow. Now, thanks to this crown and my new Spidey senses, I know exactly where to hunt. That means I've got an actual fighting chance to win this fucking challenge.

My whole body tingles and sings with an electric hum of triumph.

The hair swirls around my shoulders and the shadows lighten to violet. Psi fire spills from my eyes like Fourth of July pinwheels.

Fuck. Me. Sideways.

Just wait'll I tell my guys.

Grinning like a psycho, I spin away from the sea toward the open balcony doors.

That's when a form takes shape in the shadows.

Right there against the wall, where the darkest shadows gather.

This whole time, I've been alone on this balcony. Now, with zero warning, a strange guy is lurking there.

He's big, at least as tall as Ash, and just about as broad through the shoulders. A sleek curtain of midnight blue hair parts around pointed ears and swirls around the muscled flex of his shirtless body, all the way down to his sinewy hips. In a sharp Dark Fae face, clever eyes pulse a wicked purple. A sleeve of ink encases one brawny arm from wrist to shoulder in a tapestry of indigo scales. Sleek black armor clings to corded thighs. I can't be sure in the starlight, even with my shifty senses, but this guy's barefooted, and looks like his toes are webbed.

He's like a blue-haired version of Jason Momoa from *Aquaman* standing on this balcony. He's even gripping a trident taller than he is in casual threat.

"All hail the Gemini queen." A deep baritone rumble, like a real radio voice, rolls from his cavernous chest.

Every hair on my body rises. Fight or flight instinct gooses my vitals. I mainline an adrenaline rush like it's heroin. My inner dragon uncurls from her sex-sated sleep with a long hiss of menace.

Despite the adrenaline headrush, my thoughts are crystal clear. Even if I summon my guys through our bond to help, this POS has more time than he needs to act.

He's bided his time and chosen his game.

Nothing to do now but play it.

I plant my feet wide and fold my arms across my chest. Like I'm not just wearing a guy's shirt and a crown, with Seelie cum dripping down my thighs.

"So I'm guessing you're our missing demon." I make my voice hard like the badass I am. "Mordred, right? You here to make a play for this crown? Because if you are? Fair warning. That's not gonna end well for you."

His head tilts and his lips curl in a cocky grin I wanna smack right off him. "You know what I am."

"Yeah, you're like this half-Fae, half-kraken, *Clash of the Titans* demon."

"That ain't all I am, baby. What else." He leans his big trident against the wall and prowls toward me like sex on a stick. I swear to fuck, this guy walks like sin. (At least there's not a tentacle in sight.) "I wanna hear you say it. What else am I, Zara Gemini."

I clear my throat and say huskily, "Incubus. And don't try sexing me up like you did in that dream last night either. I'm onto you and your shit. This time I'm fucking wide awake."

Of course, this piece of work keeps right on coming.

But he takes his time, with a casual confidence to his swagger that goes way beyond cocky. "I could make you sleep. Make you beg. Make you burn. Do whatever the hells I want with you. But I ain't here to nick your crown, baby. And I ain't here to haul you off down below to my watery bed."

"Well, that's a relief. Then maybe I won't need to wipe what's left of you off this floor when I'm finished." He's not getting me trapped against this balustrade either, so I levitate a few inches and let my power rise. It rushes through me like an elixir, making my hair float and my fingers spark. "If you're not here for the crown, Aquaman, what the fuck do you want?"

He rumbles a deep chuckle, but at least he stops moving. "Hells, I want a lotta shit. Too much to spill all at once, true? How 'bout we start with this. Straight up, I'm here to hop on the harem train. Lend some demon muscle to you and your warlock homeboys."

My mouth falls open.

My levitation witchcraft (which is still a new thing for me) exits the building in a rush. I drop to the floor with a thud.

"S-sweet baby Jesus." For fuck's sake. I'm actually stammering. "A-are you trying to say…?"

I can't finish. The sentence is literally too awful to finish.

But Mordred the demon, Zephyr's mortal enemy and therefore mine, finishes that horrible sentence for me.

"Not trying, baby. I'm telling you true. I'm here to join your harem."

## THANK YOU!

Hey, witchlet! Thank you sooooo much for reading *Gemini Wicked*! What did you think??? I write to bring joy to readers like you—you're my "why" for this crazy author life!—so I'm dying to hear from you. If you loved spending time with Zara and her seven sword-crossing warlocks in their spicy secret world, please leave a quick review on Amazon, Goodreads, or BookBub. **Just a few words makes a huge difference!** Your feedback is so important to me. It helps readers like you give writers like me a chance. **Here's the link to leave feedback for** *Gemini Wicked* **on Amazon**

**(https://www.amazon.com/gp/product/B0CMCCCLXR).**

**Here's the Goodreads link:
(https://www.goodreads.com/book/show/201330031-gemini-wicked).**

**Here's the BookBub link (https://www.bookbub.com/books/gemini-wicked-a-dark-witch-academy-paranormal-romance-by-laura-navarre), if that's your thing!**

Finally, the Witching World would not exist without you–my wonderful readers! I'm thrilled to announce the elite readers who've slipped behind the magical wards that hide the Witching World from the casual reader to join Zara & her warlocks on the Icarus Academy class roster, as follows:

<u>Sexy Seniors</u>
Vasili

<u>Juicy Juniors</u>
Neo

<u>Sassy Sophomores (Zara's Belfry cohort)</u>
Amanda – Amarie - Barbara - Cheryl - Draco - George - Jenna - Katrin - Keri - Kristin - Kristy - Lisa - Lyssa - Mali - Mallory - Mary - Mary Elizabeth - Melly - Melissa - Nhbuggy - Nikki - Primmy - Rachel D. - Rachel K. - Ronin - Serafina - Serena - Shannon - Teresa

<u>Frisky Freshmen (Common Magics 101 cohort)</u>
Camoblu - Christina - Danielle - EP - Jana - Jean-Emilien - Jess - Jessie - Joel - Joelle - Juliet - Kallie - Kat - Katelyn - Kiki - Lara - Maekayelee - Maxim - Mbeck - Mendy - Nadia - Penelope - Persephone - Renate - Sheila - Zara

If you'd like to slip behind the magical wards and be recognized in my next book as well, join us in the Witching World–my intimate, immersive, inclusive reader community on Ream–at
https://reamstories.com/witchingworld

**Wanna know what happens next with Zara, Mordred, Cleo, and the warlocks… without having to wait?**

*You're in luck, Book Babe, cuz you can keep right on reading!!
Join the Witching World, my secret reader community, for instant
access here! (https://reamstories.com/witchingworld/public)*

*You want a sneak peek at Zara-Zephyr bonus content from* Gemini
Wicked *you can't find anywhere else? Or a spicy secret chapter they
won't let me publish You Know Where that features Vasili & Max's
mating flight from their POV?*
*Free follow me here in the Witching World for bonus content going
live in August 2024!  (https://reamstories.com/witchingworld/public)*

*How about secret prequel content that happens* before *Gemini
Wicked?*

*Plus access to the next Gemini novel early, months before everyone
else?*

*You ready for an exclusive, extra-steamy Zara-Vasili-Neo MMF
novella about Neo's first heat that's only available to tease and tempt
you in one super-secret place?*
*Then you're ready to join Common Magics 101!
(https://reamstories.com/witchingworld/public)*

*From Academy outsider to witchy insider, my intimate reader
community whisks you through the magical wards that hide the
Icarus Academy from the average reader to inhabit the enchanted
secret world of Zara Gemini and her sword-crossing warlocks.
Join the Witching World here!
(https://reamstories.com/witchingworld/public)*
*Keep scrolling down for a sexy sneak peek at GEMINI HEAT: A
Spicy Dark Witch Academy First-Time MMF Vasili-Zara-Neo
Novella (about Neo's first heat!), exclusively available in the
Witching World!*

# Gemini Heat:
## A Spicy Dark Witch Academy First-Time MMF
## Exclusive Novella
## By Laura Navarre

## Chapter One
### Neo

Lord, I'm burning up.

Even though this is literally the exact transformative experience I've been dying to share with my queen and the rest of our warlocks, you know, forever? Having me go into my very first mating heat at this precise moment—when there's so much in our harem that's all unsettled—well, that's not totally a good thing.

Which isn't to say I don't appreciate the upside of having five insanely hot mates and suddenly being this out-of-control horny.

But for an awkward bookworm like me, a shy guy who was a literal virgin until, like, yesterday? A guy who only just figured out I'm actually bi instead of straight?

Am I allowed to admit my first heat has been kinda… overwhelming?

Right now, I mean, I'm just trying to take the edge off this whole intense experience.

I'm stripped down to my skin and immersed to my chin in the cold plunge pool in the *caldarium*. That's part of the Roman bath under the *domus* in our residential college at the Academy. I'm alone in here at this hour, and that's by choice, just trying to focus on the icy water encasing my steamy skin.

And *not* on the hot need pulsing through my rock-hard junk. Basically, my relentless boner is totally unfazed by this whole ice bath I'm immersed in.

Wow.

This freaking heat.

It's, like, unstoppable.

I shift around on the submerged stone bench and, ugh, I just can't help it. I let out a groan. Despite this long solo soak in the *thermae*, my well-stretched and pounded hole's definitely tender with the aftermath of all that's been going on back there, really intensely with both Lucius and Ronin, since I started my heat.

My groan echoes off the glass that separates this little room from the big underground pool. This late at night, way after midnight on a school night, the whole complex is still and shadowy. Facets of green light glimmer on the walls.

Plus it's nice and quiet, except for the gurgle of water bubbling up from the hot springs under the island.

Trying like heck to ease all my assorted discomforts at once, I breathe in deep the familiar reek of sulfur and minerals, laced with the residue of Lucius' wolfish mating scent.

Huh.

Our wolf shifter headmaster must've been in here earlier. And judging by the warm spice of ambergris I can just sniff out with these sharpened shifty senses that seem to come with my heat (even though I'm not a shifter myself), Lucius was in here with Ronin.

Probably reaming him up against the wall. Or maybe bending him over the bench in the locker room next door. Or, you know, both.

My neglected dick throbs at the visual.

"Oh, sugar," I moan softly.

Usually Zara giggles and Vasili sneers at what he calls my pathetic Sunday school swearing.

Well, that's how I was raised.

I'm just hoping I can soak the ache out of this brand-new mating bite Vasili sank into my shoulder last week. And really hoping I can cope with this whole mating heat.

Because the last thing I need tonight, as in the very last, is for Vasili to see the way I—

"Mercury?" Like I've summoned him with my thoughts, the Goblin King's voice curls through the *caldarium* like a whiplash. The sound of my last name snaps against my senses from behind. "What the everloving fuck do you imagine you're *doing* in here? You've been soaking in that plunge pool for so long your precious balls must be shriveled to the size of raisins."

"If only." I heave a sigh of resignation and let my head fall back against the basin.

Actually, my balls are *not* shriveled to the size of raisins, dickhead, thank you very much. They're swollen to the size of plums and starving for attention, like the rest of my junk.

But Vasili Romanov the Goblin King, the unapproachable top-dog alpha in our cobbled-together polycule, definitely doesn't need to know that.

Since, you know, the two of us were enemies all the way from freshman year (when he bullied and hazed me so hard I almost quit) pretty much till the exact moment I lost my mind and asked him to bite me and then fuck me.

Now I think he's ruined me.

My non-response to my new alpha's sudden appearance doesn't seem to make him very happy, because he gives an annoyed-sounding huff.

Well, too bad.

If that snake had his way, we'd all genuflect whenever he slithers in.

The soft suck of the glass door closing really makes me hope he's given up and gone away. That for once, he's decided not to torment me and left me in peace. Of course, my temporary spurt of relief (and maybe a *teeny* bit of disappointment) doesn't last very long.

Because the invisible fist of his telekinetic witchcraft clamps hard and heavy around my whole body, like I've just been encased in concrete.

"Hey! Stop that, you big bully." I stiffen right up and struggle to break free. Needless to say, that's a wasted effort. He's not even letting me turn my head. He's annoyed at me and he wants me to know it.

"For cripes' sake," I grumble. "Would you please—?"

*"Silence."* His ruthless grip crushes my whole body like an iron glove.

Next thing I know (before I even have time to worry about my airway or what I can do to stop him), I'm dragged naked from the pool, spun around to face my nemesis, and dropped hard on the tile floor.

I barely manage to get my legs under me in time to save myself from landing at his feet on my butt.

Now he rears between me and the only exit like a hooded cobra, all slim and sinewy in his silky sleep pants and a black lace cami that clings obscenely to his sexy body, with the underwater light from the big pool glowing like an emerald halo in his rock-star hair. That kind of backlight makes it hard to see his David Bowie face.

Like Zara says, he's sexy-pretty.

The way I see it, that only makes him more terrifying.

I swallow hard to get some moisture down my suddenly dry throat. I'm a good size and I work out on the daily to stay buff for Zara.

Still, even barefoot, my new alpha looms over me.

"Jerk." I simultaneously glare at him and try to cover up the evidence of my condition down below with my cupped hands. (Not easy to do, because I'm not exactly tiny. I've got what Zara calls a monster cock.) "You're a real jerk sometimes, you know that, V?"

"Hmmm." His unamused stare skates over me from top to bottom, which makes goosebumps erupt down my arms and race across my shoulders. Now that I'm out of the water and all exposed, even in the humid warmth down here, I finally start shivering.

His voice lashes out like a snakebite. "Why are you hiding from all of us?"

Resentment lurks in my comeback. "For your information, I'm not hiding from *all* of you."

*Only you, snake.*

In the green-tinged shadows, I can barely see his lip curl in a sneer.

"I thought so," he purrs. "But how pathetic to hear that suspicion confirmed. You'll have to hide *much* better than this, First Boy, if you intend to hide from me."

My face tightens in a wince. He's Mogadon and I'm Kryll, which means we're both warlocks, but from non-telepathic races. The problem is, V also turned out to be part shifter—very appropriately, he shifts into a giant flying serpent. Then he bit me and fucked me, which means now we have a mating bond.

Due to that, he's reading my mind.

Which is, you know, awkward?

"Look, I'm allowed to be alone if I want." I start to fold my arms across my chest, till I remember that I'm nakey. Feeling more ridiculous by the second, I decide to keep my hands where they are, folded protectively over my dick.

By now, Vasili's not the only one feeling annoyed.

I square my shoulders (as much as I can with my hands in fig-leaf pose) and just brazen it out. "I don't even know why you're down here anyway, instead of asleep upstairs with everyone else, or why you care if I'm hiding. It's not like you're my real alpha—"

He hisses in warning.

My words dry right up and evaporate.

If I thought he was scary before, now he's like pulling back your sheets and finding a rattlesnake in your bed.

"Oh, aren't I?" His venomous voice coils and strikes. "Perhaps you'll indulge me. In precisely what manner am I *deficient* as your alpha?"

Oh, Lord, now I'm in for it. He's in one of his horrible Vasili tempers.

"Come on, V." I hate that my voice sounds sulky, but he definitely brings it out of me. "It's not like you need me to tell you…"

His tone's like a razor blade wrapped in silk. "You know I simply live for your critiques, Mercury. Now indulge me with your insights, *do*."

I lick my dry lips and his gaze drops to my mouth, which makes my dick pulse.

I shift around awkwardly and clear my throat. "Well, um, you don't actually take care of me very much, do you? Not like Zara does, or the way Lucius takes care of all of us, or the way even Max is trying to. You don't act like you're really my alpha."

"Be more specific," he snaps.

I can't believe he's dragging me through all this. But, then again, he's Vasili. Resigned, I hike up my (hypothetical) britches and wade in. "You don't tend my mating bite—"

"Because you won't let me near it."

I rush past that observation, because it's actually accurate, and he sounds acidic. Like maybe it bothers him. "And you definitely haven't been, you know, fucking me. Not since that first time—"

"Because you won't let me near *you*."

"That's because I don't trust you." I heave another sigh. This conversation really is pointless. We'll never be more than frenemies. Still, I can't seem to bottle up the rest. "Jesus, get a clue, V. Did you, or did you not, literally just bully me for the past three years?"

"Two and a half," he parries. "But who's counting?"

"Felt like ten to me," I mutter. Guess I do still resent him for it. "Dickhead."

He tilts his head and taps a mocking finger against his cheek. "Let's just see if I've captured the gist of your grievance, shall we? I'm not tending that pretty bite I've given you to claim your delectably buff body, because you won't let me anywhere near it. And I'm not tending your perfectly snug and insatiable little hole because you won't let me anywhere near *that* either."

"Uh…" Suddenly, somehow, I'm the bad guy. I feel like I should say something in my own defense, but hearing him talk about my hole that way pretty much leaves me speechless.

Inside I flutter and pulse.

Like I'm waiting for him to fill me.

"Which means that, in order to behave properly as your alpha, darling, I'd have to ignore your modest objections to my horrible attentions and simply take whatever I want from you, whenever and wherever and however I care to take it." His voice deepens to a velvet purr. "Tell me the truth now, *do*… if you dare. Is that sort of behavior something you'd enjoy?"

"Well, gosh, I mean… no." My face is on fire and the words trip over each other in their rush to exit my mouth. "No! *Obviously* no."

"Hmmmm." He hums and muses for what feels like hours. Because I'm twisting in the wind, of course that snake's enjoying himself. "First Boy, I do believe you're blushing. And, I must say, that sounds like a *very* formulaic protest. One that's meant to be overcome."

Of course, that observation only makes me blush worse. I'm fiery-blushing, it's the curse of being a natural redhead (even though lately I dye my hair purple), and I hate that I want him so much, I hate it.

But I can't help it.

The truth is, I wanted him way before I asked him to bite me.

Still, you can't just give in to the guy, he's Vasili. You have to push back or you'll be, like, consumed and devoured. So I persevere. "Listen, V, there's nothing formulaic about—"

My chest locks up tight. My indignant protest chokes off like he's twisted a spigot. That telekinetic fist of Mogadon witchcraft clamps around my body, way harder this time than before. My adrenaline spurts and my heart pounds in alarm.

"Hey!" I wheeze. "Cut it out. I mean it—"

Vasili flicks a casual hand. His witchcraft hurls me off my feet and flings me back six feet to slam against the wall.

Hard enough to bruise.

*"Ow."* Outraged, I scowl at him through the mop of wet curls that's fallen over my eyes. Of course he's all blurry now, because I'm nearsighted and not wearing my glasses. "Thank you for literally just proving my whole point. You're such a jerk."

He floats toward me (literally), levitating a few inches off the ground for effect, because he's a total show-off.

"You say you simply can't bring yourself to trust me… and truly, who could blame you?" His slim body sharpens into focus, hovering maybe three feet in front of where he has me pinned to the wall like a butterfly in a display case.

"You certainly want me." His gaze drops to my now blatantly obvious boner (because my hands are totally pinned to the wall). In the shadows, his delicate face turns all hard and predatory. "For some reason, I fancied that deferring to your wishes and indulging your virginal First Boy modesty would persuade you… in time… to trust me. Now it appears I've been mistaken." He chuffs out a snort. "Which certainly isn't a common occurrence. I blame you, of course, for distracting me with all that delicious bookworm innocence. My nefarious plot to win your trust seems to have gone disastrously awry."

"Ya think?" I mutter. Gosh, now I'm embarrassed, which is like a natural reaction when your frenemy uses a tone like that and talks about your virginal modesty and delicious innocence while staring at your dick.

I'm embarrassed and resentful as heck.

He's still not letting me move, so snark is my only recourse. My own Kryll witchcraft is alchemy and earthquakes, both useless in a situation like this.

He glides closer, still levitating, his bare feet barely skimming the tiles, which means I have to tilt my head way back (which he deigns to allow) so I can hold his stare. His lips part so just the tips of his sexy fangs are showing (which is a permanent Vasili thing he usually tries to hide). His potent scent of caramel and musk twines through my senses and makes my head spin.

That's his mating scent. The Mogadon are a scenting race.

Now he's scenting *me*.

His hand floats up to graze my cheek. I'm all stubbly because I haven't shaved. Despite everything I'm feeling, that jumbled-up knot of resentment and fear and arousal and hope that tangles my tongue and snarls my thoughts, my head turns on its own to push my hot face into his cool palm.

He's my alpha. He's scenting me to claim me. And just the smell of him, when I'm drowning this deep in my heat, has my dick dripping and my whole body tingling.

"Vasili…" I breathe in a good whiff of those yummy Mogadon pheromones he's kicking out.

God, he makes me so hard.

"Neo." He never says my actual name. The fact that he's doing it now, in this soft un-snakelike whisper that caresses me like a tongue, makes my heart pound for absolutely no reason.

His cold fingertips graze my earlobe and toy with the silver hoop he put there himself the night he pierced me.

That was the night he shoved down my sweats and briefs and got me explosively off, post-piercing, over the bathroom sink, with a hand job so epic I still relive the whole experience every time I jerk off in the shower.

Now that triggering memory rears up again and arcs straight from my brain to his through our mating bond.

Geez Louise. I barely bite back a moan.

"Hmmmm." His pale eyes narrow. A sudden sense of danger shoots down my spine. "Well. I certainly didn't disappoint *that* night, did I? If you'd prefer that I behave like a brute and simply ravage you against the wall, darling, I can certainly oblige."

Before I can even react to that idea, his hand snakes between us to close around my aching dick… and *squeezes*.

Oh. My. God.

Ohmygod. I arch into his grip with a groan I can't hold back. His commanding fingers wrap around my pulsing junk. His thumb swipes over the precum that's drizzling from my slit and smears the moisture over my crown where I'm all swollen and hypersensitive. My hips punch forward to rut into his fist and my dick begs for more.

Lord, he's gonna do exactly what he's threatening.

He's gonna get me off right up against this wall.

He's gonna jerk me off until he breaks my heat.

And I can't even decide whether that's something I should want or encourage or resist. But what I want actually doesn't matter that much, because he's not exactly asking my permission—

Still holding me frozen in place, his casting hand drifts up. His fisted knuckles skim my jaw and trail down my neck over my racing pulse. Finally, his cool hand grazes the twin punctures of that mating bite he sank into my shoulder.

"V," I whisper on a tiny puff of breath that's (almost) a plea.

It's too much sensory overload at once, the slow rhythmic knead of his free hand teasing my dick, coupled with the way his casting hand's teasing my bite.

Wow. His touch feels so good there, so soothing against those tiny swollen wounds that have been so slow to heal without his care. Even though Zara and Lucius have both been tending my bite so carefully, licking me to heal me with the biochemicals in their shifter saliva. Max wants to tend me too, I think, despite still being the new guy in our harem, because he's pure dragon shifter and he operates on pure alpha instinct. (Which causes a lot of problems.)

But the dynamic between him and Vasili is electric, and technically V's my alpha, and since Max doesn't want to trigger him—

V's soft snarl sends a tingle shooting down my spine. He releases my dick so fast I want to howl in protest.

"At least do me the common courtesy, as your alpha, of not thinking about that fucking dragon while *I'm* touching you," he snaps. "Particularly when I'm jerking you off, for fuck's sake."

Which pretty much validates my whole point about that charged energy between the two of them.

Even though I don't trust him, Vasili I mean, paradoxically I want him to want me. Good God, I absolutely *need* him to want me.

"You want me thinking about you and only you?" I suck in a big breath and lock onto his stare. "Make me."

Geez, I must be crazy, jerking his chain like that. His touch on my bite drives me insane. Must be this mating heat frying my brain.

Squirming with tension and embarrassment, I bite my lower lip.

Which I know perfectly well is one of his triggers.

He hisses like a teakettle and snakes in to lock his mouth over mine. Ohmygod, *yes*. This is what I want. *This*. Not his dark and snaky games, not him all difficult and complicated and evasive, just the simplicity and directness of his mouth on mine.

He runs cool like any Scorpio and his lips are cold, especially by contrast, with me all feverish and all sexed up. But his hot tongue darts inside my mouth and just plunders me like he means business. He tastes like juniper and Russian vodka and Vasili, all abrasive and unapproachable but totally addictive. I suck on his wicked tongue and chase his ruthless mouth and basically do every single thing I can think of to entice him.

The sharp sting of his fangs against my tender lower lip draws blood.

A husky moan rolls up my throat. It's loud enough to be embarrassing. But he swallows the sound with a little growl of his own and deepens the kiss like he's trying to crawl inside my mouth and down my throat.

Gosh, he kisses me like he wants to gut me.

Some belated sense of self-preservation jolts awake and kicks in. I'd have to be seriously crazy to trust him. I try to ease back, just so I can tap the brakes and breathe, but he's having none of it. His free hand spears through my wet curls to trap me.

His casting hand falls back to his side, but stays in a fist. Because he's still nowhere near ready to let me go.

He's my predator.

I'm his prey.

Need pools in my balls and pulses hard and heavy in my dick. My chest clenches till I can barely breathe and butterflies flutter in my belly. Just the bare possibility that he can do what he's threatening, he can make me take his cock, he can do whatever he wants to do to me and I'll have to take it (Lord, that's such a turn on!), just the possibility of that makes me tingle all over.

"You're such a naughty boy," he murmurs between deep sucking kisses that totally ruin me. "It's all rather shocking, truly, given your tiresome reputation as an apple-polishing teacher's pet."

"I'm only Lucius' pet," I mumble against his lips. *And yours.*

(Since Vasili's provisionally on the faculty now.)

He hums over my secret confession. "And you're so… deliciously… needy. Aren't you? I can sense your greedy hole just aching for me to fill you. Your insatiable little hole that's going to milk me dry."

"God, will you stop talking about it," I mutter with my eyes squeezed shut, because every time he mentions my hole, another spurt of precum drizzles down my dick.

"I'll say whatever I please. You certainly should have learned that much about me by now." He nips my lip until it stings and I whimper. "I'm your alpha. You're my mate. And, starting tonight, we're both going to begin acting that way. Aren't we?"

If this jerk thinks I'm just gonna bend over for him now that he's (sort of) claiming me as my alpha, he's definitely got another think coming. My brows rush together in protest.

But, tonight, he owns me.

At least, he owns me right now.

But I want to own *him*. I do. If I have to feel this way about him, I want us to be equal.

I lean into his kiss.

But he's such a tease he backs away. He makes me chase his kiss. I strain forward and tease his cruel mouth with mine until he relents and gives me the kiss I'm craving. The hot wet slide of our tongues lacing makes him hum low in his throat with pleasure.

A dart of happiness wiggles through me.

I'm pleasing him.

His horrible casting hand's still balled at his side, but he's finally loosened his grip enough to give me a free hand myself. My palm falls away from the wall behind me where the rest of me's still pinned. My hand drifts forward to nudge against his. Slowly my fingers curl around his casting hand, teasing gently at his little finger until it unfolds.

That telekinetic clench around my body loosens a little bit more.

I smile against his mouth and start tugging at his next finger—

*"Goblin King?"* Zara's queen voice freezes us both in our tracks. "What the fuck are you doing to him?"

A frisson of tension zings through his body, so close to mine. His fist clenches hard under my touch. The sudden vise of telekinetic pressure makes me groan. His mouth wrenches free from mine (which almost makes me whine in protest).

But his gaze finds mine and doesn't veer.

"Tormenting him until he begs for mercy," he says coolly, his stare biting into mine and daring me to contradict him. "What else do you suppose?"

"Huh." I can't see my precious fated mate with V's tall body still standing obstructively between us, but it sounds like she might be fighting a grin. "Well, stop it this instant."

"But he makes it so *easy*, little queen." Heat races across my cheeks (of course) and makes him smirk. Then his gaze drops to my blatant erection. "Besides, rather obviously, our Mr. Mercury enjoys my horrible advances. Don't you, darling?"

I just blush furiously and don't answer. Anyway, it's not like I can lie about it. Not with the physical evidence of my raging hard-on staring them both in the face.

Not to mention I'm a horrible liar.

Like really awful at it.

And Vasili's such a snake he always knows.

"Well, at least stop pinning him to the wall." Zara still sounds amused, because she definitely has a major soft spot for our snake, but I know she means what she says. "We're not having any kind of dubcon situation going on in this harem."

"Oh, why, when we all enjoy it?" he pouts, and his voice turns to velvet. "You as well, little queen. Don't deny it."

"Yeah, no. We're not talking about me right now, so no changing the subject." Under all that badass, she's fighting not to laugh. Great. Even my beloved one is laughing at my dilemma.

But underneath, she means it. She always has my back.

"Then indulge me, darling, *do*." V's gaze locks on mine, one eyebrow lifting with a wicked smirk. "Whatever will you do if I refuse to release him?"

"Sure you wanna know?" she volleys right back. "Don't make me come over there."

My belly warms and flutters and my heart goes all soft and gooey.

My love for her—my first alpha, my fated mate, the confident queen I adore, pulses through the bond between us.

And because we're seriously bonded, she can feel everything I feel.

"Whoa." That arc of connection to my various physical discomforts strips all the laughter from her tone. The quick patter of bare feet on the tiles precedes her sudden appearance at Vasili's side.

"Yo, Goblin King." Her teal brows pucker under the wild sea of blue curls tangled around her frowning face. "You're holding him way too tight. Let him go right now. I mean it."

Now she's definitely using her queen voice. Electric witchcraft crackles at her fingertips and lifts the heavy mane of curls to float around her tiny body. Through the bond between us, I can sense her inner dragon bugling and bating her wings.

Yeah, my Zara's definitely what you'd call a badass. Not only the queen of the whole witching world, and not another weak witch like the current queen regnant and all the Aquarius queens before her, but finally the powerful queen in waiting we've *all* been waiting for. The Gemini queen. As an added bonus, she's also the only dragon shifter queen we've got.

She's not the queen we deserve. But she's the queen we need.

And even V, snake that he is, knows it.

My bully's stare veers from my trapped and blushing face to the force of nature that's our queen. Their gazes meet like flashing blades. Her inner dragon screams her dominance. And that flying serpent inside V coils and hisses in challenge.

Yowsa. Those two together in dragon form must *really* be something.

V's pretty lips curl in a mocking smile. But he flicks wide the fingers of his casting hand in a gesture that manages to be both dismissive and contemptuous.

And, suddenly, I'm free.

"Master has given Dobby a sock," I mutter with a glare. I hide behind the cheesy *Harry Potter* reference because I'm disgruntled it took my beloved's intervention to free me.

V fizzes with a spurt of surprised laughter.

Which of course he chokes right off.

"Welcome to the world of the clothed, baby." Zara's lush lips quirk with humor, but her mischievous gaze drops right away to my hard-on, which is still totally a thing. "But not too soon, I hope. Because, um, right now? I kinda like you naked."

***Author's note:*** *Do you like Neo naked too? Like Zara and Vasili, I'm really enjoying ruining him, but I also kinda want him to keep his sweet bookworm innocence forever.*

**The complete *Gemini Heat* novella is only available behind the magical wards of the Witching World here at https://reamstories.com/witchingworld.**

# About The Author

Amazon category bestselling author Laura Navarre (she/her) whisks you away from your unmagical with extra spicy, extra shifty, wild & witchy why-choose romance starring hot bi heroes and the badass witches who love them. Laura's paranormal adult academy why-choose series delivers intense and steamy out-of-this world adventure with powerful heroines who never have to choose, passionate prose that packs a punch, and enough heat to set your Academy uniform on fire.

A long time ago in a galaxy far away, Laura wrote dark fantasy romance for Harlequin, while her sinister twin Nikki Navarre wrote sexy spy romance. Now, with eighteen sexy stories released worldwide, this Washington, DC-based nomad writes erotic paranormal adult academy why-choose romance featuring bi heroes, badass heroines, sweet poly love, and extreme poly steam.

Laura is a cat lover, globetrotter, wine addict, PhD candidate, and president of Ascendant Press. When she isn't conjuring witchy worlds, she's a professional diplomat with a professional background in weapons of mass destruction and an MFA in writing popular fiction from the University of Southern Maine. She's won the New England Readers' Choice Award, the Virginia Romance Writers Holt Medallion Award for Best Book by a Virginia author, finalled in the RWA Fantasy, Futuristic, and Paranormal Chapter's PRISM contest, and is a former Golden Heart finalist. She's also relentlessly obsessive, alarmingly efficient, and a recovering perfectionist. She's deeply suspicious of the Oxford comma, but she's never met an em dash she doesn't love.

Stalk Laura across the galaxy like the queen killer stalks Zara at the Icarus Academy! Her adventures across the witching world are trackable by witches, warlocks, humans, and aliens alike at:

http://reamstories.com/witchingworld (best way to reach me and grab steamy free reads)
http://www.LauraNavarreSciFi.com (go here to join my newsletter)
https://amzn.to/3FrX5t7 (follow me on Amazon to be alerted to new releases)
http://www.goodreads.com/LauraNavarre
https://www.bookbub.com/authors/laura-navarre
https://www.facebook.com/LauraNavarreAuthor
https://www.tiktok.com/@LauraNavarreAuthor
http://www.instagram.com/LauraNavarreAuthor